"Is that a yes?" He angled his head to kiss the edge of her mouth. "Or a no?"

"Must you ask?" she pleaded, still avoiding his gaze. "Must you make me say it outright?"

"How else should I know what you want?" he countered, anticipation hovering just beneath the surface of his heated tone. "Or what your feelings toward me are?"

"You just should, that's all. At least, I thought you would. Does a savage ask to be fed? I think not." Her haughty look gave way to a softer, wistful expression. "He just takes what he wants. It's instinctive. Somehow I rather thought that when this happened, if it happened, that it would be the same, all sweeping me off my feet and ravishment. And another thing—"

"You've said quite enough," he declared. "Rest assured, madam, if it's ravishment you want, ravished you shall be."

LORD SAVAGE

Patricia Coughlin

BANTAM BOOKS
New York   Toronto   London
Sydney   Auckland

LORD SAVAGE
A Bantam Book/December 1996

All rights reserved.
Copyright © 1996 by Patricia Madden Coughlin

Cover art copyright © 1996 by George Bush

Design by Carol Malcolm Russo/Signet M Design, Inc.

ISBN 0-553-57520-1

Published simultaneously in the United States and Canada

Bantam Books are published by Bantam Books, a division of Bantam Doubleday Dell Publishing Group, Inc. Its trademark, consisting of the words "Bantam Books" and the portrayal of a rooster, is Registered in U.S. Patent and Trademark Office and in other countries. Marca Registrada. Bantam Books, 1540 Broadway, New York, New York 10036.

PRINTED IN THE UNITED STATES OF AMERICA

OPM   10   9   8   7   6   5   4   3   2   1

To Eileen Fallon for challenging me to try something new . . .

To Beth de Guzman for making the dream a reality . . .

To Dee Holmes and Kristine Rolofson for encouraging me . . .

And to Bill—as always—for being there.

Prologue

London
February 1823

The Earl of Castleton poured himself a brandy, carried it to his favorite chair, and settled in to do what he had been doing with dismaying frequency of late, pondering The Problem.

Each day Tanner or Bennett or one of the other gentlemen who shared his interest in the matter dropped by to see if he had managed to come up with a suitable solution, and each day he was forced to admit to them that he had not. Until today. Castleton smiled in anticipation, if not of a solution per se, at least of the prospect of discharging The Problem to someone else. It was a chance visit by his nephew Christian that had inspired him as to who that someone else should be.

Christian, his sister's eldest offspring, had been a notoriously rambunctious youth, ousted and banned from every school he set foot in, in spite of the enormous sums of bribery his doting mother had been willing to pay in the guise of tuition. He'd made something of a name for himself by being expelled from Eton for stealing into the headmaster's office in the dead of night and tying a sheep to his chair. His mother insisted it wasn't so much the ruined chair that had sealed Christian's fate as the fact that the sheep had been wearing the headmaster's favorite robe at the time. After that his desperate parents had shipped the boy off to the Penrose School in nearby Paddington, where, miracle of miracles, he had not only lasted, but graduated with honors and emerged a quite gracious fellow.

Since a miracle was exactly what was called for at the moment, Castleton had wasted no time in contacting Phillip Penrose about The Problem. Penrose, son of the school's late founder, had been exceedingly understanding of the matter and most eager to help. He had even gone so far as to assure Castleton that he knew precisely the right person for the task. What's more, he wasn't in the least daunted by the time constraints involved. Which was more than he could say for himself, Castleton reflected anxiously. The mere thought of all that needed to be accomplished in eight weeks sent him reaching for his brandy snifter.

In eight weeks, Julia Duvanne, the Dowager Lady Sage, would be returning from her annual sojourn to France to find a surprise awaiting her here at home—a brand new grandson, fully grown and fresh from the wilds of the Sandwich Islands. If all went well, she would be as thrilled as Castleton and his friends were at the discovery that her son, the fourth Marquis of Sage, had not died heirless after all. She would give her long-lost grandson her blessing and use her considerable influence with her old friend the king to secure the title for him. That is, if all went well, and all would definitely not go well if said grandson were to greet her wearing a bloody loincloth.

Castleton shuddered and took another gulp of his brandy. Lady Sage was, to put it delicately, a trifle demanding. To put it truthfully, she was a stubborn old witch and he was counting heavily on that working to his advantage. It was common knowledge that she was not overly fond of the only other possible candidate for the title, her daughter's son, Sir Adam Lockaby, and that she was in no hurry to see him inherit. It was also said that she was quite fond of tweaking society on occasion. What better way to do that than by turning a savage into a lord?

First, however, the savage must be persuaded to meet her halfway. The earl hadn't the faintest idea how one went about persuading a savage to do anything, which was why he needed Penrose. He knew only that the radical Lockaby could not be permitted a voice in the House of Lords, not as long as it was possible to produce a living, breathing suitable heir in his stead. It hadn't been easy, but with the help of his friends he had taken care of the living, breathing part of things. That left only *suitable,* and that, thought Castleton with relief, was now up to Penrose and whomever he had in mind for the job.

One

She would refuse. Politely. Tactfully. Wearing upon her face the most saddened and regretful expression she was able to muster, but refuse she would.

She must. The very last thing Ariel Halliday needed at the moment was to take on any added responsibility, especially one of this magnitude. She simply could not be stretched any further, not even if she were qualified to attempt what Lord Castleton was asking of her. Which she most assuredly was not.

Why, she had never so much as laid eyes on a savage, much less endeavored to tame one. What did she know of teaching a full-grown man about the myriad gallantries the ton demanded of a proper gentleman? How did one begin to convey the countless small details which to an uncultivated outsider might seem so petty as to be insignificant, but which in truth were tantamount to survival in the Polite World?

It was impossible. Nothing in her teaching experience qualified her for such a task. Her talents ran to lecturing on grammar and directing energetic nine-year-old boys in the proper way to make a bow. As awkward and uncooperative as those boys could be, most of them had twenty or more years in which to be properly domesticated and refined before they would assume their titles.

How could she be expected to take a grown man, plucked from some godforsaken island in the Pacific Ocean, and turn him into a nobleman in eight weeks' time? She couldn't. That's all there was to it. She could not imagine what Mr. Penrose had been thinking when he suggested otherwise to Lord Castleton.

At the thought of her employer, Ariel went cold inside and she lifted her gaze in his direction just long enough to see him watching her as intently as Castleton and the two other men present. They were gathered in the elegantly appointed drawing room of the earl's London home. Sir Tanner and Captain Bennett had been introduced as friends of the earl's, and they clearly shared his interest in this matter. She had learned that it was aboard the captain's ship, under somewhat dubious conditions, that the man in question had been brought to England.

Judging from the hopeful gazes around her, it was obvious they were all most eager for her to agree to help. In Mr. Penrose's eyes, however, she also detected a familiar glint of impatience.

She couldn't refuse.

She must.

She couldn't.

Ariel smoothed the folds of her gray muslin skirt and clasped her hands lightly in her lap as calmly as if she were not a frantic jumble of nerves on the inside.

It occurred to her that to deny the request outright, no matter how politely, would be to embarrass Mr.

Penrose before these gentlemen he was so clearly intent on impressing. That was, of course, out of the question. She hadn't been chasing around in circles in an attempt to curry his favor all these past weeks only to ruin everything now.

Not that she could possibly grant what they were asking, not even to further her cause with the supercilious headmaster. Between her duties at the Penrose School and helping her mother keep watch and ward over her father, who was slipping further and further into a world of his own design with each passing day, she was extended to her limit. Somehow she would have to explain that in such a way that Mr. Penrose would understand and perhaps even commiserate. But not now. Not here.

She would have to bide her time, Ariel decided. It was a most unlikely and unpracticed course for her to choose, more accustomed as she was to speaking her mind directly than biting her tongue. She would manage it somehow, however, just as she had been managing so many other unfamiliar tasks of late for the sake of her dear mother and father.

"So, Miss Halliday," Lord Castleton said at last, prompting her for an answer. "There you have it, a most unusual and demanding endeavor, as you can see. You can well imagine how eager we have been to find exactly the right person to undertake this challenge and how relieved we were when Mr. Penrose graciously volunteered your name to us."

Ariel smiled sweetly as she fumed in silence, her poor tongue nearly bit in two. Penrose could afford to be gracious, devil take the man. He was not the one being pushed forward to perform a minor miracle in a matter of weeks.

"Now I dare to place the fate of the marquis, and

perhaps the future happiness and well-being of your countrymen as well, in your hands."

Ariel lowered her gaze demurely as her mind whirled in search of a delicate way to say no to an earl. "My lord, I'm sure you overstate my importance."

"Not at all." Castle leaned closer, his thick silver brows knitting in an openly entreating expression which Ariel suspected was alien to his nature as well as his position. "I cannot overstate the case, Miss Halliday. Young Lockaby is naught but a puppet for that band of radicals he has fallen in with. For years they have been goading him and grooming him to catch the family plum as soon as the four black horses pulled up to his uncle's door. There is no telling what havoc he might wreak if granted the Sage title and influence, and no question he must be stopped at all costs. If that means turning an unsuitable heir into a suitable one, then by all that's holy in heaven, so be it. Will you lend your kind assistance to our cause, my dear Miss Halliday?"

Ariel took a deep breath and glanced from one of the men looming over her to the next, her gaze finally coming to rest on the earl's bishop-blue waistcoat, which matched precisely the blue of the satin drapery and the nubbed silk of the chair in which she sat.

"Why, Lord Castleton," she said at last, "when you put it in those terms, I can only say that I . . ." The war inside her continued to rage. She avoided any glance at all in Penrose's direction as she concluded in a rush, "I shall need some time to further consider your request."

There was a barely audible, collective sigh of disappointment in the room, pierced by an unmistakably miffed hiss, which she easily recognized as coming from her employer. Then silence.

"Of course," Castleton said after a moment, his tone as smooth and accommodating as ever as he slanted a chastising look Penrose's way. "To have the matter dumped on you without warning is enough to spin anyone's head. I only implore you to remember that time is of the essence."

"She will not be long about making up her mind," Mr. Penrose chimed in. "I can promise you that, Lord Castleton."

"I have every confidence that Miss Halliday will give us her decision in a timely fashion," Castleton replied, narrowing his gaze as he swung it from Ariel to Penrose. "With no prodding from anyone."

The earl smiled as he looked at Ariel once more. "And now I imagine you are eager to meet the man I hope will soon become your most accomplished pupil to date."

Ariel, eager only to take her leave and have a chance to plead the case for her reluctance to accept the task to Mr. Penrose privately, shook her head.

"That is really not necessary," she replied. "You did an admirable job of explaining the situation, my lord. I cannot think what advantage there would be in—"

"Nonsense," Castleton interrupted. "No lady I know would buy a bit of ribbon trim for a bonnet without first seeing the precise shade for herself, gauging the suitability of the width and feeling the drape of the fabric against her hand. I hardly expect you to embark on an undertaking such as this without the same advantages."

Ariel smiled weakly. She did not want to prolong her involvement in any way that might encourage their confidence in her and throw her inevitable refusal into an even worse light. Certainly she had no intention of personally evaluating the man's width or drape.

On the other hand, her weaker side argued, a small peek could not hurt. She was most curious after all.

"Lord Savage," as he had been dubbed, was currently the number-one topic for gossips across town, and since Castleton was already on his feet and indicating that she proceed him through the drawing room, it appeared the matter was settled. Ariel felt a tremor of excitement at the realization that she was about to make the acquaintance of the toast of all London.

Castleton guided her, with the others in tow, through a door at the far end of the lavishly decorated room into an equally ornate hallway. The wool runner beneath Ariel's feet was as much a work of art as the paintings that graced the walls, and she knew at a glance that the matched silver candelabra on the mahogany half-moon table were heirlooms of the finest order.

Amid such affluence, the imp in her was tempted to inquire of the earl what he might contemplate paying for her services should she agree to grant his request. She quickly suppressed the impulse. No matter the sum, it would never be enough to settle her father's gambling debts and also ensure a decent future for her parents and herself. At the moment, that was her number-one concern. She needed lasting security, not a sudden windfall, and that, she reminded herself stoically, was why she could ill afford to provoke Mr. Penrose in this or any other matter.

Castleton led them to the very end of the hall and stopped before a door with a heavy black curtain covering its top half.

"I had a glass installed here so that we could keep a proper watch on things without constantly locking and unlocking all this business." He indicated several heavy locks securing the door. "No need to take unnecessary risks after all."

Ariel looked at him in surprise. "Do you mean he is bent on escape?"

The earl shrugged. "Who can say what's in the fellow's mind from one moment to the next?"

"He did put up quite a fight when we took him aboard ship," Captain Bennett offered, stroking his salt-and-pepper whiskers. "Though he calmed down some once we were under way."

"Leg irons tend to have that rather settling effect," Sir Tanner remarked dryly.

The captain shrugged.

"We have not had any problems of that sort since he's been here," Castleton added quickly. "Just the same, we cannot afford to take chances."

"Just so," agreed Tanner in the same amused tone. A ready smile creased his plump face, suggesting he was quick to find the humor in any situation. "You can't just lay your hand on another marquis at every turn in the road."

"Would you expect me to be locked up with him, then?" Ariel found herself asking.

"Of course not," Castleton assured her. "I have made arrangements for you to be assisted by a couple who have been most highly recommended to me. He's said to be a handy fellow all around, and a great burly one at that. His wife is no mere slip of a thing either. They would be at your beck and call at all times to ensure your safety and peace of mind. As to precisely how and under what conditions you conduct the actual lessons, that, of course, would be a matter left entirely to your discretion and expertise."

"Yes, well . . ." Ariel gave him a small smile. "That's that, then."

Castleton reached for the cord on the curtain. "I keep this drawn most of the time," he explained. "I should think even a savage appreciates a modicum of privacy."

A modicum was apparently all he was permitted, thought Ariel uncomfortably, as with a quick flick of his wrist the earl opened the curtain fully, exposing the small room to the inquisitive gazes of those gathered outside. A knock of forewarning of any other sort was obviously deemed unnecessary. Ariel could not help but recall the caged chimpanzees she had found so amusing on a long-ago trip to the circus.

She was not amused now, however, only ill at ease and oddly embarrassed as she sensed the men behind her leaning forward and craning their necks for a better view. She shuddered to think of the humiliation for all concerned had the room's occupant been making use of the chamber pot only half hidden by the screen in the far corner.

There was no movement inside the room save for the shadow of the still-swaying curtain, and several seconds passed before Ariel's gaze came to rest on the narrow cot against the back wall and the man lying upon it. He stared straight ahead, through the room's only window, which was secured with iron bars that she rather suspected were another recent modification.

Bed linen and a pillow were heaped willy-nilly on the floor at the foot of the cot. With his back propped against the wall, he lay on the bare mattress, his arms folded across his chest, not even sparing a glance toward the door with its viewing glass, much less turning his head in that direction.

Odd, thought Ariel, certain that he must have discerned the sudden movement of the curtain. Even a dog would respond by pricking its ears and looking to see who was there.

Perhaps he slept with his eyes open, she mused, taking a closer look to gauge the rise and fall of his chest. Instantly her face warmed, and she knew if she were to peer in a mirror just then, she would see that the normally high coloring in her cheeks had blazed to the color of sin. Bright red. At least that was her estimation of sin's color. She told herself she would do well to feel sinful for gazing so boldly at a man wearing next to nothing and that she ought to look away that very instant. But she didn't feel sinful or look away.

She felt more curious than ever. This was, after all, much more of a man's body she had ever had occasion to view so directly—or might ever have the chance to view, she reminded herself. Not even for the sake of Phillip Penrose was she about to pretend to go all weak in the knees and succumb to a case of the vapors. Not right away at least.

The object of her fascination was wearing black trousers that clung tightly from hip to just below his knees, and that was all. Ariel's first impression was of a great deal of sun-browned skin and unruly jet-black hair. His chest and shoulders were broad; his arms and his long legs sculptured with lean muscle. Nowhere on him was there the slightest hint of the cursed padding of flesh that softened her own shape more than she would like.

Perhaps, Ariel thought, consciously releasing the breath she had been holding for so long it hurt, perhaps all men were built this magnificently under their layers of waistcoats and silk stockings and elaborately tied cravats. Perhaps he was not something so far out of the ordinary as to warrant this sudden pounding of excitement inside her. Perhaps, but she did not think so.

"I must apologize for his indecent appearance," Castleton said to her with a sigh of resignation. "He refuses to have any part of the clothes or bedding or anything else we endeavor to provide for him."

"What you see is what he was wearing when we found him," Captain Bennett explained. "He was"—he seemed to catch himself and cleared his throat—"swimming."

Ariel nodded, surreptitiously observing the sly look the captain exchanged with Sir Tanner. It was reminiscent of the look the more brazen midlevel boys at school passed behind her back if the sudden swish of her skirt should by chance expose a glimpse of ankle, and it suggested to her that there was more to the story of the marquis's capture than they were willing to share with her.

"When he first arrived," Castleton continued, "we summoned the footman each morning to shave his beard and dress him by force. We shed some blood and ruined a goodly amount of costly tailoring in the process. It was finally decided to let him have his way for the time being. Naturally Mr. and Mrs. Farrell, the couple I spoke of earlier, will assist you in persuading our reluctant marquis that he's no longer in the islands and must dress accordingly."

"What about food?" Ariel inquired without removing her gaze from the motionless form on the cot.

"I beg your pardon?"

"Food," she repeated. "You said he refuses everything you offer him, and I wondered about his response to the meals you serve. He does not appear to be emaciated."

"He eats enough to stay alive and at the same time little enough to make the point that he will accept no more than he must for that purpose. Bread and meat mostly. No sweets or confections of any sort. A feat that, since Cook's cakes would tempt a dead man."

"A dead man has no ax to grind," she murmured thoughtfully.

"True enough, I suppose," the earl agreed, taking her meaning. "I will say that his fortitude in that regard has given me high hopes for his character. It is one thing to be uncultured, another entirely to be without principle or self-control. Even so, he must come around in the end."

Ariel nodded, preoccupied with her own thoughts and a growing wish that the remarkable creatures on the other side of the glass would move and turn his gaze her way. What would she see in those hooded eyes? she wondered. Fear? No. She was certain of that. Anger? Contempt? Rage? Turn my way, she pleaded silently. Show me who you are.

"Does he speak English?" she asked.

Behind her, Captain Bennett snorted. "Not so you'd notice."

"He's been silent for as long as he's been here," Castleton told her.

"The same on board," Bennett concurred. "At least in front of me. A few of the mates that brought him aboard said he swore at them fluently in about seven different languages."

Ariel turned from the window for the first time and glanced over her shoulder at the captain. "Which?" she inquired.

He frowned. "Which what?"

"Languages," she replied, curbing her impatience. "You said he was fluent in seven languages. I wondered which languages they are."

"Begging your pardon, miss," Bennett said with a chuckle, "what I said was that he swore fluent in seven of 'em. I myself know a few handy words in Portuguese and Russian. Don't make me fluent in either."

"I understand," she told him. "I would still be

interested in knowing in which languages he swears fluently."

Sir Tanner smiled ruefully at her. "I wager you'll be finding out for yourself before long."

Castleton arched him a quelling look, obviously not wanting her to be dissuaded before she'd even accepted the role of savage tamer.

"English and French," the captain began, rubbing his stubbled chin with a perplexed frown. "And that island mumbo-jumbo, of course. Seems to me they might have said he threw in some choice bits in Spanish. That's all I can recall. If it matters, I could ask the boys who heard him firsthand."

"No, that won't be necessary," Ariel replied. She turned to Castleton with a properly concerned expression. "I think it would be far better if I attempted to speak with him myself. If that would be all right."

"Of course," Castleton agreed without hesitation. He reached above the door for the keys hanging on a hook there. "I'd be happy to bring you in so you might—"

"Alone," she added.

She squared her shoulders and told herself it was all for a good cause. If she could force herself to flutter her lashes and smile at her employer's insipid humor, then surely she could manage this as proof of her sincerity.

That was all that had prompted her request, she assured herself, doing her best to ignore the sense of anticipation that had set her pulse racing. She was doing this to impress Mr. Penrose alone. The man himself, this savage, was of no import. None. Truth be told, she had not the slightest notion of what she might possibly say to him if given the opportunity. Yet there she was, beseeching a clearly reluctant Earl Castleton to permit her to go alone into his heavily locked and barred room.

Lord, what was wrong with her?

She was daft, she had to be. She was overwrought. She stole another quick glance at Lord Savage. She was bedazzled.

"I really don't know what to say to your request, Miss Halliday," Castleton replied at last. "I must confess that I am most uneasy with the prospect of permitting you inside his room unescorted."

He was going to refuse her. Ariel's heart lifted and wrenched at the same time.

"Yes, come now, Miss Halliday," Mr. Penrose put in, catching Ariel's gaze with an exasperated look clearly intended to be a warning. "Do be sensible."

"But," Castleton continued, overriding him, "if you think it will assist you in making an evaluation . . ."

"I am sure of it," she said quickly, steadfastly avoiding Mr. Penrose's narrowed gaze.

"Then so be it . . . with a minor precaution taken for your safety." He excused himself and returned a minute later with a pair of long-barreled dueling pistols. Holding on to one, he handed the other to Sir Tanner, prompting a churlish pout from Penrose at being passed over.

"I don't know, Cas," said Tanner, his expression jovial as he sighted down the barrel experimentally. "I've never shot a peer before."

"You best not be shooting one today either," snapped Castleton. "But if you must fire, for God's sake aim low." He turned to Ariel. "Whenever you are ready, Miss Halliday."

"I do have one other small request," she told him, having thought of it only as she stood waiting for him to return with the pistols.

"Name it."

"Tea. I should like to bring him tea."

"Tea?"

She nodded. "Yes. Tea."

Tanner and Bennett chortled.

"Really, Miss Halliday," said a peevish Penrose. "Are you deliberately trying to test our patience?"

"Of course not. I simply would like to bring him some tea. That is, if it is not too much trouble," she added in her most docile tone.

"It is hardly trouble," replied the earl, frowning. "But . . . tea?"

"Yes. I should think," she said, judiciously stealing a few of his own earlier words, "that even a savage gets thirsty."

Ariel waited, thinking she would be lucky if Castleton refused her this ridiculous request and changed his mind entirely about letting her go into the room alone. If so, it would be out of her hands. And Mr. Penrose would not be able to accuse her of failing to contemplate the offer fully before declining.

Rather than refusing, however, Castleton was suddenly regarding her with beaming approval.

He nodded vigorously. "Of course. Tea. I see your method now, Miss Halliday. Brilliant. Damned brilliant, if you will pardon my enthusiasm."

"Thank you, my lord," she murmured, wishing she might ask him to please explain her brilliant method to her since he was so far ahead of her in figuring it out.

He turned to the footman hovering a discreet distance away and ordered that tea be brought, and quickly. As they waited, the men discussed the political implications of the situation in which they found themselves, and Ariel simply stared through the glass.

At last the tea arrived. Ariel accepted from the

servant the silver tray holding a gracefully curved pot and a pair of china cups and saucers rimmed with gold and engraved with the Castleton crest. She waited while the earl unlocked the door.

Just as he reached for the doorknob to open it for her, she said, "Will you please draw the curtain?"

He hesitated, and Ariel hastened to explain.

"If we're to work together, I think it best this first meeting seem as natural as possible, that he believe we're not being watched, and that I trust him."

Castleton nodded. "On one condition. At the first hint that something is amiss, you must shout or pound the door, anything to signal to us that you are in need of help."

"I will," she promised, and meant it.

Two

Ariel stepped inside the room and heard the door shut behind her with a click that sounded as irrevocable as a gunshot. She closed her eyes briefly, caught her breath, and took a determined step forward.

"Good afternoon," she said. Another breath. In. Out. She could do this. "I'm Miss Halliday. Miss Ariel Halliday. I know that you're Leon Nicholas Duvanne, the fifth Marquis of Sage. I'm just not sure that you know it yet," she added ruefully.

She set the tray on the small table a few feet from his cot.

"Of course you have a whole mouthful of other titles I shall not even attempt to recite for you now. I believe Lord Sav—Sage will suit nicely for the time being."

Ninny, she thought. Such a slip of the tongue might have made for a most uneasy moment. That is, if he even understood a word she was saying. There was no indication he did. For that matter, there was no obvious sign the man was alive, but for the slow, steady rise and fall of his very imposing chest.

Ariel, trying not to stare in fascination at the wedge of silky, dark chest hair, wet her suddenly dry lips with her tongue.

"Proper manners," she began, "dictate that a gentleman rise when a lady enters the room and greet her by title and name. I am prepared to overlook your failure to do so on this occasion, overtaxed as I'm sure you must be from your obviously high level of exertion thus far today." He offered no response to her sarcasm.

"I do believe, however," she continued, "that in consideration of the fact that I have gone to considerable trouble to bring you tea, you could at the very least turn your head and acknowledge that I am speaking to you."

To her amazement, the dark head began to turn her way slowly. He understood, she thought excitedly. Either her words or her chilly tone, she couldn't be certain which, but he had clearly understood something. And he had responded.

Her excitement turned to apprehension as he proceeded to swing his feet to the floor and stand, facing her fully. She fought an urge to step back. He made no move to come closer, however, and her heartbeat gradually slowed to as near normal as she expected it to be while she remained confined there alone with him.

His gaze caught and held hers, and Ariel found that the effect of his silent presence was even more daunting when he was staring directly into her eyes. He was, she concluded objectively, without question the most beautiful man she had ever seen. Never before had she thought to describe a man as beautiful, but the word came to her easily and naturally when she gazed at

Lord Sage's serene face and strong, lean body. He appeared to her as masculine perfection, chiseled by the hand of the greatest master of all.

His cheekbones were aristocratically high, his jaw beneath the short black beard classically square, his mouth full, with just enough of a slant to add interest to his otherwise perfect face. A stray lock of his long raven hair hung loosely across his forehead, and his eyes, deep-set and almond-shaped, were a quite extraordinary shade. Brown velvet swirled with gold, dark and bright at once, like sunlight on ancient brass. Tiger's eyes, Ariel mused, thinking of the gemstone by that name. Hard and gleaming and exotic.

At that moment the expression in his remarkable eyes was neither warm nor cold, neither friendly nor antagonistic. It was shuttered. She felt certain that the man was no dolt, and that although he would not permit her to be privy to it, there was a great deal of thought and evaluation going on inside his head. In fact, some instinct warned her that his lordship was taking her measure just as calculatedly as she was taking his.

She straightened, smoothing a few stray wisps of light brown hair. Why hadn't she taken more pains in arranging the chignon at the back of her neck that morning? she lamented. And perhaps worn a newer dress? One in a more flattering color? She quickly marshaled her thoughts, reminding herself that she did not possess a newer dress and that gray was a most serviceable hue for everyday wear and that besides, it mattered not at all what the man before her thought of her appearance.

Without warning he shook back his hair, dislodging the lock that hung over his forehead to reveal a two-inch-long scar there. The imperfection, which would have marred the appeal of most men, enhanced his instead. For the first time Ariel noticed the array of other small marks and scars that covered his body, souvenirs, it seemed to her, of a life far more reckless and exciting than her own. Feeling a mixture of curiosity and envy, she lifted her gaze to his to find him watching her with his eyes narrowed in suspicion.

"Forgive me," she murmured. "Here I am commenting on your manners and failing to mind my own. I neglected to thank you," she added, belatedly acknowledging his cooperation in standing and facing her. She extended her hand toward the tray resting on the table beside her. "Now then, shall I pour?"

Silence.

"The proper response to that request is a gracious, 'Yes, please do,' or perhaps, if you are on more familiar terms with the lady posing the question, a simple, 'Yes, by all means.'" She accompanied the spontaneous lesson with fluid gestures. She might as well have been reciting calculus equations for all the comprehension reflected in his unwavering gaze.

Steeling to the task she'd brought on herself, she lifted the silver teapot and filled the two cups with the steaming liquid. She glanced up to find him still staring intently at her face. She'd rather thought he would be more interested in what she was doing, certain as she was that he had not been treated to a proper tea either aboard Captain Bennett's ship or since.

"Cream and sugar?" she inquired with a small smile.

Silence.

The edges of her mouth quirked with amusement. "The strong, silent type, I see. In that case, I shall assume that you take your tea as I do mine. One sugar," she continued, carefully measuring a teaspoon of sugar into each cup, "and just a bit of cream for color. I must say that many gentlemen prefer it black, and you may find you do the same. Time will tell, my father likes to say."

She carefully lifted one cup and saucer and held it out to him. "Your tea, my lord."

For a few seconds longer his gaze remained fixed on her face. Then it lowered briefly to the cup in her hand and returned, all without a flicker of expression or any move to take the cup.

Ariel sighed and took a step closer. "At least extend me the courtesy of trying it," she urged. "If you are going to make your home in England, you have to either learn to like tea or pretend to. It's practically the law."

She would swear that her last remark sparked something inside him. There was a lightning-quick, barely perceptible movement of his lower lip, a tightening, it seemed to Ariel, minuscule, but under the circumstances enough to encourage her efforts.

"Here you go," she said, shifting the cup and saucer to her left hand as she prepared to reach for one of his hands, hanging loosely by his side, in order to guide him in accepting the cup.

"If it's the saucer that is daunting you, don't let it. I know it must seem a lot to juggle at once, but truly it is not as difficult as it appears at first and it is necessary to catch the drips before they stain the table linen or rug." She glanced at the bare table and uncovered floor. "Not that there is either linen or rug to be concerned with at the moment. Suffice it to say that it is there because good manners dictate it be there. I am afraid good manners dictate a great many silly and useless things that you will have to adapt to, my lord." She sighed, her small smile rueful. "Not always an easy task, I can assure you."

She reached for his hand and was startled when his fingers curled to capture hers rather than the other way around. Without warning the very floor beneath her feet started tilting wildly. At least it seemed so to Ariel. She could think of no other rational explanation for her sudden loss of equilibrium. Her senses were reeling, making her feel hot and cold at the same time, and all strange and ticklish on the inside, as if a feather pillow had burst open in her stomach. Her gaze jerked up to meet his and probe the depths of those mesmerizing bronze eyes and in them she saw . . .

Nothing.

Either Lord Sage was a master of self-control or he felt nothing of what the light touch of his hand had caused her to feel.

The loud clattering of the cup and saucer still gripped in her left hand helped bring Ariel to her senses. Any second she expected to see tea sloshing over the rim of the cup to stain her best white gloves. She breathed deeply and ordered herself to stop acting like a silly twit. Drawing herself to her full five feet six inches, a goodly height for a woman but one that still left her at least eight inches beneath the top of Lord Sage's head and therefore fated to stare at his very distracting chest, she drew his hand up between them and somehow succeeded in transferring the cup and saucer to his possession.

He still showed no emotion, but at least he appeared to grasp that he was now to hold on to the cup and saucer in her stead. She took the precaution of observing him for several seconds, but if anything, the Castelton china seemed safer in his strong, steady hands than in her own. Certainly it was no longer clattering.

Ariel turned back to the table to reach for her own cup. She balanced the saucer carefully in her left hand and lifted the delicate cup with her right.

"You must always use your index finger and thumb to lift the cup." She spoke slowly and formed each word as precisely as if he were without hearing and had to rely on the movement of her lips to understand. Belatedly it occurred to her that perhaps that was the case. If so, it might make matters simpler than if she had to teach him English before anything else. Or, rather, Ariel corrected herself, it would make the task simpler for whomever Castleton found to undertake it once she had declined.

She continued slowly, illustrating each step as she explained it and finally taking a small sip of hot tea and swallowing.

"Now you try." She put her cup aside to urge him to make an attempt.

Excitement raced through her as he did exactly that. He appeared not to have grasped the notion of separating the cup from the saucer before drinking, however, and, holding them as she thought a starving man might cradle a bowl of soup, he raised them to his mouth while at the same time lowering his head. When lips and cup met, he quickly gulped the entire contents before lifting his head again and bringing his watchful gaze directly back to hers.

"An excellent first attempt," Ariel exclaimed brightly, amazed that he hadn't burned his mouth with the still-hot tea in the process. "Now you must—"

She broke off, horrified as a good portion of what he'd recently quaffed came trickling from the sides of his mouth and proceeded on down to his bare chest.

"Oh, see what you've done." Her face puckered with concern and dismay as she realized he may have scalded himself after all.

For the first time Ariel saw a flicker of emotion in his eyes. Unfortunately, this was not the time to try to analyze or decipher the brittle, fleeting look he gave her. She grabbed for a napkin at the same moment he opened his hands and let the cup and saucer drop to the floor.

"Oh, no," she cried as the china landed and shattered.

Instantly the door behind her was flung open with a crash.

She half turned and had only the most fleeting glimpse of panicked faces and waving pistols before she was knocked to the floor by the savage, who followed her down and covered her body completely with his own. All the air left Ariel in a rush, whether from the fall or her sudden awareness of the overwhelming and unmistakably masculine heat and power holding her helplessly immobile, she couldn't be sure.

The shouting confused her further, only fractured portions of it penetrating her hazy state.

"By God, man . . ."

"Release her . . ."

"Low, aim low."

That was Castleton.

". . . this instant, I say."

"Bloody savage." That from Captain Bennett. "And right in front of our very eyes. I warned ye, I did."

"Don't point it this way, you idiot."

"Cease, I order you to cease that . . . whatever you are about, immediately."

The last was clearly Mr. Penrose's contribution to her rescue. Uttered in his usual nasal tone, it wavered somewhere between a complaint and a plea and served to jar Ariel back to reality.

She tipped her head back and was somehow not surprised to find the savage staring down at her with those unsettling eyes. She was quite startled, however, by the heat she saw in them. It had burned away all trace of gold so that beneath the thick curtain of his hair his eyes glittered as darkly as she always imagined black stars might. Sir Hilbert, her astronomy mentor and very good friend, insisted that black stars did not exist in this galaxy, but Ariel, in defiance of his opinion and the absence of any scientific proof, believed just as passionately that they did.

Now, staring up into the dark stars of the savage's eyes, she did her best to ignore the resurgence of that strange fluttering inside her.

The frantic wiggle of her shoulders was instinctive. "Please, sir, I cannot breathe."

He remedied that inconvenience by raising his chest the smallest fraction of an inch, a movement she was certain had been imperceptible to the men gathered around them.

Ariel gulped at the air, filling her lungs so that her chest lifted into contact with his once again, causing her to shrink away instantly. With her back pressed tightly to the hard wooden floor, she spoke again.

"Thank you. Now, my lord," she continued, "if you would please be so kind as to release me before one of them hurts the other."

With only the slightest hesitation, during which his eyes again became as shuttered as when she had first walked in, Sage levered his weight to his arms and in one graceful motion rose to his feet. Though it was exactly what they had been clamoring for him to do, his sudden movement incited another round of shouts and warnings from Castleton and the others. Ariel glanced up to see both pistols aimed in the vicinity of Lord Sage's legs as he ignored their orders to back away and instead bent and extended his hand to help her up.

It was, Ariel noted, an amazingly gallant gesture on

the part of a savage, the significance of which appeared to be lost on the four gentlemen present.

She put her hand in his, searching in vain for another sign of awareness in his gaze as he pulled her to her feet. He managed the maneuver so effortlessly that she was made to feel as delicate and graceful as a ballerina. It was, for Ariel, a stunning and unprecedented occurrence.

"Thank you," she murmured to him once again as she pulled her hand free of his.

"Thank you?" echoed Sir Tanner. "By God, that beats all. Tell me, madam, are you thanking the heathen for jumping you or having the sense to back off when a gun was put to his head?"

"I saw no gun at his head, sir," Ariel snapped without stopping to think. "Only a pair aimed in the general vicinity of his bare feet. On the theory, I suppose, that a toeless marquis is still a marquis and therefore a valuable commodity. As for my reason for thanking him, I did so because he assisted me in regaining my feet, something the other gentlemen in the room were too busy playing the hero to be bothered with."

Lord Castleton was the first to display the grace to look remorseful and offer an apology.

"You are absolutely right, my dear Miss Halliday. I can only hope that you will be kind enough to attribute our temporary lapse in manners to our overwhelming concern for your safety."

She was not that kind. Or that gullible. It was obvious they had been much more concerned about the welfare of their prized marquis than her. Nonetheless, with Mr. Penrose looking on she had no choice but to smile and nod.

"Of course, my lord," she said.

"My thanks," he responded with a small bow of his head. "And now, are you all right? Dizzy? Bruised? Perhaps I should call my physician."

She shook her head. "Thank you, but that is not necessary. I simply had the wind knocked from me momentarily."

"And why wouldn't you have?" demanded the captain. "What with the way that brute landed on you. I swear, in all me travels I never saw such a vicious attack on a member of the fair sex before."

"Attack?" Ariel blurted out. "I fail to see how the word *attack* comes close to describing the actions of Lord Sage."

Castleton cocked a brow. "Then how would you describe them, Miss Halliday? I saw with my own eyes how he shoved you to the floor."

"Yes, he shoved me. To save me from being shot in the back," she exclaimed. "The way the lot of you burst through the door with guns waving wildly, I was certain I had breathed my last. I can't fault Lord Sage for believing the same and taking whatever action he deemed necessary at the time. Should I not thank him for putting concern for my life ahead of his own?"

"At the risk of appearing argumentative, Miss Halliday, we all quite clearly heard you shout before we opened the door," Castleton pointed out.

"And the crash," Mr. Penrose added. "Let's not forget the crash."

"A cup dropped," she said simply. "I cried out because I believed Lord Sage may have been scalded by the hot tea. I must apologize to you, Lord Castleton, for the breakage of your cup and saucer."

He waved off her apology. "It is of no import, as long as you and Sage are quite all right. Perhaps we did overreact . . . but you have to understand, it is bloody hard to know what to do or how to treat the man, when he will not speak or respond or even cover himself for the sake of decency."

"I daresay," Ariel countered, "that decency may be defined differently by men of different cultures."

"This is his culture now," Castleton proclaimed loudly. "He best understand and accept that—and quickly. It is English blood running in his veins after all, and in my view that counts for everything. No matter what sort of uncivilized upbringing he had to start with, it can be overcome, the bad habits weeded out of him. He'll come around." His booming tone suggested to Ariel that he was trying to reassure himself as much as the others.

"We hope," intoned Tanner.

"We shall do a great deal more than hope," the earl countered. "With Miss Halliday's help, we shall have Sage here molded into a gentleman fit for polite company in no time."

"Maybe," allowed his friend, his expression unconvinced as he regarded Sage appraisingly. "It's just that the more I see of Sage, the more I'm inclined to think that his nickname is dead on and that our charming Lord Savage will not be easily bent to fit the mold we have in mind."

"He'll bend, by God," retorted Castleton, "or he'll break. I will not be deterred in this. Mark me well, savage or saint, Sage here will be brought to heel." He grinned, a cocky affair that made Ariel wince on Lord Sage's behalf. "And one day he will thank me for the privilege of calling England his home."

The men shared a boisterous, patriotic cheer at that and thoroughly missed the flash of resentment that blazed in Sage's eyes. Ariel took note and felt a shiver of apprehension along her spine. Something warned her that Tanner might be right, that Sage might present a greater challenge than Lord Castleton was willing to admit.

Even barefoot, half-naked, and confined to this cell-like room, he projected the cool, aristocratic self-confidence common to those with generations of wealth, breeding, and power behind them. The fact was, of course, that he did have all that on his side. He simply did not yet know it. And still, without speaking a word, his fierce pride was almost palpable in the tiny room.

Ariel's heart twisted to think of what might lay ahead for him. Who would Castleton and the others find to "bring him to heel?" And at what price to him? Would his eyes still glitter like dark stars after he had been bullied and coerced and heaven knew what else into fitting Castleton's and his cronies' notion of a proper gentleman?

As the men started moving toward the door, Ariel struggled to stop herself from thinking what she was thinking. She was thinking that the impossible might be possible. If Mr. Penrose were willing to reassign some of her duties at school for the next eight weeks and if she were to give up her weekly sessions with Sir Hilbert and the stolen moments she spent with her cherished astronomy texts, then it just might be possible for her to make time to work with Sage.

She paused beside the door and glanced back at him.

"I do hope," said Castleton beside her, "that you will not let this little ... incident adversely affect your decision as to whether or not to undertake Sage's edification."

It had been a mistake to look back. Ariel knew it instantly, in spite of the fact that Sage gave no response to the polite good-bye she extended. She had never thought to encounter a mere earthly mystery that could capture her heart and mind as thoroughly and intensely as the night sky, but now she had.

She shook her head. "It has not adversely affected my thinking at all. Much the opposite in fact. I find the situation quite . . . intriguing."

"Then you agree to take it on?"

She hesitated, her gaze finding Sage's opaque one before nodding. "Yes. If Mr. Penrose will agree to spare me from my usual duties temporarily, I will do my best to accomplish what you desire."

Castleton smiled broadly. "First rate, Miss Halliday. Penrose will give you all the time you need, isn't that right, Penrose?"

"Why, yes, I imagine . . . of course," he said, sounding as if this were the first time he'd actually considered what Ariel's involvement in this project would mean for him personally. Knowing him as she did, Ariel was certain that was the case.

"Then it is settled," the earl pronounced. "Shall we return to the drawing room to work out the details?"

From inside his despised cell of a room, Leon Nicholas Duvanne watched the door close behind the small group, listened to the now-familiar sound of the locks being secured, and told himself it mattered not at all to him whether the silly Halliday chit chose to see to his "edification" or to disappear entirely from the face of the earth. In fact, given a choice in the matter, he would greatly prefer the latter. One less Brit to foul the world.

If he had felt something akin to anxiety as he

waited to hear her response to Castleton's request, it was only in the interest of self-preservation, he assured himself. He had a very definite interest in seeing who would step forward to tame the savage beast.

As for the other, more disturbing feelings she had managed to elicit during her brief visit, they could be attributed to reflex, pure and simple. The past few moments had provided more in the way of exercise and stimulation than he'd enjoyed for longer than he cared to contemplate. It was only natural for his body to respond.

Leon frowned, recalling the precise manner in which his body had answered the stimulus of her soft curves and sweetly scented flesh as she lay trembling beneath him. Even now he felt the lingering tension in muscles that had been drawn tight from belly to foot. It was a raw, restless feeling he knew well. Reflex, he reaffirmed silently. Nothing more. After the long weeks of solitude and acrimony, he doubtless would have reacted in the same fashion to the touch of anything wearing a skirt.

Still, it wasn't a good sign. This ordeal was taking its toll, and if they didn't move to end it soon, he would be forced to.

Sidestepping the pieces of broken china, he walked to the door and for the first time since he'd been locked in the tiny room, attempted to peer through the narrow opening at the edge of the curtain. The hallway outside was deserted, however, and the thought of Miss Halliday and her cohorts gathered in the drawing room, perhaps drinking a toast to the success of their joint venture, only served to darken his mood further.

The woman was, without question, the most audacious, ill-advised, and foolhardy female he had ever encountered. That was no small accomplishment on her part, since his opinion of the female species in general was not particularly salutary. Who but a half-brained woman would venture into a locked room to confront a man who had been confined far too long with only his own unsavory company? And how had she come armed for such a confrontation? Why, with nothing more than a pot of British tea, of course. That and her confederates, the bungling crew of would-be protectors who had remained lurking like the cowards they were outside the door.

Leon smiled. It pleased him as few things did these days to contemplate how easily he could have slit her throat if he'd been in the mood to, grabbing her lily-white neck with one hand while he snatched the knife hidden inside his mattress with the other. A careless footman had left the utensil on his dinner tray and he had used the clamp that held the iron bars on the window to sharpen its dull blade to a fine, deadly edge.

If he had cared to, he could have ended Miss Halliday's noble ambitions on his behalf while her rescuers were still stumbling over each other in an effort to get the door open. He had no doubt the beast in him could have followed up by dispatching the four of them with equal efficiency.

Fortunately for Miss Halliday, slaying silly, brave maidens in homely dresses was not part of his plan for the duration of his stay in England. It was her great misfortune, however, that neither was he planning to be brought to heel, by her or any other Englishman.

"Lord Savage" she had nearly slipped and called him and then turned the color of a ripe pomegranate, as if he had never before heard the name. It had certainly been used often enough by the crew of the ship that brought him there and was whispered behind his back by the giggling housemaids who each morning brought fresh linen for him to heap upon the floor. At least Tanner, a rather useless sort as far as he could tell, had shown the courage to say it to his face. Leon smiled again, deciding he liked his new nickname. Lord Savage. It was exceedingly apropos, he thought, though not quite in the manner he was sure it had been conceived. His intentions at the moment were savage indeed.

They were also necessarily vague, he acknowledged with an impatient sigh. He couldn't make precise plans for evening the score with Castleton and the others until he understood exactly what it was they meant to use him for. Thus far he had deduced only that they meant for him to claim the title left vacant by the recent demise of his father, a man he'd had the distinct pleasure of never meeting.

Oh, and he now knew one more thing of substance. He knew that Miss Halliday was on their side.

For a deranged few moments he had come close to believing that she was different from the others, that she somehow understood what it was like for him to be locked up *there,* of all the wretched places on earth.

It was her eyes that had thrown him off, he decided. They were too blue and too bright, like the light from a sorcerer's wand. For an instant he'd thought he saw in them a gleam of subtle amusement, a reassuring look that was almost conspiratorial.

Which was utterly ridiculous, he realized now, slamming both fists against the solid wall above the door with such force, the glass panel shook. The only conspiracy here was being waged against him, and Miss Halliday was part of it. He could not afford to forget that, especially if she did indeed assume the role of his ... trainer, he thought with a contemptuous sneer.

Turning, he rested his shoulders against the door, arms folded. It irked him greatly that he, a man who prided himself on his immunity to even the most skillful practitioners of feminine wiles, had been momentarily confused in such a way, betrayed by his own loins. He struggled to make sense of such uncharacteristic weakness. There had been something in her tone that misled him, he reflected, a gentleness that seemed to imply he was deserving of her kindness, that he was not merely some wretched creature to be chained and stared at and exploited.

How she could have known such a thing hadn't occurred to him at that moment, of course, only that somehow, by some unmerited miracle issued on his behalf, she did, and that she alone possessed the insight to see past his silence and his boorishness to what lay hidden in the darkness of his heart.

He needn't have worried. It turned out she was exactly like the rest. Blindly smug and resolved in her supposed superiority. He'd realized it the instant he saw the revulsion on her face when he spat out her precious English tea.

Learn to like it, would he? he thought, rage and resentment flaring to life in his belly as he came away from the wall and stood with muscles clenched as if preparing to do battle. The feelings were as familiar and comforting as old friends. Together they comprised a beast he knew well. Learn to like it? Not in a million lifetimes. There was nothing about this cursed country that he would ever learn to like. Or trust. Or need.

Just as there was nothing the brave, misguided Miss Halliday or any other Englishman could teach him. The fact was that he would be the instructor before this game was finished, teaching fair England a lesson that had been a very long time coming.

In the meantime, however, there was his boredom to attend to.

Agitation still churned inside him as he made his way back to the cot. He was greatly looking forward to the entertainment of watching Miss Halliday give it her best effort. And he was resolved that she would find him a most accommodating pupil. He grinned as he folded his hands behind his head, cushioning it from the hard wall.

After all, if it was a savage she wanted, a savage she should have.

Three

I must say, Miss Halliday, you very nearly made a botch-up of that whole affair."

Pulling her mantle tighter against the damp bite of the wind on that cold, gray February day Ariel resisted the urge to point out to Penrose that if he hadn't dragged her into the whole affair to begin with, she wouldn't have had the opportunity to make a botch-up of it.

"I'm just relieved we were finally able to come to terms that are satisfactory to everyone concerned," she murmured, sidestepping a slick spot on the bricks as he preceded her down the steps, leaving her to make her own way to his carriage waiting at the curb. As always, she had to suppress an ironic smile as she climbed inside and settled herself on the velvet seat cushion. With its brass fittings and mahogany doors inlaid with the school crest, the ostentatious carriage was more suited to Mr. Penrose's aspirations than his station.

"And well you might be relieved," he replied, taking the seat opposite her. "It's not every day you have the chance to do a kindness for a peer. It cannot hurt, you know. Especially when it's the sons and daughters of Castleton's circle whom we most want to attract to Penrose."

In utter defiance of the terms of the school's founding grant and endowment, thought Ariel, but held her tongue.

Since Phillip's father, the school's first headmaster, had passed away and the school's governors had seen fit to install Phillip in his place, the enrollment included steadily fewer of the local, underprivileged youngsters the school had been founded to serve and more off-spring of the elite, girls and boys alike, whose difficult behavior made them unwelcome elsewhere and whose families were wealthy enough to pay the exorbitant fees Phillip required to deal with the little brats. It was becoming the school's claim to fame and was no doubt what had led Lord Castleton to them in the first place.

"I only hope that I will be able to fulfill the earl's expectations," she said.

Mr. Penrose's watery blue eyes grew wide as he pinched the bridge of his nose between his thumb and forefinger. It was a familiar gesture, the first indication of the onset of a horrific migraine that could leave him prostrate and Ariel rushing about tending to his responsibilities as well as her own for days at a stretch.

"Please," he said, drawing the word out in a tone even more nasal than usual. "Do not even suggest such a ridiculous possibility. You *will* fulfill Castleton's expectations, Miss Halliday, every last one of them. You must. There is no other way about it. Surely you can see that for yourself, can you not?"

What she could see was that, as usual, there would

be no sense in arguing the reality of the situation with him when that reality threatened to conflict with whatever he wanted most at the moment. It was obvious that what he wanted most at that moment was to ingratiate himself with Castleton. Ariel was merely his means of accomplishing that goal.

Her instinctive reaction was to tell him to go hang. However, since an ugly twist of fate decreed that what she must desire most at that moment was to ingratiate herself with Mr. Penrose himself, she had no choice but to smile sweetly and go along with the whole preposterous undertaking.

"I understand fully the importance of the task I have been asked to perform," she assured him. "I meant only that it is a great deal to accomplish in so short a time."

"You have eight weeks," he interjected, plucking at the starched crease of his cravat. "And it's not as if you have not been provided the raw material to work with. Good God, Miss Halliday, as heinous as he may appear at the moment, the man is a noble by birth. The potential is there. All you have to do is bring it out."

Is that all? thought Ariel, tempted to inquire as to precisely how he would suggest she go about bringing out the noble side of a man she couldn't say for certain knew how to speak or dress himself.

"You will need to devise a plan, of course," he proceeded to instruct without her having to ask. "As well as a list of goals and a schedule. And you will need to apply yourself most diligently," he added, lifting his chin to direct a meaningful stare down his long nose at her.

"Yes, Mr. Penrose," she replied, taking advantage of his attention to flutter her lashes rapidly, the way she'd been practicing in the mirror every morning for a week.

Penrose frowned impatiently. "Have you something in your eyes, Miss Halliday?"

"No . . . I mean yes." She lowered her gaze, feeling her cheeks growing warm. "That is, I did, but whatever it was is gone now."

"Good, we've no time to waste here. Now, where was I? Oh, yes, I was saying you will need to establish a schedule and keep to it. None of that losing yourself in a book of stars or wandering off in the dead of night in search of some ungodly comet. Do you take my meaning?"

"Entirely."

Oh, why, she thought, couldn't fate have dealt her a more pleasant cross than this to bear? Being mired in quicksand or burned at the stake, perhaps. She'd prefer almost anything to being forced to play the coquette, and for the benefit of Phillip Penrose of all people.

Pale and puny and self-absorbed beyond endurance, he was the last man she would choose if she were looking to make a match. Which she most definitely was not. At least not of her own free will, she thought miserably, defiance warring with resignation as she realized that as unsettling and humiliating as it was to admit, she was reduced to doing precisely that. Husband-hunt.

She shuddered against the tufted seat back, barely listening to the steady stream of advice and admonitions flowing from the opposite side of the coach.

At twenty-five she was well beyond the realm of romance and had been quite content, even happy, to claim as her own the relative freedom that was the only silver lining to be found in the cloud of spinsterhood. As insignificant as it might be when compared to the privileges that were the birthright of every man, Ariel had come to the conclusion that freedom from wedded bliss was the nearest thing to true independence a woman could hope to achieve in this world. And it had been hers . . . until disaster struck.

"Discipline," Mr. Penrose was saying, his tone rising as if sensing her distraction. "There is no substitute for it in all of education. And in this case I can see where it will be particularly imperative."

Ariel nodded agreement, though not quite sure if he was suggesting that the need for discipline applied to her or to Lord Sage or both.

She considered asking, tactfully of course, and mostly in an attempt to advance her cause by providing further opportunity for him to indulge in his favorite pastime, listening to the sound of his own voice. However, a glance out the window informed her that they had turned onto the road to Paddington and she quickly raised a hand to halt his soliloquy.

"I beg your pardon, Mr. Penrose, but I just noticed that we've made the turn for Paddington."

"Of course we've made the turn for Paddington. The school is located in Paddington." His derisive smile signaled his irritation at being interrupted. "Or had you forgotten?"

"No, but perhaps it has slipped your mind that Saturday is my customary day off and that I have plans to spend the afternoon at home."

"Your customary day off?" The words sputtered from him. "My dear lady, have you entirely no grasp of the situation at hand? And that there is not the least thing at all customary about it?"

"I believe I fully grasp the situation, Mr. Penrose," she replied, endeavoring to sound serene, the epitome of sweet-tempered femininity. "But I gave my mother my word that I would stop by this afternoon to check on my father's progress and see if I might help in any—"

"Really, Miss Halliday, I have quite had my fill of your father and his infernal gout and with you running over there every time you turn around. How long might I expect this to go on?"

Forever, Ariel thought.

"It is difficult to say," she replied. "You know what is said about doctors making the worst possible patients, and I confess that my father, though retired from his profession, is no exception. I must beg your indulgence for a while longer."

"My indulgence is one thing; interfering with Lord Castleton's plans is quite another."

"Of course, and I would not dream of doing such a thing. If I'd had some prior warning of the earl's request, I would never have given my mother my word that I would call today. As it is, however, I'm committed. So if you would please be so kind as to ask Brindley to turn before we get any farther from Clapham Common, I would be most grateful."

Penrose folded his arms across his chest. "I'm afraid that's out of the question." Before she could protest, he continued. "Your parents have always seemed reasonable enough sorts to me. I'm sure they'll understand why the earl's wishes must take precedence over a mere family visit. You may send word to them later, explaining your failure to call."

"But—"

"My decision is final, Miss Halliday. There will be no more social calls and no more days off for any reason until after Sage has been presented to his grandmother. Is that clear?"

"Very," she said, resentment forming a fiery lump in her throat, one she couldn't swallow and didn't dare spit out.

"You have much to accomplish in a limited time.

You said so yourself only a moment ago," he reminded her. "You can start as soon as we get back by overseeing the preparation of the cottage. I shall have no time to manage the task since I"—he thumped his chest dramatically—"shall have my hands full dealing with all the duties that you will be neglecting for the next eight weeks."

"Of course," Ariel murmured, concealing her amusement at the thought of him trying to manage his own responsibilities without assistance, much less see to hers.

Once she had a moment to consider, she decided she would actually prefer to see personally to the quarters where she would be living than leave the preparation in his incapable hands.

The original plan had been for her to travel with Lord Sage to Castleton's country estate where they could work without interruption. She had balked at that, however, and made it clear she could not be away from London, and her parents, for eight weeks. Her reluctance might have provided a reprieve, but for Mr. Penrose's hasty offer to let them use a vacant cottage on the grounds of the school.

The ivy-covered dwelling tucked into a remote corner of the wooded campus had been the headmaster's residence until Mr. Penrose decided the position called for more spacious and luxurious quarters. Ariel had often stopped while walking nearby to peer into the darkened windows, and she looked forward to at last seeing what the pretty stone house was like on the inside.

First, however, she must arrange for a message to be carried to her mother, expressing her regret at being unable to come as planned and promising to explain everything when she saw her next. Which would be very soon. Ariel was determined about that, whether Mr. Penrose approved or not.

She considered the possibility of attempting to persuade him to change his mind by telling him the truth about her father's condition, that it was not gout that had him indisposed, but something far more serious and dismaying. However, that might interfere with her plans by making her appear to be what she was, desperate. It would also mean breaking her promise to her mother that she would keep the family secret about the true nature of her father's illness as long as possible. She would simply have to go along with Penrose's edict for the time being.

Fortunately, her mother still had the assistance of Elise. Once her mother's cherished lady's maid, poor Elise was now reduced to the status of maid-of-all-work, as much a victim of circumstance as the rest of them. And there was also Horace, of course, their manservant for years and years and who, like Elise, was too fiercely loyal to desert them now, in spite of the fact that his duties had multiplied even as the salary they could afford to pay him had whittled.

As loyal and dedicated as they were, however, they were still servants. With her younger sister Caroline married and living most of the year in Derby, Ariel knew her mother had only her to turn to for the comfort and moral support she needed, and it rankled that she would be forced to abandon her for even a short while.

They passed the rest of the ride to Paddington in silence, Mr. Penrose no doubt reliving his recent moments of glory in Castleton's drawing room, while Ariel relished the thought of just how full her odious employer's hands were going to be in the coming weeks. Perhaps, she mused, there was a bright spot to all this. It was possible her absence would succeed where all her pitiful attempts at coquetry had failed, convincing Mr. Penrose of how much he needed her help to keep the school and his life running smoothly, now and in the future.

As soon as they arrived back at school, Penrose went off in search of medicine to forestall the approaching migraine, and Ariel, after sending a message to her mother, set off to explore the cottage where she was slated to perform her upcoming miracles. In spite of her dismal mood, she had to admit that the house lived up to even the most whimsical fantasies she'd woven while stretched on tiptoe to peer through its mullioned windows.

There was a curved window seat overlooking the garden, a delicate plaster-cast vine of leaves and flowers trailing along a curling staircase, and delightful nooks and crannies throughout. Before leaving she took inventory of linens and supplies and spent the rest of the evening and most of Sunday devising a plan to accomplish the task she had so foolishly agreed to undertake.

As always in times of trouble, she resorted to making lists. A well-ordered list made her feel in control even in the midst of chaos. She made lists of chores and lists of supplies. Her final list was concerned with the task itself. Sunday afternoon became Sunday evening as she sat at the desk in her small, drafty room asking herself where she might best begin the taming process.

It was, she discovered, like trying to unravel an endless ball of twine. There seemed to be no logical place to start. Which came first, the croissant or the cravat? The fencing saber or the salad fork? The art of conversation or the art of sipping tea without spitting it in the hostess's face? Finally, exhausted from thinking about it, she blew out the candle and crawled into bed, resolving to assume nothing and expect nothing and therefore be pleasantly surprised if her new pupil demonstrated any aptitude for anything at all.

By Wednesday everything in the cottage was clean, aired, and in place—thanks to a small battalion of the school's staff of housemaids and footmen. Glass sparkled, wood gleamed, and scents of burning wood and lemon oil filled the rooms.

The previous night, Ariel had paused while making up the bed in the master chamber, aware that she was humming happily. The sheer intensity of her feelings was disconcerting to her. It occurred to her that this had to be what a new bride feels as she goes about setting up the first household she will share with her husband. It was a heady mixture of pride and excitement. No, she thought, more like anticipation, as if all this preparation was intended to please an audience of one.

That morning, however, she rose early, too anxious to sleep, and watched as heavy gray storm clouds rolled in from the west, darkening the sky to a violent swirl of gray and black. During the night the temperature had dropped and the wind picked up. Shutters rattled and tree branches slapped at the windows. All in all it promised to be a most disagreeable day.

Even the air felt heavy and tense, as if nature herself were poised and waiting to see what would be unleashed by the heavens. It was fortunate she was not the fainthearted sort who believed in omens, thought Ariel, or she would be quite undone.

The rain came just before noon, the appointed hour for Lord Sage's arrival. It swept across the land in great wavering sheets that quickly turned the lawn to swamp and transformed the drive to the cottage into an obstacle course of deep ruts and puddles that the trio of carriages sent by Lord Castleton had to twist and swerve to avoid.

Inside the cottage the mood was as tense and fore-boding as the elements. Ariel, dressed in her best sage muslin, ivory lace at her throat and wrists, stood at one of a pair of tall fireside windows in the drawing room, tracking the carriages' tortuous approach. Mr. Penrose stood watch at the other. Judging from the occasional nervous giggle that drifted from the dining room across the hall, she suspected that the windows there were similarly manned by the small household staff that Mr. Penrose had reluctantly agreed to provide.

Finally the caravan reached the circle in front of the cottage and stopped. A footman disembarked and hurried to open the door of the first carriage in line. Mr. and Mrs. Farrell, the couple hired by Lord Castleton, emerged and lumbered their way to the front door, where Hodges, the butler, motioned to the waiting footmen to help deal with their wet cloaks and bags.

Ariel had already met the Farrells and found them quite dour and well suited to each other. They had stopped by earlier in the week, finding her up to her ears in soot from the fireplace screen she was polishing, and had immediately and haughtily informed her that they had not been hired to clean house. Ariel had been only too happy to send them away with instructions to return today.

She nodded to them as they made their way to the fireplace to warm their hands, then moved to join Mr. Penrose at the center of the drawing room. Together they watched a pair of burly giants alight from the second carriage. The men were clad in polished top boots and matching frock coats bearing the Castleton crest, and their stiff posture spoke of past military service. Once on the ground, they reached back into the carriage and dragged out what appeared to be a bundle of rags the size of a man. A very tall man. Bracing it between them, they made for the door.

Just as they reached the threshold, the first bolt of lightning came, splitting the sky in two and igniting the land below with a light so intense that it seemed to make time stand still for an instant. Thunder followed, quick and fierce and very close by, jolting them all back into action.

The Farrells were grumbling to each other and footmen hurried to and fro, unloading the carriages. Only Ariel and Mr. Penrose remained still, waiting as the earl's men dragged their sopping, unwieldy bag of rags inside and came to a stop directly before them.

As Penrose stammered for words and Ariel regained her breath, the rags moved. First slightly, then with a sudden, furious shaking motion that sent drops of water flying onto Mr. Penrose's favorite embroidered waistcoat. The uppermost folds of the bundle of rags parted so that Ariel could see that it was not rags at all, but rather a dingy and well-worn gray blanket.

A head emerged from inside the blanket. She focused on it in pieces as it was revealed. First the cascade of raven hair, thick and straight, and then the eyes, that deep-set, unflinching gaze of ancient bronze that was scorched into her memory and had even invaded her dreams.

She breathed deeply, instinctively avoiding the gaze, staring instead at the mouth, at the full lips surrounded by black whiskers that had grown noticeably longer and bushier in just a handful of days. Already his mouth was slouching into what might or might not be a faintly contemptuous sneer.

Ariel reminded herself that she had prepared carefully for this moment, fully anticipating her own disturbing and unexplainable physical response to the man's presence. She had been caught unawares at their first meeting, but this time she was ready, braced for the impact, and so there was no logical reason why her stomach should be threatening to take flight this way.

"I say," Mr. Penrose began, and then said nothing.

Sage stared down on him, his narrowed gaze as icy and harsh as the wind that whipped outside.

There was also no reason, she tried telling herself, that his stare should be construed as threatening. Sage was not only restrained and outnumbered after all, but thoroughly confined by the blanket.

It *was* threatening just the same, and with a sharply drawn breath Ariel accepted the fact that rules of reason did not apply the same way to this man as they did to everyone else in the world.

Without taking his eyes off their blanket-swathed guest, Mr. Penrose reached out to grasp Ariel's arm and thrust her forward.

"Talk to him," he ordered.

Refusing to tremble, Ariel lifted her chin to confront the tarnished gold gaze of the Marquis of Sage.

"Welcome, my lord," she began, bending one knee in a curtsy as she drew the well-rehearsed words from her memory. "This humble dwelling is called Placentia, which means the pleasant place, and it is the fervent hope of both Mr. Penrose and myself that your brief stay with us here will prove to be both pleasant and fruitful."

Silence.

Penrose nudged her. "Go on."

Go on? Ariel gulped. That was all she had prepared. She clasped her hands in front of her and tried to smile.

"You are wet," she observed. "And cold as well, I would wager. May I relieve you of your . . ."

Blanket. The word froze on her tongue, plunging the room back into tense silence. Her gaze remained riveted on Sage. With his black brows arched, his eyes as cold as brass coins, his lean countenance a study in grimness, he called to her mind the image of Satan in the mural at the Church of the Holy Martyrs. It was an image that had caused her to quake in her boots as a child, and it threatened to wield the same sinister power over her now if she let it.

". . . your wet things," she finished gamely.

At that instant another bolt of lightning cracked across the sky and everyone in the room jumped at once. Everyone with the exception of Sage.

It was eerie, as if he were in league with the storm and its timing was his own so that at the precise instant the thunder shattered the quiet in the room, distracting them all momentarily, he wrenched loose from the men holding his arms and with a violent toss of his head freed himself from the blanket as well.

It fell to the floor, leaving him clad only in the same tight black breeches she'd seen on him before. The bare skin of his shoulders and chest gleamed golden brown in the candlelight, the flickering shadows playing across a magnificently masculine arrangement of sinew and bone.

A lesser man would have appeared foolish, standing nearly naked in their midst. Instead, Sage's composure and his proud, defiant stance rendered him a figure of mystery and power, clearly a force to be reckoned with. The small group of onlookers was as stunned as if some ancient, mythical god had suddenly materialized before them. It was several seconds after the initial collective gasp of shock before any of them recovered enough to take action. His brawny escorts reacted first.

"Grab him," ordered one of the men, himself reaching to take Sage by the nearest arm.

Sage was quicker by far. He sidestepped their grasp and then held the two men at bay with a wild, teeth-bared glare, his fists tightly clenched at his sides. This was a look more reminiscent of a jungle painting than either a church mural or an ancient god.

Ariel stared at him uneasily. It was not at all the smooth start she had hoped for. In fact, she was thinking the moment could hardly get any worse, when suddenly it did.

The thunder spent, it had become as quiet outside the house as within, as if the very eye of the storm were upon them. Only one sound disturbed the unnatural stillness, and that was the low, feral growl coming from deep in his lordship's chest.

What in heaven's name had she gotten herself into?

Four

Castleton's henchmen stood their ground, eyeing Sage with a mixture of caution and confusion.

As well they might, thought Ariel. She could imagine what the earl's instructions to them must have been. Guard Sage, but take care not to do him injury. Be alert but unobtrusive, firm but respectful. No doubt the poor fellows were wondering just how far it was proper for them to go to subdue an unarmed, half-naked, growling marquis.

An excellent question.

Unfortunately she hadn't even the beginning of an answer.

Perplexed, she turned to Mr. Penrose and discovered that the quiet tapping noise that now presented a counterpoint to his lordship's growling was the sound of her employer's teeth chattering in fright. Obviously there would be no help from that quarter. Even the Farrells, her supposed protectors, seemed to be struck dumb. Though it was Mrs. Farrell who found her tongue before the rest of them.

"Blimey," she murmured, her wide eyes focused with undisguised fascination on Lord Sage's bare chest. "He's a right fit one, ain't he?"

Ariel squared her shoulders and stepped forward. Obviously it was up to her to do something. She positioned herself between Lord Sage and the two men, putting her back to Sage in what could prove to be either a fatal mistake or the first step in building the requisite trust between teacher and pupil.

"Enough," she said.

The growling ceased.

She glanced slowly around the room before continuing.

"It has been a trying morning for everyone. What with the storm and the no doubt perilous trip out here, none of us are at our best or most gracious. For that reason I suggest we do not prolong matters unnecessarily." She returned her gaze to the two men before her. "Please convey to the earl that Lord Sage has arrived safely and assure him that I will report to him as previously arranged."

One of the men bobbed his head and wiped the back of his hand across his mouth nervously. "Begging your pardon, ma'am, but his lordship said it might be best if we stayed on for a while, until you could be sure . . ."

The growling resumed at her back, rough, low, sending warning shivers along her spine that she somehow found the courage to ignore.

"I am sure," she said, her firm tone giving no hint of the quivering inside.

"For God's sake, Miss Halliday," exclaimed Penrose,

stepping forward only to flinch back twice the distance when Sage focused his stare on him. "It never hurts to be cautious," he said more quietly, darting her a meaningful look.

"I am being cautious." She knew he would never understand why she felt it imperative at that moment to place the successful concordance with her student ahead of her own safety.

"You may go," she told Castleton's men, who fled the room with relieved expressions.

Turning back to Penrose, she managed to keep a straight face as she said, "Under the circumstance, perhaps you would rather postpone any further conversation with his lordship until another time. I know you have pressing school matters to attend."

"Yes, yes, of course," he blurted out, already edging toward the door. He halted halfway, a guilty flush spreading across his narrow face. "That is, if you are certain you . . . that is, that you will be . . ."

"Quite certain," she assured him. "Good day, Mr. Penrose."

When he was gone, she beckoned to the Farrells.

"You have made it clear that housekeeping was not included in your arrangement with Lord Castleton," she said. "However, he has informed me that you, Mrs. Farrell, will be available to cook, as well as be on hand for any other tasks that might arise in association with his lordship's stay here."

The woman shrugged her plump shoulders. "That's true enough, I suppose."

"Very good. Then perhaps you would be so kind as to begin preparations for dinner. I believe you will find the kitchen well stocked."

"Yes, ma'am."

"We shall also be desiring tea later this afternoon, after Lord Sage has been made comfortable," she added, trying not to think about what that entailed.

"Yes, ma'am."

Ariel dismissed the woman with a nod and turned her attention to Mr. Farrell, who stood by eyeing her warily.

"I will be needing your assistance with Lord Sage periodically throughout the afternoon, but for now you may take your bags to your room. Hodges will show you the way." She smiled at Hodges, a spry, silver-haired gentleman who was thrilled with his temporary assignment at the cottage. "I shall be expecting you to join us in a half hour's time."

Farrell nodded and turned to go. Ariel couldn't deny that the sight of him hoisting a heavy bag under each arm as effortlessly as if they were filled with feathers was the most reassuring sight she had seen all day. As disagreeable as she found the Farrells personally, it was comforting to know that if bad turned to worst, the hale and hearty Farrells would be within shouting distance.

She gestured to the young housemaid hovering by the door, coaxing her forth with a smile.

"Jenny, please dispose of that." She pointed at the blanket that lay on the floor where Sage had dropped it. "Lord Sage will have no further use for it."

"As you say, ma'am," the maid replied, keeping her eyes averted from the half-clad noble as she scooted across the room to snatch the blanket and make her getaway.

Ariel envied her. She envied all of them really, all free to walk away from this debacle and tend to other matters. Matters that could be easily understood and approached in a logical and proven fashion.

She longed for her tiny office on the top floor of the school building. How happy she would be to be back at work on her tedious ledgers and boring order forms, passing the hours trying to decipher Mr. Penrose's squiggly penmanship, composing tactfully worded progress reports and letters to parents for him to sign. She even had a fond thought for her private students, the worst of the worst, who were regularly foisted on her for individual tutoring because Mr. Penrose insisted she "had a way with them."

Had a soft spot for them was more like it. She believed there was always a reason, as carefully hidden as it might be, for their sullen attitudes and the rampant misbehavior that had landed them in the school's "special program."

Perhaps it was because she understood so well what it felt like to never get things precisely right, never quite measure up, never be as pretty or witty or pleasing as she ought to be, that she was able to fathom what each of them really needed to be taught and to teach them.

Could she succeed in doing the same with the silent, untamed man behind her?

The moment had arrived to find out.

Ignoring a last surge of nerves, she slowly turned to face Lord Sage. He appeared as remote as ever. Hoping to heaven she was right in her conviction that a lively intelligence lurked beneath all that stony detachment, she offered him a smile.

"Well then," she began, instinctively clasping her hands loosely in front of her as if she were in the classroom, "it seems we will be able to get under way at last.

And not a minute too soon in light of all we have to accomplish." Her smile became edged with doubt as he continued to watch her without reaction. "Tell me, Lord Sage, do you have any understanding at all of the words I am speaking to you?"

Silence. Steady, impenetrable silence.

"Fiddlesticks," she said experimentally, careful to maintain the same even expression and tone. "Hennypenny. Hatter-scatter. Knocking nodding nabobs need not apply."

As she spoke, she observed his face intently, alert to even the slightest spontaneous flicker of surprise or amusement. There was nothing. It was a foolish notion, she supposed. Why on earth would a man want to complicate his own situation by pretending not to understand if in fact he did?

"Very well, I can see that we will need to begin at the beginning." She sighed. "Before the beginning actually, wherever that may prove to be. Please follow me." She accompanied the request with an appropriate gesture, and wonder of wonders he complied. She led him to the staircase.

"Stairs," she said slowly and clearly, tapping the carved newel post. "Stairs. Climb."

She made a walking motion with her fingers before hitching her skirt and climbing up a few steps. She stopped and turned back to encourage him to do the same, only to find him staring at her ankles. He appeared fascinated, his mouth again curved in that way that unsettled her.

"No," she said firmly, hastily lowering her skirts and again gesturing for him to follow. "Come. Climb stairs. Stairs. Climb. Follow me."

Wordlessly he moved behind her up the stairs. Still

speaking in single words and using hand signals, she led him the length of the hallway to his chamber at the back of the house. A fire had been started in the fireplace and the wall lamps lit so that there, as in the rest of the house, the mood was warm and welcoming even on so bleak a day.

The room itself was spacious, with a high ceiling and walls papered in a bold cream and evergreen stripe. A dark patterned rug covered the newly polished wood floor, and both the damask coverlet and matching silk drapes were a deep shade of gold. Even the new addition of framed woodland prints contributed to the chamber's appropriately masculine air. Ariel couldn't help feeling a twinge of pride, and it was with great anticipation that she observed his reaction as he followed her inside, gazed slowly around, and sniffed.

Sniffed.

There was no mistaking it, for he performed the act quite openly, wrinkling his nose and turning his head from side to side. He even strode about as he sniffed, rather like a dog on the scent, moving past the high mahogany bed with its embroidered canopy, past the freshly stocked toilet table, at last coming to a stop in front of a tallboy of Hepplewhite design.

With nostrils flaring, he sought Ariel's gaze. Seeing the inquisitiveness that burned in his eyes, she hurried across the room to stand beside him. She inhaled deeply and smiled.

"Sandalwood," she told him. "You smell sandalwood. Smell." She touched her nose and sniffed enthusiastically. "Nose. Smell." More sniffing. "Sandalwood."

He inhaled again, deeply, and looked about.

"Sandalwood," she repeated. "Here. See for yourself." She pulled open the tallboy's doors, revealing the neat arrangement of drawers within. Sliding open a drawer, she scooped out a handful of the fragrant wood chips and held them up to him.

"Smell," she urged. "Sandalwood."

He pushed his nose into the wood chips.

Ariel shivered as his whiskers brushed the sensitive flesh at the inside of her wrist, and his breath warmed her palm.

"Sandalwood," she said again, aware of a change in her tone, a hesitancy that had nothing to do with the woodsy fragrance and everything to do with the man and the tiny ripples of sensation that his touch sent racing the length of her arm. She plodded on. "At home we always scattered bits of it in the drawers and closets. It counteracts the dampness and leaves the most wonderful scent on everything that is kept there."

With a final sniff he lifted his head, breaking their contact, to Ariel's great relief. She was startled to see his mouth slant in what seemed to be an ironic smile.

"So," she said, "we have made our first discovery together. We found out that you like the scent of sandalwood. Good. It will make your stay in this room that much more pleasant."

She dumped the chips back into the drawer and closed it.

She turned her attention to his trunk, which had been placed at the foot of the bed, and to the matched valises lined up on the cushioned bench nearby.

"Ordinarily your belongings would be unpacked by the upstairs maid," she explained, having decided beforehand to speak to him as if he did comprehend what she was saying in the hope that eventually, in bits and pieces, he would. "However, I shall tend to it myself so that I might become acquainted with your personal effects and the extent of your wardrobe. In that way, if anything is lacking, I will be able to remedy the situation as quickly as possible."

As she spoke, she went about removing from the trunk a variety of finely tailored garments made of the choicest fabrics—silk and kerseymere and damask. The Earl of Castleton was a renowned follower of fashion, and he had obviously spared nothing in assembling a wardrobe befitting a marquis.

There were a dozen ruffled shirts of fine white lawn, an equal number of snowy silk cravats, and nearly twice that many waistcoats, vibrant colors for day and elegant black and white for evening, many with an overlay of intricate gold or silver embroidery. The buckskin trousers were all buff, but in subtly different hues of that most fashionable color, enough pairs for each day of the week. Also included was the full assortment of coats a gentleman required. From the most simple morning coat to an elegant, fitted greatcoat, they were made of wool in black and deep, rich shades of brown and green.

"I can see that my concerns were ill placed," she said as she hung the last of the coats in the deep dressing closet. "Lord Castleton has provided everything you will need to appear the perfect English lord and gentleman. Now it is up to us to see to the rest."

Ariel paused, gathering herself for the next, and most potentially difficult, phase of the day's agenda.

"The very first requirement for any gentleman, or lady for that matter, is cleanliness," she told him. "It was not always so, and unfortunately there are those in society who still ignore the most basic dictates of personal hygiene, to an end that no amount of sandalwood chips can overcome, I assure you."

To her amazement, he sniffed the air enthusiastically.

"Yes, yes, sandalwood," she exclaimed, reaching

out without thinking to touch his arm encouragingly, the way she would with any other student. Any other student, however, would not be standing there shirtless. Her fingertips sizzled as if his skin were on fire, and she jerked her hand away.

His bottom lip curled.

"Sandalwood," she murmured again, her concentration shattered. "Where was I? Oh, yes, cleanliness. A gentleman ignores the matter at great social peril. Brummell himself set the standard, and to be fresh and naturally fragrant from the inside out is now quite the rage. George Brummell was, of course . . ."

She saw his gaze cloud and wander to where she held her hands loosely clasped at her waist.

"Brummell is a topic that can wait till another day," she concluded. "For now, please come with me. Come."

She beckoned and led him to the tiled bathing chamber several doors away. Stepping inside, she indicated the oversized metal tub in the center of the room.

"This is a tub for bathing. Tub. Bath." She pointed to the buckets of water lined up against the wall, waiting to be heated on the coal stove in the corner. A large cauldron was already steaming on top of the stove, and the tub itself had begun to be filled in accordance with her orders.

"Water. For washing." She dipped her fingers into the tub and made circular motions over her face and neck. "Water. Wash. Bath. Water."

He watched her and then lifted his hand to his chin and rubbed his beard.

She smiled broadly. "Yes, that's it. You will do fine. Now we only have to wait for Mr. Farrell to arrive to assist you."

He continued to stare at her.

Ariel continued to smile. "I am sure he will not be long."

She was glancing around the room, wondering why on earth Mr. Penrose hadn't thought to install a bell there, when Sage moved toward her. He stopped between her and the tub and bent to trail his fingers in the water. Before she realized what he intended, he had lifted his wet hand to her face and was moving it over her cheek and chin the same as she had done a moment earlier. The effect, however, was entirely different.

The water was warm, his fingertips slightly rough, and together they produced a sensation that left Ariel momentarily speechless.

Her eyes grew wide as his hand slipped lower, stroking the skin beneath her chin, then drifting lower stiff, moving down her throat in what could only be called a caress.

Warm drops of water from his fingers slid along her cheek and neck, leaving it moist and slippery and adding to the tantalizing effect of his touch. Slowly, his fingertips began to trace the slant of her collarbone. Ariel shivered and drew breath to order him to cease at once, but managed to say nothing.

Throughout it all, his dark gaze held hers captive. Now he shifted his attention to that place where his fingers had come to rest at the center of her chest, just above the lace trim of her gathered neckline. Instinctively, Ariel also lowered her head and watched, transfixed, as he lifted his thumb away from her, then lowered it again, using the callused pad to blot a drop of water that had pooled at the very top of the shadow between her breasts.

He rested his other hand on her shoulder, as if to

hold her near him as he casually raised his hand to his mouth and slowly drew his thumb across his tongue.

Ariel swayed weakly.

She was certain that what he had just done was the most erotic thing she had ever witnessed, without fully understanding why. A man's tongue, licking up water he'd taken from her breast, his heavy lidded gaze . . . Good God, what was there to understand, she chided herself, even as she continued to stand immobile beneath his light touch.

His gaze had grown hooded and speculative. He stared down at her, the haughty backward tilt of his head accentuating his high cheekbones, watching, waiting, daring her, it seemed.

To do what? she found herself wondering.

It didn't matter.

Decency demanded that she put a stop to what he was doing without another instant of delay, chastise him severely, and then put it from her mind forever.

She knew all that. And still she stood before him, dazed and dizzy, a docile prisoner of his, his wrist draped carelessly across her shoulder as if he had every right in the world to put his hands on her.

Not until his grip tightened and she felt him begin to slowly draw her closer did she regain some semblance of reason.

"No," she exclaimed, twisting to break free of him at last. Instinctively she clasped her arms across her chest. "No. No, no, no. You must never—" She paused for air, breathing suddenly an arduous task. "Never touch a lady . . . without her permission. Touch," she said, gesturing and shaking her head and wondering when this strange dizziness would leave her. "No."

He frowned.

"I'm very sorry if that does not meet with your lordship's approval," she snapped, irritated as much with the fact that she was still weak in the knees as with his impertinence. "Perhaps in your island society you are accustomed to unrestricted liberties of this nature, but I assure you it is not acceptable here. In England there is much protocol to be observed in affairs of the heart as in everything else." Her mouth quirked. "Perhaps more. But that is also a topic for another day. For now it is enough that you understand that you must not touch."

"Problem, missy?"

Ariel jumped and turned to find Mr. Farrell standing in the doorway, eyeing Sage with suspicion. She ought to feel a great surge of relief to have him there, she told herself. Instead, she felt a wisp of annoyance and a vague sense of disappointment.

"Not at all, Mr. Farrell," she replied, avoiding his gaze.

"You sure?" He looked from her to Sage and back. "You sounded riled to me."

"You're mistaken," she told him with a crisp air of finality. Since she intended to make certain that what had just transpired never happened again, there was really no need to mention it to Farrell.

"Now that you're here, however," she continued, "you may get on with his lordship's bath."

"His bath?" Farrell echoed, his face puckering. "You want me to bathe him? Like a babe?"

"No, I want you to teach him how to bathe."

"You mean he don't already know?"

"I'm not sure what he knows, Mr. Farrell. I expect we will discover that as we go along. For the moment I would say it's safest to assume you must start at the beginning and show him everything."

Farrell looked at the tub, then at Sage, then back to Ariel. "Everything?"

"Yes. Everything. You will find soap and towels on the bench by the window. There's also water heating on the stove. I shall leave it to you to finish filling the tub and warming the water in those pails for rinsing." She moved toward the door.

"While you're busy here, I will see to laying out his clothes." Drawing to a stop beside Farrell, she added in a quieter tone, "When he removes his breeches, you may place them outside the door and I'll see to their disposal."

Farrell's nose wrinkled. "Yes, ma'am."

"I will leave his dressing gown hanging on the doorknob."

He snickered. "If he even knows how to get such a thing on."

"I believe you are being paid to show him. If the arrangement is not satisfactory to you, perhaps you should say so now."

"No, ma'am," he said, sobering instantly. "It's plenty satisfactory."

"Good. Then get on with it." She smiled past him at a grim-looking Sage. "I'll leave you in very capable hands, I'm sure."

It was a vast overstatement. She was already beginning to question the judgment of whoever had recommended the Farrells to Castleton and to wonder how capable they would prove at anything useful. At that moment, however, she had more pressing concerns.

She went directly from the bath to the master chamber, maintaining a normal pace and stepping inside and closing the door calmly behind her. Then she threw her back against it and squeezed her eyes shut, her breath coming as hard and as fast as if she'd just run uphill.

She lifted her palms to her cheeks, not at all surprised to discover that her hands were shaking and her face was as warm as a fireplace stone. She shook her head, releasing a small, mirthless laugh at her own foolishness. She had thought herself so well prepared, she with all her lists and her vast experience with wayward youths and her meticulous plans for the future.

Well, you weren't prepared for this, were you? she thought wryly. You weren't prepared for *him*.

She opened her eyes and still couldn't halt the flood of excruciating memories. She recalled in vivid detail the moment he had touched her, the shadow of his long, dark lashes on his cheek as his gaze narrowed on her, and the way her senses had leapt at the sight of him licking the taste of her from his thumb, and the sudden swirl of heat and sweetness that had pooled in her stomach and held her spellbound.

How could she possibly have prepared herself? she wondered, when she had not even dreamed such things occurred . . . or that such feelings existed.

Forewarned was forearmed and all that, but how could she arm herself against something she did not even understand?

Obviously, through no fault of his own, his lordship was quite without even the most basic concept of civilized restraint. He was like a child, she decided, putting it in terms she did understand. He saw something that interested him and reached out to touch it.

That sort of impulse was something she knew how to deal with very well. Now all she had to do was remember that whenever she was in his presence.

Hoping to turn her thoughts in a different direction, she went to the overcrowded closet. She reached for a waistcoat, only to discover that the selection of the proper one was not a simple matter. One after another she lay the possible choices on the bed, imagining the effect of each with Sage's dark skin and dramatic features.

The procedure dragged on for several minutes before she recognized the absurdity of it. Snatching up the armful of waistcoats, she returned them to the closet, leaving by default an understated stripe in crimson and charcoal. She would do better to concern herself with how to get the clothes on Sage's back than whether or not they would flatter him.

Turning to the drawers, she quickly pulled out stockings, a cravat, and a shirt, stopping as she was about to toss the last on the bed to press it to her cheek, savoring the soft crispness unique to fine new fabric. There was a time not so long ago when she had taken such small pleasures for granted, a time when the smell and feel of new clothes were simply facts of her life as the elder daughter of a physician baronet.

She inhaled, detecting the hint of sandalwood that had already clung to the cloth, and had to smile.

"Sandalwood," she whispered, and suddenly without warning it wasn't finely woven linen she was feeling against her skin, but Sage's hands, warm and wet and rough. She closed her eyes, swamped by the abrupt intensity of the recollection. It was as if he were touching her again, and it took tenacious self-control for her to open her eyes and cast the shirt aside.

"Boots," she muttered, looking around distractedly. "He will need boots."

She found footwear in a bag she hadn't noticed earlier and quickly selected a pair of glossy black Wellingtons, propping them on the boot rack by the side of the bed. With the same determined efficiency she located his dressing gown, a simple black silk design with gold accents and piping, and carried it, along with extra towels, with her back to the bathing chamber.

She was still several yards from the tightly closed door, when she heard the noise. It was sharp and distinct and Ariel's brow wrinkled as she tried to identify it.

Oh, please, don't have let him fall into the tub, she prayed. But it hadn't sounded like a fall exactly. That would have been a thud. This was more like . . . a crack, she decided. Like a slap, but louder. Much louder.

As she drew closer, she heard Farrell's voice, low and unmistakably angry, and she quickly rapped on the heavy door.

"Mr. Farrell?"

"We're not done," he shouted.

"What is going on in there?"

"You wanted the heathen bathed. I'm bathing him."

"I heard noises." she said, pressing her ear to the solid door.

" 'Tis a noisy job," he retorted. "Now go away and let me see to it."

Ariel drew herself up, indignant. "I most certainly will not go away. Nor will I have you speaking to me in that tone."

From inside the room she heard what sounded like splashing and furniture being dragged. Then another of those cracks followed by grunting and a long, offensive oath by Farrell.

She rapped on the door. "Mr. Farrell, I would like to see you out here for a moment."

There was more furniture-dragging and grunting.

"Not—damn you back to the netherworld that sent ye—now."

"That is quite enough, Mr. Farrell. If you refuse to come out, I am coming in. On the count of three. Please make whatever . . . adjustments are necessary for the sake of propriety. One. Two . . ."

"I'm warning you, missy," Farrell shouted. "You oughtn't . . ."

The rest was lost in a series of cracks and thuds.

"Three," she shouted, and flung open the door.

She stopped dead in her tracks at the sight before her. She wasn't sure whether to be relieved or irritated to see that Sage was still wearing his britches. He stood in the far corner, glaring at her, as dry as when she had last seen him.

If anyone appeared to have been bathed in her absence, it was Mr. Farrell . . . and the room itself, she noted with exasperation. Water dripped from the tile walls and formed pools on the floor. Towels floated in the tub, empty buckets were scattered about, and the bench lay toppled on the other side of the room, one leg missing. Belatedly she noticed that Sage was holding what remained of the splintered wooden leg in his hand.

It was what Farrell was holding, however, that interested and angered her the most.

"Did you strike him with that?" she demanded, her voice shaking uncontrollably as she stared at the two-inch-wide brown leather strap he was trying unsuccessfully to conceal at his side.

"He hit me with a wooden plank," Farrell told her, pointing to an already red and raised spot on his forehead. The heat in his tone warned that the situation could quickly get more out of hand than it already was.

Ariel struggled to compose herself. "How did he come to be holding the wood in the first place? Was it to defend himself from your strap?"

"Defend himself? He's a savage, for God's sake. Did

you expect an ordinary man like myself to go into a room with him unarmed?"

"I did so," she reminded him.

He shrugged and muttered under his breath something about women that she decided she would prefer not to hear repeated.

"You told me to bathe him. I did it the best way I know how." He flicked a look at Sage. "Tried to anyhow. He don't take to the idea much, I can tell you."

"I instructed you to *teach* him to bathe," she corrected Farrell, "not *force* him. The whole point of our being here is to teach him to behave properly. Do you really believe you can accomplish that with a strap?"

"It's been known to teach others a thing or two."

"Oh, really? And how do you propose we manage it when he leaves here and takes his place in society? Follow him about with a whip to get him to use the proper fork? Sit beside him in Parliament, rapping his knuckles, when it is time to cast a vote?"

Farrell grunted and looked at his feet. "You didn't say nothing about Parliament, missy. Only to bathe him."

"Yes, my oversight, of course." She glanced around her at the mess. "Obviously even with the benefit of the strap you failed at the task."

"I told you already, he don't like the whole idea. I must outweigh him by four stone, at least, but it will take more men than me to get him out of them breeches and into a tub, and that's a fact."

"Perhaps," she murmured even as she met Sage's dark gaze and saw the truth of what Farrell said in the fierce obstinacy reflected there.

"You would have done well to let the earl's men stay on like he wanted them to," he pointed out.

"Thank you for your valuable counsel," she replied, her tone dripping sarcasm. "Now, please leave."

"Leave?"

"Yes. I can barely get his lordship to heed the most simple gestures and commands as it is. Surely you can see how agitated you've made him. With that and his lack of English, the water will freeze over before I can manage to convince him that you can be trusted and he can safely climb into the tub with you here."

"But I thought you wanted him bathed?"

"I do. I shall tend to it myself. You may see to the disposal of that filthy strap. If I catch sight of it in your hand again, or suspect that you have struck his lordship in any mannner, I will urge Lord Castleton to have you arrested. Is that clear?

Farrell's florid complexion grew even redder. "Yes, ma'am."

"Good. You may go."

"Now?" he asked, surprised.

"Immediately."

He didn't move. "Begging your pardon, ma'am . . ."

"I said you may go, Mr. Farrell," she broke in, not wanting to hear whatever reasons he might offer for why she should not remain there alone with Sage. She didn't need to hear them. They were already reverberating inside her head.

She did her best to ignore them, telling herself she had no choice but to assume the task. Besides, it wouldn't be the first time a female servant had tended her master's bath.

Except that she was not a servant. And Sage was not her master.

It didn't matter. She had given her word. The bath must be accomplished, and seeing the tension that radiated from him, she hadn't the heart to send in someone he had never seen before to start plucking at him.

She was, she told herself in an effort to buoy her own confidence, the perfect person to handle it. After all, if she could teach the little Higglesby monster to chew with his mouth closed and spoon-feed Latin to the notoriously thick youngest son of the Duke of Far-lingsworth, surely she could teach the Marquis of Sage to wash behind his ears.

She only wished that were all they would be washing.

Alone with Sage, she faced him across the flooded chamber. "I am sorry for what happened," she told him. "Mr. Farrell should not have struck you, and he will not do so again. I give you my word. From my heart," she said, placing her right hand on her chest. "I promise you that you will be safe here."

To her surprise, he placed his hand over his heart as well.

"But you must promise me something too, that you will cooperate, with Mr. Farrell and with me. It will make life easier for all of us."

He tilted his head to the side, his look bewildered.

"Of course," she said, sighing. "You can hardly give your promise on something you don't even understand, can you? Only an addle-brained twit would think to ask such a thing. All right, then, let's get on with it, shall we?" Her smile faded as she approached the tub. "I suppose the first thing is to get the towels out so that you may get in."

She was aware of his gaze resting on her as she dragged the sodden towels from the tub, wrung them as best as she could, and put them in a pile by the door. The silence made her uneasy.

"It's a good thing I brought extra," she said to fill the void. "In fact, it appears a good many towels will be needed to mop up this mess."

As she glanced at the puddles all around, she noticed that the bottom of her skirt was already soaked about eight inches up and the thin muslin gathers clung to her in front, where it had gotten wet as she bent over the tub. Ariel grimaced, thinking it was likely to get worse before it got better. At least the heat from the coal stove would keep her from freezing to death.

When the room was restored to a semblance of order, she added hot water to the tub, put the single bucket that remained upright on to heat, and realized that at last she had run out of reasons to delay.

Holding a washcloth and a bar of imported soap, a luxury she had deemed de rigueur for a marquis, she positioned herself beside the tub.

"Bath," she said, pointing to the tub.

He was standing with his shoulders resting on the tile wall, watching her. When she beckoned, he pushed away from it and moved closer.

Ariel's pulse quickened. Control, she reminded herself. She must remain in control at all times around him and remember that essentially, he was no different from any other student she had taught.

He sauntered to the end of the tub, opposite her, and stopped.

She waited.

He stared at her.

"Oh," she exclaimed finally. "You must get in. In." She pointed to the water. "Get in."

His gaze shifted from her face to where she pointed and back, but he made no move to climb into the tub.

Ariel bent and plunged her hand into the water so

that she was now wet to the elbow as well as the knees. "In. To bathe, you must get in the tub."

He watched, then bent and plunged his hand into the water as she had done.

"Not only your hand," she explained. "All of you. Your whole body." She lifted her foot and held it poised over the water.

He followed suit.

"Oh, dear," she murmured. "How on earth can I make you understand?"

The answer was obvious. And impossible. She could make him understand the same way she had gotten Edward Higglesby to chew with his mouth closed, by demonstrating precisely how it was done.

Ariel dismissed the idea as quickly as it came to her. She could not possibly climb into the tub with him, not even if it meant his lordship did not bathe for the entire eight weeks that he was in her care. Not even if it meant failing to deliver on her promise to Lord Castleton. Not even if it meant being dismissed by Mr. Penrose and forfeiting the one chance she had of securing a decent future for herself and her parents.

She would have to be daft to even consider doing such an unseemly thing.

She would have to be reckless beyond belief.

She would have to be desperate.

Five

Catching her bottom lip between her teeth, Ariel darted a glance over her shoulder at the door. Before she could think herself out of her plan, she hurried to close and lock the door.

"All right," she said curtly. "Please pay attention, because I shall not be repeating this, I promise you."

Sage immediately pressed his hand to his heart.

"What?" she inquired distractedly, impatient until it occurred to her what he meant, and her expression softened. "You remembered. A promise. Yes, that's right." She covered her heart. "A promise comes from the heart. Now, please do watch carefully."

She reached down and pulled off her kid slippers. "I don't know why I'm bothering, since they are already soaked through," she grumbled, "but there. As I was saying, to bathe properly you must get into the tub."

As she spoke, she lifted her skirt, stepped into the

water, and was rewarded for her insanity when, without hesitation, Sage did the same.

"Excellent, my lord. Of course there is still the small matter of your breeches." She stared at them, her mouth gathered in a thoughtful frown that quickly gave way to a smile. "I have it."

By bracing one hand on the tub's curved rim and stretching, she was able to reach the towels she'd placed on a nearby chair. She grabbed one and shook it open so that it hung between them.

"There, now that you have some privacy, you may remove your breeches," she told him. "Breeches." She pointed. "Off."

He glanced down briefly, then tilted his head to the side.

Ariel sighed. "I will not be demonstrating this," she muttered. "There must be another way."

Still holding the towel so that it shielded his body from her gaze, she inched toward him, her stocking feet slipping on the smooth bottom. When she was only a foot away from him, she stopped and, gripping the top of the towel with one hand, reached around to find the buttons at the front of his breeches. Managing to locate them with only a minimum of fumbling, she began to work the top one open.

His only response was a minuscule widening of his eyes before they once again resumed the shuttered watchfulness she had come to expect.

Ariel wished she could say the same for herself. Her heart was thundering so violently, it was as if an entire tribe of savages were pounding drums inside her chest. The beating echoed everywhere, in her throat and lungs and in the frantic clenching in the pit of her stomach. As if all that weren't distracting enough, her fingers were trembling, making the blind task even more difficult, and her breath was coming in short, rapid pants that left her feeling there wasn't enough air in the small room.

She felt quite unlike herself, which was a blessing, she supposed. Perhaps later she could pretend that this act of madness had been committed by someone else, someone impersonating her. Control, control, control. She repeated the word over and over in her mind, praying to whatever saint in heaven it might be whose task it was to protect the feeble-brained from themselves.

The heavy fabric of his breeches had grown soft and pliable from much wearing, but use had also frayed the edges of the buttonholes, making the buttons difficult to free. Worse, what lay beneath the fabric was far from soft or pliable.

Ariel did her best not to let her thoughts linger on what she was uncovering as she struggled to dislodge one button after another. Neither task was easy.

For one thing, she'd had no idea it required quite so many buttons to fasten a man's breeches. Two endless rows of them. As she worked her way down the first side, her fingers slid deeper and deeper inside the garment. With her hand thus wedged between his breeches and his startlingly warm flesh, there was no possible way she could remain unaware of the washboard ridges of his stomach muscles, or the heat and size of him in general. Doctor's daughter or not, her cheeks were flaming by the time she released the final button.

Avoiding his gaze over the top of the towel, she caught the waist of the breeches and began to tug them down, her only thought to get the job done.

"Off," she said. "You must take these off."

To her everlasting relief, Sage grasped her intent immediately and made quick work of shedding the pants and dropping them outside the tub. Ariel, over-joyed to have it done with, was caught completely off guard as he then proceeded to grasp her and pull her into his arms, landing her hard against the solid wall of his chest.

She made a small, strangled noise, something between a gasp and a whinny, she registered with disgust as her stunned gaze met his above the damp towel that was all that separated her from his naked body.

He was grinning, damn his heathen soul. For some reason she was as shocked by that grin as by his rough embrace. This was no sneer or mild, ambiguous twist of his lips. Oh, no. This was a full-out grin, wild and unabashed, forcing Ariel to recall with great haste that in fact Sage was not a schoolboy, but a man, and that some things were the same in any language.

My God, what must he be thinking?

And whatever had she been thinking not to anticipate what he would think? She had been so concerned with appearances, with the possibility of a passing housemaid catching sight of her standing fully clothed in the tub with a man and—she had to admit it—with keeping a rein on her own wayward responses to him, she hadn't spared a thought as to how that man himself might interpret her actions.

"No," she said firmly, struggling for composure as she pulled away from him.

He made no effort to stop her. It took a moment for the significance of that to penetrate her whirling thoughts, adding to her overall relief. Not that she was afraid of him, she told herself. She had simply been taken unawares by his most unwarranted advances. Again.

Afraid or not, she took the precaution of putting some distance between them, backing up until she felt the tub against her calves. She continued to hold the towel in front of her, spread wide as if it were she who needed shielding from his gaze. Too late she realized the folly of holding it thus as she moved away from him and suddenly found herself privy to an unobstructed view of his body from the knees up.

Why, he was brown all over from the sun was her initial, slightly amazed thought. It was immediately followed by a rush of fresh mortification. Shutting her eyes, she quickly repositioned the towel, though not quickly enough to prevent the image of his long, lean, blatantly masculine form, with its intriguing patterns of dark, silky hair, from being scorched into her brain.

"That was . . . most uncalled for," she told him when she was able to speak. She strained to sound firm and not rattled. "Perhaps I should have better conveyed my intentions beforehand, but as I told you earlier, touching is improper. That is to say, touching without permission is improper. Not that there is any way I would ever have granted permission under these . . . oh, whatever am I going on about when you don't understand a word of it? No touching. Period."

She noted his resentful frown and the sudden tensing of his shoulders and took a guess as to what was bothering him.

"Yes, I know I touched you first. But that was . . . different. Different in a way I could never explain to you, so we will just leave it at that. Now," she said, reaching for the soap and washcloth, which she held out to him. "Wash."

Things progressed more smoothly. Or perhaps it merely seemed that way after she had him sitting and more or less concealed by the water. She stepped out and moved around behind him to help wash his hair. The rest of the process he grasped quickly, to her immense gratitude. He applied himself enthusiastically and with an ease that suggested to her that bathing was familiar to him, though probably not indoors, with cauldrons of water steaming nearby and a man standing over him with a strap.

As he was leaning forward for her to rinse his hair with fresh water from the stove, she first noticed the raised red welt on his right shoulder.

"So he did strike you." Her anger at Farrell resurfaced as her hand moved lightly over the six-inch-long mark. He didn't flinch, but the tensing of the corded muscles at the side of his throat told her that it was costing him to remain still. It was a wonder he had done no more than fend off that bully Farrell with a stick.

"I can see that it hurts," she observed. "I will tend it for you before you dress. My father is—" She caught herself. "He was a physician and I have some salve that will take the sting from your shoulder. There. We're done."

She held open his dressing gown like a curtain, protecting his privacy as he climbed from the tub. Reaching around it, she handed him towels to dry himself and then, with eyes closed and a good deal of struggling, succeeded in actually getting him into the garment. The hallway was clear, and she hurried him directly back to his chamber.

Leaving him there, she ran across the hall to her own room to quickly fetch the salve she'd promised him. She longed to change out of her wet clothing, but didn't dare to leave him alone. Once Sage was dressed, she could entrust him to Farrell's care downstairs, where they wouldn't be alone, and steal a few moments to change.

She had intended to leave the matter of Sage's

dressing to Farrell, and so had not formed an exact plan for how it might best be accomplished. Now she studied the assortment of garments she had arranged on the bed, thinking that each one presented a different, and potentially embarrassing, challenge.

Opting to let logic dictate the order of approach, she squared her shoulders and reached for the black cotton stockings. She turned to find Lord Sage standing by the window, absorbed in the cricket match some young boys were playing on a field visible in the distance.

Ariel paused for a moment, watching him, taking note of the long, elegantly shaped hand that held the curtain aside and the careless ease with which he wore the expensive silk dressing gown. Penrose was right about one thing—the raw materials for nobility were all there. In fact, if she didn't know better, she'd think him already every inch the fine, arrogant lord she was being paid to turn him into.

He glanced up as she drew near, tilting his head to the side in a questioning manner that was already familiar to her.

"Cricket," she said. "It is a game played with a ball and wickets and you needn't even bother to look at me that way because it is one thing I am most definitely not prepared to teach you. The requisite dance lesson will be excruciating enough, I fear. I happen to be ghastly at anything requiring the least bit of coordination."

As she turned away, Ariel thought she caught the start of a smile in response to her self-effacing words. When she looked back, however, he was once more gazing impassively out the window. She shrugged.

"Shall we see to getting you dressed?" she asked. "As a rule, Mr. Farrell will be assisting you, but—"

He reared up at the mention of Farrell's name.

"But after the trouble earlier," she continued hurriedly, "I think it best to allow things between you to cool off a bit. You can be sure I will speak to him again, privately, about the business with the strap. Which reminds me," she added, rummaging in her pocket. "I brought the salve I promised you."

Hearing the word *promise*, Sage immediately placed his hand over his heart. His slightly uncertain expression was most endearing, making him look years younger than the thirty Ariel knew him to be.

"Very good," she told him, smiling. "You have certainly grasped the meaning of the word *promise* very quickly. Let's hope you are as successful in mastering everything that lies ahead."

He wouldn't be.

Leon had already made up his mind about that. In fact, he planned to be distinctly unmasterful. What's more, he intended to help Miss Halliday make a most momentous discovery of her own in that regard. She was about to learn that even the most accomplished, resourceful teacher could not teach a pupil who did not want to be taught.

Leon most definitely did not want to be taught.

What he wanted was to see Miss Halliday squirm, and he wanted it more than ever since their little encounter in the bath. The process of shedding his breeches had left him with a perplexing question about his new teacher. Was she really naive enough to think she could stick her hand down a man's pants and provoke in him nothing more dangerous than a grateful smile? Or was she a brazen hussy merely acting the part of the dowdy schoolmistress, a woman who knew exactly what she was about when she touched him and who had her own scheming ends in mind?

One thing was certain, he was going to enjoy finding out.

She dangled the black stockings before him and pointed to the chair she'd dragged to the center of the room. As usual, her gestures were accompanied by monosyllables. Leon briefly considered being obtuse about it, but decided against it. Stockings were boring. He was much more interested in finding out if she would be as delightfully inventive when it came to getting a pair of breeches on him as she had been in getting them off.

After a cursory delay, he obliged her by sitting in the straight-back chair and permitting her to demonstrate, at tedious length, the proper method of donning stockings. In an effort to move things along, he even played the apt pupil and handled the second of the pair entirely on his own. By the time he was finished she was radiant, beaming with approval and, more important, ripe for the plucking.

He leaned back in the chair, arms folded, watching as she fairly danced across the room to retrieve a pair of trousers from the bed. Chamois, he noted with satisfaction. A most uncompromising fabric. Judging from Castleton's own appearance, he would have ordered them to fit fashionably snug, making them a job to get into under the best of circumstances, which Leon was determined these would not be.

She started back toward him with the same confident gait, then became aware of his gaze on her and hesitated for a half second before proceeding more cautiously. The change in her demeanor was so slight, Leon would not have detected it had he been watching her less intently.

To his chagrin, he'd discovered that he enjoyed watching her. A simple case of deprivation, he assured himself as he had numerous times since the day she first visited him in his room at Castleton's. It had been a hideously long time since he'd glimpsed any female other than blotchy-faced housemaids too lily-livered to even look him in the eye. Miss Halliday was neither blotchy nor lily-livered, and looking was the least of what he longed to do with her at that moment.

In fact, if he was not careful, his pressing interest in Miss Halliday could become a hazard. He was rational enough to realize that, even if he weren't in any mood to try to determine why it should be so. All he knew was that in the past few hours, he'd been brought as close to freedom as he'd been in a long time, free to drink in all the different colors and sights of fresh surroundings, free to walk away if he chose to, and instead, whenever she was in the room, he was unable to take his eyes off her.

He was more fascinated than ever since her dress had become wet and clinging and, if he wasn't mistaken, nearly transparent in several strategic places. Which only added to his vague irritation with himself. By rights, this enhanced view of her form should have had the opposite effect, since it revealed her to be quite unlike what he'd long ago settled on as the ideal female.

The seeds for such tastes were sown early on, and he'd reached manhood surrounded by island women, with their slender hips, narrow shoulders, and small, firm breasts. He ran a critical gaze over Miss Halliday as she drew closer, and concluded that there was not a straight line or sharp angle on the woman anywhere. From the pretty arch of her cheek to the shapely ankles and calves exposed when she'd hitched up her skirts and climbed into the tub, she was all soft curves and flesh as pale and creamy as rare pearls, and he suddenly, inexplicably, found himself rethinking a lifetime of well-honed preferences.

Her very paleness intrigued him, the stark contrast she presented to most of the women he had known, as well as his own sun-darkened skin. He'd already deduced that her flawless complexion provided a charming barometer of her feelings, ranging from a tinge of pink as delicate as the inside of a shell to the full-blown crimson of the setting sun, depending on her level of agitation. He wasn't above wondering if this emotional rainbow was confined to her cheeks, or perhaps was echoed in other soft, interesting places on her body.

That, of course, led quite naturally to speculation as to how she would look when aroused. What would be the color of the prim Miss Halliday's passion? If the woman had ever experienced such a thing, Leon thought dryly. Innocent or hussy? It was difficult to decide. Of course, she herself had admitted that she was ghastly at anything requiring the least bit of coordination. But then, that could be a lie. Or, he mused, eyeing the swell of her hips and the faint, enticing outline of her belly beneath the clinging muslin, simply a case of lacking the right partner.

She came to a halt in front of him, clutching the trousers with both hands, her white knuckles yet another revelation to the careful observer. It would appear the lady was a trifle nervous, he noted with veiled amusement, and here they had barely begun their little adventure in fashion.

As he continued to level his expressionless stare on her, she caught her bottom lip between her teeth, shifting her uneasy gaze back and forth between the trousers and him.

"Please, give me another moment," she murmured finally, and left him sitting there to contemplate how even her mouth was perfectly curved, the upper lip being a delicate bow and the lower lip full and lush, equally capable, if he was any judge of such things, of presenting a man with a pout or an invitation.

He heard her rummaging through the closet, and then she was back, her smile confident once more and a different pair of chamois trousers in hand.

"There, I believe these will make a much better choice for today," she said, her sanguine tone immediately arousing his suspicion. "Buttons can be so ... cumbersome."

Leon's gaze quickly fell to the front flap of the trousers and to the fashionable laces designed to secure it in lieu of buttons, and he had to fight a grin. Maybe she really was as naive as she first appeared, if she believed that rawhide laces were enough to save her from his primitive intentions.

"Now all we have to do is get them on you and laced," she told him. The immediate prospect of lacing him up seemed to prompt second thoughts, sending her barometer sliding in a different direction. The pink glow drained from her cheeks, leaving them with an ethereal creaminess, and her smile went a bit stiff around the edges as she said, "If you could, perhaps, lift your leg."

Leon kept both feet flat on the floor and stared blankly.

Anyone else would have been discouraged. God knows, he would be. Instead, obstacles seemed to invigorate her. He watched her brows lower, her lips purse, and, as if he could also see through flesh and bone to the gears and levers working furiously inside her head, he watched her latch on to a solution to this latest dilemma and grit her teeth as she steeled herself to put it into action.

She was amazing, he thought. Naive and a little foolhardy, but amazing.

Going down on one knee before him and bending forward, she slipped her hand beneath the robe to grasp his left leg by the calf and draw it upward. Now, this was more like it, he thought, aware of a sudden increase in interest as well as a reflexive tightening of the muscles at the back of his leg where she was touching him.

"Let's see now . . ." she murmured, rearranging her grip on the trousers. "How shall I . . . ? Your legs are very strong, and quite . . . ah, heavy."

She let go abruptly, groaning from the combined effort of trying to hold his leg aloft and at the same time maneuver the trousers into position to slip them on. She paused for a few seconds, then spread the trousers in place on the floor between them before trying again.

He could have helped, he supposed, but then she wouldn't have had to bend quite so far forward, affording him a most entrancing view of the upper swell of her breasts.

"There," she said for the fifth or sixth time. He'd lost count. This time, however, she actually managed to shove his foot into the proper trouser leg and shimmy it up a short way. Puffing from the effort, she struggled to do the same with his right leg.

"There," she exclaimed again, triumphantly, as she at last succeeded in working both his feet out the bottoms of the trouser legs. Gasping for air between words, she continued. "Excellent . . . my . . . lord. Now . . . if . . . you . . . could stand . . . we'll see to the rest."

Leon barely waited for the accompanying gesture

before getting to his feet. He was most eager to "see to the rest," as she put it.

Standing so close to her, close enough for her to slip her hands beneath the dressing gown and drag his trousers up by the waist, he was struck anew by how much smaller than him she was, and how . . . delicate.

It came as something of a surprise. *Delicate* was not a word that popped to mind when he first saw her, but it was an apt description just the same. It captured not only her lush femininity, but also her manner of moving and speaking. There was a gentleness, a fineness, about her that appealed to the tender side of a man.

That is, if he should happen to have one. Which, Leon reminded himself, he did not.

If he had possessed a tender, compassionate side, it would no doubt have intervened at that moment and compelled him to brush her hands aside and take over the task she so obviously would rather avoid, that of lacing him into the snug-fitting trousers. Instead, he stood there complacently, supremely content, in fact, as her fingers fumbled with the rawhide laces.

Her first error proved to be the fatal one. He knew it at once. In her haste, she failed to pull the excess lace through from the inside as she worked. When she finally tied a hurried bow at his waist, the two of them stared down at the finished product, a front piece that gaped open in places and was noticeably puckered in others.

"Oh, dear," she cried. "We shall have to try again."

Leon smiled, more than willing do his part a second time. The buzzing inside him was a little stronger now. A warm, pleasant drone that transformed even the light brush of her fingers into a pleasure to be savored.

She studied the laces intently, gingerly tugging here and there, then sighed. "There's no way around it. I shall have to start over at the beginning," she announced, to his immense delight. "Stand absolutely, perfectly still," she ordered.

Leon supposed there might be a man somewhere, some unrivaled paragon of virtue and self-control, who could remain still and unresponsive while Miss Ariel Halliday stuck her hand down the front of his tight trousers and tugged on his laces, but it wasn't he. Not by a long shot.

This was worse than the bath. Or better. At the moment he was beyond such subtle distinctions. He knew only one thing, that the unskilled movements of her fingers against him was a dangerous delight.

He was a fool to allow it. Worse yet, he had encouraged it. Without saying a word, he himself had orchestrated this moment. Now the fierce quickening of his body warned that he had maneuvered himself into a potentially embarrassing position. For sure, his intention to rattle her was backfiring excruciatingly, just as it had when he reached for her in the tub. One moment he had been smugly amused at her vexation, the next she was in his arms and he was the one who was reeling.

He inhaled sharply as she tugged on the bottom laces, tightening the front piece and increasing the pressure of the fabric against the juncture of his thighs, an added stimulus he did not need.

Slowly her fingers climbed higher, her knuckles, jabbing, pressing, kneading.

She tugged again, drawing the cloth tighter still. Again her fingers moved against him.

Leon closed his eyes, willing himself to remain composed and . . . contained. He fell back on an old schoolboys' trick and recited mathematical calculations in his head, desperate now for her to finish before his hunger became flagrantly obvious and scared the wench all the way back to London.

Who would believe it? he thought grimly. Here he was—he, a dedicated and most skilled practitioner of the art of taking pleasure wherever and whenever he found it—standing there with a woman's hands on him for the first time in months and thinking only of bloody sums.

At last she finished and retied the knot at his waist, giving the final tug a bit more snap than necessary, it seemed to Leon, for whom each movement, each passing second, had become an unbearable risk. She muttered something under her breath as she dropped her hands to her sides. "Thank God," it sounded like to him. A sentiment he echoed heartily.

Avoiding his gaze, she hurried away to fetch the boots by the side of the bed. He took advantage of the moment to tug on the front of his trousers, making himself marginally more comfortable, and to draw a few deep breaths. When she returned with the boots, he snatched them from her and sat to pull them on without any assistance.

Enough was enough, dammit. He wasn't a dratted doll to be poked and petted and fussed over. He hated being fussed over, always had. The only reason he had succumbed today was because he'd been . . . curious, he decided. He still was, but he would just have to find some other way to assuage his curiosity about his new teacher.

He looked up from the boots to find her standing over him with an open jar, gesturing and uttering more monosyllables, this time about her intention to apply salve to his back. Sitting still as she moved around behind him and slipped the dressing gown off his shoulders, he experienced the gentle touch of her fingers on his skin with nearly the same trepidation he had the business with the laces. Gentleness in any form was anathema to him, something he avoided when he could and endured when he couldn't.

"We should let that soak in a bit before putting your shirt on," she said at last, covering the jar and setting it aside. She slid the dressing gown from the chair behind him and draped it over the corner of the bed a few feet away.

"I shouldn't want to stain any of your fine new clothes. In the meantime . . ." She circled back to the front of the chair and held up a silver comb.

"This is a comb," she explained. "For your hair. Your beard I shall leave to a hand more experienced with a razor, but your hair will require patience and, I daresay, a light touch. I suspect you have an implement similar to this in your culture. Carved from seashells, perhaps."

Leon could have told her that only thing he'd ever carved from a shell had been a stiletto. His recollection of the bloody use he'd put it to was shattered by his own pained yelp as she attempted to run the blasted comb through his hair.

"Forgive me, my lord," she said, only compounding the offense as she quickly yanked the comb free. "I'm afraid your hair is even more badly tangled than I thought. Beyond tangled actually," she elaborated, lifting a clump and dropping it. "It's quite matted in places. A good cutting is what is called for, but if I attempt to cut through it without combing first, your head will end up looking like a hedge cropped by a blind man." She shot him a sympathetic smile. "That would never do for a man of your position, so the comb it is."

A man of his position. Whatever the hell that was, Leon thought as she again approached him with the comb, this time starting at the very ends of his hair, which hung past his shoulders, and working the tangles out a scant fraction of an inch at a time.

Gradually he relaxed, growing accustomed to her touch. Sometimes she used her fingers to release a tangle instead of the comb, and sometimes she held his head lightly as she worked, almost as if signaling him ahead of time that this would be a bad one. In spite of himself, he found her touch on his scalp and the movement of her fingers through his hair relaxing.

He was not a gentle man, or a man excited by gentle things. Yet this was pleasing to him and unexpectedly arousing. She hummed softly as she worked, adding to the soothing, almost hypnotic mood that built slowly around him.

She worked her way from one side of his head, around the back, to the other. When she moved to stand in front of him to reach the last section in front, he allowed his legs to loll apart to make room for her. She stepped smoothly into the opening.

Leon leaned his head back, studying her from beneath half-lowered lids, savoring her sweet, womanly nearness. How easy it would be, he mused, to tip her into his lap. She was stretched forward and just the pressure of his hand at the small of her back would do it. She would land softly against his chest, her blue eyes widening in surprise as she looked up at him. How easy it would be at that instant to slide his hand inside the bodice of her dress, to cup her breasts and discover if they could possibly fulfill the tantalizing promises born in his imagination during the past hour or so.

He lifted his hand, but before he could do more she

moved away, placing the comb on the small table behind her and picking up a pair of shears lying there. Turning back, she raised the hand with the shears and made a purposeful move toward him.

Leon was on his feet instantly. He snagged her arm and wrenched it behind her back so forcefully, she released her grip on the shears. He snatched them in midair, and with one quick motion he spun her and sent her sprawling backward into the chair. Standing over her, his legs braced apart so that her wet skirts were pooled between them, he held the open shears an inch from her throat.

"Please, my lord," she said, her voice quaking, her eyes wide not with surprise as he'd envisioned a moment ago, but with fear. "I believe you have sorely misjudged my intent. I meant only to use the shears to trim your hair. Trim," she repeated, making a scissoring motion with her fingers. "Trim. You see, the fashion of the moment is much shorter, and—"

"No." He shook his head, sending his long hair flying and bringing the shears a half inch closer to her face.

"As you please, my lord," she whispered. "It is not my desire to force you to do anything against your will. My only thought was to help. Shorter hair would be less trouble and time-consuming to care for, and it would bring you into line with current British style."

Her words enraged him, shattering any lingering lassitude and jerking him back to reality. He recalled with icy clarity who she was and why she was there with him in the first place, why she was rubbing salve on his back and combing his hair and tending him so solicitously. She was there to tame him.

And a good job she was doing of it, he thought contemptuously, remembering how he had warmed to her ministrations like a cat craving cream. No, cats were discriminating by nature. He'd responded more like a starving dog, gulping down any little scrap tossed his way, made so docile by her touch that she was free to do with him as she pleased. And what would please her was to lull him and mold him and snip away at him until he fit the mold of a proper gentleman.

A proper British gentleman, to be precise.

British. That one word was all it took to fire the rage that simmered always inside him, close to his core. It was a proper British gentleman who had taken a vow before God, then turned his back on that vow and on his own wife and child and never looked back.

It was proper British gentlemen who had murdered his mother and left him alone at the age of five, cut adrift in the world he'd thought was his home, shunned, enslaved, struggling to survive from one wretched day until the next. With his free hand he touched the mark on his forehead, the spot where a French physician renowned for his skill had done all that was humanly possible to remove the brand that had been put there when he was still a boy.

It was British gentlemen who had spawned the beast that lived inside him and set him apart from other men, an outcast even among outcasts. The beast that cared not for consequences or reason, only revenge. The beast that made the unspeakable possible.

That beast lived in the darkness deep in his heart, in blackness so vast that even he was afraid to peer into it too closely.

The beast was on him now, taunting him to act, reminding him that if he let this woman have her way, she would turn him into the very thing he most despised. He really would slit her throat before he let that happen, he thought, before he let her take her shears to him and make him look like one of them.

He stroked her throat with the open blade and watched her eyes fill with panic.

What should he do with her? He knew from the past that once roused, the beast would not be easily appeased. There would have to be some token offered, a sacrifice made, in order to forestall its craving for vengeance a while longer.

He glanced around the room and his gaze fell on the dressing gown she had tossed on the bed, and on the gold crest embroidered on the chest. He'd paid little attention to it earlier, but now it drew him.

Yanking her roughly to her feet, he shoved her ahead of him across the room. He stopped beside the bed and reached for the dressing gown, impatiently twisting the silk until he held the embroidered patch in his hand.

Shoving it in front of her, he pinned her with a hard, questioning gaze.

"It is a crest," she said, giving it a hurried glance, her voice shaking. "The Sage coat of arms perhaps. Yes, I am certain that's what it is. See, there is the lion and the dagger with the knot. Lord Castleton must have had this robe embroidered especially for you." Her lips formed a tight smile. "It's your family crest."

"No."

His eyes blazed defiantly and his lips thinned across clenched teeth as he released her. Holding the silk robe before him, he slashed at it with the shears, slicing through the intricate embroidery again and again until he held in his hands nothing but black silk streamers.

He sought her gaze and captured it as he slowly, deliberately, let the scraps fall to the floor.

"No," he said again.

Almost immediately the beast's hold on him loosened, and Leon knew that it had been placated, for the moment at least. Still he held his gaze on her, aware that she was watching him just as intently.

Her soft jaw quivered as she drew in one deep breath after another.

He panted, aware of the labored rise and fall of his bare chest.

Gradually their breathing slowed. Where only a moment before she had looked poised to flee at the first opportunity, he sensed her reassessing the situation and wondered what thoughts were twisting and turning and taking shape inside her head.

Finally, appearing the very epitome of serenity and confidence, she extended her hand to him, palm up, and said, "My shears, sir, if you please."

When he hesitated, her golden brows arched expectantly, as if it were unthinkable that he should not heed her request.

Slowly, Leon moved to return the shears to her.

This time the tactical error was his own. He knew it the instant the shears left his hand. Distracted by her unexpected composure, he unthinkingly reversed his hold on the shears before offering them to her. He presented them handle first. She accepted them that way, and thanked him in that same cool, impervious tone, but he saw the expression in her eyes grow thoughtful. Speculative. He knew then that he had erred, and badly.

It was a simple gesture, presenting the shears handle first, and one that would be routinely expected of any well-mannered child. He was not a well-mannered child, however. Or, for that matter, a well-mannered gentleman. Simply a careless one. And his careless mistake was bound to make Miss Halliday wonder exactly what kind of savage she was dealing with.

Six

"So you can see why I question exactly what kind of savage I have on my hands," Ariel concluded, glancing across the dining room table at her mother.

She was pleased to see glints of interest and amusement in the blue eyes so like her own. Millicent Halliday had little enough to smile about these days, and the knowledge that the lighthearted recitation of her own dilemma had distracted her mother from her troubles for a few moments was worth the risk of coming.

A fortnight had passed since Mr. Penrose issued his edict that there were to be no visits home until her work with Lord Sage was completed. At first she had relied on trusted couriers to relay messages and a portion of her weekly salary. Finally, however, desperate to see for herself how her parents were faring, she had arranged to slip away without Mr. Penrose's knowledge, daring to entrust Sage to Farrell's care for a few hours.

"Perhaps you've discovered a whole new breed,"

her mother suggested in reply to her query. "The polite savage." Her small smile temporarily erased some of the worry lines that made it appear she had aged ten years in the last one.

Like Ariel's sister, Caroline, Millicent Halliday was a remarkable beauty, the sort of woman who inspired sonnets even in unpoetic men and routinely drew long second glances from perfect strangers. And, like Caroline, her beauty was an all-consuming gift. Or had been until disaster struck the one thing that mattered more to her, her beloved husband. Now all her concentration and energy went to protecting him.

Ariel greatly admired her mother's devotion, even if she did not agree that his illness was a shameful family secret or with the idea that they must keep up appearances at all costs.

"*Polite* is not the word I would choose to describe the man," she told her mother, "in spite of the way he handed over the shears."

"What word would you choose?"

Ariel gave the matter some consideration, reflecting on the whirlwind of small successes and frustrating failures that had occurred in working with Sage.

"*Impossible,*" she said at last. "What makes it all the worse is that there are times when I am certain it is wholly intentional on his part. In many ways he's like a two-year-old," she declared. "A surly, oversized two-year-old."

"Then treat him as such," her mother advised.

"That's not as easy as it sounds. The man has an iron will and the strength to back it up."

Millicent Halliday's smile faded. "Oh, dear, he hasn't manhandled you, has he?"

"Not at all." Ariel hastily lifted her teacup to her lips. He had touched her, brushed against her, and stood naked with her in his arms, but he had not man-handled her.

"But is he quarrelsome?"

"Only if a propensity to grunt can be considered quarrelsome."

"He doesn't speak at all?"

"A bit. He has mastered *out, leave, brandy, more, now,* and *no.*"

"That's it?" her mother asked, eyes wide. "How difficult that must be for him."

"Save your pity. You would be amazed at how often the man manages to get his own way with only grunts and monosyllables. In fact, there are days when he'll have no tea, no silverware to eat his dinner, no napkin to wipe his mouth, and most definitely, no Mr. Farrell. And he absolutely insists on wearing nothing more than boots, buckskin breeches, and a shirt open at the neck."

Millicent Halliday stiffened, aghast. "Heavens, no jacket? No waistcoat?"

"Not even a cravat. He refuses to permit me to loop it around his throat, much less tie it properly. It's as if he's afraid I might strangle him." Ariel's mouth curved up at the corners. "Which, now that I think about it, is not that far-fetched a notion."

"Then would you say you are making no progress with him at all?"

Good question, Ariel thought. Unfortunately her answer varied from day to day, sometimes from minute to minute.

"I think I'm making progress," she replied. "Sometimes. Then at times I think . . . I think . . . I think I am losing my mind. The man is devilishly adept at creating that impression in a person."

"How so?"

"He masters very quickly those things that make his life easier or more pleasant, such as requiring hot water to shave or discerning a fine port following dinner, but somehow when it comes to more important skills, he always fails to grasp at one critical element. When it comes to lessons regarding the rudiments of English grammar, it is even worse, for he just grows bored and restless. The result is that I'm constantly feeling like a hound chasing its own tail."

Her mother looked concerned. "I do hope that changes soon."

Ariel's expressions grew thoughtful. "At times I feel that success is not completely out of reach. You see, there are instances with Sage, mere moments really, when I catch a glimmer of . . . something."

"For goodness' sake, Ariel, don't leave me in suspense. A glimmer of what?"

"I'm not sure. It's difficult to put into words. It might simply be his sudden smile at some hint of irony, signifying a sophisticated level of understanding he ought not to possess, or perhaps just the way he steps aside to give me the wall when we are descending the stairs."

"He does that?"

Ariel nodded. "And there is the way he holds himself when he's not being observed, with an innate grace that can only be bred, not taught."

Her mother leaned forward with some of her old spark for gossip and intrigue and men in general. "So it is true. Your Lord Savage is the legitimate son of the late Marquis of Sage."

"Yes, Giles Duvanne was his father. He kept it secret to spare the marchioness, supposedly. Though I suspect he was equally interested in sparing himself the charge of bigamy."

"And not until he was on his deathbed did he reveal the truth?"

"Sad, isn't it? Since Giles Duvanne had an older brother and did not stand to inherit, he signed on with Captain Cook, in search of adventure. While they were in the Sandwich Islands, he met and fell in love with a woman named Monique de la Mornay, the daughter of an island woman and a French missionary. They married, Lord Castleton is in possession of the legal certificate to that effect, but before his son was born he had returned to England to tie up loose ends and discovered that both his father and older brother were dead and that he was now the Marquis of Sage."

"He never even set eyes on the child?"

"No. He evidently decided his first responsibility lay here, and instead of sending for his wife and son, he chose to marry himself a more fitting and wealthy marchioness."

Her mother made a clucking sound. "I've heard the Sage estate was in desperate straits when he inherited."

"That's hardly an excuse for such treachery," declared Ariel. "It's ironic that his new bride's assets proved more fertile than she did. Their marriage, if you can call it such with a straight face, was childless. And so, as he lay dying, the marquis was forced to confront the fact that all his hard work and sacrifice—not to mention his abandonment of his own wife and child—would go for naught. The estate was set to pass into the hands of a nephew whom he neither liked nor trusted."

"That's when he implored his old friend, the Earl of Castleton, to find his long-lost son and bring him home at last to claim his birthright." Millicent Halliday clasped her upper arms with her hands. "Oh, Ariel, I have goose bumps. It's all so . . . noble sounding."

"Noble?" Ariel exclaimed. "If you ask me, it's

despicable. To go barging uninvited into a person's life and drag him off somewhere where he doesn't want to be for your own selfish political ends—that's noble?"

"Really, Ariel, must you always be so cynical?"

"I am not being cynical. Merely honest. I know for a fact that the overriding reason Castleton went to so much trouble to find Sage is to stop Adam Lockaby from claiming the title and, with it, a voice in the House of Lords. He considers Lockaby a radical, and still wet behind the ears."

Her mother winced delicately. "Please, sweetheart, you know how talk of politics always makes my head ache."

"Talk of anything more serious than the latest fashion makes your head ache," Ariel teased. "But I will desist just the same."

"Thank you," said her mother, kneading her temples briefly. "Now, has Mr. Penrose been by the cottage?"

"Yes." Ariel rolled her eyes as she recalled his surprise visits. "Fortunately, thus far I've managed to divert him from looking too closely at what I've accomplished with his lordship."

"But surely he doesn't expect an instantaneous transformation? Surely he understands the magnitude of—"

"Mother," she interrupted with a weary sigh, "Mr. Penrose understands only what Mr. Penrose wants at any given moment. He and Lord Sage share a kinship in that regard. Come to think of it, maybe all men are two years old at heart."

"Shh." Eyes twinkling conspiratorially, her mother pressed her finger to her lips. "Don't let that cat out of the bag, or you'll ruin things for women everywhere. After all, a two-year-old isn't really all that difficult to figure out, or control . . . provided you don't let on that you're doing the controlling."

Ariel smiled at her mother's unique brand of logic. "I'll bear that in mind."

A none-too-subtle hint of satisfaction crept into her tone as she said to Ariel, "It's true, then. You are sweet on him."

Ariel straightened so abruptly, the teacup clattered against the saucer as she rid herself of it. "Who?"

"Mr. Penrose, of course. Who else?"

"No one, of course. It's simply that I don't usually think of myself as being sweet on him, exactly. It's true that I . . . admire him, I suppose, and that he—"

Before she could go further, her mother was around the table and drawing her close. "Oh, Ariel, that's wonderful."

"Mother, please, you don't understand. . . ."

"I understand everything. I was young once myself, don't forget. Mr. Penrose is the perfect man for you, sweetheart. I've always thought so."

Penrose? The perfect man for her? What a horrendous thought.

"I can't tell you how happy it would make me, and your father as well, if he could only grasp the meaning of it, to have you married and happily settled down."

No one had to tell her, thought Ariel. It had been drilled into her since the time she could be taught to make a curtsy and embroider a sampler. A woman was meant to be a wife and mother. It was her destiny, her reward, her duty, all rolled into one. Anything else was something less, a failure, a public humiliation for the poor woman in question, not to mention the rest of her family.

"You must tell me all about it," her mother declared,

returning to her seat with so much of her old zest that Ariel dreaded saying anything to put a crimp in her hopes.

"There's really nothing to tell."

"Nonsense. Does he know how you feel?"

"I don't believe so, though I have hinted. You know, complimenting him and doing things to cast myself in the most favorable light." That much was true. Maddening and humiliating, thought Ariel, but true. At her mother's dubious expression, she quickly added, "And, of course, I am counting on my eventual success with Lord Sage to stand me in good favor. I know that such a flirtatious technique might seem a bit unorthodox to you, but . . ."

But I am not like you, she thought in exasperation. *I do not excel in the art of romantic subterfuge. I despise it. I abhor currying favor with a man who leaves me cold, and if not for Papa's debts and your insistence on maintaining appearances at all costs, a husband is the very last thing I would be hunting.*

"But," she concluded, "it is precisely the sort of thing that will make Mr. Penrose sit up and take notice."

"Phillip Penrose." Her mother sounded as if she had a pat of butter on her tongue. "Such an elegant name. And the school provides him with an ample income? Of course it does. And a secure one too, I daresay. Plus, he's just had that new residence built. I've heard it's terribly grand."

"It is," Ariel agreed, picturing the cold monstrosity for which he had abandoned the much cozier cottage. "Terribly grand."

"Can you imagine living in such a place?"

"I try not to."

"Well, you shall be living there, and before not too

long." She reached across the table and grasped her daughter's hands. "Oh, Ariel, I just know that this time everything is going to work out for you. I can feel it. What a joy it will be for me to know that both my girls are set at last."

"I know, Mother. And I will do everything in my power to make that come about for your sake, and for Papa's."

"Of course you shall. Even if it means making a marquis out of a savage." She frowned suddenly, her grip on Ariel's hands tightening. "You can do it, can't you, sweetheart?"

Ariel felt as if a lead weight had been dropped into her stomach, pinning her to the spot. She forced a smile in spite of it. "Of course I can do it."

Her mother beamed approvingly. "I knew it. You always were such a smart girl, and at last you've turned all that talent to something that truly matters."

"But my efforts will go to waste if I stay much longer and risk having Mr. Penrose discover I am gone. In case he should need me, I mean," she hastened to add, recalling that she had not shared the details of her escape with her mother.

"Of course, of course. Out of sight is out of mind, and we don't want that, now, do we?"

Ariel managed a weak smile, thinking that circumstances had rendered what she wanted quite meaningless.

She had arrived home that day to find the situation more dire than it had been only a few weeks before. Her father was lost in the regressive rambling that was slowly becoming his whole world. But even more distressing to her was the way her mother's determination to make things appear to be as they always were threatened to pull her into a dream world of her own creation. In her own way she was becoming as disconnected from reality as her father was, and it infuriated Ariel that the only way she could save them was to land a husband.

She rose, wanting a few moments before she left to say good-bye to her father. She quickly helped clear the table of the tea dishes, something that would have been unthinkable in the days when a half-dozen servants were on hand to tend to the family's every need. Everything had changed since then, she reflected sadly as she left her mother in the kitchen and went in search of her father, whom Elise had taken outside for a walk after lunch.

Finances had finally forced them to sell off the family carriage and the pair of matched ivory ponies which, next to his wife and daughters, had been Dr. Halliday's pride and joy. It was a drastic step which they had long resisted and such a public indication of their reduced circumstances that her proud mother was overcome with shame.

Privately, Ariel had harbored a secret hope that losing the horses and carriage might somehow shock her father out of his mental fog. She longed to have back the strong, witty, resourceful papa she remembered and adored. He would have sat and discussed politics with her, she thought wistfully, or anything else that was on her mind. It was those long talks she missed the most.

Instead, he had responded to the sudden disappearance of his horses and carriage with the now-familiar look of bewilderment, and he persisted in wandering off to the stables when no one was watching, as if they were still there.

That's where Ariel found him now, staring into the empty paddock, a carrot protruding from his jacket pocket, his forlorn expression enough to break even the hardest heart. She smiled at Elise, who nodded and stepped away to give them a moment alone.

"Papa," she said quietly, "I've come to say good-bye."

He turned his head and gazed down at her. Even stooped slightly, he was a head taller than she was. His cravat was as fresh and crisply tied as ever, his silver hair just as well trimmed and neatly combed, his shirt as gleaming white. Her mother saw to that. The house might be growing steadily shabbier, her hair more gray than pale blond, and her once-glowing complexion dulled by fatigue, but anyone seeing Dr. Halliday would have to smile and comment, as they always had, on what a dapper soul he was.

If only her mother's iron will could also turn back the cruel whim of fate that had glazed his once-bright gaze.

Ariel smiled broadly at him, hoping this would be one of the days when he smiled back, longing for even a trace of recognition. Perhaps he would notice her bonnet, one he'd bought for her before they had been forced to keep him away from town altogether. Her hopes sagged as his faded sherry gaze drifted past her to where the hired gig waited.

"Those aren't our horses," he said, frowning as if he'd been the victim of some trickery.

"No, Papa, they're not. That carriage is waiting to take me back to school."

His face puckered. "School?"

"Yes. The Penrose School. I teach there, remember?"

"Caroline has our horses," he said, ignoring her question and turning away. "She's gone off to a house party at the Brimswells. Edward Brimswell is quite taken with our Caroline. All the young men are. My daughter Caroline is a beautiful girl."

"Very beautiful," Ariel agreed, her heart sinking. It

had been years since Caroline attended a party at the Brimswells. She was married to Harry Hammerton and living in Derby and either unable or unwilling to involve herself in the tragic events there at home. It would be useless to try to explain any of that to her father, however.

"I have to go, Papa." She rose onto her toes to kiss his cheek. "I promise not to stay away so long next time."

As she settled back on her heels, he cupped her cheek with his hand, blinking as if trying to bring her into focus.

"Ariel?" he said in a low, uncertain tone.

"Oh, yes, Papa, it's me. It's Ariel."

"Ariel," he said, more firmly this time, and smiled at her. "Ariel. My Orionis, the brightest star in the heavens."

Orionis. He hadn't used his pet name for her in over a year, not since he started slipping away from them. Orionis was their star, the one they stood outside searching for on cloudless nights so they could make a wish together. *Be very careful what you wish for*, he would always tell her, *because a wish is very powerful*.

"I wish," he said now, pulling her back in time with him. "I wish . . ."

She caught her breath, waiting endless seconds for him to go on.

Instead, he frowned, and his gaze shifted jerkily, as if not wholly under his control, looking past her to the yard beyond.

"Those aren't our horses," he said.

Ariel blinked back a hot rush of tears. Not trusting herself to speak, she quickly touched her fingertips to her lips and then his cheek before turning away.

"Caroline has our horses," she heard him say as she

hurried to the waiting gig. "She's gone to a party at the Brimswells."

"Can't say as I have noticed any of those glimmers," Farrell replied with a derisive snort. "Ask me, we're lucky someone taught him to wipe his own arse. He's as thick as this board," he said, pounding his fist on a raised wall panel of solid oak in the drawing room. "And about as quick."

"No, I'm sure you're mistaken," Ariel said firmly. "For instance, what about yesterday?" she persisted. "When I made that play on words about bankers and bakers? You must have seen him smile at it."

"I seen." He looked unimpressed. "Begging your pardon, but I also seen him staring at your backside whenever you're turned away from him. Some things just come natural to a man no matter how much sense he has or don't have in his head."

She tapped one foot impatiently. "Are you trying to say that it's a natural reflex for a man to smile at a witty remark even when he doesn't understand what's being said?"

He shrugged. "Maybe he smiled because you did. You know, mimicking you. Like an ape would do."

"An ape," Ariel repeated, her brows lowering in a frown. "I hadn't considered that possibility."

Why the hell not?

The question nearly exploded from inside Leon as he stood with his arms folded, one shoulder resting against the curved arch of the drawing room, listening to them discuss him, debating his quirks and short-comings as if he were the prize heifer at a country fair. And why shouldn't they? After all, if he took home the first place ribbon, they would all share in the victory spoils and everyone would go away happy.

Unfortunately he had no intention of winning any ribbons on their behalf.

He would still like to know why it had not occurred to Miss Halliday that he was behaving like an ape when he'd smiled at her little joke yesterday. He had certainly gone to great lengths in the past weeks to create precisely that impression. It was definitely not his intent to permit her these little "glimmers," as she so annoyingly referred to them, hints that he may be something other than a complete and utter barbarian.

Clearly he would have to be more careful in the future.

It was a tedious thought. As amusing as it was to watch a proper English lady lower herself to his level, he was growing restless with his stay there. He was tired of the blasted dampness, and the swill that passed for food, and of that oaf Farrell staring at him from the corner of his eye everywhere he went.

The only thing he had not grown weary of was Miss Halliday herself. On the contrary, he found her endlessly fascinating. Dangerously so at times. She was mesmerizing in her tireless efforts to make a silk purse out of a sow's ear, especially when the sow's ear resisted her at every turn.

It seemed to him that a sensible, intelligent person would have given up on him long before now. Instead, for reasons he could not fathom, she possessed some extraordinary strain of optimism that actually seemed to thrive on failure.

The woman was irrepressible, immune to his surliness, undiscouraged by his lack of cooperation, forever rising above his black moods.

His best efforts to drive her away failed. She would

appear the next morning, smiling steadfastly, her hands clasped at her waist, saying, "Now, then, where shall we begin today?" in that Miss Priss way she had that made him want nothing more than to start the day by taking her hands in his and liberating her from those pristine white gloves of hers one slow, sweet, hypnotizing finger at a time.

After he had stripped her fingers bare, he would take one of her hands between his, turn hers palm-up and raise it to his mouth and he would satisfy at last his increasingly irresistible urge to taste her. Starting, but not ending, with her soft white palm.

An insolent grin curved his lips as he savored the prospect. It was a pity Miss Priss couldn't read his thoughts right then. She would need no further convincing that he was a savage in every sense of the word with which she was acquainted, and several which he'd lay odds she was not.

She had her white gloves on now, he noted, tucked into the tight cuffs of her sensible dress. Her navy blue mantle was tied snugly beneath her chin, the ribbon bow fighting for position with the much larger bow that held in place the hideous concoction atop her head. He'd observed that she rotated three bonnets on their daily walks, all of them atrocious, this one the worst of the lot.

It had a stiffly curved brim that projected at least eight inches above her forehead and stuck out on both sides of her head. Sprouting from it at odd angles was a veritable jungle of flowers and feathers in colors bright enough to make his head ache. He had to assume the thing was fashionable. What troubled him was that such frivolous concession was totally at odds with what seemed to be Miss Halliday's sensible nature. At first he'd thought her drab, but to his surprise he had slowly come to appreciate her simple, unadorned garments and the muted colors she favored. They provided the perfect backdrop for her subtle beauty, much as a simple square of black velvet provided the perfect backdrop for a flawless diamond.

Undistracted by ruffles or doodads, he was free to gaze at her, and each day he found something new to admire, the perfect symmetry of her brows, the delicate hue of her lips, the lush fan of her dark lashes as they swept demurely downward. The bonnets were a damnable distraction, and he didn't like being distracted. The very fact that she would don them at all seemed only to lend credence to his conviction that all women, even the ones who might appear to be rational, were fickle creatures at heart.

She happened to glance away from her discussion with Farrell and noticed him lounging at the door.

"There you are, sir, and with your coat already on and buttoned. Excellent."

She beamed at him as admiringly as if he'd just completed construction of the Taj Mahal. Single-handedly. And as absurd as it was, something inside him was warmed by the approving glow she cast his way.

He pushed away from the wall and joined her at the center of the room. "Out."

"Yes, it is time for our walk. The wind has quieted some since yesterday," she told him. "Perhaps we can venture to walk a bit farther than we have been. I know how much you enjoy being outdoors."

He turned and started for the door.

"Lord Sage."

Leon stopped short, hackles rising as they always did when she called him that. He hesitated a second to control his expression before glancing back over his shoulder to find her standing in the same spot. Farrell stood at her elbow, smirking broadly.

"Aren't you forgetting something?" she asked. "Your arm?" she prompted him, lifting her own arm with her elbow bent in an apparent attempt to jog his memory. "You always offer a lady your arm when you are entering or leaving a room together."

Leon hesitated. He didn't want to offer her his arm. He didn't want to feel her slender fingers curl against him, he didn't want her skirts to rustle against his legs as they walked side by side. He didn't want to risk anything that might cause that sudden, sizzling awareness that suggested he felt for her anything other than what a lifetime of bitterness told he ought to feel.

Reluctantly, he walked back and looped his arm under hers, managing a stiff version of the maneuver she had been laboring for days to teach him.

Miss Halliday sighed, sliding her arm forward a few inches so that their shoulders bumped and his muscles jerked in response.

"I suppose that will do for today," she said. "Shall we go?"

Farrell immediately fell into step behind them as he did every afternoon. Leon could almost feel the chill emanating from his great, hulking shadow. He halted once more and glared at him with the full weight of his own self-contempt at that moment.

"No Farrell," he said.

"Now, see here," Farrell began.

Miss Halliday silenced him with a look.

"Perhaps this would be a good time for you to see about the loose shutter on his lordship's window," she suggested.

He tugged on his woolen cap. "I can see to that

later. I always go along on the walk. It's safer that way. If you take my meaning," he added, sliding a glance toward Leon.

Miss Halliday appeared to waver.

"No Farrell." Leon thrust his chin forward. If she required a scene, she'd have one. He had taken his last walk with that goon dogging his heels.

"I understand your concern," she said to Farrell, "but it is unnecessary. His lordship and I will manage on our own for today."

"But—"

"That will be all, Mr. Farrell." She dismissed him with a nod.

Leon risked directing a small retaliatory smirk at the other man over her head and was rewarded by the sound of his indignant sputtering as he charged past, sending a spray of spittle before him. It was all Leon could do not to chuckle at the irony of the moment. After all, he was the savage in residence there, and he had yet to foam at the mouth.

They proceeded outside with her clinging lightly to his arm and him pretending to be unaffected by her touch. Deprivation, deprivation, he repeated over and over to himself. He experienced only what any man would at being so close to a woman who felt so good and smelled so good and whose slightest movement promised an antidote to his long months of forced celibacy.

He paused on the brick path outside the back door to drag in deep breaths of fresh air. The cold made his chest feel tight and achy, but it was an effective distraction from his own inconvenient desires. And even frigid fresh air was an improvement over being confined in that house. He couldn't decide which he detested most about the place, the infernal drafts that seemed to arise from nowhere and find him everywhere he went, or the stench of burning wood and coal that fouled the very air he breathed.

It mystified him why anyone would freely choose to live in such a hostile climate. He could attribute it only to total ignorance of what else the world had to offer. Of course, not every Englishman could claim ignorance as an excuse. If he lived forever, he would never understand why the man who had fathered him had chosen to leave paradise to return to this god-forsaken country.

They followed the path around to the back of the cottage, taking their usual route alongside the high stone wall that enclosed the school grounds. This was his favorite moment of the day, and being alone with Miss Halliday and without Farrell made it even more pleasurable than usual.

From his window he often gazed out over the rolling fields and neat gardens surrounded by boxwood hedges, all dormant now. Perhaps it was better there in spring and summer and that was why people stayed. Perhaps, but he still could not comprehend it. Compromise of any sort went against his nature.

Although they never strayed far from the house during their walks, he knew the land around him well. From his vantage point at the window he had learned the dips and swells of the earth, the growth pattern of the forest, and where the open stretches lay, the places where a man could run flat out until his breath was gone and his muscles throbbed from the pleasure-pain of pushing himself to his limit. He also knew where the wall was high and strong and he knew the places where boys chasing balls had worn holes between the stones, making it easy to scale and reach the other side.

"It is much milder out today, don't you agree?" inquired Miss Halliday beside him.

He made a noncommittal sound and fisted his gloved hands against the cold.

"We can walk all the way to the end of the wall if you'd care to."

If he cared to. As if she could stop him if he cared to walk right over the damn wall and keep going. How could she possibly trust him out there with her alone?

His keeper, he thought with grim amusement as they plodded on across the frozen, uneven terrain. All that stood between him and freedom.

At times like this he was overcome with the absurdity of it. He felt the same way when Farrell, puffed up even more than usual with self-importance, would swagger to his chamber door at bedtime and make a show of locking the savage in for the night. He found it difficult to actually believe that they could think they possessed the power to keep him there against his will, or that a bolt and chain were enough to protect them if he should wake in the night and get it into his head to slaughter them all in their beds.

Not that he would need to kill them to escape. A hundred times since he'd been there he could have tossed Miss Halliday aside and taken his leave. He could have simply walked away from the whole inconvenient mess.

Part of him longed to do exactly that, but it was too late. At some point while he was still shackled, sick, and shivering in that stinking ship's hold, the moment when it might have been possible to walk away had passed and was gone forever. Turning the other cheek was no longer an option. No, the beast in him was bent on vengeance, and one way or another he was going to have it.

"On days like this," she was saying, drawing Leon from his own thoughts, "I feel as if spring is right around the corner and I can hardly wait for it to come. Spring is my favorite time of year. The flowers, the colors, the warmth of the sun on your face, I love it all."

Leon continued walking, excruciatingly aware of her hand on him and of the unwanted effect of her enthusiasm on his own senses. He didn't want to know about her favorite season or color or anything else.

"I expect it won't be too long," she went on, "till we see the first of the crocus popping their little heads through the earth. I love crocus. They seem to symbolize hope against all odds."

He slanted a look at her. If he wanted to, he could have told her about torch ginger and frangipani blossoms, about petals as soft as silk and as big as a man's hand, and about how their fragrance could fill the night and take your breath away. He could have told her about the bloodred anthuriums that grew like wildfire near the sea and about how the radiance and the sweetness of his home was there for him year-round.

Instead, he kicked a clump of hard earth with the toe of his boot. Damn this frigid place with its murky days and leafless trees, and damn him for letting himself be tempted by a woman who believed that the promise of a few miserable blades of grass and a crocus was cause for celebration.

The clump of earth he kicked came loose, lifting a few inches and then landing with a muffled thud in front of Miss Halliday just as she raised one booted foot to take the next step. He heard her small gasp of surprise and felt her grip tighten on his arm as she stumbled against him.

Leon moved without thinking to break her fall, easily catching her with one arm while the other moved behind her to anchor her safely against him. As quickly and effortlessly as that, he had her where he had thought so often of having her, in his arms, her chest pressed to his, her face tipped up to him and her delectable mouth only a slow, purposeful movement of his head away.

Seven

They stared into each other's eyes. His hand pressed against the small of her back. He longed to draw her closer and feared seriously offending her sensibilities if he did.

As it was, the heavy bulk of their coats prevented him from actually feeling a bit of her. It didn't matter. Just holding her at last released a powerful rush of images that had been accumulating in his imagination, and suddenly he wasn't cold any longer. On the contrary, he felt as if he'd been dragged headfirst into a furnace.

His breath came in short, rapid pants and his muscles clenched, all his muscles, demanding to be used, fast and hard. If he were in his room, he would work through this powerful urge that gripped him by laying his palms flat on the wall and pushing his weight away a hundred times, five hundred times, whatever it took to spend his pent-up energy and bring himself under control.

There were no walls to push against out here, however, or to hold him in. There was only him and her, and the sudden reckless hunger to take her, even if it meant losing himself.

With a frustrated groan he pulled away. Acting on pure instinct, he yanked off his coat and gloves and tossed them to her.

"My lord," she exclaimed. "What in heaven's name—" She paused, bending to retrieve a glove that had missed its mark. "What do you think you're doing? You'll catch your death of pneumonia."

"Spring," he said, lifting his arms in the air like the madman he was.

"No, not yet. I said soon it will be spring. Soon."

"Soon."

"Yes, soon. Not now."

"You wait."

"Yes, yes," she said, nodding with amazement and excitement at his sudden verbosity. "We must wait for spring. Now, please, put your coat—"

He pushed it away. "Wait for me."

"Wait for you?" she echoed, her proud teacher expression growing cloudy.

The words were barely out of her mouth when he turned and started running, running for his life it looked like. Her alarmed shouts chased after him, and Leon cursed softly. She would have Farrell out there in no time with all that panicky yelling . . . if he wasn't already watching them from the window, just waiting for the chance to use his strap again. Reluctantly, he turned and made a wide loop back to her.

"Thank heavens," she breathed when he drew to a halt. "I feared you were . . . well, never mind about that. You must not run away."

"Run."

"No," she said, shaking her head emphatically.

"Yes. Run. Need. Wait for me."

It was the most words he'd strung together for her yet, but it was worth it, he decided, if she would be quiet while he burned off what was simmering inside him, threatening to push him over the edge. He felt as if he were going mad, losing control of his own thoughts and feelings.

This time he didn't hear her calling to him as he ran away, and he kept going, across the lawn and the drive, leaping the low hedge on the other side and heading for the wall beyond.

He felt as if he could run forever. He wanted to run barefoot alongside the ocean, hearing it pound endlessly against the cliffs, feeling the warmth of the sun on his back and the perfumed breeze touching his face. He fantasized about that sometimes too, while he lay awake and restless in his bed at night.

He ran hard, pushing himself, taking every hill full speed and straight on, running until he felt spent and safe. He ended up back where he started, panting and grinning, more at ease in his own skin than he had been in weeks.

She was waiting for him, her stern expression undercut considerably by the gleam of amusement in her eye.

"Are you quite pleased with yourself, sir? For your information, your little . . . excursion," she said with a wave of her hand, "could have caused us both a great deal of trouble. I can't imagine what Mr. Penrose would have thought if he'd seen you running across his cricket field like a . . . a gazelle. On second thought, yes, I can. He would have thought the absolute worst and all my hard work would have been for naught." Somehow the bow beneath her chin had shifted so that one side of it stuck up in front of her face. She paused to bat it away before adding, "I certainly hope it was worth it."

Leon tilted his head and gave her the heavy-lidded stare that, he'd observed, always made her fidget uneasily. Hell, yes, it had been worth it.

"You must promise me never to do that again," she continued, holding his coat open for him.

He put his hand over his heart on cue.

"Yes, promise me," she urged.

He shook his head. "No."

"Yes. You must. I cannot have you—"

"I run," he said over her protest.

"No."

"Yes. You wait." He lifted his arm, elbow bent at precisely the correct angle, a direct challenge in the gaze he leveled at her. "I run, you wait."

She glanced at the arm he proffered, then back to his face, her expression a mingling of amazement and slowly dawning understanding of the bargain he was proposing. Of course, she had no way of knowing the significance of such an offer, or that it went against every principle he lived by to compromise with anyone for any reason. Yet he was doing precisely that. If she would allow him the physical exercise he needed and craved, he would be more cooperative in other matters, such as this silly business of escorting her in and out of rooms.

"All right," she said at last. "You may have a period of exercise each afternoon. Weather permitting."

"No Farrell," he said.

She laughed and nodded. "Agreed. No Farrell . . . provided you run only as far as I can see you."

Ignoring that, he took his coat from her. He would run where he pleased, and they both knew it.

His runs became part of their daily routine. He even managed to get her to go back on her condition regarding the weather, and she would stand huddled beneath the eaves in back, waiting, while he ran through the fog and mist. In return, he felt obliged to step up the pace of his edification process just enough to fulfill his side of the bargain.

As far as Leon was concerned, he won on both counts. Running took the edge off his growing restlessness. It left him feeling less agitated and more focused, which could only bode well for his future plans, whatever they turned out to be. And the improved communication between himself and Miss Halliday made the long days more tolerable. For both of them, he surmised. It was infinitely more interesting to pretend not to understand chess than to not understand which end of a fork to hold.

At times the mood between them was so easy, he almost forgot why they were there and what her role in this scheme was, and he would find himself smiling at something she said or impulsively reaching to brush the hair from her cheek and wanting her as fiercely as he had the day of their "exercise" walk. Then he would remember that it was her intent to break him and make him "British" enough for polite company, and with a surge of renewed resentment he would go out of his way to punish her by making it clear that in spite of all her work, he was still a long way from being tamed.

Unfortunately, neither recalling her purpose nor punishing her for it stopped him from becoming mesmerized at the most unexpected moments by something as innocuous as the downy soft nape of her neck.

As the days passed, he regained the physical stamina that weeks of forced idleness had cost him. He was able to run longer and farther all the time. He expected her to protest as the time he was gone lengthened, but she always greeted his return with the same placid smile. Slowly it dawned on him that she was able to be so relaxed because she trusted him. She trusted him. Amazing thought. There was no reason she should trust him and every reason she shouldn't. The fact that she did introduced yet another threat into the already tangled skein of his thoughts about her.

Today he'd purposely cut short his run and approached from a different direction, curious to see what she did to pass the time while he was gone.

Rounding the corner of the house, he saw her at the far side of the yard. She had her back to him, sitting on a low stone wall that encircled a small garden with a toppled birdbath at its center. He slowed his steps to watch as she bent and offered what looked like a carrot to a brown and white spotted rabbit sitting on the ground at her feet. Drawing closer, he heard her speaking to the creature as well.

"Rabbits are supposed to like carrots," she was saying in an implacable tone Leon recognized well.

The rabbit tilted his head to one side, much the way he often did to signal his lack of understanding. Leon grinned as he noted that Miss Halliday accorded the rabbit the same patience she always did him.

"Carrots are good for you. Biscuits are not, so no more biscuits."

She offered the carrot once more. Leon was close enough now to see the little bugger's whiskers twitch with distaste as he turned his head away.

"Oh, all right, then, perhaps just a half a biscuit, but that's the end of it. You'll be getting as fat as Prinny himself if you're not careful." She reached into her pocket and produced a piece of sugar biscuit. "Here you go, then." She smiled as she watched him gobble it down. "In fact, I think I shall call you Prinny. The name suits you perfectly."

She glanced around suddenly, startled by the sound of Leon's soft chuckle behind her.

The rabbit's gaze darted in his direction as well. Aside from a slight arching of its back, however, it stood its ground and kept chewing, evidently more fond of biscuits than it was afraid of a stranger.

"Friend?" Leon asked her softly, nodding at the bundle of spotted fur.

Her mouth curved in a sheepish smile. "It appears so. At least for as long as I go on feeding him."

"Why?"

"Why? Oh, you mean why do I feed him?" She shrugged. "Believe it or not, I thought he looked hungry. I first spotted him from the window, shivering out here in the rain one morning. The silly thing hasn't the sense to hibernate, or whatever it is rabbits do in winter."

"Likes biscuits," he observed.

"Too much so. I daresay he's half again the size he was at first."

"How long?"

Her expression grew sheepish once more. "How long have you been running? At least a couple of weeks, I suppose."

"Not afraid."

She sighed. "No, he's not. I've spoiled him so utterly rotten, he no doubt thinks all humans come bearing biscuits and lumps of sugar."

Crouching down, Leon regarded the rabbit soberly. "No. Only Hallidays."

She laughed. "He doesn't appear to be convinced."

It was true. The rabbit had inched closer and was sniffing Leon's hands, a hopeful gleam in his eye.

"No biscuits," he told him firmly.

She tapped his arm lightly and handed him a small piece. He in turn offered it to the rabbit. To his amazement, it stretched its neck and plucked it from his fingertips with more delicacy than some women he'd known. When he finished chewing and looked around for more, she laughed and scooped him up in her arms as she stood.

"No more, you piggy bunny."

Leon watched, captivated. Amazing, he thought. The little he knew about rabbits told him that this one should have hightailed it under the nearest bush at the sound of his footsteps. Instead, it was snuggling into her arms like the pampered family pet.

"You can pet him if you like," she said as if reading his thoughts.

Leon reached out and stroked the fur between the long white ears that flopped down on either side of his head. The rabbit responded by nuzzling his hand. He half expected the damn thing to purr.

How had she done it? he wondered. What spell did she cast to make wild things docile? What mystical power did she wield to make this untamed creature act against its own nature when she was around? If he knew the answer, perhaps he could understand the effect she was having on him. Just as she fed the rabbit the biscuits he favored, she had silently observed his own preferences, and each afternoon now she personally prepared a tea tray with morsels that tempted him in spite of himself. He couldn't recall anyone ever taking the trouble to please him in such a simple way, and he found himself looking forward to teatime with her.

As he continued to pet the rabbit, he allowed his hand to gradually glide closer to hers until the tips of his fingers were brushing the side of hers with each slow stroke. Leon found it very interesting that both she and the rabbit seemed to relax under his touch, while his own heart beat faster and faster.

They were standing side by side, her shoulder brushing his arm. He caught the light scent of rosewater that always clung to her skin. It was mixed with sandalwood, the smell of home, and with the fresh crispness of the air. It had been a long time since he'd been this close to anything that smelled so good to him. He leaned closer, yearning and feeling reckless.

What would she do, he wondered, if he were to turn his head and . . .

"Miss Halliday? Where the devil . . . oh, there you are."

She jumped at the sound of her name. Even the rabbit picked up its head and looked around frantically.

Turning, Leon saw the headmaster hurrying toward them and groaned inwardly. Just what he was not in the mood for, another visit from Penrose the Nose, as he had taken to thinking of him. The last time he stopped by to see how they were doing, the everresourceful Miss Halliday had shoved Leon into a chair in front of the chessboard and tried to imply that he had learned to play well enough that they were involved in a rousing match. An impression he hastened to correct by casually biting the head off the black knight as the two of them stood talking.

"Farrell suggested I might find you back here," Penrose said. "I must say, while you're busy teaching manners, you ought to try teaching some to that fellow."

"Was he rude to you?" Miss Halliday asked.

"Extremely so. I wonder if he's been made aware of exactly who is in charge here."

"I'm so sorry. I'll speak to him and make sure he understands that you are the headmaster of the Penrose School and are to be accorded the respect commensurate with your position."

There was a strange new pitch to her voice that caused Leon to stare at her curiously. At first he thought she must be struggling not to laugh at the pompous ass the same as he was. A closer look convinced him otherwise. Her cheeks were scorched with color, the way they were whenever she was very angry or very excited. He didn't think she'd had long enough to get angry. Her eyes had changed as well. Usually the shade of a soft summer sky, they had turned a bright, brittle blue. It was her smile, however, that disturbed him most.

In their long days together he had seen her try to resist smiling at him; he'd seen her smirk and grin sheepishly and throw back her head and laugh out loud. It had not escaped him that the woman had an unusually expressive mouth. But he had never before seen her mouth curled up stiffly at both ends as if someone had dropped strings behind her eyeballs to hold it that way.

For just a fraction of a second, as she continued to try to smooth the Nose's ruffled feathers, her gaze caught his. She took advantage of the eye contact to shove the rabbit at him. The abrupt move caught both Leon and the rabbit by surprise, and it took a moment of squirming before they made themselves comfortable with the arrangement. He looked up once again just in time to see the Nose slanting a cautious glance his way.

"How are . . . things?" he inquired of Miss Halliday.

So he was "things" today, Leon noted. He supposed it was no better or worse than being referred to as he had been on other occasions as "matters" or "this business," as in "How is this business coming along?"

"Splendidly," she replied with that same high-pitched, almost giddy catch in her voice. "His lordship is progressing in leaps and bounds in all areas."

"How are his table manners?" the Nose asked.

"Excellent. Why, just yesterday we ate an entire meal without a single slip."

A lie.

Leon observed her closely as she elaborated on this fictitious account of last evening's meal, leaving out the part where he stuck his fingers in the sugar bowl before licking them clean. Her enthusiasm bordered on the hysterical. He'd never seen her like this before, all agitated and fluttery, as if the Nose were damn royalty or the Second Coming or— Leon's thoughts thudded to a halt. Or the man of her dreams.

Impossible.

He looked again.

It was true. There was no other conceivable explanation for the way she was behaving. She was flirting with him, for God's sake. Or, rather, trying to, and doing such a pitiful job of it that it was no wonder the Nose didn't have the slightest notion of what she was about.

Miss Priss and the Nose.

Why hadn't he seen it sooner? Recalling the headmaster's previous visits, he realized that even then her demeanor had changed in his presence, that she had become more animated in a jangled, unstrung sort of way. He had assumed she was simply nervous and trying overly hard to impress her employer. And so she had been, he realized with disdain, only not for the reasons he'd thought.

The difference was that on those occasions she had been prepared for his arrival, whereas today she'd been taken by surprise.

And was still reeling from the impact, he noted malevolently, observing her skittish gestures and twitching smile.

Miss Priss and the Nose.

As distasteful as it was to accept such a notion, he had no choice.

Not that it mattered to him whom she set her sights on, he reminded himself. If he was vexed, and he had to admit he was, it was simply with his own obtuseness in not grasping the situation sooner. He refused to see his lack of perception as a reflection on his knowledge of the fairer sex, however. He prided himself on being extremely discerning in that area, if only as a means of self-defense. He would not be held accountable for the fact that Miss Halliday's approach to romance was more reminiscent of a scalded cat than a femme fatale.

He continued to listen, sullen and isolated, while the two of them discussed his behavior as if he were deaf as well as uncivilized. As if, he brooded, he were of no more consequence than the damn rabbit in his arms. He glanced down to find its glassy brown eyes riveted on Miss Halliday.

Give it up, fur ball, he thought, she's forgotten you exist as well. The only way the creature was likely to regain her attention now was if the Nose expressed a sudden fancy for rabbit stew. Leon's hold on the rabbit tightened reflexively, spurred by a protective urge he hadn't known he possessed. Suddenly it seemed that he and the fur ball had more in common than a distaste for raw carrots. They shared the bond of those who had been cast aside, deserted, forgotten. It was hardly a new experience, he thought, but to be cast off in favor of the Nose? It rankled enough to sour the best of moods, and at the moment his was far from that. He wondered now if when she had mysteriously disappeared that afternoon, leaving him alone with Farrell for hours, she had run off to see Penrose. The very idea of her throwing herself so blatantly at such a poor excuse for a Romeo irritated Leon more with each passing second. He didn't like it. Worse, he didn't like not liking it.

"Tomorrow?" he heard her say, the color draining from her face. "I'm afraid that's quite impossible."

The Nose drew himself to his full height, which put his gaze about level with Leon's armpit.

"Nothing is impossible if you are willing to apply yourself," he informed her. "Castleton wishes to see for himself what sort of progress you are making with Sage, and since you've spoken so highly of his accomplishments recently, I felt confident in telling him that dinner tomorrow evening would provide the perfect opportunity to ease his concern." His eyes became slits. "He is progressing, is he not?"

"Yes. Yes, of course he is. It's just that . . . I really do wish you had spoken to me before making such a commitment."

"Nonsense. It appears that I have more confidence in your ability than you do. It's settled, then. Dinner here tomorrow—"

"Here?" she gasped.

"Of course. Where else?"

"But surely—"

"My dear Miss Halliday, you do eat dinner here, do you not?"

"Yes, but—"

"Then there should be no problem in adding two extra chairs at the table."

"The problem, Mr. Penrose, is that . . ."

Leon listened intently, eager to hear how she would word her objection to sitting down to dine with the earl, the cherished object of her affections, and her star pupil. If anyone were to ask him, it sounded like the makings of a most memorable occasion. In fact, he decided then and there, he would see to it personally that the evening was seared into all their memories forever.

With a silent, defiant sneer, he told her so.

"Mrs. Farrell," she finished in a hollow tone. "The problem is Mrs. Farrell . . . or, rather, her cooking. It's quite dismal, I'm afraid."

The Nose waved off her excuse. "Direct her to prepare something simple and I'm sure it will be fine. Besides, we will not be here to evaluate Mrs. Farrell's culinary skills."

"No, I understand that you won't," she said, her voice sounding smaller still.

The Nose turned and looked at Leon directly for the first time.

"You're looking well, Sage."

Leon bared his teeth by way of reply.

Penrose shot Miss Halliday an alarmed look.

"I believe he's cold," she said quickly, as if that explained his feral response. "Shivering even."

She leveled a warning glare at Leon as she plucked his coat from the wall beside her. "You really should put this back on now, my lord."

"Why does he have his coat off in the first place?" inquired the Nose. "And why is he holding that filthy animal in his arms?"

Leon stroked the rabbit's head and curled his lip at the Nose. "Friend," he said.

Penrose looked to Miss Halliday. "Did he say . . . friend?"

"He's joking. You can put the rabbit down now."

"No."

Clenching her teeth determinedly, she reached for the rabbit. "I said you can—"

Leon easily avoided her grasp. "No."

"He doesn't intend to bring the filthy thing inside, does he?" asked the Nose.

She shook her head. "No."

"Yes," said Leon, the sum total of his desire and energy suddenly concentrated on doing that very thing.

And she knew it. He saw in her eyes that she correctly identified the tenacity in his, and wisely opted to change the subject.

She turned back to the Nose, her strung-up smile once more in place. "We were just about to go in to tea. Will you do us the honor of joining us, Mr. Penrose?"

No, Leon raged silently. Teatime was theirs. He refused to share it—or her—with this useless twit.

"I'm afraid I can't," Penrose replied, sparing Leon drastic action. He was still eyeing the rabbit with disapproval. "I have an engagement."

"But surely you can favor us with a few moments?" she ventured eagerly. "I have prepared a new musical piece to entertain his lordship, and I thought perhaps . . ."

The Nose waved off her offer as if she were of no more significance than a troublesome gnat, and Leon felt a sudden urge to wipe the haughty expression off the whiny headmaster's face.

"I'll be late as it is," Penrose told her as from beneath one arm he pulled a long, narrow leather-bound book. "I am having a problem with this ledger, however. The receipts and expenditures won't tally and the . . . oh, just have a look for yourself, will you? When you have a free moment, I mean."

Leon waited to hear her tell him that the only free moments she had were precious few and she spent them sleeping. Instead, the strings tightened, the corners of her mouth lifted once again, and out came "Of course, I'd be happy to see if I can find the problem. Perhaps it can be traced back to an earlier error of my own making."

"Yes." The Nose instantly brightened at the suggestion that she was at fault and not him. "Yes, I'm sure that must be it. You'll have it done for me by tomorrow night?"

"Of course."

"Very good."

Leon watched the Nose hurry out of sight, then turned back to Miss Halliday with a smug air. He was prepared to be reprimanded for his obstinacy with the rabbit. He was prepared to hear a lecture on the mountains that needed to be moved before tomorrow evening's command performance. He was even prepared to endure a brief period of lovesick afterglow on her part, though he was definitely not looking forward to it.

He was, in fact, prepared for anything but what came next.

In a shaking, defeated whisper that did not belong to her, Ariel said, "I am doomed."

Five minutes of sitting across the table from Lord Savage would be more than enough to convince anyone that he was nowhere close to being ready for the role he was expected to assume. For all that Ariel had managed to teach him, she had failed in the larger sense. He was not a fitting marquis. There would be no miracle. Perhaps the earl would even be so upset that he would refuse to let her continue her efforts for the two weeks remaining.

What then? She supposed if she were lucky Mr. Penrose might permit her to resume her regular duties, but he certainly would not regard her in a favorable light, much less the affectionate one she needed to inspire. Her heart constricted as she reflected on what that loss would ultimately mean for her family.

And Sage? She wasn't naive enough to believe Castleton would abandon his efforts entirely simply because she had proven unequal to the task. No, he would look elsewhere for assistance. Perhaps to someone who would take a firmer approach. Someone like Farrell, she thought miserably, recalling the marks his strap had left on Sage.

Her heart wrenched at the memory, forcefully enough to cause her to press her hand to her chest to still its sudden pounding. It was only natural that she feel some concern for him, she told herself. After all, they had spent a great deal of time together these past weeks, working side by side, taking long walks, searching to find ways to communicate in spite of the barriers between them.

Over time they had settled into their own system of communication, often relying on eye contact or touch to convey what simple words could not. She had been amazed to learn how much it was possible to express without speaking at all. Sage was capable of revealing more of what he was feeling with a raised brow than many men she knew could in an hour's work of pontificating.

Strangely, she felt as if they knew each other far better, or at least in a different way, than they now would if they had been able to rely on the usual social conventions that govern conduct between men and women. There were times, when their eyes met and held, that Ariel had the breathtaking sense that she was seeing all the way to his soul, and that he in turn saw all the way to hers. It was an unsettling feeling, and she was always the first to look away, invariably prompting one of his slow, lazy smiles that only served to confuse her more.

The feelings he caused inside her were much harder to escape than his gaze was. They lingered, often drifting back to claim her when she thought she was safe from him, at night, alone in her bed. She would toss and turn, praying for sleep to release her from the temptation dished up by her own imagination. But all too often lately, sleep waited stubbornly at the end of a long procession of deliciously unsettling images.

Such as the day she had stumbled and ended up in his arms.

She was not an expert on either men or kissing. Far from it actually. But she knew, the way a woman knows certain things, that if he had held her just a few seconds longer that day, he would have kissed her. And she knew, in the same way, that his kiss would be beyond anything she had ever imagined or read about or could conceivably conjure up. She knew that his kiss would be as savage and ruthless as he himself could be. The only thing she didn't know was how she would have responded.

It was a good thing, she decided, that their association was going to end soon, before she was forced to find out.

In spite of her feelings of foreboding, she planned for the dinner party with her usual thoroughness. She was determined to approach the occasion with her head held high, and to do her very best to fulfill her obligations. After much consideration, she decided to leave the choice of menu to Mrs. Farrell so that she might concentrate her efforts on what was certain to be the focal point of the evening, Sage's performance at the dinner table.

She worked diligently, staying up until long after they were both exhausted and getting up at dawn to try again. And again. Late the following afternoon she was finally forced to admit that her approach may have been a tactical error of the first magnitude.

She had been so engrossed in her own work that she had no idea of what the foul-smelling concoction being prepared by Mrs. Farrell might be, or what had been laid out for Sage to wear—or not to wear as his whim dictated—and for all her grueling efforts to polish his manners, he still lowered his head to his soup bowl, gripped his goblet with two fists, and remained unable to grasp the concept of starting a meal with the utensils farthest from his plate and working his way in as the courses progressed.

"No, this fork first," she said, pounding her fist on the table so forcefully that the fork in question bounced up and then landed with a clatter. "This, then this, then this. First course, second course, dessert. It is not difficult."

She pointed to each utensil in turn, then looked up to see Sage staring over her shoulder through the window behind her.

"You're not paying attention," she accused him

tersely. "It is little wonder you persist in eating your soup with a teaspoon."

He slid his gaze to meet hers. "Out."

"I've already told you, we will not be going outside today. We have too much work to do here. Please pick up your dinner fork."

He folded his arms and leaned back in his chair. They were seated across from each other at one end of the dining table, a full place setting in front of each of them.

"No," he said with the same undercurrent of defiance she had sensed in him ever since Penrose's visit the previous day. Just when she most needed him to be cooperative, he had become more sullen and aloof than ever.

She squared her shoulders. "Yes."

"No," he said again.

He lifted his arm, and before she realized what he intended, he had swept every last piece of china and crystal to the floor. The sound of shattering glass seemed to echo in the room forever. Or at least long enough for Ariel to rein in her temper. She stared at the mess on the floor with a mixture of outrage and exasperation, and to her horror felt tears threatening all over again.

No. She would not cry, especially not in front of this immature, ill-mannered lout seated across from her. She didn't care if he was a peer and had suffered the distinct disadvantage of being raised by savages; the man was a boor beyond description and she would be glad to see the last of him. He more than deserved whatever treatment he would receive at the hands of her replacement.

She jerked as if burned as he reached across the

table and slid his finger beneath her chin. He tipped her face up and peered at her as if she were a constellation he was having trouble identifying.

"Cry?" he said softly.

Ariel sniffed and blinked back the tears that pooled inside her lower lids.

"I most certainly am not crying. I am simply grateful we didn't attempt this afternoon's lesson with full soup bowls." Placing her hands on the table edge, she rose. "The lesson is over. I will arrange to have this debris swept up. You may go to your room and dress for dinner. It is time."

He got to his feet, carelessly kicking aside a large chunk of plate.

"You will need to wear a waistcoat and jacket tonight as well as a cravat."

She said it offhandedly, as if it were something he did with some regularity. It was the approach she had decided was most likely to meet with success. Or, at least, avoid outright rebellion.

He stood with his weight on one hip, arms folded, his expression remote.

"Farrell can assist you if you like."

"No," he said quickly.

"Very well. I will be up—"

"No."

"Then who?" she demanded, her patience finally worn thin. "Mrs. Farrell refuses to be in the same room with you since you threw soup at her. The housemaids live in terror of crossing your path. And you will never be able to knot your cravat properly yourself on your first attempt."

"No cravat."

She nodded, not totally unprepared for this

pronouncement. "As you wish, my lord. I have done my best on your behalf. Whatever happens from here on, you will have brought on yourself."

Turning quickly, she marched from the room, leaving him to his own devices for the first time since his arrival.

Eight

Ariel was waiting in the drawing room when the earl and Mr. Penrose arrived. Firelight added to the warm glow there and sent soft shadows dancing over the rose sateen draperies and comfortably overstuffed chairs. It was a room that invited one to sit down and relax, but its beckoning mood was lost on Ariel. She had spent the previous half hour pacing and rehearsing so that she might greet them without appearing to be what she was, nervous enough to jump out of her own skin.

She was wearing her best evening dress, first worn for her sister Caroline's wedding three years earlier. Made of shimmering ivory crepe with crystal beads sprinkled across the bodice, it had a twisted band of emerald-green velvet around the deep neckline and a matching velvet sash at the high waist. With it she wore ivory kid slippers laced with gold, and at her neck a delicate seed-pearl brooch given her by her mother.

Even her stubbornly straight hair had for once cooperated, permitting itself to be tortured into loose ringlets that fell softly at her cheeks.

As a rule, Ariel paid little attention to her appearance beyond a desire to appear tasteful and well groomed, and even less attention to the latest dictates of fashion. Even she knew enough, however, to recognize that the outfit she wore this evening flattered her, bringing her as close to beautiful as she was ever likely to come.

It was for that very reason that she had once thought to save the dress for a more momentous occasion, such as that time when it seemed Mr. Penrose might at last be ready to declare his intentions. Having first been led to understand that he had intentions toward her, of course. Since that now seemed an increasingly remote possibility, she'd opted to go ahead and wear the dress for tonight's dinner, ignoring the feeling that she was primping for the guillotine.

Moving to greet Castleton and Penrose as they were shown into the room, she immediately launched into a strained attempt to divert them with conversation, hoping to postpone the moment of truth as long as possible.

She had not seen Sage since she abandoned him in the dining room and had no idea if he had followed her directions and dressed for dinner or was simply holed up in his room, brooding and drinking too much brandy. Beyond taking the precaution of telling Farrell that his lordship was not to leave the house, she had not concerned herself with the matter. She'd meant what she said to him. She had done her best and now it was out of her hands.

Still, it had taken all the willpower she possessed to refrain from going to him and trying once more to somehow make him understand how important this evening was to his future. She'd even considered locking him in his room and claiming that he'd suddenly taken ill and could not join them for dinner after all. In the end, however, she had done what she always did, lifted her chin and prepared to meet the challenge head-on.

Even so, her throat constricted when the earl at last interrupted her to inquire when Sage would be joining them.

"Shortly," she replied, fighting panic and smiling even as her heart slid low in her chest.

Summoning Farrell, who was waiting just outside the room, she said, "Will you please go upstairs and ask Lord Sage to join us now?"

"Yes, Miss Halliday," he replied, hesitating. "But if he—"

"No matter what," she interrupted, "he is to join us."

The burly Farrell flushed and darted an embarrassed look in the direction of the other two men. Then, lowering his voice, he said to her, "But what if he won't come?"

"Persuade him," she said.

Farrell was backing away, still giving her a doubtful look, when an unfamiliar voice from somewhere behind stopped him in his tracks.

"That won't be necessary."

They turned as one, four pairs of eyes drawn by the unmistakable note of authority in the smooth, deep voice. Four jaws went slack at the sight. Four breaths were stolen by the sheer stupefying wonder of what was before them.

Sage stood in the doorway, dressed for dinner as if Brummell himself had served as his valet. He wore a finely woven black dress coat open over a waistcoat of black and emerald paisley shot with gold. The cuffs of his snowy white shirt extended precisely the correct length below his jacket sleeves, and for once the ruffled front was buttoned all the way to the top. A fresh pair of dark tan breeches clung to his lean hips and long legs and disappeared into black knee boots so highly polished, they reflected the flickering light from the candelabra overhead. Even his hair had been combed and tied back, accentuating the lean contours of his handsome face.

It was his cravat, however, that commanded Ariel's attention and refused to release her.

The square of pristine white silk was tied at his throat in an elaborate, complex, utterly flawless knot, raising in Ariel's mind a simple, straightforward, utterly maddening question.

Who could have tied it?

Not Farrell. He was obviously as shocked as she was by his lordship's appearance. One of the housemaids? Never. They would have run away screaming if summoned to his room alone.

Then who?

There was only one possible answer, but it was so preposterous that Ariel was unable to believe it even though she was seeing the proof of it with her own eyes.

Sage.

He must have tied it himself. Studying the crisp folds and precise angles of the knot, she knew without a doubt that it could not possibly have been the result of chance or beginner's luck.

Which meant he had known how to tie it all along.

Which meant that all those times she was gesturing and pantomiming like a buffoon, endeavoring to explain to him exactly what a cravat was, he had already known and simply pretended not to.

Which meant, she concluded, her chest tightening painfully as one humiliating realization led to another, that he had most probably been pretending about other things as well.

That was confirmed for her almost immediately as her initial astonishment passed and she gradually became aware that he was actually conversing with Earl Castleton. In complete sentences. Sentences that included words of more than one syllable and were completely lacking in either grunts or tooth-gnashing, both of which she had been subjected to on a regular basis for the past six weeks.

He was a fraud from top to bottom. She had no idea why or what he stood to gain from such a deception, only that he had lied to them all and had played her in particular for a fool and that she would not be a party to it a moment longer.

Sage had by then sauntered into the drawing room and was standing only a few feet from her, smiling faintly at whatever Castleton was saying. Penrose stood slightly behind the earl, his expression frozen somewhere between baffled and stunned.

". . . a miracle, I tell you," Castleton declared in a booming voice. "A blessed miracle. No. No, on second thought, that's not it at all. A miracle is the result of divine intervention, but this . . ." He held out both hands toward Sage as if framing a masterpiece. "This is the work of a more earthly angel." He slowly turned to Ariel and bowed deeply. "Miss Halliday, you are truly a genius of the first order."

"I'm anything but that, your lordship," she said. "I'm afraid I must tell you that you are laboring under a great misapprehension."

"What Miss Halliday means," Sage cut in before she could go on, "is that you are slightly misguided in attributing my transformation to her alone. The good headmaster, Mr. Penrose," he said, nodding at him, "was instrumental in guiding her efforts during his frequent visits, and I'm sure she would be the first to insist that his contribution be recognized."

The earl turned to Penrose. "Is that right, Penrose?"

Penrose appeared dumbfounded. "Well, I . . . naturally . . . being so close by and—" He stopped stammering and threw out his chest. "It's true I did advise as to the approach she ought to take. Be firm, I said at the outset." He pounded his fist in the air for emphasis. "Proper discipline is the cornerstone of education. And, by George, you see for yourself the results."

"Yes, indeed I do," agreed Castleton, beaming at Sage. "I have to hand it to you, Penrose. I'd heard you had a certain knack for turning a troubled bloke around, but I had no idea, no idea at all, as to the full extent of your talents."

Penrose sniffed and flicked an invisible speck of lint from his lapel. "We all have our special gifts, I suppose."

"So we do, so we do. And you can be sure I will spread word of your unique talent far and wide," the earl assured the preening Penrose.

Ariel's teeth snapped together as her gaze met Sage's. Swine. He had her cornered. To speak the truth now and reveal that there had been no miraculous transformation but only a despicable fraud perpetrated on all of them would be to steal the glory that Mr. Penrose was busy basking in at that very moment. He would feel humiliated, as well might the earl for having been so easily hoodwinked in the first place.

It occurred to her suddenly that they might even conclude that she was part of the scam. That would surely be grounds for her dismissal. She couldn't risk that. She had no choice but to accept the fact that she was as powerless to follow her own good judgment now as she had been when the proposal was first made to her. Maybe even more so. The only difference was that this time she was being manipulated by Sage.

The discussion continued around her, the earl entertaining them with gossip of a recent scandal on Fleet Street. Sage smiled and snickered at all the right times. Damn his black heart.

How? How was this possible? How could he know when to laugh and when to nod, and how had he managed to pretend otherwise so flawlessly, and for so long? As she gradually brought her reeling emotions under control, one feeling came to dominate all others, a quiet, seething anger. *How* he had done it did not concern her nearly as much as *that* he had.

Rather than consuming her, however, her anger built slowly, layer by repressed layer. It sharpened her awareness of everything around her. She imagined herself a jungle cat on the prowl. *Watching. Waiting.* Her gaze settled on Sage. *Ready to pounce.*

Just then she realized that the entire household staff was gathered outside the drawing room, craning their necks to see as if at a cage at the zoo. Ariel excused herself and approached them. "This is not an exhibit," she said. "I would appreciate it if you would all return to your duties immediately."

There was a hushed chorus of "Yes, ma'am" as they quickly dispersed. All except Mrs. Farrell, who continued to stare, her round face dotted with smudges of everything she had cooked.

"Blimey," she whispered, transfixed. "Now I've seen it all."

"Did you come here to say something, Mrs. Farrell?" Ariel asked, her tone sharp.

The other woman dragged her gaze away reluctantly.

"What? I . . . oh, yes, Miss Halliday, matter of fact, I did. Dinner is served."

"Very good." Ariel turned to the others, a polite smile frozen in place. "Gentlemen, dinner is ready. Shall we move into the dining room?"

She started to step past Sage, but he blocked her path.

"Tsk. Tsk. Miss Halliday, aren't you forgetting something?"

Ariel was surprised to discover that she could glare and smile at the same time. "Am I?"

With exaggerated formality he extended his arm to her. "A lady always allows a gentleman to escort her when they are leaving or entering a room together."

"Of course."

"Splendid, splendid," exclaimed Castleton, rubbing his hands together with great satisfaction.

Ariel was forced to place her hand lightly atop Sage's arm, thinking she'd sooner touch a swamp rat.

The meal itself was even worse than usual. Burnt tongue with red currant sauce, overly salted chicken fricassee, and boiled leg of mutton too stringy to be edible. No one but Ariel seemed to notice, however. They were too intent on the lively and sophisticated conversation led, of course, by Sage himself. Worse, to her abhorrence, he went out of his way to compound the ruse by continuing to lavish praise on her and to tout her talents.

Lies, all lies. As much as politely possible, she kept her attention focused on her plate and did her best not to hear. Even so, long before dessert was served she feared that if the words "According to Miss Halliday ..." or "As my esteemed teacher took pains to explain ..." were to emanate from his mouth once more, she would have no recourse but to leap up and silence him with the leg of mutton.

He offered opinions on everything from Blake's *Jerusalem* to the Italian influence on the evolution of Turner's art, and even discussed whether it was wisdom or folly to invest heavily in new American markets. A thousand of the world's most learned scholars could not possibly have taught him all he knew in only six weeks.

But did that bit of inconvenient reality disturb or even occur to Castleton and Penrose, both of whom hung on his every word as if it were coated with gold? Not at all. They were too captivated by their prize specimen to be bothered by anything as trivial as common sense ... or, apparently, to notice her silence.

A good thing too. Growing resentment played havoc with her thoughts until she wasn't sure what she would do if called on to offer an opinion on anything. The tables had turned with a vengeance, and ironically she was now the one unable to put together a proper sentence.

Throughout the endless meal she consoled herself with a single thought, the only bright spot she could find in the whole wretched mess. Now that Lord Savage had been so miraculously "tamed," it was obvious that her services would no longer be required. She was free. Furious. Used. Humiliated. But free.

At last the final dish was cleared, the linen removed, and the table reset for dessert. A tall, fluted crystal of syllabub was set at each place, and a platter of fresh fruit adorned the center of the table. Not even Mrs. Farrell could ruin fruit, and Ariel helped herself to several slices of apple sprinkled with cinnamon sugar.

Sage, who was seated directly across from her in a rather unsettling recreation of that afternoon's confrontation, caught her eye as he lifted his dessert spoon. His smile was a silent, private taunt.

Ariel chewed her apple. He took a bite of syllabub.

Do not let him provoke you, she cautioned herself. No matter how infuriating tonight's little charade might be, it was only one night. When it was over, he would move ahead to whatever was in store for him and she would get on with her own life.

Toying with her spoon, she glanced at Mr. Penrose, who sat at the end of the table opposite Castleton. Perhaps, she mused, there might be another advantage to this after all. Perhaps Mr. Penrose's pride and excitement this evening would lead him to a new, warmer appreciation for her. And that perhaps would lead . . .

A sudden chill interrupted her happy speculation, and she turned to find Sage regarding her with a speculative, vaguely amused look. She was immediately struck by the irrational, paralyzing fear that he was able to read her thoughts and that he understood her joy at the prospect of imminent freedom.

Holding her gaze, he opened his grasp and let his spoon drop to his dessert saucer. The resulting clatter drew everyone's attention.

With all eyes focused on him, he reached up and very deliberately loosened his cravat so that it hung open. He then undid the button at his throat, exposing a deep triangle of sun-browned skin.

"I've grown overwarm," he said.

Seemingly oblivious of the sudden tension he had caused in the room, he reached for his spoon and scooped more of his custard, pausing with it halfway to his mouth. He slowly brought it to eye level and squinted at it. They all stilled, no doubt as gripped as she was by curiosity and revulsion as they watched him extract a long black hair from the creamy contents in the bowl of the spoon.

He held it aloft for them to see before carelessly dropping it to the floor beside him.

"One of my own, no doubt," he said. "Just the same, I don't believe I'll finish this."

"I should say not," agreed Castleton.

"Shall I have another brought for you?" Ariel asked, gritting her teeth in order to act the proper hostess.

"No, thank you. I couldn't eat another bite of this"—he hesitated—"magnificent example of English culinary artistry."

A polite response to that seemed to elude them all. The room remained silent as Sage bent and reached beneath the table.

"I shall let Prinny finish up for me," he said, and Ariel's eyes went wide as he proceeded to produce the rabbit from beneath the tablecloth with the flourish of a master magician pulling one from his hat. He plopped the creature on the table beside him and tipped the crystal so it could lap at the sweet contents.

No one spoke. But then, Ariel supposed that was to be expected. After all, what was the proper response to having a live rabbit join a dinner party?

"I say," Penrose began in a hushed tone, "did I understand him to call the thing by name?"

The earl nodded, his eyes fixed on the rabbit.

"And was the name . . . Prinny?"

Castleton nodded again.

"Oh, dear. You don't suppose he's named for . . ."

"The king?" supplied Sage, nodding. "The very one. So you see the resemblance as well?"

Ariel hastened to intercede. "Lord Sage, if you'll permit me to speak candidly—"

"Permit?" he interjected. "Miss Halliday, I demand that there be nothing but the utmost candor between us. As always."

"Of course," she agreed, her fists clenched in her lap. "I simply thought to point out that in this country it is considered the height of ill manners to place a live rabbit on the dining table during a meal. Even one named for the king."

"Really? What an odd coincidence. You see, in my country it's considered a great honor to one's guests to share a meal with the household rabbit."

"Is that so?" asked a startled Castleton.

Sage nodded.

"Really?" said Ariel. "Odd. I wouldn't have thought rabbits native to the climate of the Sandwich Islands."

"Hawaii," he corrected her.

"Of course."

"Actually the climate there is infinitely more favorable to all kinds of life than that of, say, this country."

"If you care for a hot, steamy atmosphere, I suppose."

"And do you?"

She frowned. "Do I?"

"Prefer things hot and steamy?"

His intense gaze focused on her as if they were alone in the room. The air between them seemed to vibrate.

"I really wouldn't know," she replied after a deep breath. "I'm afraid my travels have been severely limited and I've never had occasion to experience such a state."

"A pity. Perhaps someday I can repay your efforts on my behalf by providing just such an experience."

Ariel pursed her lips. "Thank you, but no."

"No? Are you so opposed to visiting the islands?" he pressed with an innocent air that was as patently false as everything else about him.

"As I said, I'm hardly a world traveler."

"A condition that is easily remedied."

"A most generous impulse, my lord, but I'm certain your future schedule will leave you much too busy to bother with my limitations."

"Never. I owe you ... all of you," he added, glancing from one end of the table to the other, "a great deal. And it is a debt I will take pleasure in repaying in full. You can be assured that nothing, nothing, will keep me from it."

The note of mockery underscoring his words was clearly lost on Castleton and Penrose. But not on Ariel. She watched Sage closely as the earl proposed a toast to the future and they all drank.

She had a sense that in spite of Sage's outward demeanor, resentment simmered inside him. If this was a game, she thought, it was a dangerous one.

"Now then, Sage," Castleton said, "you were telling us about this custom of yours with the rabbits. What is that all about?"

"Tradition," Sage replied. "Power. Honor."

"All that from eating alongside a rabbit?" asked Penrose, his nose wrinkling with distaste.

"Not simply from eating with one," Sage explained. "Eating. Sleeping. Worshiping. You see, the chosen rabbit is raised as one of the family so that, over time, it absorbs the very essence of what it is that binds them together and sets them apart from all others. It becomes an embodiment of their love and devotion and the strength that comes from it."

"So it is symbolic," she suggested.

He nodded. "Highly."

"But to what end?" asked Penrose, still looking as if he had sucked on a lemon.

Sage slowly turned to face him. "Slaughter," he said.

Ariel stiffened in her seat, her gaze drawn by the sudden violent tightening of his grip on poor Prinny's neck.

Castleton swallowed so quickly, he had to slap his chest to recover. "Do you mean to say it's your custom that after raising this thing as a bloody house pet, it's taken out and killed?"

"It's not taken out," Sage replied. "It's done right there in the home, at the table. But, yes, that's the crux of it."

"Why?" Ariel asked, still staring at Prinny, who seemed frozen in place.

"I told you . . . tradition, power, honor. It's done on the eve of battle, and by drinking its blood a warrior draws on the strength of his family to carry him through the fray."

Ariel tossed her napkin aside and pushed away from the table. "That's revolting."

Sage shrugged and continued to stroke Prinny's back. "You wouldn't think so if you were a warrior."

From the corner of her eye she saw Penrose and the earl exchange a look of alarm. She had to put a stop to this.

"I believe I've heard quite enough talk of rabbits and battles for one evening. I shall leave you gentlemen to your port," she said, rising, "and hopefully to more pleasant conversation."

Both Castleton and Penrose were on their feet before her.

"No," exclaimed the earl as if she'd proposed leaving them alone with a cobra. "That is, I'm afraid I must beg off the rest of the evening. I'm expected at my club."

"And me," chimed in Penrose. "Not at his lordship's club, of course," he added quickly. "At a . . . meeting. Of the Mathematical Society. It's a special lecture I've been looking forward to for some time."

"Really?" asked Sage, lifting his head in a show of casual interest. "May I inquire as to the topic?"

Penrose paled, shifted from one foot to the other, then smiled uneasily. "A rather advanced one," he replied, his smile edging toward smugness. "I'm sure it's well beyond what you've covered with Miss Halliday."

"No doubt. But that does serve to remind me of something."

He stood, hoisting Prinny beneath one arm as he crossed the room and reached for something from the high top of the china closet in the corner.

The ledger.

Ariel blanched. She had forgotten it completely.

"I believe this belongs to you," he said, handing it to Penrose.

"Why, yes, it does." He took it, his expression puzzled.

"Miss Halliday was busy preparing for this evening," explained Sage, "so I took the liberty of reviewing the figures myself. I found your error on page fifty-four. A simple flaw in computation which even one of my limited capacity was able to discern."

His subtle emphasis on the words *your* and *simple* were like swift, silent blows to the midsection, and Penrose reacted to them as such.

"I see," he stammered, growing red and agitated.

He glanced sideways at Castleton as he continued. "I've been so busy . . . that is, I'm not as a rule responsible for . . . I . . . my thanks."

Sage bowed his head without saying a word.

"We're off, then," said Castleton. "To be totally truthful about it, there are others waiting for me, and they are most eager to hear word of your progress, Sage. I'm pleased to be able to report such encouraging news." He glanced at Ariel. "A moment with you alone, please, Miss Halliday?"

Ariel knew before she stepped into the drawing room with him what he would say. After all, "encouraging news," as he had phrased it, was not conclusive news. No, Sage had cleverly and deviously seen to that. A man who opened his shirt at dinner and shared his dessert with a rabbit was not quite ready for polite company.

He had outmaneuvered her from start to finish. Perhaps if she had been quicker, she might have surmised his intent and diverted him before he had a chance to tell of his disgusting tribal warfare customs. If so, things might have ended differently. But she hadn't, and he had, and so there was nothing for her to do but to smile as the earl exhorted her to keep up the good work and to watch helplessly as her one bright hope of freedom flickered into oblivion like a shooting star.

As soon as the front door had closed behind their guests, she whirled around to go in search of Sage. He headed her off by sauntering into the drawing room, the dratted rabbit still cradled in his arms. Any other man would appear ridiculous, Ariel thought, but not Sage. Oh, no, he was far too sure of himself to ever be the object of ridicule. She would love to think the effect went no deeper than his fine clothes or the air of grace bordering on arrogance that he had donned that evening. Unfortunately, she recalled all too well that even silent and clad in a tattered blanket he had inspired not scorn, but awe.

There was no denying that what set him apart from other men ran deeper than manners or the way he filled out his waistcoat or the startlingly perfect arrangement of his features. It was something mercurial and elusive, impossible to define, much less acquire. It was innate. Primal. Unmistakable. And formidable enough to cause Ariel to gather her defenses securely around her as she squared off to face him.

"Are they gone?" he inquired, one long finger stroking the top of the rabbit's head.

"Yes, they're gone. And now I demand to know . . . oh, do put down that silly creature," she ordered. "Better still, return him to the outdoors, where he belongs."

"No."

That single defiant syllable set off the angry volcano that had been churning and building inside her all evening.

"Don't you say no to me," she lashed out. "Don't you ever, as long as your rotten, scheming, lying life continues, ever say no to me again. Don't grunt," she went on, walking toward him, her steps measured, her tone a soft, sharp blade of contempt. "Don't bare your teeth. And don't you ever, ever growl at me. Is that clear?"

"As clear as Penrose's skull. I see now that I ought to have said that I am regretfully unable to return him to the outdoors because I've grown rather fond of the little bugger. Like it or not, Prinny stays."

"I do not like it, not at all. You see," she said,

narrowing her gaze on him, "I have a rule against sharing a home with more than one animal at a time."

Sage flashed her a sardonic smile. "I'd offer to let you choose between us, but I have my own rule against sleeping outdoors unless the weather is balmy or I'm too soused to care. It's cold, I'm not soused, and I refuse to believe you're really heartless enough to turn Prinny out on such a night."

"Believe it," she retorted. "What's more, I find your choice of name for him to be highly disrespectful."

"It was your choice," he reminded her.

"You eavesdropped," she snapped. "I may have said it privately, in jest, but I certainly never meant it to be bandied about in polite company."

"Then you needn't worry, it wasn't."

His insolence only fueled her anger. She reached for the rabbit. "Very well. If you won't put him out, I will."

"Sorry, I gave him my word he'd be treated like royalty. Isn't that right, fur ball?" he asked, turning to block her efforts with his shoulder.

"Then you needn't worry either, since your word isn't worth a bucket of spit," she declared, still trying to get her hands on the rabbit.

"If you were a man, we'd be counting off paces," he said, still fending her off.

"If I were a man, you'd have a broken jaw by now and be counting the teeth I knocked out, not paces."

"Careful, Prinny," he murmured as she changed tactics and dipped under the immovable blockade of his arm, "it appears the lady has a hidden violent streak. Up you go."

In one smooth movement he spun face-to-face with Ariel and extended his arms overhead so that Prinny was out of reach. He was taller than she was and his arms were longer, but Ariel was beyond such rational considerations. Stretching her arms as far as she could, she jumped and made a wild grab for the rabbit. She missed, of course, and as she landed, Sage stepped forward so that she slid against him all the way down and ended up with the front of her body pressed to his, swaying for balance.

"Care to try that again?" he invited her with a satisfied smile as she took a quick step backward.

Ariel glared at him, then at the rabbit, furious.

"Put him down," she ordered.

"No."

"Fine." If reason wouldn't work, perhaps action would. She drew her arm back and landed a hard punch to his midsection.

Sage's only reaction was to sag in the middle for an instant as all the air whooshed out of him. Oh, that felt good, she thought. After weeks of frustration and an evening of keeping the lid on a whole cauldron of emotions, it felt very good. It would have felt even better, of course, if her fingers weren't throbbing painfully as a result. Hitting him was like ramming her fist into granite, and she had to resist the urge to rub her knuckles.

He recovered quickly. "Hell, woman, so much for you having a *hidden* violent streak," he muttered.

"Now will you drop the rabbit?"

"I can't," he said, sounding as if he wished he could.

"Why not?"

"Because I'm a man, and my manhood demands that I allow you to pummel me black and blue rather than surrender."

"Suit yourself." She raised her arm again.

"Wait," he ordered. "Do you really want to waste time bickering about a silly rabbit? Or do you want to call a truce and let me put him down with dignity, so we can bicker about what's really got you breathing fire?"

Ariel considered the proposal and nodded. "All right. For now. We can discuss the matter of whether he stays later."

Sage kept his eye on her as he slowly lowered the rabbit. As if, thought Ariel indignantly, *she* were the one who couldn't be trusted. As soon as his paws hit the floor, the rabbit hopped out of sight behind the piano.

Sage watched him go, then turned to her. "Now, where were we?"

"I was saying that I demand to hear what you have to say for yourself."

He crossed to the mahogany serving cart in the corner to pour two brandies before replying. "I suppose that if pressed I would have to say it went rather well, all things considered."

Ariel stared at him incredulously as he approached and offered her a brandy nonchalantly. She ignored the snifter, fixing him with an appalled stare. "All . . . things . . . considered?"

"That's right." He tossed down the contents of the glass she had disdained before putting it aside and turning his attention to the snifter in his other hand.

"What exactly does that mean? All things considered?"

"It means the evening went as well as one might expect given the company provided. Do you suppose the Nose tries to appear so stunningly asisine, or is it a purely instinctive condition?"

Ariel's brow furrowed. "The Nose?"

"Penrose," he offered by way of explanation. "For obvious reasons."

Ariel refused to be amused or diverted. "The reasons for your rudeness are no more obvious to me than the reason for your duplicity. It is not Mr. Penrose's behavior this evening that enraged me, but your own."

He leaned one shoulder on the mantel and regarded her imperiously. "My behavior was impeccable."

"Oh, yes," she agreed, pacing restlessly toward the piano so that they stood like boxers in opposite corners of the ring. "At least up to that memorable moment when you bared your chest and tossed a rabbit onto the dinner table."

"I explained that."

"So you did," she agreed with false calm.

"Then what, precisely, is the nature of your complaint?"

"My complaint," she said, whirling on him, "is that until tonight I have seen no trace of these impeccable manners of yours, or your quite remarkable gift for scintillating conversation. Indeed, in six weeks I have not seen or heard anything to suggest that you are the most accomplished, intelligent, entertaining savage to ever grace a bloody loincloth."

"Your flattery is too kind," he murmured.

"I haven't finished." She started toward him, once more feeling like a jungle cat stalking its prey. "You are also the most callous, underhanded, and deceitful—"

"There's no need to be nasty."

"There is every need," she uttered, striding closer to him, savoring his wary expression. "I couldn't possibly be nasty enough to express the wrath I feel over your astounding performance this evening."

"I think to call it astounding might be going a bit far."

"I don't."

"In that case I should say that I owe it all to you."

"Should say it? You did say it. Over and over, ad

nauseam. Miss Halliday said this, Miss Halliday told me that," she mimicked, her eyes flashing angrily. "Lies. All of it."

He placed his hand over his heart. "You wound me, dear teacher."

"Don't you dare mock me," she chided. "I am not your teacher. You are not my student."

Setting the second empty glass on the mantel, he folded his arms across his chest.

"Then what am I?" he inquired, his smile a blatant challenge.

"You—" She paused, a dozen unflattering terms colliding in her head, not one of them suitably scathing. Opting for understatement, she said, "You, sir, are no gentleman."

"You, madam, are right." He came away from the fireplace with a smooth, sudden movement and took a step toward her. "I make no claim to be. I have no desire to be. Most important, I have absolutely no intention of ever becoming that most spineless and odious of creatures, an English gentleman."

"Then why go to all the trouble of putting on a show?"

"You mean tonight?"

"Tonight. Six weeks ago. All of it. It's obvious you've known from the start which fork to use, how to tie your bloody cravat, and how to make yourself understood."

"True."

Of course it was true. She had known that. And still, to hear his careless confirmation of just how thoroughly she had been duped jolted her all over again, adding new, more personal shades and angles to her anger.

"You were pretending," she said quietly, as if to herself. "All along, it was just a pretense."

He nodded.

Ariel drew herself up. "Why? I deserve an explanation for your spurious conduct, since I am the one who was made to look the fool."

Now he was the one who looked startled. "Please believe me when I tell you it was never my intent to make you feel foolish."

Ariel laughed harshly. "Believe you? I wouldn't believe you if you swallowed a Bible, whole, as a gesture of good faith."

He studied her as intently as a chess master contemplating his next move before asking, "What if I were to tell you that I did it for you?"

"Then I would know you're a liar along with all the rest," she retorted.

"All the rest?" He appeared puzzled. "Could you be more specific?"

"Gladly. I'd know you for a liar as well as a fraud, a charlatan without conscience or remorse, a scoundrel of the first order—"

"Oh. All that," he said, cutting short her accusations. "But how can you be so sure it's a lie?"

"You have the nerve to ask?"

"I have no choice. You see, the fact is that I did do it for you."

Ariel shook her head. The man's audacity was beyond belief.

"You expect me to believe that you schemed and put on this masterful performance—"

"Masterful?" he interjected, looking amused. He rubbed his jaw with an exaggerated air of contemplation. "Did you really think so?"

"And made a complete fool of me on a daily basis," she continued, ignoring his interruption. "All for me?"

"Not that part of it. But tonight, tonight was entirely for you, Ariel. Will you grant me the privilege of calling you Ariel?"

"Would it please you to do so?"

"Very much."

"Then the answer is no."

Sage chuckled softly, the hooded gaze he ran over her one of stark reevaluation. "Do you boast an aversion to pleasing me?"

"I boast an aversion to being in the same room with you," she retorted. "I suffer it only in the interest of securing an explanation for your behavior this evening."

"I've already provided it. I have no aversion to pleasing you, you see. I did what I did tonight to please you, Ariel, and for no other reason. Quite honestly, it went quite against my grain to expose my hand so early in the game."

He looked utterly sincere, which only made her distrust him more.

"I did not give you leave to use my given name," she reminded him.

"Forgive me. I can't seem to help myself. It's as if a barrier between us has been lowered. Do you feel it too?"

"No."

Behind him, a log shifted in the fireplace, causing a hissing cascade of sparks, but his warm, somber gaze remained steady on her.

"I was under the distinct impression," he went on, taking a step closer to her, "that this was what you wanted. That you wished me to dress and speak and act as befits a marquis."

His closeness made her uneasy, but she refused to show it by backing away.

"You did want that, didn't you?" he pressed.

"I did."

"You wanted to win the approval of Castleton and the Nose. You wanted them to deem all your hard work these past weeks a success?"

"Yes."

"And so they did. At least it seemed so to me. Do you agree?"

"I think it was obvious they were both amazed at your progress, to say the least. Overwhelmed, in fact." Sarcasm sharpened her tone as she crossed her arms across her chest and added, "As well they should be. All things considered."

"So my plan worked. It seems to me you should be grateful rather than angry."

"Does it really, you self-satisfied, bamboozling blackleg? Well, I'm not grateful. Not even a little tiny bit."

"You—"

"And don't think I'm gullible enough to fall for that smooth-talker's nonsense about doing it all for me," she went on.

"It—"

Again she cut him off. "Because I don't believe a word of it. But even if I were cockbrained enough to swallow your story, it would still leave an even more interesting question unanswered, wouldn't it?"

"Namely?"

"Don't play dumb with me. Are you so afraid to answer the question?"

"Are you so afraid to ask it directly?"

"Not at all. Why did you pretend to be a savage in the first place?"

"I didn't."

"You most certainly—"

Now he cut her off. "From the start I said nothing and made no claims at all. The men who shanghaied me interpreted that to mean I was a savage. I was different from them after all, so what else could I be?" His tone was biting and sarcastic. "Castleton and the others were only too willing to accept that assumption. And so were you."

"Only because you reinforced that assumption from the first moment I laid eyes on you, and at every turn since, I might add."

"Did I?"

His eyes were dark and accusing. In them Ariel saw the flickering reflection of the moment when his body was stretched protectively atop hers and their eyes met, of the sense of connection she'd felt at that instant. She recalled the way he had ignored the pistols aimed at him in order to offer his hand up afterward and the dozens of suspicious "glimmers" since then, all signs that she had obviously failed to give proper consideration.

"Tell me, Ariel, was it easier to believe me a savage?" he asked softly. "Or simply more enticing?"

"What is that supposed to mean?" she asked, suddenly feeling more confused than righteous. Not that she had any intention of letting him know that.

"You tell me." His voice was low and rough and seemed to be directly attached to the heated shivers that were moving along her spine. "How did it feel to be alone with a wild man? A man without rules or restraint? What was it like to teach me to bathe, and to dress? To show me how to hold a fork and take your arm?"

"It was mostly frustrating."

He laughed knowingly. "I know all about frustration. Tell me what it felt like to touch me." He continued to speak over her sharply drawn breath. "Or to have my hand brush against you, like this." He ran the back of his hand along her arm while Ariel tried to feel nothing, and failed. "Did my touch make your heart race with fear? Or with something else? Something stronger. Did it make you wonder what it would be like to—"

"The only thing I am wondering at this moment," she interrupted sharply, "is why I am standing here wasting my time listening to your drivel. I urge you to produce a more accurate and much less fanciful explanation for Lord Castleton, sir. You will soon need one, as I have no intention of continuing this charade for another moment, much less two more weeks."

She slipped past him and was halfway to the door when his deep voice stopped her.

"So you're willing to throw it all away?" he asked. "For what? A bit of wounded pride?"

She turned slowly.

"As usual, I haven't the faintest idea what you're talking about," she said, counting on a careless shrug to conceal the fact that his words had struck a nerve.

"I'm talking about the fact that the past six weeks have not been easy for you, and yet you endured whatever I dished out. Now, either because you feel I've made you look foolish or because you take offense at some of my remarks, you're willing to throw it all away." He shook his head, a grim, almost regretful set to his mouth. "I'd rather thought you were made of stronger stuff."

Ariel regarded him scornfully. "Don't try to manipulate me."

His grin took her by surprise. "All right, I won't. I can be as straightforward as you can tolerate. You've been kind to me during my stay here, kinder than you had to be and certainly kinder than most would have been in your place. For that I am grateful. I hate to see you toss it all in now, when you're so close to winning the prize."

"What prize?" Ariel asked, watching cautiously as he moved to refill his brandy snifter.

She told herself there was no way he could know why she had agreed to undertake this project or how much she would be giving up if she went ahead with her impulsive threat to quit. But then, only hours earlier she had been just as convinced there was no way Sage could quote Shakespeare.

He was right and she hated him for it. It would be stupid for her to quit now. She didn't understand how, but he had trumped her. For the third time tonight. And each time the stakes were higher.

"What prize?" she repeated as he returned with his brandy.

"Now who's playing dumb, Ariel? It's obvious what you have your sights set on."

"Not to me."

"Then permit me to help clarify the matter. The prize," he said, eyeing her with stunning clarity, "is Penrose."

Nine

Leon watched her eyes widen with astonishment. Had she really believed him so obtuse he couldn't see her fawning attention to the little twit for what it was?

"Penrose?" she asked. "Do you mean *Mr.* Penrose?"

"Of course I mean Mr. Penrose," he snapped. "Do you know another Penrose? Or would you prefer I refer to your beloved in more familiar terms, such as the Nose?"

"My beloved?" She gave him a look that suggested he had two heads, both of them empty. "Have you lost your mind?"

Yes, he thought. What else would account for his behavior this evening?

After the Nose's unexpected visit yesterday, he had been determined to play the savage to the hilt and bring Ariel's dinner party crashing down around her pretty little ears. He'd told himself she deserved to be taught a lesson. Then he had glimpsed the anguish on her face as she fled from him earlier that day. In the space of a heartbeat everything had changed. No matter that it was the loss of Penrose's good opinion that she was mourning, he would do anything to keep from seeing that look on her face again.

And so he had broken bread with Castleton instead of his head. As if all that weren't humbling enough, he was standing there now, frustrated as hell and spoiling for a fight, because a woman he shouldn't want wanted another man and not him.

"Have I lost my mind?" he echoed with lofty detachment. "Quite the opposite, in fact. I think it quite astute of me to discern the very essence of your situation."

"Which is?"

"That you're openly besotted with the fool."

He watched the color drain from her face. Proof, it seemed to Leon, of the accuracy of his deduction. He felt both vindicated and dejected. Color returned to her in a rush, transforming her cheeks from alabaster to crimson in a matter of seconds. She looked startled and indignant and bewitching.

"How dare you stand there and imply that I am in love with Phillip Penrose?"

"I didn't imply anything. I stated a fact. And I believe *besotted* was the word I used," he added. "What you're really asking is how I dare to speak the truth."

"The truth? Ha! You wouldn't know the truth if it dropped from the sky and bit you on the—" She halted, folded her arms stiffly, and with a haughty shrug concluded, "Toe."

"Really? Odd that I didn't have to be bitten on the toe or anywhere else to recognize what was going on during the headmaster's little visit yesterday."

"Are you referring to the visit during which you

made a total rattlepate of yourself with that foolish rabbit?" she inquired with feigned innocence.

He countered with an equally contrived look of surprise. "You noticed? I assumed you were too busy fawning over your employer to remember that I was even present."

"Fawning?" she repeated, her tone frosty.

"Ad nauseam, to use your own word. Smiling like a lovesick calf, begging him to stay for an impromptu piano recital, all the while your eyelashes fluttering like a flock of deranged geese. It was, if I might be permitted to speak bluntly, an altogether embarrassing display."

"Deranged geese?"

"I'm afraid so. A less perspective observer surely would have concluded that you were in the thralls of some sort of fit."

"Some sort of fit?"

Leon noted with satisfaction that guilt seemed to have reduced her to echoing him in short, sputtering bursts.

He nodded. "But having some experience in these matters, I was able to detect what I'm convinced even the Nose did not, that you were flirting with him. Or, rather, attempting to."

"Flirting?"

"Do you deny it?"

Her mouth opened and shut in rapid succession. She shrugged. She frowned.

"You know very well I cannot deny it," she said at last, glaring at him as if he were responsible for her poor judgment. "You know very well that I— That is to say, you saw how— Oh, you saw everything." She winced and pressed her palms to her cheeks and looked miserable. Dropping her hands after a minute, she squared her shoulders and looked him in the eye again. "All right, it's true. In a manner of speaking, I suppose you could say that I was ..." She shuddered faintly. "Flirting."

Leon merely arched one dark brow skeptically.

"But it was not because I care for him," she continued emphatically. "And I am certainly not besotted. Why, I'm not fond of him in the least actually. I can barely abide being near him. In truth, I think he's the most odious, self-centered, whiny excuse for a man I've ever had the misfortune to encounter."

Squelching a ridiculous urge to grin with satisfaction, Leon eyed her consideringly. "Then it's my turn to ask you the same question you posed to me earlier. Why the charade?"

"Because," she said, having the grace to look sheepish at the comparison of her little deception with his own, "I design to marry him."

It was like having her fist planted in his gut all over again. No, this was worse. Much worse. He took a gulp of brandy, trying not to look as unsettled as he felt. Unsettled? Hell, he felt dizzy. Carrying the glass with him, he dropped into one of two comfortable high-back chairs by the fire, arranged himself in a suitably lazy slouch, and waited for his heart to unclench. Only then did he turn his attention back to her.

"Same question," he said. "Why?"

"I have to," she replied.

Her resigned expression and heavy tone slammed him upright in his seat. His gaze arrowed in on the sash at her waist. "You have to? Do you mean that you are—"

She pressed her hands flat on her stomach, her eyes blazing. "Of course I am not. How dare you even suggest—"

"Let me settle this dare business for you once and for all," he said, feeling relieved all over again, like a blasted dinghy caught in a crosscurrent, his heart being jerked this way and then that. "I have a long-standing habit of daring to say and do whatever I please, whenever I please. For you to repeatedly question me on the subject is not merely tiresome, it is a waste of your breath and my time. Understood?"

"Understanding does not signify approval," she told him.

"I'm not seeking your approval," Leon retorted.

She shrugged. "In that case, it's understood."

"Good. Now come and sit down."

He indicated the chair across from him. She hesitated only briefly before complying, looking as grateful as he was to be sitting for this.

"Let's try again," he said. "If you are not compromised, why do you have to marry Penrose?"

"I suppose it would have been more accurate to say I have to marry, and it is my unenviable luck that Mr. Penrose is the most likely candidate."

With his elbows braced on the chair's generously upholstered arms, he peered at her over steepled fingertips.

"Oh, all right," she said after an awkwardly silent moment. "He is the only candidate."

"I see. And the reason for this sudden matrimonial urgency?

"How do you know it's sudden?" she countered, evading his real question. "Perhaps this is my last-ditch effort. After all, most women my age are long married, with clusters of little ones dashing about."

She wiggled her fingers in the air, to represent, he assumed, the dashing little ones.

Leon gave a dry smile. "Lucky them. Tell me, your

advanced age for this last-ditch effort is all of—" He paused to run an appraising gaze over her.

"Twenty-five," she informed him with a defiant toss of her head.

"Ah, twenty-five. As well along as that, are you?"

"Yes, nearly as decrepit as you are, I fear."

He grinned. "Age certainly hasn't sweetened your tongue any. My advice is to say as little as possible if you want to catch a husband."

She leaned forward as if to strike back and then caught herself and laughed softly, almost as if it were against her will to share even that with him tonight.

"It's not a joking matter," she told him, easing herself back into the chair. "I'll have you know my mother does not find my lack of a husband and children to be amusing in the least."

"Your mother. Why do I have the feeling that we're getting close to solving this mystery at last?"

"It's not much of a mystery. The simple fact of the matter is that I must marry for reasons of financial security. Not my own," she hastened to add even as Leon felt his lip begin to curl derisively.

"Then whose? Penrose's?" he suggested with a smirk, oddly disappointed to learn she was nothing more than an ordinary, everyday fortune hunter.

"Of course not." She sighed, looking hesitant, then said, "If you must know, I am doing it for my parents' sake, so that I might provide them with a measure of security in the years to come."

Maybe not such an ordinary fortune hunter after all, thought Leon, but rather one with a lively imagination.

"I see. They failed to plan and provide for their final years, so now you're called upon to play the sacrificial lamb on their behalf, is that what you would have me believe?"

"Not at all," she exclaimed, looking offended now, and very convincingly so. "I would have you believe the truth, that my father is a baronet, and that he was a prominent and successful physician. He provided very well for his family all his life and would have continued to do so with savings and investments, but for . . ."

"But for?" he prompted.

"But for an inauspicious twist of fate."

"Sounds fascinating," he remarked. "I want to hear everything."

Ariel made as if to rise. "I fear it's a rather long and tedious story."

She looked almost as distressed as she had that afternoon, and as quickly as that Leon decided that she wasn't feigning sorrow or fabricating a tale to justify her blatantly mercenary play for a husband. The sight of her perched at the edge of her seat as if she might bolt any second bothered him more than he would have guessed possible. She looked forlorn, and worse. She looked alone. He knew how that felt, and he knew that when the reasons for feeling that way really mattered, there was nothing anyone could say to take the pain away. So he had no idea why he was about to try.

This time when he filled the brandy snifter he returned and handed it to her, sweeping aside her polite refusal.

"Take a sip," he ordered. "You look as if you could use it."

"Thank you." She sipped the brandy, still looking poised for flight if he pushed too hard.

So he wouldn't push. At least he would try not to. Resisting his natural instinct to demand to hear the rest

of her story without delay, he glanced around for something gentle and reassuring to do for her and spied a
small needlepoint footstool. He bent and repositioned it
so she could reach it.

Slanting a look up at her, he said more gruffly than
he had intended, "Don't make me lift your feet onto it."

"You wouldn't da—" She stopped and took in
the arch of his brows, which, he'd been told, could be
quite diabolic. Then she sat back and put her feet upon
the stool.

Leon reclaimed his seat. "Now," he said, "tell me all
about this inauspicious twist of fate."

Ariel shifted in her seat, her gaze moving restlessly
from his attentive expression to the oil painting above
his shoulder to the glowing logs in the fireplace.

"It's not easy," she said at last. "The fact is, I've
never before discussed this with another living soul.
Except my mother, and even with her I feel I have to
skitter all around the edges of it."

"If it helps any, I abhor skittering in any form. Just
have out with it, Ariel. Who knows? Maybe I can help."

She glanced at him in surprise.

He shrugged, a little surprised by the offer himself.
"Stranger things have happened."

"To be sure," she agreed with a trace of a smile that
as weak and fleeting as it was, for some reason made
it easier for him to breathe. "Stranger things have
happened recently, and in this very room, as a matter
of fact."

He returned her smile, gently, and forced himself to
wait without speaking until she was ready to.

"I've already told you that my father was a physician," she began, her tone quieter and more tentative
than usual, "and a very good one. He counted nobles

and common folk alike among his patients, and he prided himself on treating them all the same. Then, about a year and a half ago, my mother began to notice little things about him, nothing of consequence really. He might return home without his coat or get up and dress for Sunday services on a Friday, things like that." A wistful smile lifted the edges of her mouth. "We even teased him about it. At first.

"Gradually the little things became more serious, and more frequent," she went on. "Finally there were several incidents at his office. Nothing that resulted in injury to anyone, thank heaven," she quickly added, "but remarkable enough that my mother knew she must consult someone more knowledgeable about the changes in his behavior."

"Was your father aware of these changes?" he inquired.

Ariel nodded. "At times he was. At other times . . ." She again stared into the fire. "He did agree to be examined by an old friend and colleague, who in turn referred him to another physician, and by the time all the reports were written and examinations performed, he had slipped badly. I'm not sure he ever fully understood the diagnosis, and perhaps that's a blessing. Senile dementia is the official name for his affliction. Rapidly advancing in his case and irreversible. His old friend recommended that he retire from practice immediately, before a tragedy occurred that would cause injury and destroy his good name."

"Did he agree to that?" he asked, fighting the urge to lean forward and take her hands in his.

"Yes. Though there are days even now when he dresses and goes in search of his medical valise, insisting he must get to the office to see some patient who's been dead and buried for years." She pressed her lips together briefly. "The look on his face when he's told he cannot go is enough to break your heart."

That was how she looked, he realized, as if her heart had been broken and scattered in pieces. His urge to gather those pieces and fit them back together was unprecedented. And absurd, he told himself. He didn't even know her father. He hardly knew her. And he was not the sort of man who went around repairing broken hearts.

"I understand now," he told her quietly. "You needn't put yourself through a rehashing of the details, since the subject is obviously very painful for you."

"Actually in a way it feels good to speak freely of it at last," she admitted. "My mother is bound and determined that no one outside the household is to know the truth about the state he's in. And so we go on living as if everything is the same as it was, or trying to at least. Lately it's become nearly impossible to keep up the pretense or to maintain even a semblance of normalcy."

"Because of your father's deteriorating condition?"

"That and finances."

He frowned, recalling what she had said about being forced to marry for financial reasons. "But surely a successful physician had savings of some sort. You mentioned investments."

She sighed. "Yes, there were savings and investments. My father was a prudent man, which makes this all the more tragic. It turns out that during those early months when we were teasing him for misplacing his watch and walking past his own house, we failed to notice that he was also spending more time than usual at his club, accumulating gaming debts, thousands and thousands of pounds worth of them. And that's only what we've paid off so far. We've no way of knowing where it will end or when. At least once a week someone comes around or sends their representative to collect from Dr. Halliday on their gentleman's wager that it would rain on a certain day or that a particular ship would arrive in dock before another or that some share of stock would rise or fall by a specified date. The most preposterous things imaginable, but all duly recorded in the club's gaming book."

Leon was dumbstruck. "Let me get this straight. These men come to you with their claims and you pay what they say they're owed? Just like that?"

"My mother insists upon it. She says Dr. Halliday never welshed on a bet in his life, and she will not permit it to occur at this late date."

"That's admirable, but surely if he was not in his right mind when these wagers were made—"

"Don't you see?" she interrupted. "She refuses to acknowledge publicly that his senses were, or are, in any way diminished. My mother is a proud woman. She has suffered more than anyone from this cruel turn, and I fear that the added strain of public shame and pity would be more than she could bear."

Leon dragged his fingers through his hair, snagging them in the rawhide lace at the back. Impatiently, he tugged it loose and tossed it aside. "Ah, civilization," he said, his tone bitter. "Where a man's illness is cause for shame and pity."

"It is not the illness that is hardest on my mother. Though she greatly misses my father's company, she is happy to care for him. It is the debts and the way that settling them has reduced our circumstances so drastically that is taking its toll."

"But if your mother would appeal to those holding the wagers and tell them the truth . . ."

"She won't."

"Because of pride," he snapped.

"No, because of love," Ariel corrected Sage gently. "She loves my father and she's protecting him in the only way she knows how."

"That's utter nonsense," he declared with an impatient grimace. "Only a woman would allow herself to make critical financial decisions based on her emotions of the moment."

"I'd hardly call forty years of marriage the emotions of the moment," she argued.

"It's still emotion. Pure drivel. And now you're aiding and abetting her by sacrificing yourself in marriage to the Nose to provide her with the means to continue with this foolishness."

"You look so outraged, one might think I was asking you to settle the debts," she declared.

"Perhaps I should," he retorted. "Have you no man in the family to handle this matter on your mother's behalf? No brothers? An uncle perhaps?"

She shook her head in reply to each question. "I have only a younger sister, but she's married and living in Derby."

"Then she has a husband. Surely he could step in and resolve this to everyone's benefit."

"I'm afraid Harry is not one to involve himself unduly."

"Nor financially either, is that it?"

"They have not offered. I prefer to leave it at that."

He shook his head, disgusted. The situation she described was unfortunate, but not a disaster, not unless her mother, with Ariel's help, insisted on making it one. Which, apparently, she did. He had no doubt he could settle the entire matter with a minimal outlay of cash in less than an hour. Only not without violating her mother's strict, asinine dictates about appearances.

He glared at the dying fire and got up to toss more logs onto the grate. So half the blades in London would be paid off, a good man would be stripped of the savings of a lifetime, and, most senseless and disturbing to him of all, Ariel would be forced to barter herself into a lifetime of joyless servitude. Marriage to Penrose could not possibly amount to anything else, he thought, resuming his slouch in the chair opposite where she sat silently.

"What about love?" he asked so abruptly, Ariel jumped.

"Love?"

"Yes. Love. It is supposed to play some small role in marriage, is it not? At least for a woman."

"Yes, I suppose it is. And I expect I could learn to love Mr. Penrose." She took a deep breath. "In time."

He slanted her a disparaging look. "Be serious. Eternity isn't time enough for a lesson of that magnitude."

With a small laugh, she nodded agreement. "It's true. I probably will never come to love him. But I will make him a good wife just the same. I'll continue to keep the books and run the school as I have been doing." Her eyes widened guiltily. "I mean to say, I'll continue to assist him with its operation."

"Don't bother covering for him. I saw the books. I know who it is keeps this place going."

"And a good thing I'm able to," she countered wryly. "My unique talents in that regard shall be my dowry."

"How very innovative. I assume your father wagered away your conventional dowry as well?"

"Certainly not. I was the one who insisted it be

tossed in with the rest of the family assets in our time of crisis—against my mother's objections, I might add. The sacrifice of my dowry crushed her aspirations on my behalf much more than it did any of my own."

"Until you thought further on the matter and concluded that marriage was your best hope of salvation?"

"Yes," she conceded, her deep sigh tinged with both resignation and resentment. "I had no idea at first that the debts would keep coming and coming as they have, quite overtaking our ability to meet them. You see now why I say that Mr. Penrose is the only conceivable prospect for me, a woman of no rank," she added, lifting her chin as if to flaunt what society decreed was a fatal liability.

Interesting, he mused. He personally put no stock in society's stupid conventions and dictates, but he had not grown up having them shoved down his throat at every turn. She had. Interesting.

"In short," she told him, "'I shall provide him with what he needs to live a comfortable, successful life and trust him to do the same for me."

Leon snorted rudely. "How sickeningly romantic."

"I am not interested in romance."

"No?" he parried with open disbelief. "Then you're the only woman in the world who isn't."

"Then I'm the only woman in the world who isn't," she concurred, shrugging. "Because in fact I have no interest in that regard. Not in the least."

Her announcement only increased his fascination with her. Not that he believed it for a second. *All* women were interested in romance, ruled by it, in fact. He straightened in his seat and observed her thoughtfully.

"Which returns us to the question of love," he said

at last. "If you're not interested in romance, is it correct for me to assume you have no interest in love itself? That is, shall we say, in its more corporeal expression?"

Ariel waved aside his flagrant attempt to shock a response from her.

"Oh, I may take lovers," she replied airily, toying with the satin cording on the arm of her chair. "Discreetly, of course."

"Of course," he murmured.

"But I have vowed never to permit any man to engage my emotions."

"I see. And this is something you believe you can control with a vow?"

"Most certainly. Perhaps not when I was younger," she said with a small frown, "but I am most definitely in control now."

"So you will never actually fall in love with any of these discreet lovers of yours?"

"Never. Love is an impediment to a woman's happiness, not to mention undermining whatever small amount of independence she can claim as her own. I see how it's influenced my mother and sister, and I have no desire to end up in the same fashion," she insisted. "Far better, I say, for a woman to design a rational, financially sound plan for the future and adhere to it."

"Such as your own plan to marry Penrose?"

"Precisely. It was not the independent life plan I envisioned for myself to be sure, but it is a plan."

"Oh, yes, it is most definitely a plan," he agreed.

He could see that the amusement in his tone prickled her composure.

"Do you not think it feasible?" she asked.

"I am hardly the one to judge, having not the slightest personal interest in the subject of marriage."

"I see. Then perhaps you think me indelicate to pursue such a strategy regardless of the outcome?"

"Quite the contrary. It is refreshing to meet the one woman in existence who is detached from the emotional turmoil and fluctuations which, in my experience, seem to plague the rest of your gender."

She smoothed her skirt and smiled. "It is equally refreshing to meet a man who is not intimidated by such a woman."

"Intimidated? Me? Perish the thought. In fact," he continued, "I am so impressed by your rational approach that I am prepared to offer my assistance to your cause."

"You are?" Her surprise quickly gave way to caution as he flashed her his most disreputable smile. "In what way?"

"It did not escape my notice that you are an exceedingly unaccomplished flirt."

"I believe I have already acknowledged that failing."

"It so happens, however, that I am an exceedingly *accomplished* flirt."

"Splendid," she retorted with a caustic smile. "But I fail to see how your flirting with Mr. Penrose is going to help me to win him."

"You will," he assured her, getting to his feet. "Starting first thing in the morning, the tables will be turned around here. I'll be the one teaching the lessons and you, sweet teacher, will learn."

"Learn to flirt?" she exclaimed, gazing up at him in disbelief. "How?"

He was counting on her to ask.

"Like this."

He easily tugged her to her feet so that she was

standing in front of him. Holding her gaze, he lifted one end of the velvet sash at her waist and began to slowly wind it around his finger. One turn, then another, working with such restraint, she would barely be able to discern that they were drawing closer with each turn. Yet the watchful glitter in her eyes told him she was very aware of what he was doing.

"Poor teacher," he murmured. "You really are an innocent, aren't you?"

Her gaze flew to his, bright with panic—which was the very last thing he wanted her to be feeling at that moment—and curiosity, which he didn't mind at all. Curiosity could lead to some very pleasurable discoveries. For both of them.

"Truly I would not describe myself as such," she said quietly.

He laughed softly. "Do not be uneasy," he said, his deep voice practiced and soothing. "I can teach you everything you need to know."

"What exactly do I need to know?"

He sensed the uncertainty that rippled through her and tightened his hold on the velvet sash so that his fist formed a bridge between her waist and his belly. His mouth was so close to her cheek, he could almost taste her, and when he glanced down, the view of her soft, bare shoulders and plump, creamy breasts made his chest feel heavy and tight.

"For now," he replied, "all you need to know is this."

He had fantasized about that moment for weeks, envisioning it in his mind when he was awake and dreaming about it at night with annoying regularity. He would have wagered that he'd anticipated it far too well and that the moment itself would have to be a disappointment or, at the least, anticlimactic.

He would have lost.

With one hand holding her close and the other cradling her head, he tipped her face up to his. For a split second their eyes locked. In hers he saw uncertainty and excitement, a heady mix. God only knew what she saw in his. Feelings and desires were exploding inside him so rapidly, he couldn't sort them out. He could only heed the instinct driving him to act.

Lowering his head, his mouth took hers with the combined heat and recklessness of six months' worth of denial, six weeks' worth of longing, and one endless evening's worth of mounting frustration. For hours he'd been looking at her in that dress, the shimmering fabric as insubstantial as moonlight, and wondering if it could possibly feel as soft as it looked. It did. *She* did.

He'd been told that among other attributes, he was a patient lover, but that studied patience wasn't in him tonight. Tonight he was all raw need and white-hot desire. He used his tongue to part her lips and then pushed inside, searching, stroking, desperate to lose himself in the silk and heat of her.

She remained still in his arms. He slid his fingertips along her back, down, then up, gliding over the fabric so sheer, he felt through it the warmth of her skin and the fine, small ridges of her spine. He cupped the back of her neck, and the downy smoothness of her skin there invested the caress with an unexpected intimacy that sent his senses soaring even higher. Dragging in a quick, harsh breath, he repositioned his mouth across hers, needing to get closer, deeper.

She moved toward him then, and he groaned, undone by the gentle pressure of her breasts against his chest. He sensed her hands rising to his shoulders and waited for the push he was sure would come. Instead, to his amazement, her fingers clutched the fine wool of his coat and held on.

He'd expected the havoc her soft body would wreak inside his own. He'd expected her to taste and smell like heaven, and that once he put his hands on her and started kissing her, it would be close to impossible to stop. What he hadn't expected was for her to kiss him back.

He'd hoped she would, of course, and in his fantasies she always opened to him with a passion that matched his own, urging him on with soft cries of surrender and saying the sort of things men usually paid a courtesan to say. She wasn't saying anything now, but she was kissing him. There was no mistaking that, and Leon felt a fresh, hard surge of desire.

Her tongue moved tentatively against his, with a soft fluttering motion that sparked his imagination, creating visions of all sorts of erotic applications of her natural talent. He drew back slightly to lick at her full bottom lip, slowly tracing its lush curve. When he paused, she mimicked him. Too well, he thought, straining for control as she painted lines of hot delight across his parted lips, making the ground beneath his feet rock wildly.

He clasped her to him, holding on, dragging her close, releasing his hold on the sash so that not even his hand was between them as their bodies came together, swaying, arching, straining. He kissed her hard, pulling her against him, his impatient hands making a shambles of her hair so that the loose curls tumbled to her shoulders.

When he looked at her that way, tousled, her eyes wide and overbright, her lips wet and swollen, reason failed him. His usual careful control unraveled inside him, like a spool rolling out of reach. Without thinking, he followed the pulsating urge to touch her and hooked his fingers inside her softly gathered bodice, a raspy sound coming from deep in his chest as for just an instant her softness spilled into his hand.

She wrenched away and placed her palms firmly against his heaving chest. "Please, my lord, you must not."

"No," he countered, curling his hands over her shoulders to keep her close. "It's you who must not. You must not say no to a marquis. That's the law, isn't it?"

She shook her head, her cheeks as bright as wild roses. "Not at all."

"Then it ought to be," he muttered, caressing her cheek with his thumb as he gazed hungrily at her mouth. "Otherwise what's the sense in being one?"

"I'm sure you'll find ample reward in your title."

"I've found the only reward that interests me at the moment. Come here, Ariel."

She stiffened her arms, holding him at bay. "Really, sir . . ."

"Leon," he interjected. "It's jarring to hear a woman call me sir when I'm making love to her."

"You are not making love to me," she told him, reaching to put a halt to the meandering progress of his fingertips along her throat.

"I am certainly trying."

"Admirably well," she said with a flicker of the humor he'd come to expect from her, "but you cannot continue."

"I can," he insisted, grazing the side of her throat with his mouth, smiling as he felt her shiver in response in spite of her protest. "I'm a noble by birth, remember? I believe that in fair England that means I can do pretty much anything I choose to do. And what I choose to do at the moment, and for the rest of the night as well, is make love to you, sweet Ariel."

His mouth closed over hers once more, and for a second he could swear he heard her whimper, feel acquiescence spreading through her like warm honey. Then she jerked her face aside and spoke out loud, and there was nothing the least bit whimpering or acquiescent in her tone.

"Stop," she ordered. "This instant."

He lifted his head enough to slant her a darkly amused look. "Why?"

"Because I said so."

That brought his head up fully. He searched her expression for signs of teasing or lunacy and detected neither. The softness was gone from her eyes and from her posture, however. She stood with her shoulders squared, her jaw high, the same serious look about her as the day she'd demanded the return of her shears. She was determined. Dauntless. Exquisite.

He smiled at her. "I want—"

"I don't."

Leon straightened to his full height, glaring down at her from a lofty eight-inch advantage. Still she didn't waver. He could easily name a half dozen more weighty reasons she might have given for ordering him to stop. Morality, their surroundings, the straitlaced dictates of society. None of them would have mattered a damn to him of course, or deterred him in the least. But this one did. Damn her honesty.

Because I said so.

He didn't particularly care what society thought or what the parlor maids saw or what some hypocritical bishop of somewhere or other decreed to be moral and immoral. It appeared, however, that he did care what this woman thought.

This woman who had shown him more concern and patience than had anyone else in the whole cursed land. No doubt a good deal more than he merited, he acknowledged a bit sheepishly. This woman who had taken his abuse and tolerated his boorishness and who possessed an unprecedented knack both for making him furious and making him ache with longing.

She was also in league with his enemies, he reminded himself. In league? Hell, she was planning to marry one of them, and for that heinous reason alone it shouldn't matter to him at all what she said or thought or felt. He shouldn't care, but he did. He hadn't realized how much until that moment and he didn't like it.

But he could not look her in the eye and force himself on her. Not even if the forcing were accomplished with a connoisseur's velvet touch, couched in skilled caresses and pretty lies. He couldn't do it. No matter how badly his body was throbbing and clamoring for him to get on with it.

He might have attributed the uncharacteristic failing to his conscience, if he had one. As it was, he had to shoulder the entire blame himself. So now he was his own enemy as well, he thought contemptuously. Thanks to her, he must deny himself even this small bit of well-earned solace. The more he thought about it, the more it irritated him. Resentment gathered inside him hard and heavy.

He released her abruptly. His gaze darkened and chilled as it honed in on his target.

"You are true to your word, I see. Pretty kisses, but no—how did you put it? Emotional entanglement." His words were as cold as the air in the room this far from the hearth.

"I never led you to think otherwise, my lord."

She had him there.

"True," he said, "you didn't." He managed a sardonic smile and a condescending drawl. "I shall have to be very careful not to lose my heart during our upcoming lessons."

"You cannot be serious about that."

"I assure you, I've never been more serious, or more determined, about anything in my life. Get a good night's rest, Ariel, you shall need it."

Upstairs he found Farrell waiting at his chamber door, key in hand. Leon was primed and ready for him.

"Not tonight, my fat friend," said Leon. "You've locked my cage for the last time." Holding out his open palm, he added, "The key."

Farrell tightened his grip on the cord from which the key dangled. "Miss Halliday didn't say nothing about giving you the key."

"Didn't she? It must have slipped her mind. As you're aware, she's had a most taxing evening."

Farrell grunted, his eyes mere slits in his bacon-faced countenance. "Just the same—"

"Just the same," Leon interrupted, "you will hand over the key before I am forced to take it from you." His lips curved in a feral smile. "Do you doubt that I can? Bear in mind you've no leather strap to ward me off this time."

The big man twitched uneasily. "I was just doing me job. You can't blame a fellow for that."

"Can't I? You would be surprised by what I've done with far less provocation."

Farrell glanced over his shoulder anxiously, kneading the cord between his fingers. "I don't know about this. My orders have been to lock you in for the night."

"Ah, but that was prior to my miraculous transformation. Your orders were to lock up Lord Savage, were they not?"

The other man shifted his feet nervously and nodded.

"As you can plainly see, the situation has changed. I am Leon Duvanne, the Marquis of Sage," he said, surprised he didn't choke on the words, "and you continue to refuse me that key at your own peril."

"Yes, sir," Farrell replied, his head bobbing. "I mean to say, yes, my lord. Yes, Lord Sage. The key. Right away, sir."

It was hurriedly dropped in Leon's outstretched palm, and he closed his fingers around it, amazed by the swiftness of Farrell's capitulation. It was no wonder titles were so highly prized by the British, if the simple invocation of one that had yet to be officially sanctioned could produce such magical results. The fact that the Sage title, and all that went along with it, meant less to him than the dirt beneath his feet would not deter him from exploiting it to his full advantage in the days ahead.

"Is there anything else you'll be wanting this evening, my lord?" inquired a far humbler Mr. Farrell than he had ever seen.

"As a matter of fact, there is," replied Leon. "There is something you can do for me tonight, and every night henceforth."

"Yes, my lord, just name it."

"Stay the hell out of my sight."

Leon stepped into the room and slammed the door shut behind him. Tossing the key in a silver dish on the bedside table, he tore off his cravat and stretched out on the bed. He needed to think clearly, and that was not easy to do with the feel of Ariel seared into his brain. He could still taste her, he could still smell her, he still wanted her. And she, if her claim were to be believed, was not the least bit emotionally engaged.

How dare she say she could not be emotionally engaged by a man? *Any* man. It didn't lessen his irritation at all to know that the little minx had a whole head full of such outrageous and fraudulent ideas. Anyone's emotions would respond if the stimulus were right. *Anyone's.* Hell, he was proof of that. Hadn't he also thought himself immune? And he was a man. After years of dallying with some of the most beautiful, most sexually adventurous and accomplished women in the world, how was he to have known that the right stimulus for him would be a rebellious schoolmistress with eyes the color of a summer sea?

Ariel was a woman predisposed to falling in and out of love at whim. She simply didn't realize it. Something had to be done. It would mean putting any plan to deal with Castleton and the others on hold for a while longer, but it could not be helped. Ariel Halliday could not possibly understand the irresistible challenge she'd presented him when she boasted of her immunity to emotional entanglement.

He realized now that at that very instant his mind had been made up as to how to proceed. He would help her win her repugnant little headmaster, and in the process he would also peel off the layers of her defenses and find a way to prove to her, and to himself, that she was no different from every other silly, treacherous female on earth. Before he was through he would engage the cool and calculating Miss Halliday's emotions fully. Repeatedly. Overwhelmingly.

If it was a lover she wanted, a lover she would have.

Ten

Leon Duvanne may not be a savage, Ariel decided the next morning, but he was clearly deranged. The notion that he could teach her to flirt was not only mad, it was a lost cause.

She rose at her usual time and washed and dressed routinely. Routinely, that is, except for the sudden impulse to add an ivory lace collar to the neckline of her best gray muslin and secure it with a cameo that had once belonged to her grandmother, an adornment ordinarily reserved for special occasions.

Her routine varied in another way as well, it occurred to her as she descended the stairs. For the first time since arriving at the cottage she had no plan for the day that lay ahead. She had a sense that the previous evening had changed everything as surely as if an omnipotent hand had reached from above to draw a thick black line across her life, separating all that had gone before from whatever might follow. Ariel couldn't deny that she was curious to see what that would be. More troubling to her was the accompanying feeling that she was no longer in control. If, she thought ruefully, she ever truly had been.

As was her custom, she waited in the drawing room for Sage to join her so that they might breakfast together, though she rather doubted it would be necessary for her to monitor his table manners this morning. It served him right, she thought, grinning. Her tedious lectures were the least he deserved for hoodwinking her all this time.

"What are you reading that's so amusing?"

She glanced up from the book she was holding to find Sage standing with one broad shoulder resting against the doorjamb, watching her. Immediately her breath caught in her throat and the book fell shut in her lap.

She'd thought the dazzling effect his changed appearance had exerted on her senses the past evening was due to shock and could not be repeated. She was wrong. The sight of him, clean shaven and impeccably dressed in a dark gray cutaway and snug doeskin trousers, looking every inch the arrogant noble, sent a tingle of awareness through her.

"Well?" he said from the doorway. He moved quickly without seeming to and he reached her before she had a chance to work a reply past her suddenly dry throat. He glanced at the book she had plucked from the shelf at random, without so much as glancing at the title before launching into her daydream. *"Modern Methods of Land Irrigation,"* he read, and looked at her. "You must have an amazing sense of humor."

"I do," she countered, marshaling her wits. "How else could I have possibly endured these past weeks with you?"

He flashed her a smile. "Of course, I should have realized that. So tell me, has a night's rest softened your mood and changed your mind about letting me call you Ariel?"

"It certainly seems to have softened yours," she observed.

"I am in a good mood," he replied. "Today promises to be most stimulating."

Stimulating? Of all the words she would have chosen to describe the sight of her trying to be flirtatious, stimulating was not one.

"I should warn you that you are setting yourself up for failure, my lord. I—"

"Leon."

"I beg your pardon?"

"Leon," he repeated. "That's my name, and I would prefer you use it when addressing me in the future."

"I'm afraid I cannot oblige you. To do so would be extremely discourteous."

"To whom?"

"To you, of course. You are a marquis and must be addressed accordingly."

"I am hardly a marquis," he argued. "Hell, I'm not even a real Englishman, at least not by choice, and I refuse to allow the fanciful machinations of those who are dictate what I will and will not be called."

"As you wish, my lord."

"For God's sake, woman," he exploded. "I just—"

"Oh, all right," she said, cutting short his reprimand.

"Very good. And now you can scarcely deny me leave to call you by your given name in turn."

She was outmaneuvered. Again. He was alarmingly good at doing that. "I suppose I cannot. But only when we are alone."

"Then it's settled." He moved to her side and

offered his arm. "Shall we go in to breakfast, Ariel? I find my appetite ravenous this morning."

If Mrs. Farrell's cooking had a bright spot, it was breakfast. Either that, Ariel often thought, or their typical evening fare left her so hungry by morning that breakfast tasted better than the rest. This morning, however, a bowl of pickled pig's feet could have been set before her without impressing her one way or the other. Her unruly thoughts were elsewhere—on heat and darkness and a soft, damp mouth moving ruthlessly on her own.

No matter how scrupulously she tried to turn those thoughts in another direction, all she had to do was lift her gaze from her plate to confront the unwavering perusal of the man seated opposite, and she was plunged back into the indecent reverie within.

"Are you not hungry this morning?" he inquired, wiping his mouth and putting his napkin aside as the maid hurried to clear away his empty plate.

Ariel looked with surprise at the large portion of ham and Dutch pudding remaining on her own plate. She felt as if she had been sitting there eating, or trying to, for hours.

"Not terribly," she replied, signaling that her plate could also be removed.

"Did you sleep well?" he asked.

The undercurrent of laughter in his husky tone made her loathe to admit the truth, that questions about him had kept her awake most of the night. In the end, however, curiosity won out over pride.

"Actually, I did not sleep well at all. I lay awake thinking about you a good part of the night."

"What a coincidence." The heat from his gaze reached her across the table. "Were you having second thoughts?" he drawled.

"Not exactly. You must have something upon which to base second thoughts you see, and aside from knowing that you are immensely educated, impeccably mannered, and well versed on an impressive array of subjects, I know nothing at all about you."

He leaned back in his chair. "What do you wish to know about me?"

Everything, she wanted to say. She wanted to know everything about him. But while his expression remained casual, caution had replaced the amusement in his eyes, warning her to tread carefully.

"To start with, I suppose I would like to know how you came to be so accomplished."

"In the usual manner, I expect. I was taught."

She shot him a wry look. "Please elaborate."

"All right. Schooling, like most things, is considerably less formal in the islands, so as a boy I was taught to read and write by one of the—" He hesitated, an enigmatic slant to his mouth. "I suppose you could call him an elder statesman of the group I was living with at the time. Later, when I moved to court, I had private tutors, and then I was shipped off to be finished at the university in Paris."

Ariel shook her head, amazed by the offhand recitation. "That is your idea of being educated in *the usual manner?*"

He shrugged. "More or less. Whatever else I know I learned even more informally, otherwise known as the hard way."

Ariel pushed aside her teacup and leaned forward excitedly. "I have a million questions I want to ask you."

"We don't have time for a million questions," he told her. "You may ask me two."

"Any two?"

She meant it teasingly, but the cornered look that suddenly shadowed his face reinforced her sense that he would rather not be having this conversation. His reluctance only added to the mystery that surrounded him. What was it about himself or his past that he did not want to talk about? And how could she ferret it out of him in only two questions?

Who are you? she wanted to ask exactly as she had wanted to the very first time she set sight on him. It was strange that in spite of being with him day in and day out for weeks now, observing him so closely that she knew he preferred tart berry jam and a window left open while he slept, she really did not know much of substance about him at all.

"Tell me about your mother," she said at last.

"That's not a question."

She rolled her eyes in exasperation. "Fine. Will you please tell me about your mother?"

"Yes. You have one question left."

"That's not fair," she protested. "Yes is not a proper answer."

"Is it any fairer to sit there and peck away at me for your own amusement?"

"That was not my intent," she said with quick regret. "Nor did I mean to give offence. I think it only natural that I should be interested in your background. After all—"

"Please," he said, raising his hand to stop her. He shook his head, his faint smile one of self-derision. "Do not be uneasy. I've no doubt your interest is perfectly normal. It's just that I'm not accustomed to what is normal, or, for that matter, to having someone take an interest in me without some personal gain at stake."

"Just the same, I'm sorry for making you feel put upon."

He smile deepened. "I don't. You have one question left. Make it good."

"All right." Curious though she was, she had lost her enthusiasm for the game but didn't want to make the situation any more strained by saying so. Still, she settled on repeating herself.

"What was your mother like?"

For an instant she thought he was going to stalk angrily from the room. It was as if a wall of ice had dropped between them, transparent but impenetrable, turning the air so cold, her own breath seemed to sear her lungs. Castleton's investigation had revealed only that his mother had died of unknown causes when Sage was quite young. Having never known his father, she had assumed his memories of his mother would be warm and cherished. His black expression suggested otherwise.

At last he drew his gaze from whatever it was above her head that it had been fixed on, and looked at her.

"She was beautiful," he said finally, "and she never laughed. Not really anyway. Not the way you do. When you laugh I think of a waterfall I played in when I was a boy, of how good the warm water felt pouring over me and how I wanted it to never stop."

She shook her head with a rueful smile. "Not laughing the way I do could probably be counted as one of your mother's greatest virtues," she told him, hoping to lighten the mood. "There are those who would say I laugh a bit too much."

"They're wrong," he said. He turned his head to stare out the window overlooking the garden, again letting the silence stretch. Without looking at her, he asked, "Have you ever stood outside on a summer night, when the sky was so clear it seemed to be hanging right over your head?"

"All the time," Ariel replied, understanding exactly the sort of sky he described.

"My mother was like the stars in that sky, shimmering and bright and seeming so close, you felt as if you could reach out and touch them, but when you tried, they were always too far away. When she was killed I—"

He stopped abruptly, still not looking at her.

A lump formed in Ariel's throat at the forlorn image his words conjured. Her own family had been exceedingly close, and she couldn't bear to think what it must have been like for the little boy Leon had once been to have felt that his own mother was beyond his reach, felt it so strongly that even as a grown man his entire body tensed when he spoke of her. She yearned for the right words to say to comfort him, wondering at the same time if those words even existed.

"Leon," she began.

At the sound of her voice he jerked his head around to look at her, almost as if he'd forgotten she was there, or that anyone was there listening to what he was saying. One thing was certain, she thought, taking in the thrust of his jaw and the contempt that appeared in his eyes, he had said more than he'd wanted to.

It's all right, she longed to say, but there was no time before he was on his feet.

"Shall we get started?" he asked, his deep voice markedly serene considering his black expression. It was as if he had drawn a line of his own and put the discussion behind him. "Last night I pledged my unwavering support to your cause, and it is a pledge I intend to honor fully."

"My cause?" She laughed softly. "You make it sound so noble."

"You're right. *Noble* is not the right word to describe the seduction of Mr. Penrose."

She came out of her seat to face him, her eyes wide. "Seduction?"

"Seduction, flirtation . . . you may quibble over the choice of word if you wish, Ariel, but make no mistake, the result is one and the same." He cocked one dark brow. "Or hadn't you considered the inevitable outcome should your plan meet with success?"

Actually, she did her best not to think at all about "the inevitable outcome." Oh, she knew that she would be required to share the marriage bed with Penrose should they wed, but in her methodical approach to the matter, that fell under the heading of Bridges to Be Crossed When She Came to Them. She was of the opinion that dwelling on unpleasantness beforehand did nothing but make it worse.

"You do understand the rights and privileges accorded a man in marriage?" he pressed.

"Of course," she replied, indignant. "I understand all of that. I am not some green girl fresh from her mother's side."

"I'm glad to hear it," he said, sounding either cynical or relieved, she couldn't be sure. "That advances our cause considerably."

"But I do not agree that smiling at a man and attempting to win his good favors are one and the same as seducing him."

"They are if you're playing to win, the prize being a ring on your finger and financial security for life. There's no need to blush," he admonished her. "It's no more shameful an endeavor than applying for any other position. You do desire to fill the position of Mrs. Phillip Penrose, do you not?"

"I do," she acknowledged reluctantly.

"Then you must understand the true nature of your goal and focus on it relentlessly. It is not your goal to be his friend, his valet, or his solicitor, is it?"

She shook her head.

"Then stop applying for those positions," he ordered with all the bluntness he had warned her of.

"But—"

"Your goal is to be his wife, his confidante, his lover. Yes?"

She clenched her teeth and nodded.

"Then say it," he ordered. "Tell me what you want, Ariel. Tell me exactly."

"I want to be his wife."

"And?"

"His confidante." She hesitated, gripping the edge of the table beside her with one hand. "And . . . oh, is this really necessary?"

"Yes. If you can't even bring yourself to say it, you can't focus on it, and if you cannot focus on it, you will never be able to take the steps required to get you where you want to go."

"But I thought—"

"You thought what?" he challenged, his slight smile mocking. "That keeping tidy ledgers would excite him? That he would find himself fantasizing about your well-wrought lesson plans? That playing the doormat for the man would arouse his unbridled lust?"

"Heavens, no. Trust me," she said, resentment driving out any trace of embarrassment at the turn the conversation had taken, "I have no desire to arouse Phillip Penrose's unbridled lust."

"Trust me," he retorted, "you'd better plan on doing exactly that if you hope to have him slip a ring through your nose. Pardon me, I mean on your finger."

"That may be the way to some men's hearts," she said pointedly, "but I had hoped that being a gentleman, he would in time come to recognize the true value of a decent, loyal, resourceful woman."

"Well, you hoped in vain. If you want him, you must first make him want you. It's as simple as that. The question is, do you have what it takes to do it, or am I wasting my time¿"

Ariel hesitated, clasping her cold, damp hands together. She would like nothing more than to tell him that yes, he was wasting his time as well as hers, and that she neither needed nor desired his assistance in this matter or any other. However, in spite of her irritation with his high-handed manner and the awkwardness of the entire discussion, there was a knowledgeable, logical core to his argument that appealed to her pragmatic side.

If they'd been discussing celestial theory, she would have adhered to her position even in the face of his dictatorial stance. Unfortunately, however, she knew a great deal more about heavenly bodies than earthly ones. He, on the other hand, appeared to be quite well versed in this subject. At the very least, he seemed to have given the matter extensive thought. If she was serious about approaching this in the most rational manner possible, she could not logically refuse expert assistance regardless of the source.

"I'm not sure if I have what it takes," she confessed at last. "Only that circumstances demand that I do whatever necessary to become Mr. Penrose's wife."

"And¿"

"Oh, all right," she snapped. "And his confidante and . . . lover."

"Louder," he coached, "and with feeling."

"And his confidante and lover."

"Better. The volume is good, but the feeling is all wrong. Work on it."

"How?" she demanded, throwing her hands in the air. "I do not even know how to begin to adopt the strategy you propose."

"That's easy," he said with a smile that made her think this might just work after all. "We'll begin with the way you walk. Go put on your walking boots, Ariel. We're going outside."

Though a chilly March wind blew from the east, the temperature outside had warmed enough to thaw the uppermost layers of the earth, turning the lawns to muddy mush and creating dips in the stone walks, where puddles had formed. Ariel couldn't imagine how a walk in such a mess was going to advance her cause, not even when he started off by saying to her, "I'm Penrose, come to take a turn with you. Now, let's proceed."

They walked, dodging puddles. Ariel was very glad she had heeded Leon's suggestion to wear her boots.

Leon. In spite of her earlier objection, she was already becoming accustomed to calling him by his given name.

Leon. It suited him, she mused, envisioning a proud, fierce lion, the undisputed king of the jungle, a lion with a mesmerizing bronze gaze and a wild, unruly mane. Tilting her head slightly, she slanted a sideways glance up at him, noting the way his long, unbound hair gleamed in the morning sun.

"Not like that," he said sternly.

"I beg your pardon?"

"I said, not like that," he repeated more emphatically. "That look you were giving me is all wrong."

"You are mistaken, I'm sure. I was not giving you a look of any sort at all," she insisted, quickly looking away.

"You were. It was an undecided look, and now you're flustered instead, and that's even worse."

"Pray tell, how am I supposed to look at you?"

"Assuming I'm Penrose," he reminded her, "you should be looking at me like a woman who knows what she wants, not one who's trying to make up her mind if a certain piece of beef would be suitable for that night's stew."

"I assure you I was not thinking of stew when I glanced your way."

"Then what were you thinking of?" he demanded.

"I was thinking of . . . avoiding the next puddle," she lied.

"How irresistibly alluring of you," he retorted, his tone disparaging. "Try thinking of me when you look at me, that is to say, Penrose, and of all the incredible, intimate things you eventually plan to do with me."

She halted in her tracks. "I can't possibly do that. It's just so . . . so . . ."

"Personal?" he suggested, transforming the word into a silky challenge. "Romantic?"

"Stupid," she said. "It's all so stupid and calculated. I can't do this."

"You can," he said, stopping and turning to face her. "And you must if you are to have any hope of salvaging this sinking ship of yours."

She arched her brows. "Sinking?"

He nodded. "And fast. You've no doubt heard of the import of first impressions? Well, suffice it to say that the impression you've made on the schoolmaster has been at odds with your intent. We're starting at a disadvantage and so you must double your efforts merely to pull even. Do you understand?"

"Yes. Unfortunately." She blew out a troubled sigh. "I knew I was not proficient at my task when I set about it, but I had no idea I was actually losing ground."

"You were. But it can be remedied if you do exactly what I tell you."

"Oh, all right," she agreed as unwillingly as if he were asking her to swim the Channel to fetch him a pint. "How's this?"

She gazed at him with a smile so utterly forced, the look in her eyes so brittle and eager, Leon had no doubt she was giving it her all.

"That's very ... passable," he said. "What I want you to do is to look at me with a promise in your eyes. Can you do that?"

"Yes," she replied without hesitation. "A promise." Her gaze clouded. "What shall I promise?"

"Everything. More than you intend to deliver. In fact, your look must promise more than you could possibly deliver. It's your intent to bewitch this man, to burn from his consciousness all thoughts but those of you and the pleasure you could give him if you deigned to, to bring him to his knees before you."

"That's dishonest."

"This isn't a court of law, Ariel. Honesty isn't required."

"But wont he be angry? In the end, I mean. When he discovers, as he surely will, that I have promised more than is mine to provide?"

"Take my word for it—if you do this properly, he'll be so besotted by the time he finally gets around to collecting that he won't know, much less give a damn, that he's been had."

"It still seems deceitful. And not at all the proper start for a successful marriage."

"Look, do you want there to be a marriage or not?"

"I have no choice."

"Remember that. And remember this, all's fair in love and war. Now, stop arguing and look lovingly at me, dammit."

She squared her shoulders and peered at him, her eyes bright and round as saucers. "How's this?"

"Terrible. Try again." He shook his head. "Stop fluttering your eyelids as if you might take flight at any instant. No. Again."

"I can't. Those are all the looks I know how to give. Is not even one of them suitable?"

"Not even close." He sighed dramatically, as if on the verge of tossing it all in. Manufacturing a frown, he studied her face, lifting his hands to frame it without touching her. "Perhaps I can guide you through it."

Instantly suspicion replaced the impatience in her dark blue eyes. "How?"

"To start, I can see now that the trouble is not limited to the eyes alone."

"It's not?"

"No, I'm afraid it's much more pervasive than that. But let's see what we can do. We'll start with your mouth."

"What shall I do with my mouth?"

Oh, Lord, he was a saint, he decided. He had to be. Only a saint could hear that question, look at her soft, beautiful mouth, and suppress the suggestion that sprang readily to mind.

"Wet your lips," he said, his tone rougher than usual. "Run your tongue across them. Just do it," he ordered when she hesitated. "That's better. Wet is always better than dry."

"Why?"

"Because . . . because it is, that's why. It's enticing to a man. Don't ask why; just believe it. Now purse them, just a bit. That will do. Now for the angle of your head." He laid his open hand against her cheek to adjust the tilt. Her skin was soft and pleasantly cool and he was in no hurry. "There," he said eventually. "That's good. Now for your hair."

"What about my hair?"

"No need to panic. I won't be coming at you with a pair of shears," he assured her with a sardonic look. "To start with, I ought to be able to see for myself that you have some of the stuff." He tried unsuccessfully to pull a few wisps of hair from beneath her bonnet before giving up and reaching for the bow at her chin. "May I?"

"Must you?"

"Yes."

"I've come this far, so I suppose you might as well."

She lifted her chin stiffly. Hell, he'd seen condemned men react less stoically. He was tempted to remind her that she hadn't found his touch so loathsome the evening before, but he didn't want to do anything to endanger her cooperation. He would do well to take his own advice and stay focused on the goal. His goal was Ariel herself, warm and willing and, most important, emotionally engaged.

Before she could withdraw her consent, he gave a tug and the bow opened. He half expected her to wince, but no, she was braced for the supreme indignity of having a man remove her bonnet.

"You're sure all this is really necessary?" she inquired.

"Will you stop asking me that? You'll have your answer when you're making your way down the aisle," he retorted as he tossed the bonnet atop a nearby bush and used his fingers to gently loosen her hair from its tight arrangement at the back of her head. Strands curled gently round her face, and, satisfied at last, Sage dropped his hands to his sides and examined the results. Damn, he was even better at this than he'd thought.

"Will that suit?" she asked tentatively when he continued to gaze at her in silence, ensnared in a web of his own thoughts. In daylight her hair appeared to be shot through with spun gold, and he had a sudden vivid image of it spilled across his pillow in the morning sun, and of waking to find her smiling at him exactly as she was smiling at him then.

"Yes, it will suit," he murmured finally, unable to take his eyes off her as she gazed up at him from beneath lush fans of half-lowered lashes. Last night, dizzy; today, mesmerized. What was happening to him? "It's perfect actually. By God, you're perfect."

"I am?"

She sounded as stunned as he felt, summoning Leon back to himself.

"I mean to say the look is perfect. You did it."

"*You* did it," she corrected him, her pouting vixen pose giving way to an eager smile that shouldn't have been nearly as alluring as the first, but somehow it was.

"Let's call it a joint venture, shall we?" He frowned at her hesitant expression. "What now?"

She shook her head self-consciously. "Nothing, I . . . all right. It's silly. And rude as well, I'm sure."

"Which only makes me more determined to get it out of you," he said. "Let's hear it."

"I was simply curious about the mark on your forehead. You see⸮" she added hurriedly. "I told you it was rude. I wondered if it happened aboard Captain Bennett's ship, the result of an accident perhaps. If so, I know of an ointment my father used on burns that you might . . . Never mind. I'm sorry I asked, really."

Aware that he was glowering at her, Leon struggled to bring his feelings under control.

"It wasn't an accident," he said, aware of the chill in his voice. "And it wasn't rude," he added to try to make up for it. "It's just something I don't talk about."

"Of course."

Unnerved by the exchange and his response to it, Leon resumed walking. Ariel fell into step beside him.

"I am sorry," she said after they'd walked a few paces.

"Forget it."

They'd walked a few more, when he felt a tug on his sleeve.

"Leon, wait. I forgot my bonnet."

"Leave it," he said without breaking stride. "We'll retrieve it on the way back." Under his breath he added, "Unless we get lucky and a crow carries it off in the meantime."

"Is that meant to be a joke⸮" she inquired, pursing her lips the way he'd taught her. That may have been a mistake, he thought, looking away, annoyed to feel the impact in the sudden tightening of his chest.

"Far from it," he retorted, seizing her bonnet as a target for his irritation with himself. "The fact is, Ariel, it's a god-awful bonnet. The worst I've ever seen."

"Oh, really⸮"

"Really."

With an indignant toss of her head that sent her loosened hair rippling like sun-scorched silk, she quickened her pace so her back was to him. Over her shoulder she said, "I'll have you know my father bought me that bonnet, a pair of them actually, the same style but different colors."

"Yes, I couldn't help taking note of the other as well," he said, his longer stride easily closing the distance she tried to put between them. "And upon rethinking it, I see I may have been wrong about today's being the worst. It would take a coin toss to settle it."

"Go ahead and laugh. I am not ignorant of the fact that they are a bit on the overdone side, or that they make me look like—"

"Like a walking market stall?" he suggested dryly.

The sudden self-effacing curve of her lips took him by surprise, breaking the awkwardness of the moment before and freeing them both to laugh openly. "That bad?"

He nodded.

Again she tossed her head, making him want to reach out and catch that silken bounty in his hands and bury his face in it. "I don't care. They are likely to be my last present from Papa, and I shall treasure them because of it."

A derisive retort rose to his tongue and died there. Who was he to mock her fierce loyalty to a man who, according to her own description, was beyond knowing whether or not she wore the bonnets he'd given her? He'd never received acknowledgment, much less gifts of any sort, from his own father. At least, Leon thought bitterly, not until it was too late. What did that kind of deep bond feel like? he couldn't help wondering. What sort of love from a parent inspired such tenacious devotion in a child? Or was it not inspired or taught at all? Was it simply a matter that Ariel had been born with a generous heart? And he had not.

Either way, it suggested that she was not the emotionless ice fortress she claimed to be.

"And so you should treasure them," he told her quietly, the gentle turn of his tone drawing a curious glance from her. "However," he went on before she became overly curious, "if you're smart, between now and the wedding you'll use them to adorn the mantel or keep the garden free of blue jays, anything rather than be seen with one of them atop your head."

"Agreed," she said. "I shall retire them to their hatboxes, at least temporarily."

They walked in silence for a few moments, before Sage cleared his throat and said, "Your dress last evening, it was not at all like the bonnets. It was really quite splendid."

"It is lovely, isn't it? It was my dress for Caroline's wedding and quite unlike any I've ever owned. Caroline said it would make even a dormouse look fetching."

"Caroline sounds like a charmer," he said dryly, certain of her type without ever having met her. "It wasn't merely the dress, Ariel. A dress, any dress, is only a handful of cloth and a bit of imagination. It was *you* in the dress that made it memorable." So bloody memorable, he thought, that he couldn't get the image out of his mind. "You looked beautiful in it, Ariel."

A sideways glance at her flushed face and tentative smile assured him that she was not accustomed to receiving compliments from men. Another encouraging sign for his campaign.

"I thank you for saying it flattered me," she said, her

tone somewhere between breathless and teasing, "though I'm sure you're simply being overkind to make up for calling my bonnet ugly."

"Not at all," he assured her. "The bonnet is ugly, and you did look beautiful. The one has nothing to do with the other."

"I see. Well then." Clasping her hands tightly at her waist, she rushed on. "I think that's quite enough about dresses and bonnets, don't you? Our purpose in coming out here was to work on my walk. You did say that was the first step, did you not?"

"I did. You may consider the other lesson a bonus." He stopped beside the stone wall at the edge of the property and held out his hand to her. "All right, up you go."

"You want me to climb over the wall?" she asked, clearly on the verge of mutiny.

"No, I want you to climb onto the wall."

"Whatever for?"

"To practice your walk."

"I'll have you know I spent hours practicing my walk and perfecting my posture in the drawing room at home. My mother insisted upon it. You can tell a lady by her carriage, she would say as Caroline and I went round and round, a half hour each morning, with medical texts balanced atop our heads to keep them from bobbing."

"That would explain it."

"Explain what?"

"Why you walk as if there's an iron rod strapped inside your chemise."

"I do no such thing."

"Trust me, Ariel. I've spent enough time observing you from the rear quarter to know what I'm talking about. You—"

"Enough," she snapped. "As grateful as I am for

your assistance, I must admonish you for your brashness."

"Fine. Consider me admonished," he said briskly. "Forget what you mother told you, Ariel, bobbing is good."

She caught her bottom lip between her teeth, gazing at him with all the certitude of a woman with one foot onshore and the other on a ship pulling rapidly out to sea. "It is?"

He nodded. "But not your head. It's all right to hold that steady if you choose."

"Then what on earth should I be bobbing?"

He reached out and bracketed her shapely hips with his hands, silently applauding the current fashion for a minimum of layers and petticoats, which enabled him to assess her attributes with blissful accuracy. Her figure was exactly as he had surmised, luscious.

"These," he said, feeling her go stiff. "But perhaps *bob* isn't the right word to describe what I have in mind." He pretended to give the matter due consideration, exploiting the excuse to keep his hands on her for as long as he dared.

"Sway," he announced finally, decisively. "That's what I want from you, Ariel, swaying. Slow and smooth. Like this." Still holding her hips, he endeavored to show her the range and rhythm of what he had in mind and found her as loose and malleable as a block of granite. He sighed heavily. "Never mind. We'll work on this too."

"How? By making me walk on walls?" she demanded, incredulous. "You can't be serious."

"You walk as if you're afraid you'll break," he explained. "The unevenness of the wall will help you to find your stride, loosen up your muscles, take some of the starch out of your backbone."

"And if I fall?" she asked pointedly.

"If you fall," he countered, tightening his hold slightly, just enough to make sure she felt it, "I'll catch you."

Releasing her, he offered her his hand. She glanced at it briefly, then met his gaze once again. It occurred to him at that moment that they had never formally sealed their bargain. He had offered his assistance and she had not refused it. In a way it was as if she'd been swept along by the power of his own enthusiasm. Until now.

The air was heavy all around them, and the moment held the silent import of an official ceremony. She might balk. If she did, that would end it right there and then. He would be free to walk away and get on with the matters that really should be commanding his full attention. It would be best if she did end it now, Leon told himself, even as he realized that it was not what he wanted to happen.

What he suddenly wanted, for some irrational reason he couldn't name, was for her to trust him. No matter that his motives were suspect and his intentions dishonorable, he wanted to know that for better or worse, they were in this together.

Just when he despaired of that happening, and was about to start searching for a suitably acerbic comment to mark his leave-taking, she surprised him for a change by placing her hand atop his.

"Help me up," she said.

For the next ten minutes he walked beside the wall as she traipsed along the top. After the first few steps she paused to toss her mantle to him, insisting it was getting in her way. There was something vaguely unsettling about the fact that he was now the one holding her coat while she forged ahead.

She didn't fall. He didn't get to catch her, though she did reach for his hand a few times to steady herself, and each time he was there for her, holding her hand until she felt secure enough to pull away. The simple act imparted more of a thrill than ought to be possible for one of his jaded sensibilities. When she reached the end of that section of wall, she turned to him, grinning, her expression an unguarded appeal for his approval.

The protectiveness he'd felt holding her hand was nothing compared to what he felt seeing her look at him in that unguarded way. Didn't she know how dangerous it was to expose her feelings so openly for anyone to tread on? Her fortress walls were proving to be amazing easy to scale, he thought, without any of the satisfaction he expected to feel.

"How am I doing?" she asked.

"Better. Shall we see if you can apply the technique on solid ground?"

He reached out to provide support as she climbed down, and was surprised when instead she leapt into his open arms. Surprise turned to delight and something more as their bodies collided and his arms closed around her.

She tipped her back and gazed up at him, laughing, a new and beguiling looseness about her. Her lips were parted and her cheeks rosy. She was part disheveled minx and part provocative woman, and desire for *all* of her began to surge and rush warmly through his veins.

He cupped her chin and bent his head and watched the excitement in her eyes turn to smoke.

Then he saw the cameo at her throat and hesitated.

"A mermaid?" he murmured, compelled to touch it. "You've never worn this before, I'm sure."

"No. I save it for—" She blinked and said, "Services on Sundays. It belonged to my grandmother."

"Really? Services on Sundays?" His mouth curved knowingly as he took note of the froth of lace it was pinned to.

He tilted the carving so that the sunlight illuminated its fine workmanship. The stone itself was an unusual deep amber and was banded with gold. But it was the rendering of the mythical sea creature itself that startled and fascinated him most. She was unabashedly voluptuous, the insouciant tilt of her head sending her long hair falling back, baring one lush breast and most of another. Definitely fantasy material.

He cleared his throat. "It's a beautiful piece. Though not what I would expect a proper British lady to pass on as a family heirloom."

"What did you expect?" she countered, amusement in her tone. "A likeness of Wellington, or, better yet, a bowl of jelly wearing a crown?"

"Either would make an exquisite brooch, I'm sure."

"It so happens this was a gift to my grandmother from a dashing sea captain who courted her before she wed my grandfather."

"And which she in turn wore only to Sunday services?" he inquired, a gleam in his eye.

"As a matter of fact, she wore it whenever she was piqued at my grandfather and wanted to tweak him. She was not, I am proud to say, a very proper British lady at all. Rather, she was a great deal of fun."

She sighed, her small smile wistful as she fingered the small pin. "I miss her. Whenever she wore this brooch she would let me touch it and make a wish and she told me the mermaid would make it come true."

A strange sensation, almost like being weightless and leaden at once, gripped Leon. "That is . . . very odd," he told her. Seeing her prickly defenses rising, he hurriedly added, "Not your grandmother, but the fact that while she was telling you to make a wish on a mermaid, thousands of miles away, my mother was telling me the same thing."

"Is that really true?"

He nodded. "She didn't have a brooch for me to touch," he told her, "but she had a lagoon, a lagoon full of beautiful mermaids, according to her, and she had a son who was deathly afraid of the water. The water, you see, had taken my father away, and in my six-year-old mind it made sense not to risk disappearing the same way."

He still had one arm around her waist, her hands resting lightly on his biceps. He felt them tighten slightly.

"To me that sounds eminently logical for a six-year-old," she said simply.

"It was also eminently dangerous for a young boy living on an island, surrounded by water, not to know how to swim. My mother used the mermaids to entice me to learn. She told me that if you swam underwater and caught one by the tail, the mermaid would trade you a wish for her freedom. I was hooked. And I knew exactly what I wanted to wish for," he said, the memory drifting forth from a place deep inside him that he'd thought was locked forever.

"Did it work?" Ariel asked softly.

"I learned to swim, if that's what you mean, better than anyone else in our village. I could swim the width of the lagoon both ways underwater."

"And did you ever catch a mermaid?"

He shook his head, remembering the disappointment that had been the other side of his excitement and pride in learning. Remembering the wish that never had come true.

"No, I never did." His thumb caressed the soft place beneath her ear. "Not until today. I wish—" He stopped abruptly, uncertain what he wished for, without words for the yearning that was opening up inside him, afraid to even try to put a name to it.

She saved him, gently covering his mouth with her hand so he didn't have to try to speak.

"You mustn't speak your wish out loud," she admonished Sage.

Leon wrinkled his brow, his voice muffled by her hand. "Why?"

"Because if you do, it won't come true. That's the rule about wishes. Didn't your mother tell you that?"

He moved her hand away from his mouth and placed it on his chest. "No, she didn't. Maybe because she didn't know the rules either, not about wishes or . . . anything else."

He stopped her as she went to pull away.

"You tell me," he said. "Why am I not allowed to speak my wish out loud?"

"I didn't say I knew why," she replied. "Only that it is the rule. When I was younger, I believed it simply because my grandmother said it was so."

"And now?"

She made a vague gesture, her smile haunted and more disturbing to him than his own unwanted memories.

"Now I think that it's because to speak it out loud makes it seem real, and making it real makes it hurt even more when your wish does not come true."

That was something he understood. Hiding what you were thinking, never letting anyone know when you wanted something, or, worse, needed it, and how badly—that was all familiar terrain to him. But, he thought, recalling her eager expression of a few moments before, when she turned to seek his approval, it shouldn't be that way for someone like her.

"I see what you mean," he said. "On the other hand, if you say it out loud and let someone else hear what you are wishing for, perhaps that person would have the power to help make it come true."

Ariel considered his conjecture as seriously as if they were discussing the properties of life and matter, and not wishes and mermaids.

"You mean like a fairy godmother?" she asked.

Leon tried not to look astonished. "Do fairies have godmothers here?"

There was no malice in her laughter. "Fairy godmothers are not godmothers to fairies," she explained. "A fairy godmother is a fairy sent by the other fairies to be someone's godmother, to take care of them and help them make their dreams come true. Now do you see?"

He did, but he was in no hurry to say so, not when holding her in his arms and listening to her explain was so enjoyable. He was willing to let the moment spin out. Maybe he would kiss her this morning, maybe he wouldn't. He was learning that there were times when restraint could be as intimate as a kiss.

"I think I have it straight," he said. "Wishes have rules and fairies have godmothers. Is that it?"

She regarded him ruefully. "And to think that only last evening I was so sure there was nothing that I could possibly teach you."

"Am I not even close?" he asked.

"Don't worry," she told him. "We'll work on it."

Eleven

Ariel had never truly believed that she could be transformed from her plain, candid self into a veritable coquette. Now, to her amazement, slowly but surely, it was happening.

Leon's unorthodox approach over the past week had added to her skepticism. Not that she was sure what conventional lessons in flirtation might be. She surmised they would involve lectures on the use of clever bits to brighten one's conversation, lest one be thought a milk-and-water miss, and perhaps reminders not to best a gentleman at whist or gobble down every last scrap on your plate when dining in his company.

Leon never lectured her at all. Instead, he placed great emphasis on determining how she ought to think and look and respond in a given situation to best captivate Penrose's interest and approval. He had a knack for cutting to the heart of the matter and making it sound simple, but what with trying to summon the proper thought to elicit the precise facial expression he desired of her from moment to moment, Ariel found it all got very confusing.

Further complicating matters was his insistence that she pretend he was Penrose. Ariel imagined this was what it was like to perform in a play, except that she was playing herself, or, rather, a more provocative, sophisticated, evolving version of herself, playing opposite Leon, cast in the role of the man she was trying to seduce. She only hoped she did not end up the laughingstock before the final curtain fell. It was a distinct and distressing possibility since, with each passing day, she was becoming more adept at her role of seductress and less certain of Leon's.

Perversely, the more he spoke to her of the subtleties of enticing Penrose, the more she felt enticed by Leon. The more he urged her to imagine Penrose's response to her, the more she found herself imagining his instead. And whenever he would begin an exercise by taking her hands in his and instructing her to close her eyes and think of Penrose, she could not conjure up even a vague image of the man she'd worked beside daily for over three years. At those moments there was but one image that filled her thoughts, filled them so completely, they overflowed and drizzled through her body like warm, soft rain. That image was Leon's.

It was all very confusing indeed.

For weeks she'd thought of Leon as a magnificent symbol of man's ultimate freedom, a freedom she had secretly envied. She had anguished over her part in taking that freedom from him and making him into something he did not want to be. Now suddenly their positions were reversed. He was the one bringing her to heel, training her in the civilized art of entrapping a man she did not want but must have. The very idea of it made her want to run away screaming. It only made it worse that in the process, Leon was awakening feelings in her that she knew would be impossible to transfer to Penrose, or to forget.

At times Ariel wondered if Leon felt the same ambiguity over their roles and was simply better at concealing it. Hiding his feelings seemed to be his forte after all. He made a point of not talking about himself, adopting a black scowl if he should slip and inadvertently reveal something personal in the midst of one of their lively debates.

That was how she had discovered he was a hero.

"Payment for services rendered," he had snapped at her one afternoon when their discussion of royal privilege grew heated and she had endeavored to bolster her position by reminding him how his own education had been advanced by his presence at the Hawaiian court of King Kamehameha.

They were playing chess at the time, the legal moves of the king versus the queen having somehow inspired the fiery debate. It never took much.

"Technically I was never a part of the court," he insisted. "The king was merely repaying a debt he thought he owed, rendering your argument inapplicable."

"What did he think he owed you for?" Ariel asked, more than willing to concede the argument if it meant learning more about him.

Immediately the familiar cornered look tightened his jaw and narrowed his gaze. Before he could change the subject as he usually did at such moments, she spoke.

"Please tell me. I've never been anywhere more exotic and exciting than Bath. Hearing you talk about your life in the islands, I feel as if I'm there."

It was a shameless generalization, but as he had

said, this was not a court of law. In truth, it was Leon who seemed exotic and exciting to her. He was the mystery that consumed her.

His scowl grew blacker still, but he nodded. "If you insist."

"I do," she said quickly.

He moved his rook, gave a negligent shrug, and said, "I saved his youngest brother's life and for that he brought me to court, where, as you pointed out, I learned all sorts of new things." He nodded at the chessboard. "Your move."

Ariel waved off the reminder. "How did you save his life? I want to hear everything."

"You always do," he muttered, looking as if she'd asked him to walk barefoot across hot coals. "The boy was only nine and blessed with an inflated sense of his athletic prowess. There was a typhoon building when, on a dare, he tried to swim out past some breakers and didn't make it."

"So you went in after him? In the middle of a typhoon?"

"Not quite in the middle, and stop looking at me that way," he ordered her gruffly. "The boy couldn't swim. I could. That doesn't make me some sort of bloody hero."

It did in her eyes, and the glowing smile she bestowed on him told him so. She didn't care if he liked it or not.

"Just make your damn move, will you?" he growled, ending the discussion but not the mystery.

In spite of her sense that Leon avoided lowering his own guard while constantly hammering away at hers, Ariel did not find his company unpleasant. They took long walks together and in the evening she read to him by the fire, evocative passages he selected from

Shakespeare's sonnets or Byron, or else they sat at the piano and played duets. Since neither of them could be mistaken for an accomplished pianist, their attempts more often than not ended in a tangle of misplaced fingers and laughter. She tended to forget that she was being paid to be there, and felt as if she were attending a continuous house party, the pampered only guest of a handsome and charming, if somewhat enigmatic, host.

The scattered insights she had managed to get of Leon's past, and his glowering resistance to revealing the little he did, only added to the mystery surrounding him. Who was Leon Nicholas Duvanne? Lord Savage or Lord Sage? Gentleman or villain? A nobleman in spirit as well as by birth, honestly committed to helping her win the affection of Mr. Penrose? Or a clever blackheart, amusing himself at her expense?

Just thinking about it made the skin at the back of her neck prickle and her fists clench. Perhaps he was even using her and her wretched situation for some nefarious purpose of his own. She'd known from the start that he resented being there, but she was still no closer to knowing why he stayed. And now, by confiding in him and accepting his offer to help, she had, in a way, linked her fate to his.

Could she trust him? Whenever her heart said yes, her mind countered with a resounding maybe. He had fooled her once already. He was not only capable of deceit, but devilishly adept at it. Then there was the darkness in him to consider. That was something she sensed with both her head and her heart. But while her head cautioned that he was a man to be held at arm's length, her heart refused to listen.

Her heart knew pain when it saw it. Her heart understood secrets and disappointment and was neither frightened by his coldness nor deterred by his arrogance. Her heart understood what her head resisted, that from the start she was drawn to this man as she had never been drawn to another, not in spite of his aura of danger and mystery, but because of it.

She ought to know better, Ariel told herself. She'd thought she did, that she had learned from the grievous mistakes of the past. It was a tug-of-war between her head and her heart that had led her to commit a costly indiscretion with the son of distant acquaintances when she was barely eighteen, and still hopelessly naive. Her second mistake had been in confessing the first to a gentleman she had believed cared enough for her to understand. More naivete on her part, she supposed, thinking back on how soon after her unburdening he had taken his leave, never to reappear at her door.

It was then that she had vowed never again to become emotionally engaged with a man. The rest of what she'd told Leon, about taking lovers without falling in love with them, had been an impulse fabrication that she had embellished and warmed to as she went along. It had made her feel deliciously adventurous, when in fact she'd learned the hard way to listen to her head and not her heart, and to live according to a carefully wrought plan. Leon challenged all of that. He refused to conform or be categorized.

They had been at it for exactly a week, with only a week remaining in their time together, when she was summoned to the drawing room one afternoon, arriving to find the rug rolled back to expose the highly polished parquet floor beneath. Miss Earnhardt, the school's new music teacher, was seated at the piano, performing complicated finger exercises. She stopped playing when she noticed Ariel pause uncertainly in the doorway, and though they didn't know each other well, she flashed her an encouraging smile.

The bare floor, the music, the smile—all of it made Ariel suspicious.

She looked around and found Leon standing by the window, a black-booted toe resting on the thick baseboard, staring with an incongruously brooding expression at one of the finest days they'd enjoyed in a fortnight.

He turned at the sudden quiet in the room and started toward her, no brightening of his expression.

"Don't just hang there," he directed, "I've a hunch we've no time to waste."

Her vague suspicion began to take shape, and she clasped her hands tightly at her waist, determined not to reveal to him just how anxious this made her. "It appears you're in the mood for spring cleaning. How clever of you to think to arrange for a musical accompaniment. I'm sure it will make the drudgery pass more quickly."

"Don't be tiresome. What I'm not in the mood for is entertaining arguments from a stubborn woman. Now, come here."

She shrugged, still hanging back. "I can hardly argue until I've been presented with something to argue against."

"Very well. You once claimed to be ghastly at anything requiring the least coordination."

He paused, his brooding gaze roaming over her, seeming to scorch a dark and predatory path everywhere it touched. Ariel sensed anger in him, simmering just below his cool reserve. Though why *he* should be

angry when she was the one summoned into a trap of
some sort was beyond her ability to reason. Each time
she thought she was beginning to understand the man
at last, a setback occurred and he withdrew into the
curt, intimidating shell of a stranger.

This latest followed yesterday's impromptu visit by
Penrose to discuss a school matter with her. With Leon
looking on, she had swallowed her pride and forced herself to put into practice everything he'd taught her. And,
if she did say so herself, she'd performed admirably,
even going so far as to touch Phillip's arm lightly, linger-
ingly, precisely the way Leon had rehearsed with her
over and over. But did that please the man? Heavens no.
When she later asked how he thought she'd done, he
glowered and nitpicked and drove her even harder.

And now this.

"I am uncoordinated," she told him. "So whatever
you have in mind here, you can just forget it."

"Not a chance," he said. "What I have in mind,
madam, is dancing."

Her stomach clenched. Dancing. She knew it was
to be that the instant she saw the turned-back rug.

"Then you shall need to find a more suitable
partner. I cannot name anything at which I am more
inept than dancing. My mother warned that my lack of
serious effort in learning would plague me one day, and
it appears that day has arrived."

"Are you finished?"

Ariel nodded, giving serious thought to bolting or
feigning a swoon.

"Good. It's time I see for myself exactly how uncoordinated you are."

She sighed, resigning herself to the fact that if
she ran, he'd catch her, and if she pretended to faint,

he'd probably take pleasure in slapping her back to consciousness.

"I'll save you the bother," she told him. "Previous partners have rated my dancing skill between adequate and insufferable, with the former opinion coming from my own father. Plainly put, I can hardly dance at all."

"What do you do at balls?"

"Count the minutes mostly. I've no patience for all the silly preening and positioning and gossiping behind fans that goes on at such gatherings. Balls have never been a priority for me. Nor a particular pleasure."

"Then what is?"

"My family, of course. My position here at the school and insomuch as it relates to—"

"Not your priorities," he interrupted with obvious impatience. "Those are patently obvious. I want to hear what your particular pleasures are, Ariel."

"Oh, that." She considered briefly. "I suppose I should again mention my family first. At least prior to my father's illness it was pure pleasure to spend time at home with them. And my work, of course, my reading and—"

"You mean your work here?" he cut in, looking exasperated. "Good God, woman, do you see no difference between work and play?"

"I am certainly able to see the value in serious pursuits over frivolous," she retorted. "However, I should point out that before I was interrupted by your lordship for the second time, I was referring to my work away from the school, specifically my studies in astronomy."

She savored his look of surprise. Let him go ahead and think he had poor, dull, workhorse Ariel all figured out. She'd show him there was more to her than met his cynical eye.

"Astronomy," he echoed, folding his arms across

his chest and finding his ease by bracing one shoulder against the solid oak frame of the arch. "A rather unusual pursuit for a young lady, isn't it?"

"Since we've already concluded that I am no longer young, I don't see how your observation pertains."

Now he was amused and made no effort to temper the curve of his wide mouth. "Touché. Tell me, Ariel, how you came to develop such a rare interest."

"It began when I *was* still young," she explained. "No more than ten or eleven. Our closest neighbor, Sir Hilbert, is a serious astronomer. His essays have been widely published and he's been instrumental in planning for the establishment of the Royal Astronomical Society. He and my father were fast friends, and whenever he visited I would beg to sit in the room with them, fascinated by their discussion of the stars and the planets. Sir Hilbert was good enough to foster my interest in spite of the piteous fact of my femininity," she inserted dryly, "by lending me texts and allowing me the free use of the equipment in the tower room he turned into a laboratory. In short, I daresay I caught the passion from him."

"Hilbert sounds like a wise man. I daresay I do not find your femininity piteous in the least."

Ariel shrugged. "Call it a drawback, then."

"Nor that," he countered. "So how did you end up here, teaching, instead of off stargazing in your own tower laboratory somewhere?"

She gave another shrug, this one accompanied by a weary laugh. "To misquote Pope, practical concerns spring eternal. I never found the right moment to just turn my back on everything else and pursue my studies the way I dream of doing."

"Were your parents not supportive of your ambition?"

"My father was, wholeheartedly so. Indeed, both he and Sir Hilbert urged me to pursue a path of formal study and research, with Sir Hilbert even making inquiries on my behalf with influential colleagues."

"And your mother?"

"She was decidedly less enthusiastic."

"Of course, she was the one holding out for marriage and clusters of little ones."

Ariel laughed. "Exactly."

"And in the end you bowed to her wishes and gave up on your own."

"Not at all," she denied hotly. "I still have every intention of pursuing my dream when the time is right. I was, in fact, on one occasion set to leave for Plymouth and a course of study with a Professor Perry, who was most highly recommended to me by Sir Hilbert, when my aunt Catherine took ill and I felt obliged to go to Bath to tend her instead. By the time she was recuperated, my sister Caroline was about to formalize her attachment to Harry Hammerton and Mother requested that I postpone any activities that might give rise to unkind gossip until after her wedding."

"A younger sister's duty," he observed.

"Actually, Caroline is younger than I am by several years."

His brows lifted in silence. The comment was quite enough. Fortunately, Ariel had grown all but immune to the conjecture and sympathy directed at her when people discovered Caroline had married before her.

"How long ago was that?" he asked.

"Three years. No, closer to four actually. Of course, there was the engagement to get through, several times, really, since they are both high-strung and were betrothed in fits and starts. By the time the actual event came round, I had found my way through a private tutoring maze to my position here. Right off I discerned that Mr. Penrose was in dire straits and had allowed affairs to deteriorate so sorely that he was in far greater need of a business manager than a grammar instructor. I ended up doing both."

"Let me guess, for the same pay you would have received for teaching alone?"

She gestured sheepishly. "I could hardly stand by and watch the place dwindle into bankruptcy, punishing everyone involved over a few shillings. I committed myself to staying on until matters were put right. There were also my students' needs to consider. Of course I never anticipated that my father would be afflicted so dreadfully, causing me to alter my own plans and . . . well, you know my situation at present.

Leon nodded without comment.

He had nothing to say. Her pattern of letting the needs of anyone and everyone interfere with her own desires was so outrageous, so totally alien to him, as to leave him speechless. She may not feel as if she had been used and abused and her kindness taken for granted, but he felt it on her behalf and it made him furious with people he'd never even met.

He signaled for the music teacher to begin, and the opening notes of the first piece he had selected filled the room.

Ariel's eyes grew wide when she heard the melody, as he had known they would. "A waltz?"

She was already shaking her head, as he had known she would. Ariel, he had discovered, did not like taking risks.

"Are you familiar with its form?"

"Only enough to know I do not care to become familiar."

"Don't be a prude. The waltz is now quite acceptable in the upper reaches," he assured her.

"Which is precisely why I have no need to learn it. As luck would have it, I am almost never called upon to dance in the upper reaches."

He laughed, taking her by the wrists and drawing her inexorably closer.

"What's more," she went on, "I have no reason to believe that Mr. Penrose has any desire to dance with me, much less to waltz."

"Perhaps not," he allowed, lifting her right hand to his shoulder. "But I do."

She appeared to lack a ready response to that. No argument, no alternative suggestion, no great plan for bringing him around to her way of thinking. She docilely permitted him to close his right hand over her left. With his other hand resting lightly on the small of her back, he waited for the pianist to reach the proper note and began to move.

He had known women who lied about their talent for a specific activity, downplaying it severely, so that when their true aptitude was revealed they would be the recipient of the most lavish and astounded praise.

Ariel was not one of those women.

Her dancing truly was atrocious. She was impervious to his efforts to lead her and held herself so tightly wound he felt as if he were embracing a spool of wire. Far from being discouraged, however, Leon was elated, and looked forward to the hours and hours of lessons that would obviously be required. His only regret was that he had wasted so much time before coming up with such a simple excuse to touch her and hold her the way he longed to.

The first piece ended and the second began.

"Was that so bad?" he murmured during the brief silence between.

"Yes," she retorted without looking up.

He caught her to him briefly. "Don't worry, love, it will get easier."

The start of the music precluded a reply, but Leon felt the ripple of surprise that passed through her at his familiarity and he cursed himself silently. Not for hugging her, but for calling her "love." Damn it, where had that come from? He disdained such endearments only slightly less than he did lovers' pet names. He never uttered such drivel himself and forbade any woman who shared his bed to do so. Those who transgressed found their first invitation to his chamber to be their last.

Of course, there was no accounting for what he might say or do lately. Being close to Ariel all day, every day, had incited a hunger deeper and sharper than any he had known, and now this, holding her in his arms, feeling the sway of her gently curved body, absorbing the pressure of her thighs sliding against his each time she took yet another wrong step, the sensations building and building inside him until he thought he would have to do something about it or go mad.

He used the excuse of a turn at the edge of the room to pull her even closer, savoring the contact for the scant seconds it took for her to squirm away and reestablish the proper space between them. Then he had to settle for the less tactile pleasure of the view afforded him by his greater height, an enchanting vision of the twin swells of her breasts above the gathered neckline of her deep blue dress.

Their creaminess was tinged with pink from exertion, and the desire to let his tongue explore the sweet valley between was so all-consuming that at first he did not hear the butler's attempts to gain their attention. Only when he rapped heavily and repeatedly on the open door of the drawing room did Leon lift his head.

Ariel turned at the same time.

"Excuse me, Miss Halliday, but Mr. Penrose is here to see you," Hodges announced.

Sure enough, there was the Nose, standing at Hodges's elbow in all his dubious splendor.

Leon felt Ariel go as still as death in his arms before ripping free of him, her face as guilt-ridden as if they'd been caught in flagrante delicto. With stiff fingers she smoothed the folds of her skirt.

"Thank you, Hodges," she said, running her tongue over her lips as she stepped forward to greet Penrose.

Leon frowned at the sight of her mouth, soft and wet and smiling for that pompous fool.

"Mr. Penrose, what a delightful surprise," she said. "Isn't it, Lord Sage?"

Leon said nothing, simply staring at the unwanted visitor with only a fraction of the contempt he actually felt for him as the music dwindled and died. Finally he turned to confront Ariel's desperate glare.

He glared back. "I'm sorry, were you speaking to me? I don't believe I heard you say my name."

She clenched her teeth with a warning glare. "I said, isn't it a surprise to see Mr. Penrose?"

"A stunning surprise," he agreed, but only because she had not persisted in calling him Lord Sage a second time. "Why, by my calculation it's been nearly twenty-four hours since he called last."

His sarcasm was wasted on the other man, who seemed unable to turn his head in any direction other than that which made Ariel the center of his focus. Leon felt his annoyance increase, scratching like nails at the back of his neck.

"I see you're now teaching our Lord Sage here to dance," the headmaster observed. "Splendid, splendid. I had no idea you were so accomplished, my dear lady."

"She's not," Leon told him. "It so happens I am teaching the waltz to Ariel."

"You don't say," Penrose countered, sparing him a glance at last. "My error. Though surely you can understand how I would draw such a conclusion when Miss Halliday's, that is to say," he amended, his gaze suddenly skittish, "Ariel's, movements are so smooth, so graceful, so divine."

She smiled coyly. "You flatter me, I'm sure, Mr. Penrose."

"Not at all." He cleared his throat and tugged at his cravat. "But if I might be permitted a bit of self-flattery, I'm no novice on the dance floor myself."

"Really?" Ariel responded, sounding so utterly fascinated that Leon could almost believe she meant it.

She certainly looked sincere. As sincere as she had looked when she confided in him that her desire to wed the headmaster was strictly a matter of necessity. For all he knew, she really was in love with Penrose and he was being played for a fool.

"Now it is I who must admit to being surprised," she was saying to Penrose, her tone the quietly caressing one that he himself had taught her. "I had no idea you were fond of dancing."

He'd had no idea it would sting so much to hear her use that tone with another man.

The Nose was preening. Leon couldn't help noting that Ariel's proclaimed distaste for such behavior was nowhere in evidence.

"Very fond indeed," he assured her. "In fact, I wonder if it would be too presumptuous of me to request that you take a turn around the room with me so that I might demonstrate?"

"Not at all. I would be delighted to dance with you," Ariel replied before Leon had a chance to remind the little weasel that he was interrupting them.

"Miss Earnhardt," said the Nose turning to the music teacher still seated uncertainly at the piano. "Hummel's Opus 27, if you please." To Ariel he added, "Not the latest piece, my dear, but in my humble view the best for waltzing. They played it at the Hoskinses' soiree on Saturday last," he went on, rambling even as the music began and they made their bows and moved together. "The pianist that night inserted a clever allemande. Of course, in those circles one cannot help but be . . ."

The rest of his soliloquy was mercifully lost to Leon as their mincing steps carried them to the far side of the room. He found a piece of open wall and leaned against it, arms crossed, watching.

The Nose's bony white fingers were curled like claws against the dark blue fabric of her dress. Seeing his hand there, Leon was swamped by the memory of how the supple cloth had felt to his own touch, the way it moved against her skin, and the heat of her coming through it to warm his palm. Was it his imagination, or was she having more success at following the Nose's lead than she had his?

They made one full-turn around the room and part of another before he decided he'd had all he could stomach.

"Was this your only reason for coming, then, Penrose?" he inquired loudly enough to be heard over the music. "For a dance lesson?"

"My reason?" repeated the headmaster, glancing Leon's way with obvious reluctance. "My reason . . ." He seemed to be having trouble digesting the notion. Then he stumbled as if the words had landed at his feet and tripped him. Stopping abruptly, he released Ariel and began frantically patting his coat pockets, looking aghast.

"My reason for coming. By all that's holy, I nearly forgot what it is that brought me here. The music, the dancing . . . where is my head? Where is that letter?"

He pulled a crumpled sheet of parchment from his inside pocket at last.

"The letter," he announced, waving it about triumphantly. "Just arrived by special messenger from Castleton. She's back."

"Who's back?" Leon asked, ignoring the letter that was being thrust at him.

"The marchioness. The Dowager Lady Sage. Your dearest grandmother, sir. She's heard of you, you see. The talk reached her all the way over in France, and she cut short her visit there and returned to see for herself if the rumors about you held water—her words, not mine—and—" Out of breath, he stopped and waved the letter some more. "See for yourself. It's all in here."

Ariel stepped forward and took the letter from him.

"It's true," she said, glancing quickly at it. "Lady Sage has returned to her home in London and desires that you be presented to her there forthwith." She looked up at him. "Tomorrow. Leon, she wants to meet with you tomorrow."

"Leon?" echoed Penrose, swinging a befuddled gaze from one of them to the other. "Did you call him Leon?"

Leon yawned as he came away from the wall. "It's

the dowager's loss, I'm afraid. I am otherwise engaged tomorrow."

"Engaged how?" she demanded.

"I promised to take you riding," he reminded her.

"Don't be daft," Ariel scolded. "If you gain her support, all that you have endured will have been worthwhile. Her approval is imperative if you are to claim the title. Besides, the woman is your *grandmother,* Leon. Your own flesh and blood. Think what that means. Think what this meeting could mean for you."

"For all of us," Penrose chimed in. "That is to say, relatively speaking, of course," he added when they both looked askance at him. "It's all spelled out there in the letter. Lady Sage desires to meet personally everyone involved in his lordship's miraculous transformation. As headmaster of the Penrose School, I am to be included, and naturally you are to be there too, Miss Halliday. Orders from the earl, you know. It's all there."

Ariel read further and nodded. "According to this, I am to accompany you to tomorrow's meeting and Mr. Penrose is to attend as well. Lord Castleton will call for us with his town carriage at one."

Penrose was nodding vigorously. "Just so. However, I have given the matter some thought and realize that for all we know, Castleton may be bringing along Tanner or some of the others he's in with. We shouldn't want to be squashed arriving for our presentation to Lady Sage. First impressions and all that, you know."

It was all Leon could do not to grab his scrawny neck and choke off his inane rambling.

"So," he went on, "I am offering my own fine barouche to transport myself and Miss Halliday to town. We will arrive in a cavalcade." He seemed to shiver with delight. "Most impressive."

Ariel glanced at Leon, who was clenching and

unclenching his jaw, and moved quickly to step between the headmaster and him.

"Thank you, Mr. Penrose—"

"Call me Phillip."

"Phillip, I would be pleased to share your—"

"No," Leon said, his tone slicing through her cordial reply. He strode from the room, returning in less than a minute with the Nose's hat and coat in hand. He shoved them at him, being sure to land his walking stick on top with a little jab. "Tomorrow. One o'clock. She rides with me."

Penrose thrust his arms into his coat and fled, hat and walking stick in hand. Ariel could hardly blame him. Leon's erratic demeanor and ferocious expression were so reminiscent of his behavior when he first arrived that any sane person would flee. She intended to do the same, just as soon as she'd burdened him with her opinion of his actions.

"I suppose you are happy now," she remarked the instant they were alone, Miss Earnhardt having escaped on Penrose's heels.

"Delirious. Why do you ask?"

"I ask because of your atrocious behavior toward Mr. Penrose. You were insufferably rude to the man, when he came here only to relay an important message from the earl."

"I saw the message he was relaying," he drawled, his mouth curled contemptuously. "His hands were all over you."

"Ha. His hands were no more impertinent than your own, and, indeed, if you will recall certain earlier occasions, a good deal less so."

"Signifying what?"

"Signifying . . . signifying . . ." She searched for a retort that would stand up to the cold arrogance in his gaze. "Signifying that he is a gentleman in the truest sense of the word."

"And me? What am I?" he goaded, looming over her fiercely. "A sham?"

"Yes. It is not my manner to intentionally speak ill of anyone or to hurl someone's faults in their face, but since we have come to this, I will tell you that I have seen a side of you in the past week or so that has been most baffling, sir, and which has thrown all my earlier opinions of you, both bad and good, into disarray."

"So now I am to be held accountable for your cloudy judgment?"

"It is clouded no longer," she told him. "There was a time when I believed your performance as a savage had been merely that, an act, a facade employed for your own nefarious purposes, whatever they may be. Now I see that the opposite is true. You may act the gentleman on the outside, but you are a savage at heart."

"And what," he asked, jaw rigid, "has led you to this reversal?"

"The obvious fact that you care for no one's feelings but your own. Therein lies the truest form of savagery."

"What the hell do you know of savagery?"

"I know how it feels to have my hopes built up and then cruelly dashed, ground beneath your polished heel," she cried, demonstrating by twisting the heel of her slipper against the wood floor, "as if they were of no more consequence than a speck of lint brushed from your lapel. You led me on, you pledged your help in securing Mr. Penrose's favor, and when that very thing appeared within my grasp just now, you dashed it away."

"All that simply by suggesting to him that it was time to leave?"

"Do not insult me by attempting to lessen your offense."

"I wouldn't dream of it. Only could you please name my offense directly so I might be sure I am flagellating myself for the proper reason?"

"You know what you did," she snapped. "You . . . glowered. And you stopped me from accepting his offer to join him in his barouche, when anyone can see that such an invitation would be a most positive step forward."

"I stopped you from throwing yourself at the man, you mean."

Ariel drew in a sharp breath. "I did naught but what you suggested to me."

"Well, you did it a bit too enthusiastically for my taste."

Ariel folded her arms tightly in front of her. A hot surge of frustration and something else, something much more confusing and hurtful, pressed at the back of her throat.

"I swear I cannot abide this," she said, stopping to press her lips together between sentences. "First I am criticized for being too subtle in my approach and now for being too enthusiastic. Either I'm boring and unremarkable or so outrageously forward I must be censured for it. I cannot do this. I will not. There has to be another way."

"You can do it," Leon snapped, turning his back on her struggle to regain control. Had he done as she accused? Had he ground her hopes beneath his heel when all he wanted to do was make up to her for all the hopes she'd had to abandon in her life?

He crossed the room and faced her again from that distance. "And you will do it. Now that I rethink the matter, I see you may have been right yesterday after

all. Perhaps you have piqued the man's interest."
Piqued, he thought, the little wretch had been nearly salivating as they danced.

"If that is the case," he continued, "now is the time to let the realization of his new regard for you sink in fully, by absenting yourself from his company. That was my only thought in declining his offer on your behalf."

"Without so much as consulting me?" she demanded.

"Would you have preferred I asked him to stick his fingers in his ears while we debated strategy?"

"According to your brilliant strategy, I'm now expected to charm him by staying away from him?" She rolled her eyes. "I begin to question your technique as well as your sanity."

"Do you indeed?" He approached her once more, his pace slow and ominous, his silky tone pitched low. "On what basis do you criticize my strategy, madam? Are you, perhaps, the veteran of numerous liaisons in which you have observed firsthand a man's technique?"

"Certainly not."

"Ah. Then I take it you have had the benefit of a great many purely romantic conquests to assist your judgment?"

"You know that I have not."

He stopped in front of her, only a few inches separating them. "Exactly. But I have. So if you don't mind, I think we'll go with my instincts for the time being."

"But—"

"Trust me," he said, and left.

Trust him? Ariel shook her head and wished him back there, if only to provide her with a target for her resentment. Trust him? How could she trust him when she could no longer trust even herself?

Twelve

Leon was in no mood to be presented to anyone. Most especially not to some stuffy old dowager who was no doubt expecting him to grovel and bow and jump through hoops at her behest, all in pursuit of the almighty Sage title. Well, the dowager was in for a disappointment, he mused, a smile of sardonic anticipation curving his lips as he gazed out the window of the earl's overcrowded carriage.

He shifted his weight, jockeying for shoulder room. Having been denied the pleasure of Ariel's company, the Nose had decided to squash in with the rest of them after all. They were five altogether, though Tanner, beside him, took up room enough for two and talked enough for half a dozen men. Together, he and Penrose had ensured that the headache Leon awoke with would be with him for quite some time to come.

After delivering as brief a greeting as he could get away with, he had been required to endure a lengthy warning lecture from Castleton relative to his grand-mother's likes and dislikes. It boiled down to the fact that she liked fine food, animals more than people—her pair of pet pugs in particular—and having her own way in all things. She disliked impertinence, boring conversation, and the prospect of Adam Lockaby inheriting.

Castleton added his own harsh denunciation of Lockaby. In spite of all he heard, or more likely because of it, Leon was beginning to feel a perverse kinship for the man. Better an honest enemy than a false friend, he reflected. As soon as possible, he put an end to the one-sided conversation and discouraged further overtures by turning to stare out the window at the passing scenery. It was his first decent look at London, and he was captivated in spite of himself.

Big cities cast a spell all their own, and as loathe as he was to admit it, London was one of the most lively and exhilarating he had ever seen. It spun around him like a kaleidoscope, the activity growing more frantic and colorful as they made their way from the city out-skirts toward Mayfair, where his grandmother's home was located at one of London's most prestigious ad-dresses. This according to the Nose, who was obvi-ously a connoisseur of such drivel.

Peddlers and street urchins and penny sweeps filled the streets, expertly weaving their way through the traffic and the afternoon parade of pedestrians. The pun-gent aroma of spices wafted from an open air cook stall, and the distant music of a German band was punctuated by the clatter of horseshoes on street stones. After observing a dozen mounted riders pass, Leon grudgingly conceded that if nothing else, the British were excellent judges of horseflesh.

There was one among their party whose attempts at conversation he did not have to discourage, for the simple reason that none were forthcoming. Ariel. Except for a curt greeting at breakfast that morning, she had not spoken a word to him since yesterday afternoon's shouting match. She was, he felt it safe to say, still angry with him.

Which only proved his point about women and the absolute irrationality of their emotions, he told himself. Here he was, doing his best to help her win the affections of a man he personally disdained, and she was annoyed with him for the manner in which he chose to do it.

Men were different. More treacherous and avaricious, it might be argued, but constantly so. If a man stuck a knife in your back today, he could be trusted to do the same tomorrow. There was something reassuring about that. It was also something Leon knew how to deal with. But a woman ... A woman could drive you mindless with passion by running her fingernails down your spine one moment and then use them to scratch your eyes out the next. With no predicting when or why the change would come.

He had decided long before that there was but one defense against the shifting whims of femininity and that was to never, ever lower his guard, to never let any woman get too close to him. To let a woman know she could get under your skin was to put oneself forever at her mercy, and that he would never do again.

It irked him to think how close he had come to violating his own code of aloofness yesterday. For an instant after Ariel had called him a savage, he'd seen nothing but red, as if his heart had exploded inside his head. The near loss of control alarmed him, and he still wasn't sure why he'd reacted so violently. He'd certainly been called a savage frequently enough of late that it shouldn't have left a mark.

Ariel, however, had managed to twist the knife deeper than any of the others. She had called him a savage *in his heart*. What was a savage but a beast? Could the fact that she had called it so closely mean that she knew? That somehow she had gotten near enough to see past what he wanted everyone to see, to what was hidden in his heart?

It didn't matter. He would prevail. He calculated that his advantage lay in the fact that he was objective by nature and dispassionate by choice. A study in detachment. He prided himself on it. He was the absolute master of his own emotions and never the other way around.

The carriage drew to a halt on the west side of Berkeley Square. The footmen leapt from their stations at the rear before it reached a full stop and opened the carriage doors for them to alight. Leon, seated closest to the door, went first and took advantage of the brief wait for the others to join him to inspect Lady Sage's town house for flaws. It was, he was forced to conclude after examining the stately brick front and black wrought iron terraces, a most handsome and dignified residence. Penrose appeared at this elbow, pointing out to him the home of Lord and Lady Claremont only two doors away and informing him that the king had dined at both homes on occasion. As if, thought Leon rancorously, such a thing should possibly be of interest to anyone.

Castleton led their party to the front door. They were quickly admitted by a manservant in green and gold livery and full powder, passed on to the small regiment of waiting footmen who relieved them of their coats, and finally given over to the stiff-spined butler who personally ushered them up the stairs to the salon, where "Madame" awaited.

The house's simple facade belied the ornate design of the interior. Everywhere Leon looked there was silk on satin and silver on gold. He noticed that on the velvet drapes that framed the arched windows of the upstairs hall, even the trim had trim.

The salon itself was a room of massive proportions, its high ceilings embellished with elaborate filigree and white plaster cornices that reached their full overblown glory in framing the outwardly curved bank of high windows overlooking the rear courtyard. The furnishings were of such ample design that the oversized grand piano in the corner appeared almost dainty. He turned to see Ariel gazing around in wonderment, as if she'd never seen anything quite like it. He wasn't surprised. It all struck Leon as calculatedly excessive, and as soon as he cast eyes on the dowager, he understood why.

Lady Julia Sage was a large woman, and as Castleton had forewarned, an opinionated one. The intimidating room, with its bold colors and uncompromising decor, was the perfect setting for her, and Leon was certain the arrangement was no accident. Even the chair in which she sat was positioned on a low platform built into the curve of the windows, with all the others set in a row before her, leaving no doubt as to who held court in that chamber. On either side of her was a stool topped with a fringed satin cushion. Perched on each was one of her precious pugs.

Only after taking in the ridiculously ensconced dogs did Leon notice that two of the chairs in front were also occupied. The first, he soon learned, by Lady Elizabeth Lockaby, Lady Sage's daughter and his aunt, Leon reflected grimly as he made his unsmiling bow to her. Also present was the Reverend Mr. Botts, rector of Ashbury, which straddled the border between Sage and

Devon. Botts was a squat, bald, and altogether unremarkable man who, Leon had no doubt, had been singled out by his benefactor precisely for that accommodating quality.

As they approached, he felt a slight pressure on his arm. Glancing in that direction, he saw Ariel smile reassuringly at him.

"Good luck," she said softly, her smile not enough to distract him from the concern in her blue eyes. She was worried about him, he realized, and any irritation with her he'd felt in the carriage evaporated.

I don't need luck, he wanted to tell her, but there was no time.

The introductions were handled by Castleton and Lady Sage, and included an affectionate mention by the latter of Faith and Felicity, the pugs. As soon as the stilted preliminaries had been gotten through, Lady Elizabeth Lockaby turned to her mother.

"Mother, as you know, I question the very necessity of arranging for this little meeting." She paused for a pointed glance in Leon's direction, her long, narrow face dour beneath a cap of crimped hair the dullish color of soot and ash. "But as you seem, for some unfathomable reason, to have your heart set on giving credence to what amounts to no more than a ridiculous rumor of—"

"For heaven's sake, Elizabeth, if you have something to say, spit it out," ordered the dowager.

"I only want to urge you to reserve any discussion of consequence until Adam arrives," her daughter concluded in a rush.

"Why should I delay anything for the arrival of someone who wasn't invited?"

Lady Lockaby blanched. "Adam not invited? But he's your only grandson."

"Yes, yes, and he was here with you at Christmas-time and will, I suppose, have to be welcomed for that same occasion again next year," she added with an obvious dearth of enthusiasm. "If I don't have to endure his endless, overzealous prattle again until then, I shall be well pleased indeed."

"May I remind you that this is hardly a social occasion, Mother? But a meeting that could, if certain clever and ambitious individuals have their way," she said, her quick glare at the earl and Sir Tanner accompanied by a haughty sniff, "have a devastating effect on matters of a strictly private family nature."

"The membership of the House of Lords is hardly a family matter," Castleton pointed out.

Lady Lockaby whirled on him, venomous in defense of her absent cub. "You have your seat there, Castleton," she hissed at him. "Concern yourself with that and leave my son alone."

"Gladly, dear lady. Provided he pledge to do the same toward me and all that I hold dear in this great country of ours."

"Hear, hear," cried Tanner enthusiastically.

"Enough," decreed Lady Sage, her irate tone causing the pugs to growl in unison. "I should have followed my own counsel to leave out the lot of you and handle this myself. I'll do so yet if you don't cease. Now, be seated, all of you," she ordered, dismissing the butler with no request for refreshments, obliterating any lingering illusion Leon might be harboring that he was there to be entertained rather than inspected.

She wasted no time getting started.

"You," she said to Leon. "Come closer, where I can get a decent look at you."

He stepped forward, stopping directly in front of her, where the light from the windows was brightest, and silently withstood her frank, unhurried perusal. He entertained himself by returning the favor. He gauged Lady Sage to be in her early seventies, and with a figure that in a man of the same age would be kindly referred to as substantial. She had keen green eyes and a reddish tint to her hair that flattered her healthy complexion and did not foolishly aspire to appear natural, and though she was not smiling, Leon noted that the laugh lines around her mouth and eyes were deep and many.

"You're not at all what I expected," she said at last with a dismissive wave of her hand.

"Nor you I," Leon countered. "But if you'll tell me what it is about my person that displeases you, perhaps I can rearrange it to suit. Would you prefer me shorter? Taller? With a broader jaw, or fewer arms perhaps?"

"Your impertinence displeases me," she snapped, but her sharp gaze reflected interest and not displeasure.

"My apologies," he murmured with a negligent bow of his head. "I regret if you mistook for impertinence my eagerness to please."

"Your apology is accepted in spite of my overriding suspicion that the only person you are eager to please is yourself."

He unleashed a slow, infallible smile. "My single fault, madam. Since you've seen through me so quickly, I feel at ease to say that what pleases me now is to take my seat."

Tossing in another offhand bow for good measure, he moved to join the others. A quick glance along the row to his left revealed the array of expressions to be exactly what he would have predicted. Castleton and Penrose looked aghast, Tanner wickedly amused, and Lady Lockaby smug bordering on triumphant. The rector didn't count because he appeared to be dozing. Ariel, the only one whose reaction mattered to him at all, seemed to be caught between laughter and uncertainty. Hoping to encourage the first, Leon gave her a wink.

"It is a devilishly long haul up those stairs," he remarked after settling himself comfortably.

"Are you infirm?" Lady Sage inquired suspiciously.

"No, merely lazy."

She leaned forward sharply, like a duelist preparing to lunge. "That's two faults."

"Do you really think so?" He gave an indifferent shrug. "From my observations, I'd rather thought indolence a prerequisite for a title."

"And that is what you seek? The title of Marquis of Sage?"

"It would be more accurate to say that it sought me," he observed dryly.

Lady Sage drew back, eyeing him thoughtfully, and evidently elected not to lock swords just yet. Her gaze passed down the row to the Nose and Ariel instead.

"Mr. Penrose, Miss Halliday, I understand that you two are responsible for the comportment of this man?"

Penrose stammered and shrank in his seat, recognizing a trick question when he heard one.

"Yes, Lady Sage," Ariel replied, her voice striking the first true, clear note Leon had heard uttered in the room. "Mr. Penrose provided guidance and oversight, but I handled everything that was done on a day-to-day basis. It follows that any failing you might find is attributable to me alone."

"I see," replied Lady Sage, studying Ariel more closely. "If that's so, and one tenth of the stories that reached me abroad are true, you are a most remarkable woman."

Ariel bowed her head sheepishly, feeling the prick of her guilty conscience, no doubt, thought Leon.

"Thank you, ma'am," she murmured.

The dowager, revitalized, set her sights on Leon once again.

"So, you were raised in the Sandwich Islands, were you?"

"No. Hawaii."

"Is there a difference?"

"There is to a Hawaiian."

"And to an Englishman?"

"I wouldn't know about that."

"How so? When you freely call yourself a Duvanne, do you not?"

He lifted one broad shoulder slightly. "I seldom call myself by any name at all, but it's true that I answer to that one readily enough."

"And yet you sit there and boldly deny the country of your father's birth?"

"If I had a father, Lady Sage, I have no personal knowledge of the man, much less a certainty of what country he called home."

There was an indignant gasp from Lady Lockaby's end of the row. "Mother, really. I cannot believe that you intend to sit there and allow this—"

"Please, Lady Sage," entreated the earl, on his feet at once and sounding shaken. His trained savage was not performing up to expectations, thought Leon with great satisfaction. "Let me explain to you that what he means to say—"

"Sit down, Castleton," she ordered, at the same time quieting her daughter with a look. "It strikes me that the man demonstrates no lack of ability to say precisely what he means. On the contrary, he does a better job of it than most I'm burdened with around here. Let him speak for himself."

"Thank you, madam," said Leon.

She nodded. "Now then, you were saying⸮ About your father⸮"

"I believe I was saying that I had nothing to say about him."

"Humph. And your mother ... Monique something-or-other, I believe⸮"

There was a quick, painful wrench in his chest, the same one that accompanied any mention or thought of his mother. It was a weakness he'd once expected to outgrow, and having failed that, had learned to live with. He waited for it to pass before replying.

"My mother died when I was very young."

"Yes, of course, I was told that. How young exactly⸮"

"Six."

"Not an infant surely. And yet you remember nothing of her either⸮" she pressed, her expression openly skeptical.

"I remember a little."

"Tell me what you remember of her."

"I remember that she loved your son enough to die for him."

Leon was aware of the heavy silence that fell over the room and seemed to enclose the dowager and him like ropes strung around a boxing ring.

Folding her hands on the pillow of her lap, she said, "Will you tell me how she died⸮"

"I'm not entirely certain. I was watching from the shore, some distance away. She always made me wait there whenever she rowed out to the edge of the cove with the other villagers to greet an incoming British ship. She thought I would be safer onshore and," he said, his small smile brittle, "she was right."

"Please go on," encouraged Lady Sage. "Why on earth would anyone bother to row out to meet an inbound ship?"

"The others wanted to be the first to reach the foreigners. They filled their canoes with whatever they had to offer and pulled up as close to the ship as they dared, eager to trade for silk and mirrors and other worthless, shiny trinkets." He paused to rein in his simmering bitterness, thinking it might have been a mistake to get into this now. "My mother went out with them to search the row of strange men's faces hanging over the rail, hoping to see one particular Englishman. Your son. He had given her his solemn promise that he would return, and she believed him."

"I see," said Lady Sage, her thin lips barely moving. "I regret that an accident befell your mother, but—"

"It was no accident," he declared. He got to his feet, too agitated to sit. The pugs watched him as he paced a few feet and then turned. "I am sure of that much. But the rest is in doubt. You see, from where I stood it was impossible for me to tell if she drowned after she and the others were knocked from the canoe with the butt of a British firearm, or if she burned to death after the sailors poured kerosene on them and set them afire."

The horrified gasp he heard clearly over the shocked murmurs came from Ariel. He was certain of it, though for some reason he didn't trust himself right then to turn and confront the anguish and the pity he was sure he would see in her eyes.

"Afterward," he went on, determined that since he had started, they would hear it all. "Afterward, the water in the cove ran red with blood. It stained the sand and my legs up to my knees, which was as deep as I was allowed to go in by myself, and I waited. I waited there until the screaming had stopped and the men from the village had dragged in all the bodies that the tide didn't carry away." His eyes were dark and glinting, still focused on the windows behind the dowager but seeing only the past.

"There were rows and rows of them," he said, "some with no clothes, some with no faces. Or worse. I walked up and down the rows all night, and I waited, but if her body ever washed to shore, I never found it."

He tossed his head and drew a deep breath, using all his will to force the stiffness from his clenched muscles, reclaiming the air of nonchalance that he had honed to perfection in the years since that day.

"That," he said to Lady Sage, "is how my mother died."

"Mon Dieu," she whispered, her soft face pale. He heard the others behind him echo that grossly ineffectual sentiment.

"But why?" she asked him. "Why?"

"Retaliation," he replied, shrugging. "Revenge for something that had happened at another stop in another village a week earlier. Mostly, however, simply to teach the 'savages' a lesson. To put the fear of the almighty British in them so they wouldn't try to interfere with the ships as they pulled in to steal from them. Official policy, you know, the best defense is a good offense."

"Now, see here, Sage," Castleton said, getting to his feet with an indignant frown. "I won't have you—"

He was interrupted by a sudden commotion at the door as it was flung open and a man charged into the salon, shouting too frantically to be clearly understood. He was being chased by the same butler who had shown them in earlier, looking considerably more spry now, Leon observed. Instantly the pugs were off their perches and into the fray.

They ran laps around the two men as they approached, yapping and lunging until one of them, Felicity, he believed, though it was hard to tell, latched on to the calf of the intruder. The man howled a most ungentlemanlylike oath and shook his leg fiercely in an unsuccessful attempt to dislodge the tenacious little dog.

"Land's sake, Adam, hold still," Lady Sage shouted. The man was younger than Leon expected, very young to have generated so much ill will. "You'll only excite her more with all that shaking about. Felicity, my sweetling," she cooed. "Come to Mummy. Faith, come here, that's my angel."

Faith obediently reclaimed her post by her mistress's side, but Felicity appeared to be in it for the long haul, thought Leon. It occurred to him that the wisest course might be to forget any thoughts of forming an unholy alliance with Lockaby and throw in with the pugs instead.

The frenzied skirmish continued until the man finally reached down and backhanded the dog across the snout. Felicity released with a yelp and scurried away, ending up tangled in the ruffle of the embroidered cloth draped over a small table.

"Now see what you've done," Lady Sage admonished Lockaby. "She's upset."

"So am I," the young man growled, stooping to rub his lower leg where she had bitten clean through his stocking.

"Bring her to me," she directed him.

"Me bring her?" he countered, incredulous. "So she can rip into my other leg? If you're so fond of the mutt, why don't you—"

"Adam," said his mother sharply. When he looked

her way, she thrust out her jaw several times to indicate that he should do as he was told. With obvious reluctance he gritted his teeth and slowly moved in the direction of the dog.

"Be gentle," warned his grandmother with what sounded like an undercurrent of amusement. That in turn amused Leon. He liked the old fox, he decided on the spot. Under different circumstances he suspected he could become very fond of her indeed. "I'm sure this has been trying for the little dear," she added.

Lockaby hunkered down and called the dog by name. He whistled, patted the floor, and got on his hands and knees to try to cajole her from her hiding place as his mother stood by offering insipid suggestions. Felicity's only response was to stare at him with wounded eyes.

After enjoying the spectacle for several moments, Leon stepped forward to help.

"Leon Duvanne," he said, extending his hand to the other man.

Lockaby looked up, hesitating before taking his hand and shaking it. "Lockaby," he said curtly.

"Mind if I give it a try?" Leon asked him, indicating the dog.

He gave Leon a look that said he was the last person he wanted help from. Then, red-faced from exertion, he took another look at the crouching dog.

"Be my guest," he said, eagerly withdrawing.

Leon hunkered down beside the table and murmured to the dog in the island dialect that rolled easily from his tongue. Felicity picked up her ears. He kept it up, speaking softly and moving slowly as he slid his hand steadily closer to her. When it was only inches away, the dog lowered her head and sniffed his fingers.

Immediately her stubby tail began to twitch and her tongue came out to lick him happily. Even Leon was surprised by the fervor of her response until he remembered that he'd been petting Prinny before setting out. Evidently Felicity was fond of rabbits.

Confident she was his friend for life, he scooped her up and carried her to Lady Sage, who thanked him briefly and fussed over Felicity for several minutes before returning her to her perch.

The crisis past, the butler stepped forward.

"My apologies, madam," he said to Lady Sage. "I explained to Sir Lockaby that you were unable to receive callers, but he refused—"

"I understand," she said, waving him away. She turned to her grandson. "I realize, Adam, that you find not to your liking much of what holds polite society together, but I had thought that even you tolerated the concept of private property. Or have you rounded even that bend in your steady descent into radical lunacy and decided you have some innate right to force yourself in wherever you please, invited or not?

"Not at all," he replied. "It so happens my mother invited me to be here."

Lady Sage swung a scathing look in her daughter's direction.

"What choice did I have?" whined the younger woman. "I was afraid to rely on you to inform him of what you were doing, and I can see my fear was justified. Adam has a right to be here."

"Adam has no rights here."

"Only because you've been dillying and dallying about signing the inheritance papers. First you're too upset and then you're off on your everlasting travels. If you weren't my own mother, I'd swear you knew something like this savage business would crop up and you were stalling on purpose for your own entertainment."

Lady Sage regarded her drolly. "Why should being your mother interfere with my entertainment any more than absolutely necessary?"

Lady Lockaby huffed and exchanged a long-suffering look with her son.

Adam Lockaby was nearly Leon's height and sturdily built, with dark eyes unusual in one with his fair complexion and pale hair. He didn't look to be the demonic threat to the empire that Leon had been warned of. In fact, if first impressions could be trusted, he appeared to be rather unsure of himself and, at least at the moment, sadly henpecked.

"Since you've gone to such painful lengths to be here," Lady Sage said to him, "I suppose you can stay." She nodded for him to sit and he did so with a triumphant swagger, apparently oblivious of the mockery in his grandmother's tone. The others slowly reclaimed their seats as well, until only she and Leon remained standing.

"Try to amuse yourselves," she told them. "I desire to speak with Mr. Duvanne in the library. Privately," she added before any of them could make a move to join them.

Leon followed her from the salon to the library that adjoined, walking behind her canine honor guard. The library was a stark contrast to the salon. It was softly lit and smelled pleasant, the aroma coming from the hundreds of books that lined the walls and, if he wasn't mistaken, good cigars. Here, too, the furniture was comfortably ample, but the soft fabrics and subtle colors were much easier on the eye. It would be a serious mistake, he mused, for a man to draw conclusions too quickly about Lady Sage.

"Vultures," she muttered, shutting the door tightly behind them. "Picking at me from both ends, conniving to get the old lady to do what they want her to do. You might as well know right now, young man, I do what I want to do."

"So do I," he told her, their gazes locking in silence before she gave a slow nod.

"Good." She moved to the desk in the corner of the room and flipped open an engraved mahogany box. "Cigar?" she offered, holding up a cheroot.

Leon grinned. "I knew I smelled fine tobacco."

"The best. They're Garcias," she informed him. "Cuban. They're shipped to Port Isaac and I have a man there who brings them to me the first of each month like clockwork. I acquired the taste in France."

"So did I," he told her, accepting the cigar.

Lady Sage expertly trimmed the tip of hers with a small clipper produced from her pocket, then passed it to Leon so that he could do the same. They lit up and retired to the massive wing chairs flanking the fireplace, all without speaking a word that might interfere with the pleasurable moment.

"Excellent," he told her, savoring the first mellow taste.

She nodded, looking as pleased by the compliment as if she'd harvested the tobacco herself. After another moment or so of silence she said, "Elizabeth doesn't approve."

"Which, I imagine, adds immensely to your enjoyment."

She threw back her head and laughed out loud,

confirming his earlier conjecture about the origin of the lines she sported about her eyes and mouth. It was impossible for Leon not to laugh along with her.

She gazed at him afterward, her smile slowly fading and taking on a wistful cast.

"You favor my father when you laugh," she told him.

The quiet comment caught Leon off guard.

"That's right," she said, observing his reaction. "I have no doubt that you are who they say you are. The resemblance to your own father is very slight, but it's there. You are most appallingly handsome, you know."

"Thank you. I think," he murmured.

"My son was not nearly so good-looking, but then, perhaps your mother contributed in that regard."

"My mother was a very beautiful woman."

"I'm sure she was," she told him, her voice suddenly gentle. "And I am deeply sorry for the manner of her loss."

He nodded without comment.

"I only wish I could have . . . well, that's neither here nor there at this late date. So," she went on crisply, "you are my grandson. Since I make it a rule never to try to fool myself, I must accept the truth, at least within these four walls. What I decide to acknowledge publicly is an entirely different matter." She sighed. "You do present me with a thorny dilemma."

"How to proceed without offending Sir Adam and your daughter."

The dowager snorted. "That's the least of it. Thanks to your father's clever management of funds, I can well afford the price of my daughter's continued goodwill, even if I decide to thwart her in this. As for Adam, he's not fit for the title, or he'd have it already. Elizabeth is correct when she says I have been delaying intentionally, but not without good reason. You see, Castleton is not the only one your father confided in upon his deathbed."

"He spoke to you of me?" Leon asked, loathing the fact that he cared even enough to ask.

She nodded. "For the first time ever, and at great length. He spoke of your mother as well and of ... regrets. I was stunned by his revelations, to say the least. Perhaps the day will come when I feel free to share his thoughts with you."

"Thank you, but I feel certain the day will never come when I am interested in hearing them."

It should have made him feel good to say that, to at last have the satisfaction of rejecting, even in a small way, the man who had rejected him. But he did not feel satisfied. He felt hollow. The part of him that would always remain a scared, lonely six-year-old boy longed to hear the reasons and the explanations and the excuses that the rest of him understood could never make up for a lifetime of betrayal.

"Never is a long time," she said in a soothing voice. "Perhaps you will change your mind, perhaps not. My uncertainty about you only increases my quandary. I know exactly the threat that Adam presents, you see."

"Yes, I know as well. He's a radical who wants to bring down the empire by feeding the hungry and paying a man an honest wage for an honest day's labor."

"You've been listening to Castleton."

"I've had damned little choice recently."

She chuckled. "Some would say you deserve the title on those grounds alone." She puffed her cigar. "Castleton is a good man, but he has a tendency to panic far too easily. Deep down, like most of us, he understands the need for change."

"Of course," he agreed, a heavy note of sarcasm in his voice, "but let it come on the nobility's terms."

"Let it come in doses we can all digest," she shot back. "Those who would push too hard, too fast, will create a mess no one will be able to stomach. A little something else I picked up from the French," she added, the crafty glint in her eye unmistakable.

"Adam is guilty of pushing too hard, too fast, is that it?"

"Adam himself is harmless," she retorted. "It is his misfortune that he has been coddled by his mother his entire life and as a result has trouble standing on his own two feet even on a windless day."

"And that is your reason for denying him the title?" he challenged.

"I *may* deny him the title," she responded, "because his spinelessness makes him far too easily influenced. It is a regrettable trait that I have high hopes he will over-come if forced to make his own way in the world. In the meantime, if given a platform in the House of Lords to spout the radical philosophy that is his cause of the moment, he will only help to drown out the voices of those who have been bravely working to bring about necessary reform. Men like your father," she added pointedly.

Leon sat in stony silence. If Giles Duvanne had good points, he didn't want to hear about them.

His grandmother ignored his lapse in manners. "Your father was well aware of the dangerous pressures that would be brought to bear on Adam if he inherited the title and the fortune that goes with it, and he knew the boy was not seasoned enough to withstand it.

Someday Adam will understand that it was to protect him, as well as the Sage name, that he acted as he did. Family was very important to your father."

Leon laughed out loud. "Was it really? Not *all* family apparently. To protect his poor, spineless nephew, he was willing to toss his own son to the wolves."

"Ha. Something tells me that if you were ever tossed to the wolves, the wolves would soon be sorry."

"Perhaps that's true. But he could not have known it when he sent his goons to kidnap me and drag me here."

"You're right. He had no idea what kind of man you were. But he knew you were your mother's son, and his, and so he told me he decided to do what he should have done thirty years ago." She leaned forward, refusing to let him escape her steely gaze. "He listened to his heart. Now it's time for you to listen to yours."

Leon stood and crushed his cigar into the glass tray on the desk.

"Impossible," he told her. "I don't have a heart."

She chortled, stealing a great deal of his righteous indignation.

"All the better," she said. "*If* it proves to be true. For now, we'll listen to mine, and my heart tells me your father was right on the money."

She lifted the cigar to her lips and held it there without taking a puff, her lined face settling into a shrewd frown. "Of course, as you will no doubt learn, the beau monde as a whole does not share my easy, accommodating spirit."

Leon's brows shot up. Easy and accommodating? Determined and shamelessly manipulative was more like it.

"It won't be easy," she continued, "but somehow I shall have to devise a way to see you Marquis of Sage without jeopardizing my standing at Almack's this season."

T h i r t e e n

Ariel felt as if she were marooned on a tiny island of neutral territory between two enemy camps. On her left sat Sir Adam, looking ill-tempered and impatient as his mother whispered feverishly in his ear. On her right, in a conspiratorial huddle of their own, were the earl and Sir Tanner, leaving her, for all intents and purposes, alone with Mr. Penrose.

He seemed not at all displeased with the situation and talked to her incessantly and in far more amicable fashion than in all the years she had known him. It was precisely the sort of opportunity she had been hoping for and plotting to bring about for months now, and if she could have dropped a pail over his head to shut him up she would have done so without hesitation. Fortunately he required little by way of response, no more than an occasional nod or smile. She was far too preoccupied to actually pay attention to what he was saying.

Her feelings were in turmoil. On the one hand, she

was proud of Leon for refusing to be intimidated there today. At the same time, she worried that his own stubborn pride would blind him to what was best for his future. All the way there she had told herself she shouldn't even care what happened to him after his despicable behavior toward her the previous day. She did care, however. She had not realized how much until she had been forced to sit and listen to him describe the nightmare of his mother's death.

Once she had worried about breaking his spirit. Now she blamed herself for not having seen how tormented that reckless spirit was, and for having played a role in reopening old wounds.

She suspected that in Leon's eyes, his mother had been taken from him long before the day he watched her climb into that canoe and row away. She had loved him, that was obvious to Ariel from things Leon had told her, but she had been young and heartbroken, pining for a man who had promised her he would return and never did. No doubt it must have seemed to Leon that his mother loved that mythical man more than she did her own son.

Loved him enough to die for him, those were his words. Leaving him all alone, with neither father nor mother, his English blood making him an outsider in his own homeland. It was little wonder he hated England.

She had a feeling that Leon had not acted the part of a savage, or remained there when he could easily have left, or agreed to today's presentation to the dowager duchess because he had a deep yearning for either the Sage title or the spoils that it would bring him. She had no proof of what she was feeling, but the suspicion alone was a cold, hard knot in her belly. Something warned her that Leon didn't want the title at all. He wanted revenge.

At last, when she thought she could not endure waiting another second or force even one more interested nod for Mr. Penrose's benefit, the door opened and they reappeared. A hush fell over the room as Lady Sage reclaimed her seat before them. Leon stood beside her at the edge of the platform, his gaze immediately seeking Ariel's. He gave her that faint smile that hinted at things untame and which, she had learned, could signify any number of things, none of them particularly reassuring to her at that moment.

"I have reached a decision," Lady Sage announced without preamble.

Elizabeth Lockaby gasped, and Ariel felt her own stomach seesaw apprehensively. She wasn't sure what she had expected the outcome of their private meeting to be, but this was not it. Her gaze swung to Leon, but he did not look anxious in the least. On the contrary, he appeared insolently at ease. Was that because he knew he was about to be named Marquis of Sage? she wondered. Or because he knew he wasn't?

Regardless, she flashed him her most encouraging smile, only half hearing Lady Lockaby's indignant protest that Adam ought to be granted a private audience before any decisions were made.

"Quiet," Lady Sage ordered. "I know all I need to know of Adam, I assure you. Now then, my decision involves a sword that has been in the Duvanne family for seven generations."

Castleton nearly came out of his chair. "A sword? What has a sword to do with—"

"This sword was carried by the first Marquis of Sage at the Battle of Sedgemoor," she continued over him, only to be interrupted a second time by her daughter.

"Mother, Sedgemoor was nearly two centuries ago and—"

"And the legend," Lady Sage went on doggedly, "is that when cut off from the two regiments supporting him and facing certain death at the hands of the invaders, Sage held on through the night and just before dawn raised high his sword as he prayed for the strength and the courage to mount one final, desperate assault."

She looked around, clearly warming to her role as storyteller. Ariel found curiosity slowly overtaking her anxiety.

"It was then that he saw three suns on the still-dark horizon, hovering just above the tip of his sword so that it appeared to glow like a flame against the night sky. The marquis took it to be a sign that he should wait for sunrise to strike and that if he did, the separated regiments would again be there to flank him. He waited, and when he struck, they were with him.

"Afterward he learned that it had taken his men all night to regain their position, falling into place only minutes before he charged into what otherwise would have been certain annihilation. From that day forward that same basket-handled sword accompanied the Duvanne men into battle, and it has never once failed the men who wielded it in defense of right and honor."

"An inspiring tale to be sure, madam," said the earl, "but, if I might be frank, I fail to see how it relates to the problem at hand. Namely—"

"Namely," Lady Sage interrupted, "the question of who is most worthy to be installed as the next Marquis of Sage."

"Precisely."

"And I say, who better to claim the title than the man who can lay claim to the family sword?"

"But the sword is hidden away, God only knows where," her daughter reminded her impatiently, "and has been for years and years. You left out that little bit of the family legend."

"It is hidden, to be sure," Lady Sage agreed. "In Devon I should think. Perhaps even within the very walls of Restormel. The exact whereabouts has always been a closely guarded secret, passed down along with the sword from father to son. At least that was the case until the regrettable situation we are faced with now. However, the title must be passed on, and since I have determined that there are two possible candidates, each of whom—"

"Two? You can't mean—"

Lady Sage lifted both hands in disgust. "By my word, Elizabeth, if you interrupt me one more time, I will have you gagged. As there are two candidates, I have decided to follow the good example of the first man to bear this title and trust the power of the sword to reveal which of these two men should be the next marquis. Simply put," she concluded, looking from Adam Lockaby to Leon, "the one of you who brings me the Sage sword will be assured of my support for his claim."

"But first we have to find the bloody thing, is that it?" Lockaby blurted out.

"That would seem the logical place to start," his grandmother agreed dryly. "Naturally you are both welcome to stay at Restormel should you decide to search near there. Who knows? You might even find you enjoy each other's company."

"Duvanne can suit himself, but I decline your most generous offer," Lockaby retorted, making no effort to blunt his sarcasm. "I have numerous friends in the area who will be only too happy to extend their hospitality, I'm sure. Mark this, the next night I spend at Restormel will be as lord of the manor."

He left the room in a huff, his mother at his heels. Ariel, not yet certain if the dowager's challenge was good news for Leon or very bad, found encouragement in the exchange between him and Lady Sage, which she overheard as they took their leave a few minutes later.

"The arrangements we discussed?" Leon queried softly as he made his parting bow. He spoke to her easily, as if there had been "arrangements" being made between them for years.

"I'll see to it by the close of business today," the dowager had replied. "You have my word on it."

At the very least, it appeared the two of them had hammered out the beginning of some sort of relationship. While Ariel couldn't predict what that might mean for the dowager and the eventual marquis, whoever it might be, it seemed to bode well for grandmother and grandson. She couldn't help thinking that for Leon, that may prove to be far more important.

In the carriage, Leon alone appeared totally undaunted by the prospect of locating the infamous sword before Lockaby did. He evidently intended to follow the dowager's advice and begin his search at Restormel and to take advantage of her invitation to stay at Restormel, the Sage estate. After Castleton and Tanner had been dropped off, he questioned Mr. Penrose extensively about the trip from London to Devon. Were the roads macadamized all the way to the coast? Would it be quicker to travel by private coach or in a rented hack that would include provisions for fresh horses along the way?

He didn't share his final plans with Penrose, but as soon as they arrived back at the cottage he summoned Farrell to ask if he knew where to arrange for a hired chaise to take him to Restormel.

Farrell stood a respectful distance away from Leon, as Ariel had observed he always did these days, and nodded. "Aye. The White Horse in Piccadilly would be as good a place as any."

"Then see to it straightaway. Specify that I want their four best horses and a driver who is both fast and steady." In a wry drawl he added, "I should like to arrive this year, and with my neck intact."

"I'll say so to them. Should I handle it from the household account, sir?" Farrell asked.

She was surprised to see Leon shake his head firmly. "No. From now on I'll bear full responsibility for my own expenses. You may secure the agreement with household funds for the moment, but I will provide you with a private draft by day's end."

Well, that would appear to explain the nature of his "arrangements" with his grandmother, mused Ariel, her curiosity increased rather than sated. She must have agreed to advance him funds. Was it a loan? And if so, how had he secured it? Or was Lady Sage confident that he was a safe risk because she had sound reason to believe he would soon be inheriting the Sage fortune?

"When should I say you'll be leaving, sir?" she heard Farrell ask, pulling her from her own thoughts.

"As soon as possible," Leon replied. "Tomorrow afternoon at the latest."

Ariel turned and left the room with a sudden tightness in her chest.

So it was over at last, or would be in a matter of

hours. She was relieved, she told herself. Vastly so.
Now she could get back to her own life at last. Which,
all in all, was looking more promising than it had a few
weeks earlier. The recent change in Mr. Penrose's
demeanor toward her could be interpreted only as an
encouraging sign. It was exactly what she had hoped
for, Ariel reminded herself without managing to produce so much as a speck of satisfaction, much less joy.

She spent the afternoon in her room, working on a
piece of embroidery. Then deciding that her last
evening together with Leon was an occasion of sorts,
she dressed carefully for dinner. But when she reached
the drawing room, she was informed by Farrell that *his
lordship* wished him to relay his regrets that he would
be away for the evening.

Ariel's first reaction was panic. He was gone.
Escaped. She quickly reined in her fear, reminding herself that Leon was neither prisoner nor child. Nor, she
supposed, was he any longer her responsibility. He was
a grown man, and as such free to go out for the evening
if he so desired.

But where on earth would he go? And why?

It was not her concern, she tried telling herself over
and over as she picked her way through dinner and
then tried to pass the evening reading and catching up
on letters to friends. She retired early and lay awake listening for the sound of his return. Her thoughts were
divided between speculating on where he might be and
where the Sage sword might be hidden. The latter
problem being the one *he* ought to be concerned about
this evening, she thought, instead of being off for himself, gadding about heaven only knew where.

Not that it mattered to her where he went. Or with
whom. Or if he beat Lockaby to the sword.

Still, purely as an intellectual exercise, she couldn't

resist thinking about how she would undertake the search if it were up to her. She lay in bed organizing lists in her head, enumerating the stages of the search and the materials that would be needed and all the potential pitfalls Leon might encounter along the way.

All right, she conceded at last, so she was a bit concerned about the outcome. After all, she had yet to be formally relieved of her task, and she had never been one for ignoring her responsibilities. See a job through to the end, that was her motto.

With that in mind, she added one final item to her mental list of things Leon must bring with him to Restormel.

"We missed your company at dinner last evening," she remarked over breakfast the next morning, the smile she sent him across the table as sweetly subtle as she'd decided her approach should be.

Leon regarded her over the piece of toast he was about to bite into, his dark brows lifting. "We?"

"I suppose I should have said I missed you. Missed your company, that is," she added, aware that the hasty qualification had brought a gleam of amusement to his gold eyes. "Though it was unfortunate that given such late notice, Mrs. Farrell did trouble herself to cook for two as customary."

"To Prinny's benefit, I trust." He took a bite of his bacon. "Have you noticed how fond he's become of table scraps?"

"I've noticed how you spoil him by always saving some of your meal for him. He'll miss you when you're gone."

"No, he won't. He's coming with me."

"To Restormel?" she queried, piqued that he'd thought to include the rabbit in his plans and not her.

The amusement in his eyes spread to his mouth, lifting the corners in a lopsided smile. "Why not? Don't they allow rabbits at Restormel? Not that it matters, since I'll soon be deciding what is and is not allowed there, assuring Prinny of a place of honor."

It was Ariel's turn to lift her brows speculatively. "Are you so certain of your success?"

"I am."

"May I inquire whether your confidence is a result of your activities last evening?"

"You may." He grinned. "The answer is no."

"I see. I thought perhaps you might have ventured out to discuss strategy with Lord Castleton and his friends."

"God, no. I'd hardly go seeking new opportunities, to be bored in the same old way."

Ariel smiled cordially and sipped her tea. So, whatever his activities of last evening, they were not to be classified as boring. How very . . . intriguing. She patted her lips with her napkin, rearranged the knife on her plate, and chose her words carefully.

"Well then, I hope that however you passed the time, you found it to be enjoyable."

"Very much so, thank you."

He was laughing at her.

Let him. She was too intrigued to care.

"And productive," she added.

"That too."

Now what? There had to be a way to find out what she wanted to know without asking him directly, like some shrew demanding he account for his time. Never mind that that's exactly what she was doing, and they both knew it, Ariel refused to give him the satisfaction of admitting that she was interested enough to ask.

"You don't have to beat about the bush with me, you know," he said.

She looked up from the absent drumming of her fingers on the table to find him watching her with an indulgent smile. "I beg your pardon?"

"I said—"

"I heard you. Judging by your responses, I rather thought that beating around the bush was the order of the day."

"It doesn't have to be. If you're so obsessed with knowing where I was last evening, just come straight out and ask me."

"Me? Obsessed?" She appeared befuddled. "I'm sure I do not know where you got such an idea."

"I'm not exactly sure myself," he countered, laughter lurking in his deep voice. "It must have been either the questions you've been firing at my head like buckshot or that mysterious green tinge to your complexion this morning."

"I do not have a tinge, green or otherwise," she said, shaking her head as if he were too ridiculous to be believed. "Was your remark somehow meant to suggest that I am jealous over whatever it was you were involved with last night?"

"Or whomever," he countered smoothly, a blackguard enjoying himself thoroughly. At her expense.

"Well, I'm not. Please pass the jam."

He handed over the small crock of strawberry preserves, accompanied by a pirate's smile. "Then you're not interested in hearing all the fascinating details of my assignation last evening?"

"Not in the least." She smeared jam on a piece of

scone as if it were her mortal enemy. "I was merely endeavoring to show a polite attention to your activities."

"Liar."

The word was a soft, insidious challenge.

Ariel tossed down the scone and opened her mouth to deny the charge, and could not. That exotic, searing gaze that seemed to see all the way to her soul wouldn't let her.

"All right. Maybe I was concerned about where you had gone last evening. Can you blame me? London is a dangerous place if you don't know the spots to avoid. The truth is—" She gripped the edges of the table. "The truth is I was worried sick about you, you great, thoughtless oaf. I couldn't sleep picturing you clunked on the head and left in some dark alley somewhere to bleed to death. Or worse."

"If there's anything worse than clunked and bleeding, I'm sure I don't know what it is," Leon said, managing to maintain a teasing posture in spite of the way everything inside him was spinning out of control.

She had been worried about him.

He couldn't begin to absorb the sheer, unprecedented wonder of someone caring where he went or what he did or what might happen to him while he was doing it.

He had been amused by her curiosity about his whereabouts last night, and charmed by the delicate but determined way she went about finding out what she wanted to know. Like a terrier with silk teeth. It was so typically Ariel, he thought, an unfamiliar tugging sensation near his heart.

For all his vast experience with women, that sort of friendly sparring over breakfast was new to him. He never allowed questions about his personal affairs and couldn't quite believe that not only was he permitting

Ariel to question him, but, to his amazement, was finding the process quite enjoyable. Of course, he had no intention of admitting to her where he had gone the evening before or why. In that way their lively exchange had reminded him of a fencing match. He'd admired her skill as an adversary, but never doubted he was in control. At least not until the very end, when she had appeared to go all soft and vulnerable, only to rally and deliver the final lunge by announcing she had been worried about him.

I was concerned . . . Concerned enough, he dared to wonder, to come with him to Restormel? It was one thing to toss the rabbit in a cage and haul him halfway across the country. Ariel, he was certain, would have to be approached with a great deal more finesse. Maybe even more finesse than he had at his disposal. That's why he had been putting off broaching the subject. Somehow, with Ariel, all his old rules for dealing with women failed him.

"I regret if I caused you undue concern last evening," he said to her. An apology seemed a safe place to start. "Or interfered with your night's rest."

She shrugged. "I slept very well once I heard you return."

"Had I known you were still awake," he said in his most solicitous tone, "I would have knocked on your chamber door and brought you a cup of warm milk."

"I despise warm milk."

"A brandy, then."

She wrinkled her nose.

Fussy little minx. Leon gritted his teeth, refusing to be daunted. "Tell me what I could have brought you to help you sleep."

"A map of Restormel."

He blinked. "I'm not sure I understand."

An understatement. He knew bloody well he didn't understand what a map had to do with either her sleeping or his attempt to be charming.

"Since I was awake anyway," she explained, "I decided to give some thought to how you might approach this business of searching for the sword."

"I see."

"Have you decided what method you will employ?"

"Method?"

"Yes, your strategy, your tactics. You must have some sort of plan in mind," she declared with obvious impatience.

"I do. I plan to think about it when the time comes."

Ariel tossed her napkin aside, her eyes wide with disbelief. "When the time comes?" she echoed.

"Yes," he said, thinking she look adorable when she was questioning his sanity. "I believe it's more formally known as the impromptu method. It's the one I generally prefer to rely on in most instances."

"Fine, go ahead, mock me. It's a little-known fact that misplaced objects are recovered in direct proportion to the organization that goes into the search for them. I assure you that Sir Adam's search will be well organized. His mother will see to it. And you, sir, will not be laughing when he beats you to the sword and the title along with it."

"Don't be so sure," Leon muttered, then quickly lifted an appeasing hand. "I'm sorry. I assure you I am not laughing at your concern. I know it is well intended and with my own best interests in mind. Tell me, Ariel, what method would you employ in my place?"

Without hesitation or false modesty she pushed her plate aside and leaned forward.

"The quadrant method." Using flatware to create boundaries, she marked off a space on the table in front of her. "It would be much easier to explain if I had a map, but for now this will have to suffice. Here is Restormel," she began, positioning her saucer in the middle of the marked space. "Now imagine a line about here, bisecting the property from north to south . . . "

Leon folded his arms on the table and leaned forward, listening without interruption as she outlined a plan for searching every last, blessed inch of the mammoth estate. Her bizarre strategy was to compile a list of every building on the property, right down to the tiniest shack for grain or pen for pigs. Next would come lists of every room in every building, and then lists for each room listing the furnishings in each.

She explained to him that there should be a separate list dealing solely with walls, complete with corresponding boxes to be checked off as each wall was verified to be solid and not harboring any secret compartments where a sword might be concealed. Finally there would be a master list of all the other lists to ensure order and control.

The thought of all those lists boggled his mind. No, that wasn't exactly true. *She* boggled his mind. He was transfixed by the sound of her voice and her smallest gesture, captivated by the way the sun shaded her cheek, and he feared it would be the same no matter what she was talking about.

"Amazing," he said when she had finished, his attention focused on her soft mouth.

She noticed and swept her tongue across her bottom lip as if concerned she might have a speck of jam caught at the corner. It was a thoroughly innocent, utterly provocative movement which, of course, only intensified his interest.

"I'm glad you approve," she murmured, glancing at the array of spoons, forks, and cups that were now arranged before her to represent Restormel and the surrounding countryside. "I'm afraid I got a bit carried away."

"Not at all," he assured her. "I was fascinated by your presentation."

"Really?"

"Really." He was also grateful as hell for it. If he'd been in need of a plan, hers would be as good as any, he supposed. But as a means to an end, it stood without equal. Straightening, he dragged his fingers through his hair and endeavored to look perplexed. "However, the beauty of your approach lies in its specificity and, ironically, that is also the aspect that most troubles me. You see, I question my own ability to manage so many lists and at the same time apply my full attention to the search itself."

Her eyes flashed with excitement. "You won't have to if you take me with you to Restormel. Please," she said, raising her palm to forestall any protest he might make, "hear me out before you refuse."

Refuse? Leon thought he might throw back his head and laugh, or jump across the table and hug her, but refusing to let her come with him was not even within the realm of possible reactions. Still, there was no need to appear too easily conquered. He waited for her to present her arguments, curious to see if they would be the same ones he'd been concocting on his own.

"First of all, Mrs. Farrell will accompany us as chaperone," she began. "I've already checked with her and she is agreeable."

He hadn't considered a chaperone. Not a single one of the fantasies he'd been entertaining about Ariel and him and a long carriage drive through the countryside required a chaperone. Evidently, she did require one, however. It served as proof of how much he desired her company that he was prepared to agree to a package deal that included the formidable Mrs. Farrell.

"I won't be missed at school, since they're not anticipating my return for another week yet," she went on. "Likewise, my parents will not be expecting me. I'll simply send word to them that my work for Lord Castleton requires me to be away for a short period. Then, of course, there is the fact that I am notoriously adept at making lists and sticking to them."

He nodded. It was all very reasonable, though not anything close to his own reasons for wishing her to come along. They had run more along the lines of his having grown accustomed to having her around to talk with, and his apprehension about being in his father's home for the first time, and a strong aversion to the idea of leaving her alone with Penrose.

"And lastly," she said, "you need me."

His head jerked up. "Do I indeed?"

"Yes, you do." The jut of her chin reflected a familiar stubbornness. "You see, I am the only one who sees through this new act of yours and understands the truth about what's going on."

Leon felt his pulse pick up speed. Was he that transparent? Impossible, he told himself. How could she understand what was going on inside him when he didn't?

Ignoring his racing pulse, he leaned back, crossed his arms, and regarded her with vaguely amused indulgence. "And what is the truth about what's going on?"

"That you're up to something." She folded her arms in the same manner he had. "I just haven't figured out exactly what it is. Yet."

"So you expect me to bring you along so you can figure it out?"

She shook her head. "I expect you to bring me along because I can help you find the sword. And just maybe, at the same time, I can keep you from doing something foolish." Her defiant expression softened. "I know the past has afforded you good reason to resent England and the people who wield power here, but this is not as small or uncomplicated a place as Hawaii. You have no idea what you are up against."

Leon breathed a sigh of relief. Is that what this was all about? She evidently suspected him of being less than sincere and playing both ends against the middle in this little game of "find the sword and claim the title." Which he was, of course. He'd much prefer she occupy herself with that and not catch on to what was really wreaking havoc with him, namely the problem of how to engage her emotions without surrendering another decimeter of his own.

"Are you trying to warn me that there are dark alleys and people waiting to clunk me on the head even in Devon?" he asked lightly.

"I'm warning that that is the least of what could happen to you if you step on the wrong toes here."

"Then it appears I shall have to bring you along to see to it that I step on only the right toes," he said, oddly touched by this new evidence of her concern, as misguided as it was.

Her explosive smile caught him off guard, and he felt its power all the way to the pit of his stomach. "You won't be sorry, Leon."

"I do have one admonition, however," he told her. "Since you've been so scrupulous in looking out for my welfare, I feel obligated to warn you that you may be in considerable danger yourself."

"What sort of danger?"

"You may be in danger of violating your vow not to become emotionally engaged with a man."

He observed her carefully, looking for chinks in her armor as understanding slowly replaced the apprehension in her beautiful eyes. She batted her thick lashes with recently acquired expertise. "Which man might that be?" she asked.

"Me," he retorted. "First, by your own admission, you lose sleep over me, and now you're willing to travel to the ends of the earth—"

"Devon is hardly—"

"It's bloody well close enough. And you're willing to go all that way to try to save me from incurring the British wrath."

"Thank you, Leon. It was very sweet of you to warn me," she said, getting to her feet with a small, enigmatic smile. "But what makes you so sure I'm not going along to try to save Britain from you?"

F o u r t e e n

Ariel packed simply for the trip and carried her own valise downstairs, placing it in the hall alongside Leon's bag and Prinny's cage. Mrs. Farrell had been very vocal in her opposition to sharing a carriage with "that crazy, filthy animal," and while the glint in Leon's eye suggested she was pressing her luck by forcing a choice, he had reluctantly agreed that things would be more comfortable and tidier for all of them if Prinny were not given the free run of the coach.

Ariel also arranged to bring a lunch, thus eliminating one stop. She personally oversaw the packing of the wicker hamper to make sure it included none of Mrs. Farrell's inedible surprises.

The sound of wheels on the stone drive announced the arrival of the hired coach. Mrs. Farrell hurried outside to supervise the loading of their luggage and, no doubt, to lay claim to the choicest seat, Ariel thought resignedly. She found it hard to be annoyed. She really didn't care where she sat as long as she got to go, and without Mrs. Farrell that would not be possible.

The carriage's arrival brought Leon from the study, still engrossed in conversation with Mr. Farrell. As they approached, he snapped shut a small leather-bound book Ariel recognized as an account register and handed it to Farrell.

"Those listed on the final page are to be paid in full as well," she heard him say.

Farrell's face became scrunched with confusion. "In advance? You can see for yourself that the dates—"

"Yes, in advance," Leon interjected. "I shall require signed receipts from the gentlemen involved in those transactions, just like the others. Have it all settled by the time I return, and there will be a bonus in it for you."

He didn't appear to be wasting any time in spending the money he borrowed from his grandmother, Ariel observed, wondering all over again what he was up to.

He motioned Farrell away with the register and joined her.

"Ready to go?" he asked, his gaze moving over her with warm, lazy interest, as if she were wearing something much more remarkable than a simple pale blue dress and her everyday navy mantle.

"Yes," she replied. "The bags are already in the carriage, along with Mrs. Farrell."

"Don't be redundant," he remarked dryly.

"Don't be cruel," she countered, at the same time pressing her lips together to smother a laugh. "The three of us shall be cooped up together for at least the next day and a half, and we have to try to be cordial."

"If my strategy works, that may not be as difficult as it seems," he told her as they walked outside.

"What strategy?" she asked, instantly suspicious.

"I suppose you could call it the 'fetch and conquer' approach," he explained. "I managed to *forget* a number of critical items while I was packing this morning and was forced to ask Mrs. Farrell to run upstairs and fetch them from my chamber." He glanced at her with a look of wicked satisfaction. "One after another after—"

Ariel cut in. "But the poor woman hates climbing stairs. She must be . . . exhausted," she concluded as understanding dawned.

"Exactly. If we're lucky, she'll sleep all the way to Devon."

Ariel tried, and failed, to look disapproving, and ended up grinning at him as she gave him her hand to be helped into the carriage. Hesitating in the doorway, she whispered, "You're completely incorrigible, you know."

"I know," he murmured, grinning back.

He was about to swing up behind her, when Mr. Penrose's familiar voice detained him. They all turned to see the headmaster hurrying toward the carriage.

"Greetings, greetings," he called out as he drew near, wheezing from the exertion. He pulled a white silk handkerchief from his pocket and dabbed his face as he bowed. "I'm so glad I made it here before you left. I wanted to wish you the very best of luck in your quest," he said, ostensibly to Leon, Ariel thought, though his pinprick gaze kept veering toward her. "And to bid you a safe journey."

"Thanks," said Leon, and he stepped into the carriage, joining Ariel on the seat behind the driver since Mrs. Farrell was situated dead center on the bench facing forward.

"How long do you expect to be away?" inquired Penrose.

"A week," Leon replied, reaching for the door handle. "Assuming we get under way sometime today."

Penrose stepped aside. "Of course, of course, I shan't detain you a moment longer."

Taking pity on him, Ariel leaned forward to offer him a smile. "Thank you for coming to see us off. It was very thoughtful of you."

"My pleasure," he said, beaming at her and reaching for whatever was clamped beneath his arm. "I did have a thought that during your long drive you might see your way clear to . . ."

He sputtered to a halt under Leon's hawkish glare, and belatedly Ariel realized that what he had under his arm was the ledger he kept managing to botch up and expected her to put right. No wonder he had been in such a hurry to catch her before she left.

"On second thought," he said, "never mind."

Leon gave him a nod and yanked the door shut. "Drive on," he called.

Mr. Penrose followed to the edge of the lawn, then stood waving until they made the turn at the end of the drive. He looked so silly doing it that in spite of herself, Ariel felt a moral responsibility to acknowledge his effort by waving back. She was the only one of them who did feel so obliged. Mrs. Farrell was busy rearranging her bulk in a more comfortable position, and Leon sat with his arms folded, watching Ariel, his lips curved in a cynical smile.

When at last they pulled out of sight, she sat back with a relieved sigh.

"Parting is such sweet sorrow," he whispered. "Try to look on the bright side. If old Penrose couldn't tolerate a carriage ride into town without you, a week's absence is sure to drive him over the edge . . . or straight to the altar, as the case may be."

Ariel frowned. "Do you really think we will be gone a week?"

He nodded, making Ariel sorry she had even asked. They were just getting under way. The last thing she wanted to think about was how soon it would all be over. No, actually that was the second to the last thing she wanted to think about. The last was Mr. Penrose himself, and what was almost certainly to be her fate upon her return from Restormel.

She had an agonizing sense that the last eight weeks had changed everything and nothing at all. Her financial situation remained the same. Dismal. If she were to help her parents survive, she needed the security of marriage, and Mr. Penrose was still the only viable candidate to be her husband. What had changed, irrevocably she feared, was her confidence in her ability to settle for the sort of bland existence such a marriage would provide. What had changed it was knowing Leon. He had opened her eyes to the kinds of feelings and longings that are possible between a man and a woman, and there was no going back.

Turning away from the sight of Mrs. Farrell wrestling with the pillow she had pulled from the voluminous satchel beside her, she gazed out the window without really seeing the familiar landscape. A week. That was the bright side she was expected to look at? Seven days never seemed so paltry and insignificant a period of time. She wished he had said a month or a year or, better still, nothing at all. That would have left the trip in the exciting realm of the unknown, where anything at all was possible.

Still, she refused to brood about it. A seven-day reprieve was still a reprieve. This trip may well be her last taste of freedom before assuming a lifelong obligation she would never choose willingly. That being so, she decided, drawing herself up on her seat and leaning a little closer to the window, she was going to live every minute of it to the fullest, without being haunted by dismal thoughts of Mr. Penrose and what lay ahead.

She'd much rather think about what waited at the end of the journey. Restormel. Even the name had intrigued her the very first time she heard it. It was while visiting her aunt in Bath that she met a woman who had actually been to a ball at the renowned estate on the craggy western coastline near Devon. She'd told Ariel it was easily the most romantic-looking house in all of England, like a castle belonging in a fairy tale.

Personally Ariel had never put much stock in fairy tales, but she was still eager to see such a place for herself. The visit would also provide her with her first glimpse of the ocean, and the thought of standing at its edge, looking up at a night sky without end, was unbearably exciting. Almost as exciting, she thought ruefully, as the thought of spending another whole week with Leon.

The sound of Mrs. Farrell's muffled snoring soon filled the carriage. She turned with a conspiratorial smile, only to find Leon slouched in the corner, his black hat tipped down so the brim covered his eyes. Apparently Mrs. Farrell wasn't the only one who had been worn out by his packing. So much for the lively conversation she had been looking forward to, she thought.

From beneath his hat Leon watched her smile fade to disappointment and her expression grow wistful as she turned away. He ought to say something to let her know he was awake, he thought. But then, he ought to have done a great many things he failed to do.

If she knew he was awake, she would talk to him, and he didn't feel like talking. The trip, for which he'd had such high hopes, had gotten off to a miserable start. Thanks to the Nose. And Ariel. She'd asked to come along, pleaded with him really, and then had gone all sad and mopey-eyed when she realized it was going to mean being away for an entire week. He didn't know if it was Penrose she would miss or the chance to practice her burgeoning wiles on the man.

It was better that they didn't talk. So he feigned sleep until boredom overtook him and then dropped his hat to his lap and stretched. Silently. He didn't want to say or do anything to wake their chaperone.

"You're awake. Good," said Ariel. "I was about to eat lunch by myself, and I hate eating alone. I was so busy recreating Restormel over breakfast, I think I forgot to eat."

Leon smiled wryly at the recollection. He had eaten breakfast, but that was hours earlier and the mention of lunch had him eyeing the wicker hamper hungrily.

Ariel slid the hamper so it was in front of her and lifted the lid. "Will you join me?" she invited.

"I'm not sure," replied Leon, weighing the extent of his hunger against his knowledge of Mrs. Farrell's cooking.

Obviously discerning the reason for his hesitancy, Ariel slanted him a beguiling smile. "I prepared it myself."

"In that case, I'll join you."

"Good. Let's see," she said, pulling out plates and napkins and handing them to him, "we have cold chicken and sliced beef, with horseradish sauce made the way my mother prepares it to spread on top. I also made sure to pack some of those little pickles you like and two kinds of bread, and to wash it all down . . . " With a flourish she held aloft something vaguely bottle-shaped and swathed in a white linen towel. "Ale."

"The damp towel is to keep it cold," she explained. "I considered bringing wine, but that seemed so unimaginative. Every picnic includes wine. Ale is more adventuresome, don't you think?"

"Definitely. For sheer recklessness I should say it rivals the pickles. In fact, the whole meal has a decidedly brash and daring appeal. Was that the theme you had in mind?"

"If you're trying to get a rise out of me, you're sure to be disappointed," she told him, calmly removing the stopper from the ale bottle and reaching for a glass. "I've grown quite accustomed to your mockery, you see. It rolls off my back like water."

"Is that the puddle I've been sitting in?"

"Very funny." She handed him the glass. "And as long as you asked, the answer is yes, adventure was most decidedly the theme I had in mind, and not just for the lunch, for the entire trip."

He made a scoffing sound. "Some adventure. Thirty-six hours in a coach with no leg room and a snoring chaperone."

"Well, if you insist on looking for problems, I suppose you'll find them fast enough. *I'm* having a wonderful time."

"You are?" he asked, slightly amazed.

She nodded, the excitement in her eyes leaving no doubt that she was sincere. So much for her pining over Penrose, he thought, his own mood rapidly improving.

Out of sight, out of mind was suddenly his favorite proverb.

He reached for another glass from the hamper and held it out to her. "It so happens I abhor drinking by myself as much as you do eating alone," he said. "Please join me."

She barely hesitated before giving her head a careless toss and lifting the bottle to pour. "Why not?" she replied with a laugh that seemed to wrap around him like velvet and pull him closer. "I've never drunk ale on a picnic before."

Leon eyed her curiously. "Where have you drunk it?"

"Nowhere," she admitted.

"That's what I thought."

"But don't you see? That's the whole point of an adventure, to do things you wouldn't ordinarily dare to do. I want this time away to be different," she told him, the enthusiasm in her tone a stark contrast to the cynicism that had been lurking in his own. "I've decided that it's to serve as a holiday from everything that is dull and ordinary and routine in my life." Her mouth tilted in a rueful smile. "Which is nearly all of it, not that I think about it. Which I suppose makes this a holiday from myself." Her smile quickly gave way to a more earnest look. "That is, when I'm not assisting you in your search for the sword, of course."

"Of course," Leon agreed, the sword the very last thing on his mind at that moment.

This was how she did it, he mused, fascinated and alarmed and enchanted all at the same time. This was how she drew him into her mood, her world, and made him forget. It wasn't magic. It was simple. She laughed, and she gazed up at him with that silvery-blue look of excitement that made him want to move mountains, conquer continents, bring down the moon, whatever it took to make her keep smiling and looking at him exactly that way. More dangerous still, at moments like that, he *believed* he could do it.

"I am determined to see everything there is to see between home and Restormel," she was saying. "Then, when I get there, I want to stick my bare foot in the ocean even if the water is so cold my toes turn blue, and I want to stare out over the waves at the horizon until my eyes get tired of looking, and I want to . . . to do all the things I've never done before," she concluded, her level of exhilaration suggesting that the things in question were so out of the ordinary that they defied naming.

"Such as drink ale?"

"It's a start."

Indeed it was. Her soft mouth curved upward, and expectations shimmered in her eyes. Thoughts of all the scorchingly sensual ways he longed to expand her horizons and fulfill her expectations beat inside him, turning his palms damp and his defenses to jelly.

"Then you shall see and do it all," he said on a husky note of conviction she could not possibly understand. "I'll see to it personally." He lifted his glass in the air. "Here's to new experiences."

Smiling with guileless abandon, she touched her glass to his and took a sip, wrinkling her nose at the taste.

"Does it go down easier with practice?"

Leon unleashed a lethal smile. "Most things do."

After they finished eating and packed away the leftovers, she curled up on the seat beside him and proceeded to fall asleep. Why not? thought Leon, positioning his left shoulder to catch her head as it lolled to the side. *Her* appetite had been sated.

He slanted a glance at her.

Her head had found a nesting place between his jaw and his collarbone. Her gently rounded chin rested against his chest. Her delicate lips were parted just slightly, just enough to fire his imagination. it took damn little lately.

He found himself imagining that they were somewhere else, somewhere private, where he could pull her onto his lap and ease that dress that was the same clear blue as her eyes when she laughed off her shoulders, lowering it to her waist and her chemise with it so that he could at last see her breasts, bare and lush, so he could discover for himself if they were as smooth as silk and responded to his touch like quicksilver, the way they did in all his dreams, and if the tips could possibly be as rosy as he imagined and taste as sweet, so trembling, quivering sweet that when he bent his head and used his tongue to . . .

Damn him for a fool.

What in the name of Satan was he doing to himself?

His knuckles were white and his head so filled with heat, he wouldn't have been surprised if it popped off his shoulders and landed in Mrs. Farrell's ample lap. Worse yet, his head was not the only overheated part of him. He shifted his weight, trying to reduce his discomfiture without disturbing Ariel. In spite of the fact that she was disturbing him.

He had to stop imagining, stop envisioning, stop wishing they were somewhere else. Anywhere else. Anywhere but there, piled into a rented hack with a driver, a postilion, a chaperone, and a pet rabbit for company, when all he wanted at that moment was to be alone with Ariel.

Soon he would be.

The realization flared to life inside him, hot and

wrenching. Restormel. A few minutes earlier the place had meant nothing more to him than a means to an end. Retrieving the sword was one more move in this political chess match he'd been forced into and had every intention of winning . . . if only by seeing to it that everyone else involved lost. In the space of a heart-beat, that had changed.

Restormel. Even the name was uncommonly alluring to him now. Restormel. Never in his entire life had he longed to be anywhere with the ferocious pas-sion with which he now longed to be at Restormel. Whatever the hell it turned out to be, it was sure to pro-vide him more opportunity to be alone with Ariel than this blasted coach.

The first sign he had that they were growing close to their destination was the eerie vibration that passed through him without warning, an unprecedented sensa-tion he could neither explain nor control. It brought him fully alert.

That's when he noticed the light. At first no more than a faint glow on the edge of the darkness that engulfed them, it grew steadily stronger and brighter, warming from ghostly white to soft yellow as its arc gradually climbed higher in the sky.

Leon sat close to the window, unable to look away. Across from him, Ariel slid to the edge of her seat so that their knees collided and their shoulders were pressed tightly together as they took a final turn. The sight they were presented with caused even the stal-wart driver to draw hard on the reins, slowing the horses to a walk as they followed the private brick drive that cut a wide path through the endless frost-touched meadows on either side.

Restormel.

It burst upon his senses. He'd expected nothing and prepared himself for anything and was still so struck by the sight that he neglected to breathe until his aching chest demanded it.

A meandering ring of towers and turrets and chimneys floating on the ridge above the cliff, glowing like a string of mystical gems against the blackness beyond, portentous and weightless at once, all redbrick cloaked in mist, light red, dark pink, orange, and rust, enough reds to dazzle the eyes and warm the soul, a fitting monument to mark the edge of the earth, the last stop before oblivion, pale and luminous, a fantasy, a memory, a dream.

Restormel.

He felt Ariel's fingers curl over his forearm.

"I've never seen anything so beautiful," she whispered, as if to speak loudly would break the spell and make it vanish from their sight. "Or so many lights."

Leon nodded, focusing for the first time on what it was that lent the place its ethereal glow. Flaming torches, a hundred of them at least, lined both sides of the drive, and it seemed as if a candle burned in each of the countless windows, from the tall, arched ones flanking the portico to the tiniest pieces of glass rimming the pepperpot turrets.

"Must be a pack of vampires living in the place," he muttered. "Don't they bloody sleep here?"

"Don't you see?" she said, squeezing his arm. "It must be for you, to welcome you and ensure that your first sight of Restormel would be a memorable one.

From the look on your face, I'd say they succeeded admirably."

He immediately arranged his face in a scowl, not sure what his previous look might have been, only that he didn't care for her tone when she remarked on it.

"There's only one flaw in your theory," he told her. "No one here knew I was coming."

"Didn't they?" she countered, her small smile wise. "I wouldn't put it past Lady Sage to have sent word as soon as you left her. The post chaise would certainly have gotten her message here in time for a proper welcome to be prepared."

He leaned back in his seat, disgruntled enough to detach his gaze from the spectacle. The last thing he wanted was to be welcomed there, properly or otherwise. If Ariel was right, Lady Sage should have remained out of it and left him to handle his arrival in his own fashion and with as little fanfare as possible. A place this size no doubt boasted a small army of servants, and the thought of all those overeager smiles and ever-present eyes did not fit well with his plans for their stay.

The sense that he was losing control intensified as the coach came to a stop and he climbed down. He turned to help Ariel, feeling her sway and catch herself as her feet touched ground.

"Forgive me," she said, trying to pull away. "The long ride seems to have left me a bit dizzy."

"Perhaps I should carry you," he suggested, only half joking. The thought of carrying her under Restormel's solid brick arch, through its massive oak doors and straight to its master chamber appealed to him on levels he didn't even want to think about.

"No, please," she said. "I'm quite recovered, I assure you. What would the house staff think if their first glimpse of you is with a swooning woman in your arms?"

"I couldn't care less what they think. Besides, we're not an overly impressive sight at present," he pointed out, eyeing her travel-rumpled attire as he stroked the black stubble covering his jaw.

"All the more reason . . . oh, no."

She was brought up short by the arrival of the first of the welcoming committee. A pair of hounds from hell appeared in front of them as silently as smoke, their massive black forms materializing out of the night and blending with it so completely that the only things plainly discernible about them were the matched sets of silver-white fangs snapping behind gray, curled-back lips. That and, of course, their barking, which was loud enough to raise the dead.

While they were at it, they roused Mrs. Farrell as well. She started out, got a good look at the dogs, and retreated, slamming the door behind her and leaving them to fend for themselves.

Ariel thrust herself behind him, clutching his coat.

Hell, Leon thought, and proceeded to do what came naturally. He bared his teeth and snarled back at them. They ceased barking as if on cue, looking from him to each other and back. Leon had no illusions that he'd solved the problem, but he had bought them a moment's reprieve, and as it turned out, that's all it took for what appeared to be the entire household, offspring included, to make a bleary-eyed appearance.

They streamed from the front door and around both corners of the house, as if some silent alarm had seeped through the entire dwelling and roused them from their beds. There were men with their nightshirts half-tucked inside hastily donned breeches, women with their nightcaps askew and pelisses buttoned crookedly or not at all, babies in their mothers' arms and small children being dragged alongside. Most of the children were crying crankily.

These before him fell into a ragtag arrangement, headed by a slender, stiffly erect gentleman of nearly his own height, but who was a good thirty years older. Dressed in a crisp blue and gold morning coat and impeccably powdered, he was as alert and crisply turned out as if it were three in the afternoon instead of three in the morning.

Head vampire, thought Leon.

A brisk slicing motion of his right hand brought the dogs to a full crouch at his feet. A second silent gesture sent a young man at the edge of the group scurrying forth to help with the horses and show the driver to the stables, where he could spend the night. Satisfied that it was safe, Mrs. Farrell made an appearance, and yet another footman was beckoned forth to convey her, along with their bags, inside.

"Welcome to Restormel, my lord," said the man in blue, bowing deeply.

"I'm not—"

He continued, obviously well rehearsed and not open to interruptions. "Calvin Metcalf, at your service. The entire household and I are pleased beyond measure to have you here at last, and we stand ready, day and night, to serve you."

"Yes, I couldn't help noticing," Leon remarked, gazing at the sleepy assemblage.

"Lady Sage sent us word of your imminent arrival," Calvin Metcalf explained, "and we have been on high alert ever since."

Leon exchanged looks with Ariel, conceding the accuracy of her insight.

"We have done our best to anticipate your every need," the butler continued. "Cook has prepared a hot meal in the event that you and the lady are hungry. There is also lighter fare if that suits your taste more at this hour. Your chambers have been prepared and—"

"Thank you," Leon interjected. "I can see you've gone to a great deal of trouble and I . . . thank you."

"No thanks are necessary, my lord." Another bow.

"I'm not—"

"All of us here were privileged to serve your dear father, may God rest and keep his soul, and now we are blessed to do the same for you. I cannot tell you what a relief it is to know that thanks to you, Restormel will not be falling into the wrong hands."

Leon could swear the man clicked his heels together and drew himself up straighter still.

"Tomorrow," he continued, "I will personally take you on the grand tour of your new home, and Alfred, the chief groundsman, will be honored to show you the layout of the gardens and outlying lands. There are two ponds, a waterfall, and seven fountains with statuary on the grounds proper. But I daresay that can all wait till the morning."

"Yes, it's a bit late for statuary."

"And let me not neglect to mention the children, sir. They have also anticipated your arrival by preparing a song and brief program to welcome you." His high forehead puckered with consternation. "But perhaps that should wait till morning as well."

"I think that would be best, since those children who aren't bawling appear to be sleeping, and vice versa."

"Very well, my lord."

"I'm not—"

"All that remains is for you to tell us what we may do next to make you welcome and we will hasten to render it done."

"What I would really like," Leon replied, feeling as if the entire lot of them were leaning forward in anticipation, "is for you all to go back to bed. Immediately."

"But—"

"No buts, Calvin. Back to bed," he called out, running his gaze over the gathering. "All of you."

He didn't have to issue the order twice. A collective sigh of relief seemed to drift over the entourage as they broke ranks and returned the way they had come until only the butler remained. He stared uncertainly at Leon.

"You too, Calvin. Off you go." He picked up Prinny's cage which the driver had left with him. "But if you have your heart set on rolling out the welcome mat for someone, maybe you could find my friend here a warm place for the night."

"Of course, sir." He turned to Ariel. "If the lady will be so kind as to—"

"Not her," Leon told him. "I will see to Miss Halliday's comfort personally." He held out the cage. "Here you go. Answers to the name of Prinny."

"Prinny, sir?"

"That's right."

"Just so." The butler took the cage from him, as nonplussed as if he played host to rabbits named after the king on a regular basis. "But, sir, who will show you to your chamber? Help you to disrobe? Assist Miss Halliday with—"

"To tell you the truth, old man, I rather have my heart set on bumbling my way through my first night here on my own."

"Bumbling, sir?"

"That's it."

"But, sir, your father—"

"Is no longer with us, God rest and keep his soul. Good night, Cal."

A shudder shook the butler's shoulders at the casual shortening of his name, but his upper lip remained impressively stiff as he made his bow. "Good night, my lord."

"I'm not . . . ah, the hell with it," Leon muttered.

They stood together in silence as Calvin walked away holding a wide-awake Prinny's cage a cautious distance from his side. As they looked on, still without speaking, one by one the candles in the windows were extinguished until most of the massive house was in darkness, a grandiose shadow against a night-black sky.

"That was quite a welcome you received," Ariel remarked.

Leon shrugged, uneasy with the unexpected warmth of his reception. "I might be more touched if it had been meant for me and not an empty title that's not even mine."

"I'm sure it would be yours right now if it were up to these good people. Reading between the lines, I'd say that Lockaby is not a favorite of theirs."

"So instead they're mindless enough to trust their fate to a man they never before set eyes upon?"

"It's obvious they trusted your father. Did you hear the reverence in Calvin's voice when he spoke of him?"

"I heard," he replied tersely.

How could he help hearing? The servant's tone had dripped respect and affection for his late master. Conventional wisdom held that was proof he had been a kind and just master. Conventional wisdom could go hang. There had been no kindness or justice in the way Giles Duvanne had treated his mother, or him. As far as Leon was concerned, the fact that he cared more for his servants than his own flesh and blood served only to twist the knife that had been buried in his heart years before.

"You are their dear master's long-lost son," Ariel said to him. "I daresay your very existence is a source of comfort to them, and they turned out in force at this ungodly hour to show it."

"Well, you're wrong," he snapped. "My existence, madam, is a perverted joke."

He started toward the house, covering ground with a long, angry stride.

"That is not true," she admonished Sage, doing her best to match his pace. "I know you harbor bitter feelings toward your father, but—"

"My father?" He paused at the door, turning to glare at her as she came to a hurried stop to avoid a collision with his chest. Her cheeks were flushed and she was breathing hard and he wished to hell they were back in the carriage, alone and riding away from there as fast as they had come. "My father is an even bigger joke. My father, if you are so loose with language as to call him that, was nothing more to me than a name and a betrayal and a convenient focus for the constant surplus of hatred that's my only birthright."

He watched her valiant, reassuring expression

vanish, replaced by sadness. Or pity, he thought, furious. He didn't want her pity. He didn't want anything from anyone.

"Saying such things does not help anyone," she said quietly.

"Don't tell me what to say. I'll say what I damn well please," he told her, shouting now as he strode into the grand entrance chamber and was struck speechless all over again.

He wasn't so completely jaded and lacking in tradition that he couldn't recognize that the abundance of beauty and richness surrounding them was the accumulated treasure of several lifetimes. Time-mellowed tapestries of the four seasons shrouded the high walls. White marble pedestals displayed recognizable sculptures by the masters. Greek gods, their bronze arms raised high, supported the wide balcony that hung far above their heads. Even the intricate sunburst mosaic beneath their feet was a work of art unto itself.

Ariel appeared to notice none of it as she focused her worried blue gaze on him alone.

"Your father sent for you," she reminded him. "Too late, I grant you, but it must still count for something."

"My father sent for me to use me, the same way he used my mother. That's what men who live in houses like this and collect things like these do," he said, indicating an arrangement of ornate urns on a nearby table.

"So now there is uniform offense in living well and acquiring beautiful objects?"

He turned away from her quiet challenge, overwhelmed by the sudden image of his mother as he would always remember her, young and beautiful and laughing, with head held high in anticipation as she rowed away and left him alone on the shore.

"There is offense in acquiring beautiful objects

simply to toss them aside when they have outlived the initial pleasure they brought." He picked up one of the smaller urns, this one of ebony with silver chasing, and held it without seeing it.

A flood of memories rushed past him, newly unleashed memories he suddenly felt the full weight of for the first time in his life. It was as if, along with the front door of Restormel, a gate had been opened inside him, releasing thoughts and impressions and feelings that he didn't want to own.

If coming here was like this for him, what must it have been like for his father when he returned? What had he felt, knowing it was suddenly all his to safeguard and to pass on? Leon couldn't imagine. Nor did he care to, he reminded himself. His heart was slamming against his rib cage with every thunderous beat as he continued to turn the urn in his hands, over and over.

"Don't," Ariel said softly, moving so that she stood close to his shoulder. "Don't try so hard to hide what you're feeling from me, or worse still, from yourself. It's perfectly natural for you to be affected this way walking in here for the first time."

"What way?" he asked icily, without turning.

"To become overwrought with the import of the moment," she replied.

Now he did turn, spearing her with the dangerous golden stare of a trapped animal. "Madam, you are sorely mistaken in your assessment of my mood. I am not now, nor am I ever, overwrought."

"Now who is quibbling over words?" she asked in a gentle attempt at humor which he was of no mind to tolerate. "It is plain to see that you are deeply moved to be standing in this place, where so many of your ancestors have stood before you, gazing at these same works, perhaps holding in their hands that same urn you hold in yours now. It is obvious that you care greatly—"

"No," he bellowed, and fired the urn across the room, where it missed the carved bust that had been his mark and shattered on the marble floor below. "Wrong again. I don't give a damn for any of this, or for anyone who ever did."

Hurried footsteps sounded in the distance, and seconds later Calvin appeared, entering the mammoth hall through a doorway such a distance away, he was recognizable only by his blue coat.

"Lord Sage, I heard—"

"Get out," Leon roared, stopping the butler in his tracks. "Out. Now. And don't, by God, call me lord again."

Calvin fled the room.

Leon swung his enraged attention back to Ariel. "And don't you ever say again that I care for anything about this place or I will smash the lot of them," he promised, sweeping his hand perilously close to the collection of urns. He glanced about the room with a ruthless sneer. "I'll topple all of it, I swear, and send the whole place crashing down around your pretty ears if that's what it takes to prove that I don't give a damn."

"Prove it to whom, Leon? Me? Or yourself?"

He flung himself away from her with an anguished growl that reverberated in the cavernous hall like the cry of a hundred jungle cats. His broad shoulders heaving with every labored breath, he braced his palms on a wide marble ledge and gazed out the window above. All he saw in the night-black pane was the reflection of his own tortured countenance surrounded by the bright splendor that was Restormel. With a harsh, broken laugh, he let his head drop.

Damn this place. He should never have come. He should have ended this farce back in London and not tempted whatever twisted ghosts inhabited these ancient halls. They were nothing to him, none of them, and one of them at least, the most recent Marquis of Sage, had clearly deemed him nothing in return.

Too late, too late, intoned a voice deep in his embittered soul even as that newly unlocked force inside persisted in peeling off layer after hidden layer of feeling, filling him with thoughts and yearnings he didn't understand or know how to deal with.

He hadn't heard Ariel approach, but suddenly he felt a light pressure on his shoulder, and his head jerked upright as if she'd used a rawhide lash on him instead of her hand.

She meant to console him, he knew. Instead, her touch sent a familiar sensual awareness coursing through him, driving a white-hot shaft of desire through the tangle of everything else he was feeling at that moment and setting him free.

This was something he did understand, and knew exactly how to deal with.

In one skillful motion he turned and pulled her into his arms and kissed her. Her eyes went wide as she first grasped his purpose and then fluttered shut as his mouth opened over hers. Yes, surrender to me, he thought, the thrill of it humming in his ears, blending with her small, muffled sound of surprise as his tongue pressed for entry.

He kissed her as hard as he dared, forcing her soft lips apart and plundering her mouth over and over again, as desperate and driven as a battle-scarred warrior with victory at last in his sight.

As ruthless as the kiss was, however, he held himself in check throughout, straining to keep a tight rein on the violent-edged lust that he knew was in him, threatening to engulf him and overwhelm her before he was half done. His arms trembled from the effort and his belly burned, and not until he couldn't stand the fire in his lungs another instant did he lift his head to draw breath and let her do the same.

She shivered against his solid chest and tipped her head back to gaze up at him, her eyes all dark blue smoke and mystery, questioning, uncertain, but not telling him no. Leon cupped her chin in his hand, holding her gaze as he traced with his thumb the fine high line of her cheekbone, finding her ear beneath the loosened gold-tinged wisps of her hair and slowly, slowly stroking its shallow, delicate crevices in a way that made the air between them rank with the intimacy of his intent, and still she did not bid him no.

He kissed her again, insistently drawing her tongue into play, wordlessly teaching her how to use it to make him shudder and groan. His hair fell forward, a blue-black curtain gleaming in the candlelight, closing them off from everything but the heated exchange of their breath as his hands swept aside her mantle and roamed freely over her narrow back and the full, lush curve of her hips, searching for a place to hide, a way to lose himself.

Still caressing her, he lifted his head and fixed her with an unsmiling gaze.

"I have no ale handy," he told her, his voice a husky whisper coming from deep in his chest. "But if you're truly as adventurous as you claim, I can let you taste something else for the first time tonight."

She looked down, hiding from his view the flush he knew must be spreading across her cheeks.

"Is that a yes?" he asked, angling his head to kiss the edge of her mouth. "Or a no?"

"Must you ask?" she pleaded, still avoiding his gaze. "Must you make me say it outright?"

"How else should I know what you want?" he countered, anticipation hovering just beneath the surface of his heated tone. "Or what your feelings toward me are?"

"You just should, that's all. At least, I thought you would. You with all your majestic, primitive ways. Does a savage ask to be fed? I think not," she said, her haughty look giving way to a softer, wistful expression. "He just takes what he wants. It's instinctive. Somehow I rather thought that when this happened, if it happened, with you, I mean, that it would be the same, all sweeping me off my feet and ravishment. And another thing—"

"You've said quite enough," he declared, bending and knocking her legs out from under her with one arm as he caught her with the other so that when he straightened she landed against his chest with a thud. "Rest assured, madam, if it's ravishment you want, ravished you shall be."

Ariel couldn't decide if she was staring straight into heaven or hell. With her head thrown back over Leon's muscular arm, she could see that the fresco on the domed ceiling above Restormel's flaring grand staircase was resplendent with crimson-and-gold-shrouded angels of all shapes and expressions. She just couldn't determine if they were fallen or otherwise.

Her own fate at the moment was far more certain. She was definitely falling and had no wish to stop. Leon's anguish and confusion over being there had touched her deeply, and it would be easy to tell herself that sympathy alone had propelled her into his arms, but it was not so. She was not doing this for him, but for herself. For perhaps the first time since she had learned to cater to the needs of others and deny her own, she was doing something simply because she wanted to.

Ariel was thankful for Leon's speed up the steps. She didn't want time for her head to clear or for the strange pulsing sweetness in the pit of her stomach to subside or for all the reasons that this was madness and she must call a halt to it to catch up with her.

A taste of something new was what he'd offered her, and she wanted it. God help her, she wanted it, and she wanted it from this man alone. His bronze eyes had been dark with a wild urgency she had never before seen in a man, but had understood instantly. His passion ripped aside that part of her that was bound by society's dictates, and uncovered the part of her that questioned and hungered and chafed. Tonight she was beautiful and buoyant and desired by a man strong and virile and uncivilized enough to reveal to her the mysterious temptations she'd been warned to resist at all cost.

The room was large and empty. Illuminated only by the glow from a freshly lit fire and a single candle on the mantel, it was still well lighted enough for Leon to see the only thing that interested him, the huge bed against the far wall.

The damask coverlet and linen had been turned back and his bag placed on a rack close by, but it was the inverted V formed by the velvet drapery gathered up from both carved headposts to meet at a spot above that commanded his attention. As it was plainly fashioned to do. There, mounted above the bed, was an imposing gold and enamel rendering of the same family crest he'd taken his knife to not long ago.

The Sage crest, he thought, and cursed softly.

Obviously he had stumbled upon the private chamber reserved for the Marquis of Sage.

He contemplated the crest. Then he contemplated the throbbing dimensions of his need.

The room would have to do, he decided, swiftly kicking the door closed behind him.

It took him only two strides to reach the bed and less than a heartbeat to lay Ariel on her back and follow her down. One knee sank deep in the soft bedding as he bent to kiss her the way he'd been burning to kiss her since the instant he'd stopped doing so downstairs.

"Open your mouth for me," he commanded, pressing a line of hard kisses from her ear to her lips.

Then, beyond waiting for her to comply, he forced her to it. He sucked her tongue and traced the straight line of her teeth, discovering a single imperfection, a tiny chip on one side that in his madness he found enchanting and returned to again and again between the hard, deep tongue thrusts that only agitated his hunger for her.

His famished mouth left hers to rake across her cheek and follow the satin slide of her throat. He heard the sound his whiskers made, the rasp of gravel on silk, and regretted the damage he was inflicting on her soft skin and wished he could stop, but couldn't. She tasted too good, so good, like salt and honey, and so fresh and alive, her pulse a tremor just beneath her skin, rippling like water against his open mouth, carrying him away, and he couldn't stop, he couldn't if he wanted to, and he didn't want to. He licked her dainty pink ear and felt her tremble and lost another little piece of his mind.

Drawing back enough to look at her, he framed her cheeks with his hands, struck by how big and brown they appeared in contrast to the perfect pale oval of her face. God, she was beautiful.

"I was under the impression that I had done everything a man could do in bed with a woman," he said. "But it occurs to me now that I was mistaken. Never before have I ever taken to my bed a woman still dressed in her hat and cloak and boots. And gloves," he added, catching her hand and lacing his fingers with hers.

"Shall I remove them?" she asked, her smile both challenge and invitation.

Leon shook his head and carried her hand to his mouth to nibble her gloved fingers. "No, I shall. As soon as I've dealt with my own."

Reluctantly he drew away from her and stood. Another time he might have left the shield of his clothing for the moment, playing the tender seducer out of deference to her innocent sensibilities. But she had not asked to be seduced, only ravished, and it was with that single blinding intent that he tore off his clothes.

Ariel was still sprawled where he left her on the bed, both shy to watch and unable to look away as his jacket and waistcoat and cravat landed on the floor. Plink, plink, plink went the buttons as he ripped his shirt open, his broad chest lifting and falling with each breath he dragged in.

He didn't look at her, so intent was he on his task, but if he had, he would have seen the anticipation that was surely in her eyes. She vowed to savor every moment of this night, seal each kiss and every dizzying touch deep in her memory, pressing them there like flowers between the pages of a book so they would be there for her to call on in all the sane, tedious days to come.

The sight of his naked chest, sun-darkened and muscled and shot straight down the center with a wide arrow of feathery black hair, was mesmerizing to her. Everything about his body was so different from her own. Not simply the obvious differences between a man and a woman or that he was dark where she was light and hard where she was soft. His body appeared to have been chiseled from stone by a harsh, demanding hand, while hers was more molded, its substance soft and pliable and meant to be fitted to his.

He even moved differently, she marveled, watching as he worked at the buttons on his trousers and bent to pull off his boots. As impatient as he clearly was, his motions were still smooth and graceful, marked by the same underlying sense of strength and energy she'd observed in him whether he was running or doing absolutely nothing.

He straightened suddenly, his boots off, and as he did he let his breeches fall to the floor, kicked them aside, and turned to face her, boldly naked.

Ariel heard her breath hitch and knew he must have heard it too. She couldn't help it; he was magnificent. An arrogant, primitive god bathed in firelight and fully, wondrously, amazingly aroused. The arrow of hair on his chest fanned wider across the hard, flat plane of his stomach, ending in a thick, exotically male nest from which sprang blatant proof of his desire for her.

Desire, sharp and innate, twisted inside her. Without thinking, she rose up onto her elbows. That slight movement was all it took to bring him to her.

He stood close to the bed and grasped her hands to pull her to a full sitting position. His manhood was close in front of her, fascinating and frightening and so utterly distracting to her that not until she felt a sharp tug beneath her chin was she aware that he had reached for the strings on her traveling bonnet. He lifted it from her head and sent it sailing across the room. Next he unfastened her mantle, tugging it loose and tossing it over his shoulder. Her gloves followed in the same general direction.

Ariel could hardly breathe, knowing all she had left to be taken was her dress and what lay beneath. Watching him remove his clothes had been wickedly exciting and of consuming interest. The prospect of surrendering her own and allowing a man to see her body for the first time was more daunting. Leon's taut flesh and lean, muscled contours made her unbearably conscious of her own soon to be revealed imperfections.

She braced herself, expecting him to proceed as logically as she would and relieve her of her dress next. Instead, he went down on his knees and removed first one of her kid ankle boots, then the other. Still kneeling, he pushed her skirt above her calves. Ariel started when he lifted her left leg, straightening it so that her ankle was propped on his shoulder, leaving her right leg dangling and hopelessly weak.

She rested her weight on her hands for balance and clutched a handful of bedding in each fist as he slipped his fingers inside the bottom leg of her drawers and began working it higher, proceeding an inch or so with one hand, then catching up with the other, and on and on, the friction of his fingers making her shiver as he stroked over stocking and upward until she reached the knot on her garter.

He swiftly untied it and pushed it away. Ariel felt

more than saw his gaze on the area he had exposed just above her knee, a four-inch-wide strip of flesh between her loosened stocking and bunched-up skirt. Her heart thundered erratically as he bent his head and kissed her there. There. Such a strange place to be kissed.

Hooking his finger in her stocking, he lowered it a few inches, following with his mouth, kissing her knee, the side of it, twisting her leg to get at the soft hollow behind and sending sparks shooting along her spine. She felt the edge of his teeth and then the rough heat of his tongue. He was licking her, she realized, stunned, the way he had licked her ear. She hadn't thought . . . hadn't imagined he would do . . . that he would want . . . .

She quivered and clutched the sheets tighter as he slid his other hand along the inside of her thigh, blowing on the skin he'd made wet. Without warning, a feeling unlike anything she had ever known unfurled in her belly and spread lower, a heated melting rush of sensation that alarmed her because it seemed to be taking all of her with it.

She couldn't bear this, she thought, clamping her hand over her other garter before he could get to it. Far better to unfasten it herself and be done with it.

Instantly Leon's fingers closed over her wrist.

"Don't—you—dare." Each clipped word carried with it another small gust of heated breath, warming her skin and sending fresh shivers racing through her. Removing her hand from the garter, he dropped it back by her side.

His head lifted.

At last, thought Ariel, but before she could catch her breath she realized that he had caught the top of her white silk stocking between his teeth and was slowly drawing it down her trembling leg.

She went still. She'd thought nothing could be more shockingly scandalous than the time she had watched him taste the water from her skin in the bathtub, but she was wrong. This was worse, more shocking, more scandalous. More inflaming.

The sight of him naked and kneeling before her, his long, dark hair tumbling around his shoulders like some primitive warrior, made her realize she had plunged into this far beyond her ability to tread water. She thought to pull away and didn't. Couldn't. Didn't want to.

Going still beneath his hand, she was helpless to do more than watch shadows play across the powerful muscles in his shoulders and chest as with a final jerk he pulled the stocking free of her toes, spat it out, and flashed her a wolf's smile.

Ariel breathed deeply in anticipation as he tipped his shoulder to let her left leg slide off and reached for her right to repeat the entire terrifying, delicious process. When both stockings were gone, he caressed her bare legs, running his hands up and down her calves until her stiff, resistant muscles had no choice but to relax, moving steadily higher until he was shaping the curve of her hip and she was weak with longing for she wasn't sure what.

Suddenly he leaned forward and rested both palms flat on her belly. His hands were so big, his fingertips were curled over the waist of her drawers and his outstretched thumbs rested directly on top of her pelvic bone. He stroked her there and all the air left her in a rush as that same melting sensation began again, even more powerful this time, making her feel as if she were weighted down and soaring all at the same time.

She opened her eyes to find him watching her, no longer smiling. His expression was somber, and intensely, ruthlessly masculine.

Leon drew his thumbs back and forth over her silken drawers, entranced by the slight womanly curve of her belly, pressing against the springy nest of curls below. He wasn't sure if he could actually feel the damp heat awaiting him there or simply imagined it. It didn't matter. Just the thought of it was enough to make his mouth water and drive him to the outer limit of his already sorely tested control.

There was a potent expectancy in the air, as if they were poised together above an endless black abyss.

He stroked her again, tormenting himself once more, lower, deeper, letting his thumb dip between her soft thighs, telling himself she needed more time, already knowing in the searing, grating tightening of his flesh that time and his patience had all but run out.

Ariel gave a small whimper and lifted slightly, pushing against his hand in a sudden move he knew was pure reflex. Now he did feel her sweet heat, dampening the silk, betraying her readiness and sending him hurtling over the edge.

He reared up and covered her, his force driving her two feet to the center of the bed. He was no expert on deflowering virgins, but it would seem that a quick possession would be less troublesome on both sides than a mincing dragging-out of the inevitable. If he was able to sustain any thought as he tugged and tore at her remaining garments, it was that one. Mostly his thoughts were smoke and heat, as he was overtaken by a force he didn't trust and couldn't fight.

Dark, turbulent desire filled him, narrowing his vision so severely that when she at long last lay naked beneath him, he was able only to relish her beauty in fractured, whirling snippets instead of the lush, glorious whole that had possessed his mind for weeks.

His greedy gaze followed the frantic path of his

hands as they streaked over her. He touched the full white globes of her breasts, her tiny waist, and velvety, heavenly thighs. The cloud of golden-brown curls in between trapped his fingers, drawing him deeper, to where she was hot and slick, like honey, like butter, ready for him . . .

Countless times he'd felt this need, but never this deeply. Countless times he'd satisfied it, but never before had he been so aware of the woman he was holding, of each soft sound, each movement, each breath she took. He felt joined to her already and wanted more.

Breathing harshly, he spread her, using his weight to push her legs apart as his fingers parted the dewy petals and found the small opening at their heart. He had to struggle to be gentle as he pushed just the tip of one finger inside her. She was small. Tight. Hot. Wet. His.

Already his hips were pushing restlessly, anticipating the rhythm to come.

His hands shot up to capture hers, dragging her wrists together and pinning them to the mattress above her head as he braced himself over her and then thrust forward, a scorching joy tearing through him as he entered her easily. His head came up sharply.

Too easily?

Ariel whimpered a little under his quick, ruthless possession. There was a burning, stretching sensation as he pushed into her, a rampant sense of being invaded and conquered. But there was no real pain.

Of far more concern to her than her own response at that moment was Leon's. As soon as he was fully sheathed inside her body, he went utterly still. For an instant she feared she had fallen short of his expectations. Her heart lurched upward into her throat in panic that he would end it, turning away from her with that haughty look of disdain she had seen on him so often. If that happened, she was certain she would lose her last, her *only* chance to taste true passion.

Mercifully, she felt his body relax and he began to move once again. Her flesh yielded in increments as he pushed farther, deeper with each slow stroke until she was sure there was no more of her to be taken. Body or soul.

He filled her senses as absolutely as he filled her body, dominating her whole world. The harsh, raw sounds coming from her throat wrapped around her. When she opened her eyes she saw only him, looming over her in the darkness, the glistening curve of his neck and shoulders an irresistible lure. His arms were stretched out above her, his grip like a brand at her wrists. When she lifted her head to press her lips to one bulging biceps, she tasted the tangy, primitive essence of salt and man. Even his scent inflamed her. He smelled of danger and forbidden passion.

Without planning to, she felt herself begin to move with him, lifting her hips to meet him as he pumped into her, more rapidly now.

"Oh, yes," he murmured, his open mouth suddenly a flame at her throat. "Oh . . . please."

His fractured words excited her. She bent her knees and felt him plunge even deeper, and something else, something more, a flutter, a yearning in her womb that was repeated again and a second later as he groaned and moved against her with a new grinding motion.

She gave a small cry of surprise, instinctively twisting her hips in search of that fluttering, elusive pressure. When she recaptured it, her eyes went wide with astonishment and confusion and a sudden driving need at her core to feel it again and again and again until she discovered where it would lead her. Any uneasiness about her body was forgotten. For the first time, she gloried in the womanliness of her body in the way it was designed to be a perfect receptacle for his.

The unnamed yearning inside grew steadily more insistent, causing her to strain restlessly against his hold. She wanted her hands free to touch and claw and hold on so she wouldn't hurtle out of control as the pressure built and built.

Her head was tossed back on the pillow, her teeth clamped over her bottom lip. She closed her eyes, straining upward with a new urgency just as he abruptly pressed her down and pinned her to the bed with the force of a final driving thrust. The harsh cry that ripped from his throat was muffled against her breast, and then he went taut.

Sixteen

Ariel caught her breath, awestruck that she could actually feel his life force pulsing into her, absorbing the shudders that gripped his body, then cushioning him as his bulk dropped heavily onto her.

Almost instantly he grasped that he was too much for her and levered his weight onto his elbows.

"Sorry," he murmured, panting harshly. "Can't think."

She nodded, clenching her stomach muscles in desperation as she felt his body slipping from hers, the damp friction causing a faint specter of the thrill she'd felt a moment before. She sighed and shifted in agitation.

Leon lifted his head from her breast, leaving her damp and warm where his cheek had rested. "Are you all right?"

"Yes, perfectly. I only . . ."

"Only what?"

"Wondered ... that is, I was struck by how abruptly ... I meant to say ... to inquire ... is that it, then?"

"Is that it?" he echoed, still breathing harshly. "You dratted woman. What did you expect? That I could make the ceiling part and a heavenly host appear, blowing trumpets and scattering rose petals over you?"

"Not that. Exactly."

He dragged his fingers through his hair, looking wounded, Ariel decided regretfully.

"Then what? Exactly? Perhaps you merely expected a man who could walk on water? Shall we inquire if this bloody place has a lake or a damn moat I might walk across to satisfy you? Unless a fountain would suffice. Seven damned fountains there are, that was what he said, wasn't it?"

He rolled off her onto his back and laughed up at the scrolled ceiling.

"I wish to point out that I was not complaining," she explained without venturing to look at him. Hearing him was enough. He did not sound happy. "I'm quite certain that your part of it was magnificent."

"You do have an irritating tendency to profess definitive opinions on subjects of which you're entirely ignorant. How can you be so certain I was magnificent?" he demanded to know. "I was your first, wasn't I?"

Ariel's heart lurched. Had she heard a note of suspicion in his question or was she just so guilty, she imagined it?

"Your implication is unworthy of us both," she said to the ceiling. "Do you have some foundation to question my virtue?"

There was a pause.

"No," he said. "You were as skittish and unskilled as any virgin would be."

"Thank you."

"It wasn't a compliment, Ariel."

"Oh."

Another, longer pause ensued. A sideways glance informed her that he had folded his hands beneath his head. The quick glimpse of his armpit and the flexed muscles of his upper chest was enough to make her pulse quicken and her legs shift restlessly against the tangle of bedclothes.

Leon rolled again, this time to his side, with his elbow bent to support his head. She felt him studying her for what felt like an eternity.

"So," he said at last. "You surrendered your innocence and now you would wish it back intact."

"Oh, no, not at all," she replied quickly, cognizant of a trace of regret in his deep voice. She instinctively turned her head and then just as instinctively flinched from his close scrutiny. "It isn't that."

"But clearly you found the experience less than you expected."

"That's true in a sense," she admitted. "I confess I did believe there would be . . . more."

"More."

She nodded uneasily, cursing her predilection for the truth. Better she had cooed and sighed and told him he was the world's most clever lover, which was evidently what he expected and desired to hear. He was experienced, vastly so, she surmised, and she couldn't help wondering if he was accustomed to praise because his previous lovers were all accomplished actresses, or if her disappointment was unprecedented among his partners and solely attributable to some lacking on her part.

"When you say you expected there would be *more*," he said suddenly, "do you by chance mean more of this?"

Ariel jumped, not sure if she was more startled by the sultry drawl of his voice intruding on her tangled thoughts, or the unexpected touch of his hand high on her thigh closest to him.

He trailed his fingers up and down, from her hip to her knee, coasting close to the slanted path that led to the juncture of her thighs, but never following it there.

"Or perhaps this?" he asked quietly, drawing his hand up across her belly to cup her breast.

She gasped as he caught the tingling tip between his fingers and squeezed until the sharp pain mixed with exquisite delight became unbearable.

As if he were privy to her every feeling, his tongue was there at once, soothing where his fingers had been sweetly tormenting her, lapping slow circles around the taut bud, drawing it into his mouth to suck her as she moaned and moaned, helpless now. Her knee came up and her head tipped back, and everything inside her melted and swirled around and around in a tightening vortex at her core.

"Or," he said, his voice grating against her drenched breast as he nudged her to her left side and, lying the same way, fitted his body in close behind her, "was it more of this you desired?"

She didn't answer, couldn't, could barely gather air to breathe. They were pressed together from head to toe, his mouth busy at her ear, one long, powerful leg effortlessly holding hers apart, his left hand in her hair and his right . . . oh, his right, drifting, sliding between her legs and rubbing against her in places she hadn't known existed, shallow places and deep, in and out in long, slow strokes that melded one into the next, all slippery and warm and fragrant. Her own scent reached her, mingled with the smell of slaked lust that clung to his skin, a heady, intoxicating blend.

The fluttering inside started again and quickly became something else, a twisting, clawing fiery demand at her core. She arched her back, desperate to get away and to get closer at the same time. His other arm slide beneath her, holding her securely as he brought the heel of his hand against her woman's place, pressing and easing in a sure, steady cadence as she clamped her legs together and bore down frantically.

She felt driven and desperate and freer than ever before. Strangely, she also felt more herself than ever. She hadn't known how many layers of artifice and propriety she had accumulated through the years until his touch stripped them all away, releasing the wild, untamed, *savage* side of her for the first time.

Ariel felt his lips in her hair, heard his voice without hearing the words, only an unbroken murmur that stretched her jagged senses like a lifeline tossed at sea, *angel angel shhh letme letme* and then the rapture crested and broke and she cried out his name and clung to him, holding on as wave after wave crashed and washed through her, leaving her trembling and astonished.

She worried that her heart would go on racing forever, but gradually it slowed and her breathing returned to normal.

"Dare I ask if that was more in keeping with your expectations?" Leon inquired. His tone was light, but she sensed his need to know if he had pleased her.

"Quite," she managed to reply. "It was . . ." She searched for words equal to what she was feeling and discovered his own captured it best. "It was trumpets and rose petals enough to last forever."

"Good," he said, at last sounding happy. He

reached to draw the coverlet over them both before settling against her once more. "Consider yourself ravished."

Yes, splendidly ravished, thought a suddenly drowsy Ariel. She'd wanted to experience real passion once in her life, and now she had. Now she understood. Now she knew. And knowing what it was like, knowing what he was like, how could she ever bear to live without?

Leon felt her muscles relax as she gradually surrendered to sleep. Her fingers, laced with his, loosened, her lashes lowered, her breath became a warm, steady caress across his chest. And with each breath she took, his confusion deepened.

He was accustomed to feeling restless after sex. Energized, satisfied, bored, all those things he had felt in the past, either singularly or in combination, depending upon the woman and the night. Never before after sex had he felt confused, however. Maybe, he thought, a sudden dryness in his throat, that's because what just happened with Ariel had not been simply sex, but, rather, something else.

Something that had nothing to do with titles or manners or lessons in either grooming or flirting, but with the powerful, unrelenting feeling that she was with him even when she wasn't. That her pulse was beating inside him along with his own, so that whenever he saw or heard or even thought of something, *anything,* a sunrise, a joke, a memory, his own reaction was intertwined with an innate awareness of how Ariel would react.

Lying in that bed with Ariel in his arms, he felt a sense of connection, of wholeness, of being at peace with himself and the world, that he had never felt before.

And he didn't like it one bit.

Gently disentangling himself from her arms, he rose and looked around for his clothes. He would prove to himself that this place had no power over him, and then he would deal with Ariel's sorcery. He would walk Restormel's halls, confront its dark corners and its cobwebs, and its ghosts ... that is, if they exhibited greater interest in meeting him now than when they were alive. He *would* face this feeling and he would conquer it, once and for all.

He took the candle from the mantel and made it as far as the top of the stairs before an apparition in billowing white materialized in front of him.

"Trouble sleeping, my lord?" inquired the apparition.

Leon felt his heart and lungs unknot and drop back into place.

"Dammit all, Calvin, don't you ever sleep?"

"I do, sir, but fitfully." He patted his right knee through the white nightshirt that had given Leon such a start. On his head he wore a matching cap. "Old war wound keeps me awake."

"I see." He gestured toward the stairs with the candle. "I thought I'd have a look around before turning in."

Calvin gave an enthusiastic nod. "Just the thing, young sir. No one around to get in our way. We can start in—"

"Calvin."

"Yes, sir?"

"The tour can wait until tomorrow. I want to be alone tonight."

"Of course, sir." He began to turn and stopped, obviously distressed.

Leon sighed. "What is it, Cal?"

"I don't wish to intrude, sir, or overstep my bounds."

"Go on," he urged, impatience turning to wariness.

"I only thought to take advantage of our mutual insomnia and the private moment it has allowed us to—"

"Out with it, Calvin."

"You should know, sir, that he did search for you. Your father, I mean. I know," he went on, his tone a blend of respect and the determination to say his piece, "because I am the man he sent."

"He sent you to Hawaii to search for me?" Leon asked, part of him wanting to hear what Calvin had to say, part of him already insisting it didn't matter, that it couldn't possibly change anything.

"Yes. I was the logical choice, you see, because I was familiar with the land, having gone along as manservant on his first journey there as well."

Leon's interest was hopelessly piqued. "So you knew about my mother, then? You knew that he was already married when he returned here to claim his title and a rich new wife?"

"I knew," Calvin said without emotion. "He trusted me with his secret, and I kept it all those years. For better or worse. I was the only one who did know. I was also the only one who knew how he suffered for doing what he did."

"Please," Leon said, his short laugh biting. "Spare me."

"You don't want to hear that he suffered?" the older man countered, the expression on his lined face suddenly less subservient and more consoling. "I can understand why. But truth is truth, no matter what we want to believe, and the truth is your father suffered from the day he returned home until the day he died."

"I only hope it did not end there," Leon declared, his jaw rigid. "He deserved to suffer."

"Are you the one to judge?" challenged the servant in a quiet voice.

"I think I'm more qualified than most," retorted Leon. "It was, after all, my mother he used and lied to and finally abandoned for another woman, one who better suited his ambitious purposes."

Calvin nodded. "Perhaps you're right. But before you judge a man, you should have all the facts. Please come with me."

Leon scowled as the somber servant turned and started down the hall, but he followed just the same, intrigued. Let him present all the facts he cared to, he thought. In fact, the more facts he produced, the better. Nothing would ever change his mind about the past, and when he left there, he would leave any doubts behind as well.

Calvin led him up the stairs and along another hall before turning into a cramped passageway Leon was sure he would have missed if he'd been alone. At the end of the passage was a door, and behind it a steep spiral staircase so narrow, he had to angle his shoulders to make the climb. They must be in one of the turrets, he deduced, waiting as Calvin unlocked the door at the top of the stairs and then following the servant inside.

The circular room was ringed with windows, and Leon knew that during the day it would be flooded with sunlight that might well negate his first impression. But at that moment, with the only illumination coming from the flickering candle in his hand and a crescent moon hanging above the skylight overhead, he would swear he was back home.

"The mural is amazingly lifelike, is it not?" inquired Calvin as Leon turned slowly, taking in the lush scene that had been recreated on the curved walls. The effect was intensified when Calvin nudged the door shut. It had been painted too, so that he was completely surrounded by palm trees and vegetation and tropical birds whose island names he could recite from memory.

"Who did this?" Leon asked in a hushed voice. To speak out loud seemed as inappropriate there as at a grave.

"It was painted at your father's behest by a very talented Dutch painter. The artist himself never visited Hawaii. Everything you see was painted in accordance with your father's painstaking description." A faint smile edged his thin lips. "He had the poor man paint over the portrait and try again five times before he was satisfied with the result."

Seeing Leon glance around in bewilderment, he took the candle from him and crossed to the side of the room that remained in shadows. He held the candle close to the wall so its flickering light fell on a waterfall that looked so real, the silvery spray seemed to hang in the air, and on the figure of a slender woman with long, dark hair, seated in the tall grass beside it.

A jolt of recognition passed through Leon. The woman didn't just resemble his mother, it was his mother. Exactly as he remembered her, young, beautiful, captured with such animation, he almost expected her to laugh or reach out to him. Only her expression was different. She looked happy in the painting. In his memories, even when she smiled she looked sad and lonely. And a little scared, he realized for the first time.

He looked away. Remembering her brought a crushing wave of grief that required all his willpower to bring under control.

"So he commissioned a painting of my mother," he

said, shrugging. "What man does not want a souvenir of his adventures?"

"Your father did not create this room, his Island Room, he called it, until many years after he'd put aside adventure for responsibility."

"His Island Room?" Leon repeated mockingly. "Tell me, what did his marchioness call it?"

"She never saw it," Calvin replied. "No one was allowed here. Your father gave me the key for safe-keeping when he grew too feeble to climb the stairs. I believe that along with that key, he surrendered his will to live."

Leon refused to be moved. So he had surrendered his will to live at a ripe old age. His mother's life had been ripped from her far too soon.

Calvin took advantage of his tormented silence to tell him still more things he did not want to hear.

"Your father did intend to return to the island, and to your mother, that was not a lie. Then he arrived back here to discover his father and older brother dead, the estate in disarray, and countless people depending on him to put it all right." Calvin sighed. "He was young, and young men make mistakes that old men live to regret.

"For years I watched him struggle to shoulder the burden he had allowed to be thrust upon him," Calvin went on. "Then one day he summoned me and dispatched me to Hawaii for news of your mother. It was I who brought him word of her unfortunate death."

"Unfortunate death?" The words exploded from Leon. "Her senseless slaughter is more like it."

Calvin nodded, his ashen pallor discernible even in the dim light. "You're right, of course. I elected to spare him the painful details of her murder and I have come to see I was wrong. You see? All old men have regrets."

His anguished tone precluded Leon from being angry with him. How could he blame the man for being loyal? Or compassionate?

"I was also the one who first told him he had a son," Calvin added gamely.

With a deceptive calm, Leon quickly masked the raw emotion his words unleashed, refusing to ask what his response had been.

"I'm afraid that was all I could tell him," Calvin went on. "That and the name she had given you. I searched for you, of course, after being told you'd been taken in by relatives. But you know as well as I how wary villagers are of outsiders. Every lead I followed was a dead end. I finally had to return home with no answers for the hundreds of questions your father threw at me."

Leon stared at the older man, wondering how close their paths might have come to crossing, and if things might have turned out differently if they had. *Taken in by relatives.* The words brought back bitter memories. He'd been taken in all right. Taken in, shuffled from one reluctant uncle or aunt to another like a bad penny, and finally cast out for good. It was little wonder Calvin's search had reached a dead end. His loving family was hardly likely to admit they had sent a boy to live with the dreaded *kauwa*.

"So he inquired after my mother. Bloody decent of him, considering that she was his wife. The news of my existence must have been a trifle inconvenient for the old man," he added, pacing restlessly. The cornerless room felt smaller all of a sudden.

"The news that he had a son he could not claim was devastating to your father."

"Really?" Leon whirled back to face him in the darkness. "How long did he remain *devastated* before he managed to forget all about me and return to playing lord of the manor?"

Calvin shook his head. "Forget you? He never forgot. Years later he would appear in my room in the middle of the night, asking if when I searched for you I had thought to check with this official or inquire after you at that village. It was as if he were haunted by the past even in his sleep. He was dying by the time I received a letter from an old shipmate who wrote that there was a man who called himself Duvanne living on one of the outer islands."

The old man lifted the candle in a circular motion so that the mural was revealed in sections, the vivid colors sparkling like jewels against the blackness.

"Does this look like the work of a man who wanted to forget?" he asked.

Leon made a scoffing sound. "This room is a shrine to his young lover," he declared.

"Is it?" Calvin returned the candle to him on his way out. "Take a closer look, my lord."

Leon remained where he was, listening to the door shut and the footsteps on the stairs fade to silence. Lifting the candle, he moved closer to the painting of his mother and saw instantly what Calvin had meant for him to see, what he had overlooked before. There was an infant cradled in his mother's arm, a small dark head nestled against her breast.

Slowly, instinctively, he moved the candle to the right and saw more images, a toddler, a young child, a young man, and finally the unmistakable figure of a grown man, standing and staring out over a clear blue ocean. All the images had the same straight, dark hair. Like his mother's, Leon thought. Like his own. They also shared his lanky frame. There was no way his father could have known how he was built. Had he also been tall and lean? Had he simply guessed that his son had inherited his mother's hair and his own stature?

What the hell difference did it make? The most significant thing about the painting was that with the exception of his mother, all the faces were either turned away or in shadows. Naturally. There had been no memories for him to draw on to describe to the artist his son's smile or the shape of his eyes.

Leon took a step closer to the mural, unable to look away. It was like staring at himself, but not. Like staring at what his life could have been. Should have been. An eerie feeling settled over him, and his hand holding the candle trembled slightly. Of all the ghosts he'd thought to find at Restormel, he had never expected to confront his own.

It was early morning when a sharp rap on the chamber door woke them both.

Ariel bolted upright, at first disoriented to find herself naked beneath the covers and with Leon beside her. Then the memory of the night before came roaring back. To her surprise, it came without regrets. She was at peace with what she had done, and with what she must do now.

"What is it?" Leon called out in a voice husky with sleep and muffled by the pillow they had apparently been sharing.

"A problem, sir," Calvin called in reply. "Do I have leave to enter?"

"Tell him no," she ordered Leon, recalling the abandon with which her garments had been tossed to the four corners of the room. Being at peace with what had happened was not the same as being an idiot about it. She glanced around frantically. "My . . . clothes," she finished, mystified to see not a single piece of evidence anywhere that she had spent the night there.

"I put them in my bag," he told her. "In anticipation of just such an early morning caller. Now, get down."

"But . . ." she sputtered, wondering when and why he had roused himself to protect her good name.

"Down." He pushed her under the heavy coverlet and bunched it over his flexed knee so her shape was indiscernible.

"Enter," he called.

Calvin opened the door and stepped in. "Good morning, sir."

"Good morning, Calvin. If it really is morning," he added, yawning mightily as he glanced out the window. "Is it always so dark at this hour?"

"In March, yes. We appear to be in for a storm as well. Alfred fears your tour of the grounds will have to be postponed."

"Would that be the problem you woke me to tell me about?"

"Of course not." He looked offended. "I woke you to say that one of the children inadvertently left the cage door open and, well, I'm forced to report that . . . Prinny," he said, a definite twinkle in his eye as his thin lips twisted around the name, "is, at the moment, unable to be accounted for."

"You mean he's loose, wandering around a place with—How many rooms are there?"

"Seventy, sir, not counting—"

"Close enough. Seventy rooms."

"That is the present situation, I'm afraid. But we are already acting to remedy it. I've ordered all doors and windows secured, and rallied the entire staff for the search."

Leon gave him a reassuring smile. "At ease, Cal. He is only a rabbit, you understand, not really the king of England."

"Of course, sir. Just the same, you entrusted me with his care, and I never take it lightly when a man sees fit to place his trust in me."

The look that passed between them was a silent reminder of the night before.

"I applaud your dedication, but—"

Leon broke off abruptly, puzzled by the slow, bobbing motion of Calvin's head until he realized he was tracking the progress of the brown and white fur ball that was at that moment hopping across the room in his direction.

Prinny.

Calvin clicked his heels together. "I'll call off the search at once."

"Good idea. And, Cal," he added. "I've installed Miss Halliday in the room at the opposite end of the hall. The long trip left her indisposed. She's not to be disturbed by anyone, for any reason."

"Very good, sir. I'll see to informing the rest of the staff."

Leon waited for the door to click shut before tapping the mountain of covers beside him.

"You can come out," he said quietly. "Unless of course, you'd like to—"

Ariel immediately erupted from beneath the coverlet.

"You're very pink," he observed, holding back at least a hundred other more laudatory and important things he wanted to tell her—that she was beautiful and enticing beyond anything he had imagined and that he had been imagining and fantasizing about her for weeks and was afraid he couldn't stop.

"It's very warm under there," she said, not meeting his gaze.

"That must be it," he murmured, running his hand over the curve of her shoulder. "Although I must plead to harboring a profound curiosity about your charming tendency to blush since the first moment I set eyes on you." His fingertip traced the edge of the coverlet where she had pulled it tight across her chest and anchored it beneath both arms. "Would you like to know what, in particular, I was curious about?"

"I'm sure it would not be safe to admit it to you if I did."

"Safety is boring. I'll interpret that as a yes. I have devoted an undignified amount of time and concentration to wondering if your cheeks were the only part of your anatomy that changed color with your moods, or if you blushed . . . everywhere." He ran his hand in a straight line down the velvety skin beneath her jaw to her breast and watched her tremble in response. "Everywhere. Would you like to hear the answer?"

"I think not."

"Coward. I'll tell you anyway. You do blush all over. Every last, sweet, soft, voluptuous inch of you." He lifted her hair and pressed his open mouth to the back of her neck. "Like pink petals and cream. Without question the most delicious shade of woman I have ever seen. Or tasted. Or—"

"Please, Leon, don't do this."

He went still, though not nearly as rigid as she was at that moment. Slowly he turned her face toward him and began to lower his mouth. "Would you prefer I do this instead?"

She pulled away before his lips touched hers. "I would prefer it if you would be so kind as to hand me my dress."

"Why?" he countered, forcing calmness as he stacked pillows behind him and leaning back. He was not accustomed to being rebuffed the morning after. "Are you going somewhere?"

"Yes. To the room you said was to be mine."

"I lied. This is your room for as long as we're at Restormel."

"Don't be ridiculous," she chided, turning to face him at last. "Last night cannot be repeated. For both our sakes. I will not lead you on by falsely receiving further caresses or endearments from you."

"And what of last night's caresses?" he demanded, baffled and wounded and irritated all at once. "Am I supposed to believe that they were honestly received?"

"They were," she exclaimed. "I sincerely hope you will believe me." She swallowed hard. "Last night you made me an offer, to experience something for the first time. I accepted. The circumstances were extraordinary, you must admit. We were both bone weary from traveling and deeply affected by our arrival here. We shared a vulnerable, if not volatile, combination of emotions. Not that I feel the necessity to make excuses. Whatever the cause, our bargain was honestly struck, and fulfilled with great pleasure. For both of us, I believe."

He ignored her unspoken appeal for agreement. "And that was all it was?" he asked, arms folded across his bare chest like a shield. "A purely physical bargain struck and met? No *emotional engagement* whatsoever?"

"None," she replied without equivocation. Turning so that her long, golden-brown hair hid her face, she added, "Now it is finished and I for one would like to bathe and dress for the day so that we may both get on with the serious responsibilities that await us."

"Let's see now," he said, narrowing his eyes in mock contemplation. Everything in him rejected her claim that she had felt nothing last night but a purely physical pleasure, as if he had done no more than scratch her damn back for her. How could she have felt nothing when he had felt . . . something? "My serious responsibility would be to find the Sage sword."

She nodded. "To which I have pledged you my full assistance."

"And your responsibility is—"

"To my family," she supplied when he broke off expectantly.

"Which you mean to fulfill by marrying Penrose, is that still the plan?"

She gave a small, tight nod. "Yes, if all goes well."

"How can you even think of marrying him now?" he snarled.

"For the same reason I always thought of it, because I have no choice," she declared in a voice that simmered with frustration.

"Are you so naive you believe your little plan is still viable after spending the night in my bed?"

"How dare you throw last night in my face?"

"I'm not," he retorted, "but Penrose is sure to when he finds out you—"

"Oh, she cried, twisting around to face him, her blue eyes wide and accusing. "You . . . you . . . oh. How could I let myself be fooled into believing that buried somewhere in that selfish, black heart of yours there is even an ounce, one miserly shred, of gentlemanly integrity? Only the most despicable sort of knave would carry tales of such intimate—"

"Cease," he ordered. Loudly.

Ariel tossed her head and rose from her side of the bed. He stormed from the other, both of them seething with righteous indignation.

Grabbing his breeches from the floor, he yanked them on and fastened them, missing half the buttons. By the time he was done, she had freed a cotton sheet from the bed and swathed herself in it. They squared off across the tousled battlefield of the mattress.

"Do you really think me petty enough to go running back to town bragging to that simpleton of my good fortune with the woman he fancies?" he demanded, displeasure and disappointment mingled in his tone.

"How else is he to know I *spent the night in your bed?*"

"He won't have to know you spent the night in my bed to know you spent a night in *someone's,*" retorted Leon. "Think about it." When she merely bit her lip and gave a haughty shrug, he shook his head in exasperation. "Penrose will be expecting to find a virgin in his wedding bed and, in case it's slipped your notice, you no longer are one. It was only my *gentlemanly integrity* that prompted my concern for the uncomfortable position you may soon find yourself in . . . if all goes well," he concluded in a mocking echo of her words.

His reasoning took some of the starch from her Amazon-warrior posture. "Oh," she said. "In that case, I apologize for speaking in haste, and for implying you are a knave."

His mouth twisted sardonically. "If that was an implication, I should hate to be on the receiving end of an accusation."

"Your concern is very kind, I'm sure, and much appreciated," she told him, "but you will be pleased to know I have the situation under control."

"Is that so? May I inquire how?"

"As I see it, there are two possible approaches to the problem. The simplest is to explain it away. Technically speaking, the lack of physical evidence of virginity does not mean a woman has been with another man. I've read there are any number of strictly innocuous ways a woman's hymen may be broken. A hard fall, riding astride, a childhood accident, to name a few."

"Fascinating," he said, thinking her prepared spiel on the subject was closer to downright astounding. "And the second approach?"

"That is a little more complicated," she replied with only a shade less confidence. "It involves the use of a small vial of animal blood and a sleeping garment designed to conceal—"

"I can guess the rest," he interrupted, regarding her curiously. "It appears you've given this matter considerable thought. I wonder when you had the time."

She bit her lip, one shoulder lifting in an uneasy shrug. "I had trouble sleeping."

No, thought Leon, *he* had had trouble sleeping. When he finally returned to bed, he had been reluctant to close his eyes and surrender the conscious pleasure of holding her close and watching her sleep ... and sleep she did, as peacefully as a newborn babe. So when had she managed to concoct such an involved solution to such a recent dilemma?

"Were you unable to sleep because you were worried about how last night might affect your plans?"

She nodded eagerly. "Yes, exactly. But no longer."

"Now that you have the situation under control, you mean?"

"That's right."

"It doesn't trouble you at all that in the event you

do marry the Nose, he will not be getting the entire pound of flesh to which he is entitled?"

She flinched and clenched her jaw. "Not at all," she retorted. "He will be marrying a woman. I shall be marrying a man. I do not believe there is anything in the vows that specify precisely how much flesh either of us is required to present."

Leon laughed in spite of himself. "By God, I believe you're right.

"And even if I am less than forthright in that one area," she added, her stance relaxing a little, "I will see to it he is well compensated in all other ways. I will make him a good wife."

Leon imagined her tone was the same one that Christians had used to greet the lions. Not that he had any doubt she would make Penrose a good wife, a far better one than the little snit deserved, to be sure. She was intelligent and resourceful and loyal. And beautiful and passionate and responsive, and the mere thought of Penrose or any other man touching her made him crazy.

"I'm sure you will make a splendid wife," he agreed. "I'm decidedly less certain of the Nose's potential as a husband."

"What do you mean?"

"I mean . . ." He groped for words that would say everything he yearned to say without revealing anything he didn't want to reveal. "I mean, do you think that after last night you will still find him to be all that you require in a husband?"

"All that I require, or all that I desire?" she countered with a slow, wistful smile. "Last night may well have changed me forever, but not at all my situation. I harbor no false illusions about the physical nature of any future union between Mr. Penrose and myself. You showed me what is possible between a man and a woman, and now I shall know what I am missing every night for the rest of my life. I cannot say yet if that is something to be grateful for, or to bitterly regret."

Leon let his gaze drop suggestively to the tumbled sheets that stretched temptingly between them. "Perhaps I can help you make up your mind."

She shook her head, her small, regretful smile like a vise around his heart. "That wouldn't help. It would only postpone the inevitable, and make it harder in the end. We must both put aside what happened last night and go on with our separate lives. However things turn out between Mr. Penrose and me, I belong back at the school."

"And me?" he challenged. "Since you have everything so neatly figured out, Ariel, perhaps you can you tell me where I belong."

"I wish for your sake that you could feel at home here," she said, "that you might at last find the peace of mind I don't think you've ever found anywhere. But it isn't for me to say where you belong, or Castleton or your grandmother either. Only your heart can tell you that."

His heart, he thought disgustedly. His heart had been commandeered by a stranger. Even his thoughts were no longer his own, constantly twisting and veering down paths he had always shunned. He'd spent most of the night wrestling them into submission, only to have her unwittingly let them loose on him again. *I wish you could feel at home here,* she'd said, as if such a thing were possible.

He would never, ever feel at home there, he told himself, glancing around desperately, suddenly feeling more caged, more threatened, by the room's opulent trappings than he ever had while chained in the ship's hold or locked in his cell at Castleton's.

"In that case, I have my answer," he told her. Impulsively dragging back his hair, he exposed to her the dark red mark that stood out roughly against the smooth bronze skin of his forehead. "I don't *belong* anywhere. And I have this to prove it."

Seventeen

Y ou once asked if this scar was the result of an accident," Leon said. "It was no accident. The mark was put on me deliberately."

"For what reason?" Ariel countered, stunned.

"To set me apart. It's the mark of the *kuawa*," he explained, the native word sounding strange to her ears. Beneath his carefully dispassionate tone, she sensed his temper straining at the end of a very short leash. "The untouchables. A group of outcasts kept apart from the rest of society. I was sent to live with them when I was twelve."

"How awful." She looked away from the mark on his forehead, shaken, anguished, suffering for him. She had thought nothing could be worse than hearing him tell about his mother's death, but she was wrong. Every time she thought she understood why he was the way he was, so bitter and guarded, another layer was peeled away and she realized that the darkness inside him went deeper than she had ever imagined. "It's worse than awful, Leon, it's absolutely barbaric."

"Is it?" His wide mouth curved tauntingly. "Do you think there are no outcasts here in your civilized society? People who are shunned because of something they did, or failed to do, or simply because they were thoughtless enough to allow themselves to be born with the wrong blood running in their veins?"

"It's not the same," she protested. "No one is branded here."

"Not physically," he agreed. "But only because it's a land of hypocrites. Give me an honest barbarian any day over a gentleman who slaps me on the back with one hand while he stabs me in the heart with the other."

His words struck a painful chord. Ariel couldn't help thinking of how a single, foolish mistake had, in a sense, branded her for life, and of how she had been stabbed in the heart afterward by the only person to whom she had dared to reveal the truth.

"Even if there is some merit in what you say, one cruelty does not excuse the other," she said. "What possible reason could there be to shun or brand a twelve-year-old boy?"

Shrugging, he turned away. "It doesn't matter now. In fact, the mark has recently proven to be a blessing." He lowered himself into the chair opposite the bed and hitched one long leg over the arm, his attempt to appear detached failing to convince her. "Without this reminder staring me in the face each morning when I shave, I might be careless enough to believe it when someone tells me that I'm not an outcast, that I've ceased being an outsider as suddenly and senselessly as I became one, and that it's here that I belong, in the very last place on earth I would ever choose to be."

Ariel was swept by a longing to reach out and embrace him and tell him everything would be all right, but the simmering fury beneath his casual pose forbade it.

"I know you're bitter, and that you have every right to be," she said, choosing her words with care. "You've suffered a great deal, both at the hands of my country-men and your own. But denying the truth won't change it." She moved closer to him, heedless of the fact that she was dressed in only a sheet that molded to her curves with every step. "Leon, can't you see that you have to face the past and accept it if you are to ever be truly happy?"

His eyes darkened with suspicion. "By accepting it, I assume you mean accepting the title and all that goes with it?"

Ariel shook her head. "I may have believed that once, but no longer."

"That's quite a turnabout. Are you sure it's prudent?"

"I don't know what you mean."

"I mean it's always struck me that you are a little too dedicated to my cause for someone who is, how did you put it the other day? Just doing her job? Maybe Castleton promised you an added reward if you not only taught me to bow, but delivered me to him trussed and titled as well. How far would you go to collect?" He raked her with a blatantly suggestive look. "Silly question. We already know how far you're willing to go with me, don't we?"

"You have a hell of a nerve," she declared, trem-bling with outrage. "I've received no more than my normal salary all these weeks for performing a task that was anything but normal . . . trying to teach an oaf who refused to be taught, trying to reason with the most irrational, unreasonable, ungrateful man who ever walked the earth. If the earl offers me a reward when this is over, you bet your worthless hide I'll accept it. He could not pay me enough to undertake this task a second time."

"I am not irrational," he said quietly.

"You are if you think for a moment that it was in the hope of seeing you trussed and being rewarded for it that I shared your bed last night."

"Then why did you?"

"Because . . . because . . . none of your business," she snapped. "Nor was I thinking of a reward when I offered to come here with you in the first place. I was trying to help. I wouldn't have bothered if I'd known this is the thanks I would get."

"Help me do what?" he countered, his gaze a dangerous golden blaze, the look of a swordsman poised to deliver the fatal thrust.

"Stay out of trouble," she retorted, denying him victory. "And help you get what I thought you wanted, and why wouldn't I think you wanted the title? When you seemed so bloody eager to beat Lockaby to the sword in order to claim it."

"Did it ever occur to you that maybe I just like to win?"

"No, but I'm sure it should have, it's such an appropriately insane notion to think you'd go to such lengths to claim victory over people you profess to care nothing about. I swear I don't know what you want from one moment to the next, and I'm beginning to think you don't either."

His gaze held hers. "What if I said I wanted you?"

The quiet question twisted inside her, setting off a different kind of longing, making her struggle to appear unruffled. "I'd say you were a most foolish and impulsive man and that you need to learn to look past your momentary whims. Have you ever considered the fact that aside from everything else, as the Marquis of Sage you would be in a position to help a great many other people?"

He flashed a derisive smile. "Such as Castleton and his band of self-serving schemers?"

"No," she said, impatient, "such as the men, women, and children who climbed from their warm beds in the middle of the night to welcome you here. Such as your grandmother, who clearly has more faith in you than you have in yourself." Noting the unsettling effect her earnest argument was having on him, she pressed her advantage. "Such as all the people who have no voice in this land of hypocrites, to use your words, and who desperately need a man of intelligence and compassion to speak for them."

He lifted one shoulder dismissively. "I am not that man."

"You could be if you would stop feeling sorry for yourself and show some guts." His head came up, his dark gaze impaling her, but rather than back away, Ariel took a step closer. "In spite of your best efforts to repel and intimidate me, I've come to know you, Leon, and I know the kind of man you are inside."

He sprung from the chair and moved away, his words lashing out at her. "You *think* you know me, but you're wrong. You want to know what kind of man I am? You want to know why I was sent to live with the *kauwa*? Why my own mother's family couldn't stand the sight of me? I'll tell you why. It was because I nearly beat my own cousin to death."

Ariel was shaking inside from the sheer, intimidating force of his anger, but she willed herself to remain calm and expressionless, sensing the torment that was driving his sudden fury, knowing it wasn't directed at her at all, but at the demons inside him.

"You see, it wasn't only my mother who was eager for Giles Duvanne's return," he continued. "Our whole village was counting on him and the riches he promised to bring back with him. My cousin called him a liar, and he was right. But Giles Duvanne was still my father. At twelve I understood more about family loyalty than that bastard ever did."

Ariel listened in silence as he went on.

"My cousin was older than I was, and bigger, and a bully, but none of that mattered that day. I wasn't afraid of anything or anybody, and I could have killed him easily." He brought his hard, cold gaze to bear directly on her. "I would have if my uncle hadn't stopped me in time."

"I'm sure it must have seemed that way to you back then," she said, hoping to calm him, "but you were only a child."

"Was I still a child at sixteen?" he countered harshly. "That's how old I was when I nearly killed a lackey at the royal stable for calling me Liliuoka's pet. Never mind that I knew that's exactly what I was." The admission was accompanied by a harsh laugh.

A small frown furrowed the space between her brows. "Who was Lil— Lili—"

"Liliuoka. She was one of the king's wives. The youngest and most beautiful of them," he added, looking past her, a grim, faraway expression on his face. "When I first arrived at court she taught me to read and work with numbers. I was starving for notice and she noticed me; she was the first person to take any real interest in me since my mother died. Sometimes . . . sometimes I let myself pretend she was my mother."

He shook his head, his look one of such bitter self-loathing that Ariel's heart ached for him.

"One day she summoned me to her private quarters," he continued more hesitantly, as if picking his way through memories he knew were laced with explosives. "She offered to teach me other things as well, things between a man and a woman. I was sixteen, shocked and flattered, and scared as hell. Scared to say yes, scared to say no, afraid that if I did the wrong thing, she would send me back to the *kuawa*, and I would be alone again."

Ariel, listening in silence, felt a rush of revulsion and shock. She struggled to control the tears that stung her eyes, bitter tears of resentment on behalf of the vulnerable boy he had once been. She knew him well enough to realize he wouldn't welcome her pity.

"After that day I was never sure if I was supposed to be a boy or a man around her. Before I quite figured it all out, she grew bored with me as a lover and persuaded the king I should be sent away to further my education." His mouth twisted. "Which I obligingly proceeded to do in every tavern and brothel in Paris."

She reached to touch him, only to have him wrench his arm away.

"The day she told me I was being sent away was the same day I got into the fight in the stable. It was like fighting with my cousin all over again. I hit him once and he pulled a knife on me. I took it away from him and could have ended it right then, but I didn't want to kill him with a knife." Again he looked deliberately into her eyes, as if words alone could not encompass what he was trying to tell her. "What I wanted was to kill him with my bare hands."

It took all her courage to ask. "Did you?"

Leon shook his head. "It took three men to pull me off that time."

Ariel sank onto a corner of the bed, feeling at a loss to comfort him. A dozen excuses and justifications for his violent anger, then and now, whirled in her head.

"It happened again in Paris," he said before she could speak. "Several times actually. The worst was with a supposed friend of mine, a man who sought to amuse our companions one evening with the tale of how my mother's relatives in that city had shunned me. Also absolutely true," he added, an ironic smile cracking his tight-lipped scowl. "I have a nasty habit of beating men senseless for telling the truth about me. Not exactly a sign of *nobility,* even in this country."

"You *are* noble," she told him, no trace of uncertainty in her tone now. "In ways that have nothing to do with titles or birthright, in ways I fear that even you do not recognize. Nobility does not exist only in castles and silk-swathed drawing rooms, you know."

"Trust me, it sure as hell doesn't exist in a place where the worst mankind has to offer is thrown in together, a place where you can't sleep without someone stealing your food, or the rags off your back, or—" He paused, his pulse pounding visibly in his throat, his eyes betraying nothing of what Ariel knew he must feel at reliving the unspeakable. "Or anything else you have worth taking."

"I know—"

"You don't know anything about it," he cut her off roughly. "You don't know anything about me. How could you? I've listened to you speak about your family, I've watched your face when you talk about the things your father taught you and the dreams your mother had for you. The *kuawa* was my family. Whatever I was taught, whatever I dreamed, came from them, and you will never, ever understand what that means."

"You're right. I won't insult you by telling you I can understand all you've been through. But I don't have to have been there and suffered it myself to understand this much, that nothing that happened to you was your fault, and that you have no reason to feel ashamed."

"It happened just the same. The fact that it wasn't my fault doesn't change that any more than it can change the results. Trust me, my sweet innocent, when they get done stripping everything inside you away, what's left is far from noble." His lips thinned with self-loathing. "Hell, it's not even human."

"You're wrong," Ariel argued. "Leon, please don't turn away from me." She leaned forward, determined to make him listen in spite of the fact that he looked as if he were already sorry he had revealed even this much. "There is great nobility in overcoming adversity, in understanding what it means to suffer and lose what you love most in the world, and learning from it. My father used to say that suffering teaches compassion, and he was right. Just think of it, Leon, if you choose to, you can rise above everything that's happened in the past and use your position to help those who are still—"

He stared at her incredulously. "By God, you never give up, do you? Never leave off even for a minute. What am I, one of your damn plans?" he demanded. "The subject of one of your endless lists? Tell me, how far along have we gotten? Monday, tame savage. Tuesday, fuck him. Wednesday, badger him until he agrees to accept the bloody title. Is that how it goes?"

Resentment flashed hotly inside her. Ariel strained to rein it in, understanding the torment he'd suffered and how difficult it must be to have those memories resurrected. Still, she had no intention of allowing her words to be so unfairly misconstrued.

"Is that the best you can do to shock me?" she drawled by way of reply, eyeing him with far more savoir faire than she felt. "Why, I've heard worse from my third-level boys."

"I wasn't trying to be shocking, merely truthful. It's not my problem if you don't like hearing it."

"No, your problem has more to do with avoiding the truth, of hiding behind a facade and changing the subject and feeling endlessly sorry for yourself instead of just getting up and getting on with what needs to be done." She got up and snatched her dress from his bag. "If you fear losing to Lockaby, why not just admit it and get it over with?"

"Nice try," Leon retorted, "but I don't respond well to manipulation."

She spun to face him. "Nor to obstacles, it would seem. It occurs to me that perhaps the reason you persist in standing around here, wasting the day arguing with me, is that you are afraid to try."

"Afraid?" He laughed and fumed and paced back and forth in front of her. "Afraid. That's twice you've questioned my courage, madam. On what basis, might I ask?"

Ariel shrugged with feigned nonchalance. "I see no other explanation for your reluctance to attempt to better your situation the way any sane man would when given the opportunity. It seems to me that even being the Marquis of Sage beats what you have going for you at present."

"So now I'm mad as well as cowardly." He grinned, an ominous glitter in his eye as he looked about the room. "Obviously there's only one thing to be done about it."

He dove beside the bed so suddenly, Ariel jumped

nearly a foot. He came up holding Prinny by the back of the neck. The rabbit's small pink nose twitched happily.

"What are you doing?" she asked warily, watching as he grabbed his bag and upended the contents next to where she was sitting.

He ruffled through his things with his free hand until he found a knife, then used his teeth to open the rawhide tie and pull it from its leather sheath.

"Leon, what are you doing," she asked again, trailing him across the room. "Leon, I asked—"

He silenced her by sweeping clean the desktop, sending books, pens and inkwell, and a lamp crashing to the floor, and plunking a now-disconcerted Prinny down in their place.

"What does it look like? I'm summoning my courage to look for the almighty Sage sword," he explained as calmly as if he were sane. "You do remember the story I told you at dinner that evening?"

"I remember," she replied uneasily.

"Good. I hope you're not squeamish."

"Are you trying to frighten me?"

He turned and locked gazes with her. "Are you frightened, Ariel?"

It was a test, she thought. Of what, she had no inkling, but he was testing her, and as angry as she was with him at that moment, she did not want to fail, for both their sakes. She folded her arms in front of her, clutching the sheet more tightly. His eyes were dark and murky, sand laced with gold, offering her no answers at all. She had only her instincts to guide her.

"No."

"Good." He pinned the rabbit to the desk and raised the knife.

Ariel caught her breath, forcing herself not to cry

out. In spite of her determination, a small sound escaped her throat.

His head turned sharply. "Do you bid me stop?"

She shook her head, a silent, desperate prayer circling in her head. "There's no need to."

"No need?" he roared. "I just told you what I'm like, what kind of man I am, and still you'll stand there and let me slaughter him?"

"You won't let yourself slaughter him. You see, I believe in you even if you refuse to."

He clenched his teeth, a harsh breath hissing through them as he turned from her and quickly brought the knife higher and then down, stabbing with the strength of ten men and plunging the blade deeply into the solid wood desk no more than half an inch from Prinny's quivering head.

Gripping the back of the chair beside her for support, Ariel fought a wave of latent light-headedness.

"This proves nothing," he said without looking at her.

"It does. It proves you are not the beast you claim to be." The fierce, startled look he turned on her almost made her leave it at that. "And," she continued bravely, "it proves I am not afraid of you."

"You should be," he said, and walked away.

According to Calvin, it was the worst storm to ravage the coast there in over a decade. A black squall, he called it, and Ariel's image was of a tempest rising straight from hell.

The thought of being so near the sea with nothing between to check the buffeting wind and pelting rain was frightening, and she gave thanks for the sturdy walls around her, reassuring herself that over the centuries Restormel had surely withstood worse assaults from both nature and man.

Even so, the wind rattled the windows and howled in the chimneys and the rain fell like an avalanche of hoofbeats on the stone roof. The only thing that appealed to Ariel less than being trapped in the same house with a saturnine Leon—even a house of seventy rooms—was venturing outside. Unfortunately she had no choice.

By the time she'd dressed and arrived downstairs, Leon had left. He'd gone to the cliffs to "fetch the lousy, stinking Sage sword," Calvin told her, visibly distressed at being required to pass the message on verbatim. Furthermore, his lordship did not, Calvin dutifully reported, require her damn help to do it.

Maybe he didn't need her help, Ariel thought as she overrode Calvin's protest and piled on pelisse and jacket and the heavy coat he appropriated on her behalf from one of the maids. He was going to have it just the same. She'd given her word and she would stick to it, his surly moods and raging storm notwithstanding.

With head and shoulders lowered, she battled the wind to catch up with him.

"What do you think you're doing?" he demanded, halting when he caught sight of her behind him. He had to shout at the top of his lungs to be heard over the noise of the storm.

"Going with you," Ariel shouted in reply.

They were only a short distance from the house, heading across the lawn toward the black cliffs which she could barely make out through the sheeting rain. Already she was drenched to the skin and cold to the bone. Leon looked to be the same, though he evidently possessed some magic formula to prevent his teeth from chattering the way hers were.

"The hell you are," he yelled. "Didn't Calvin give you my message?"

"He did. But I pledged my assistance to your cause and you shall have it. Even if you are going about this in the entirely wrong manner."

He pointed a gloved finger at her. "You so much as utter the word *list* and I swear—"

"It doesn't require a list to know that only a fool would begin his search for the sword outdoors in the middle of a veritable typhoon."

"Oh, really?"

"Really." She made a quick grab for her hat as a sudden blast of wind threatened to rip it from her head, wishing there were someone to hold on to her in the same manner. She didn't relish the thought of going the way of the leaves and twigs and at least one good-sized rhododendron bush that swept past them.

Leon did not appear to share her concern for his footing. He stood like a block of granite, boots apart, face into the wind, his long, black hair lashing around his hatless head. But then, he was weighted down with all those coils of rope and bits and pieces of metal gewgaws he was lugging. A list would serve him better on a day like this, she thought irritably.

"So now I'm a fool along with all the rest. At least," he bellowed, pushing his face so close to hers she could count the raindrops dripping from his black-stubbled chin, "I know that typhoons are confined to the Pacific."

"It so happens I was speaking figuratively," she said haughtily.

"Well, I'm not," retorted Leon. "Go away."

He turned and resumed walking. Ariel was at his heels, plunging heedlessly through the same puddles and mud he did, determined to keep pace. Wet was wet, she reasoned. It was little use to try to pick her steps now. His longer stride put him steadily out front even though she was nearly running. Or trying to. The bulk of her sopping, muddy skirts kept catching between her legs and slowing her down.

"For God's sake," he shouted in exasperation when he glanced back and saw her still following him. "Don't you ever listen?"

"Don't you? We could both be warm and dry inside if you would listen to reason and proceed to search the house first and in an orderly manner which—"

"Which would be a waste of time. The sword is not in the house," he told her, wiping his wet face with his wet sleeve.

Ariel frowned. "How do you know it's not?"

"Because I know where it is, drat you."

"You know . . ." She blinked rapidly. "You know where it is?"

Leon nodded. "I've always known. Giles Duvanne was lovesick enough to confide everything in my mother, and she told me. It was one of the fairy tales she used to keep his spirit alive for me until he returned." The familiar bitterness was plain even though he was straining to be heard and shaking water from his head between words.

"Then where is it?"

"There," he replied, pointing toward the edge of the cliff, now only twenty feet away. "Third formation from the end of the main house and straight down."

She scurried after him as he walked closer to the edge and peered over.

"Stay back," he ordered as she attempted to follow suit. "All it would take is one strong gust to knock a bit of fluff like you over the edge."

Ariel refused to be frightened off by either his warning or his fierce scowl. Instead, she lifted her chin and glared back. Tossing the coils of rope and the rest of it onto the mud-streaked ledge that was about six feet wide from cliff to grass, he finally relented and said what she wanted to hear. "Fine. Remain, if it pleases you. But at least get down so you'll be safer."

He hunkered down himself, and Ariel followed suit.

"You're right," she shouted. "I don't feel quite so much like the mainsail this way."

He seemed to catch himself on the verge of smiling. Instead, stripping off his coat, he pulled a heavy mallet from one deep pocket and tossed the coat to her. "Put it on. I can't climb with it and I can't stand to watch your wretched shivering."

"You don't really intend to climb down there now? In the middle of this storm?" she asked, aghast.

He slanted her a sardonic look. "I do. Unless, perhaps, you know of a way to get the sword to come to me instead?"

"Not offhand," she retorted. "But what if you get all the way down there and it's not there? Or you don't see it? Or—"

"Then I'm no worse off than I am now," he cut in. "But have no fear. The cursed thing will be there. I'm too damn unlucky for it not to be."

"Is it hidden underwater, do you know?"

He shook his head, dragging his wet hair back from his face as he got ready to drive a metal spike into the ledge. Speaking between labored breaths as he swung the mallet, he said, "There's a cave below us. The entrance is accessible only. . . . at low tide."

"This is low tide?" she asked, staring wide-eyed at the swirling gray and white sea.

"More or less. Don't worry," he said, tying the rope to the hook he had somehow attached to the spike in the ledge. "If worse comes to worst, I'm a good swimmer."

The small bit of reassurance *that* provided vanished as she clenched her fingers into a crevice in the ledge and stretched forward to view the churning waters below. No one was a good enough swimmer to survive them, she thought, paralyzed with fear as she watched Leon strip down to boots, breeches, and shirt sleeves. With swift, sure movements he secured the rope around his waist.

He reminded her of a fierce, primitive warrior about to do battle. In a way, that's exactly what he was, she realized. He was at war with the past, and with himself, and that, she feared, made this a battle he could never win. Ariel gazed up at him.

He was about to step over the edge, when she stopped him by calling his name.

"What is it?" he asked.

"Don't go," she cried. "It's not worth it. I know I was the one who—"

"Ariel," he shouted over the roar of the wind and the surf.

"Yes?"

"Shut your mouth."

That said, he braced one boot against the cliff face and swung over, sliding rapidly downward until only his head was in view and her heart and lungs were knotted in a solid lump of fear. He somehow managed to hover there briefly, gripping the rope and grinning at her, as if this were no more than a game they were playing.

"And cross your fingers," he added, then dropped swiftly from sight.

Ariel clung to her perch, flat on her belly with her eyes squeezed shut. She couldn't decide whether to open them or not. If she watched, she might jinx him and he would fall. But if she didn't watch, how would she know if he did fall and was in trouble and needed her to run for help?

What was she thinking of? He was in trouble just being out there. If she had an ounce of sense, she would go for help now, she thought, unable to tear herself away.

She opened her eyes slowly and stared out over the heaving surf. What sort of maniac would even attempt such a dangerous venture alone, and in weather like this? Even as she asked herself the question, the answer slid under her skin like a burr beneath a horse's saddle. A proud, headstrong maniac, that's what sort. Leon was doing this to prove to her that he wasn't afraid.

Lord, she was a fool to have goaded him, and he was a bigger one for listening. She had wanted him to seize control of his life, not throw it away.

Her words had been spoken impulsively and in the heat of the moment. Never for an instant had she actually believed that he was afraid of losing to Lockaby, much less afraid to try. As far as she was concerned, his courage and self-assurance had been established irrevocably the day he held his ground against four men and two loaded pistols in order to protect her.

It had taken her a while longer to figure out that all that reckless bravado and the lethal charm he wielded at will concealed a weakness in a different area altogether. He was very good at hiding it. But then, she thought sadly, he'd had a lifetime of practice. She had no doubt his aloof, often abrasive, sometimes downright hostile demeanor kept at a distance anyone who threatened to get too close. Exactly as he intended it should do.

What she didn't understand was why it hadn't worked on her. Had he simply not tried as hard to keep her at arm's length? Or was there a more fundamental explanation for the connection she had always sensed between them? Like fate, perhaps.

From the beginning, she had been drawn to him *because* he wasn't like everyone else, because he didn't do what he was expected to do or act the way he was told he was supposed to act. How she envied his freedom, his proclivity to spit in the face of all the things to which she must bend a knee and pay homage. What was it about him that enabled him to laugh at what other men craved and scrapped over?

The mystery of him had captivated her long before she realized it was nothing more than smoke and mirrors he used to hide the vast, aching emptiness inside him.

Strong, brave, cocky Leon Duvanne was hiding a broken heart and didn't want anyone to know it. But the walls he had built around himself, as high and as solid as they were, did not prevent Ariel from seeing the truth. She knew that Leon was in desperate need of love in his life, of being loved and of learning to love in return. She knew it as surely as she knew that she wanted to be the one to love him and be loved by him.

If the foolish, stubborn man lived long enough to give her a chance.

How long had he been gone? she wondered. Long enough to reach the bottom? Too long?

Tightening her hold on the rough slate ledge, she forced herself to creep forward several inches to where she had an unobstructed view of the flat rocks that dropped like a jagged sheet of jet-black ice thirty feet to the ocean surface. Leon was nowhere in sight, only the empty rope hung there, barely moving.

Ariel stopped just shy of panic when it occurred to her that was probably a good sign. If the rope wasn't swinging freely in this wind, it meant that Leon was still holding on to it, or else that he'd reached the bottom safely and had secured it somehow while he entered the hidden cave where the sword was hidden. Or, she thought, edging back toward panic, that the rope was being held steady by the weight of his drowned and lifeless body as it sank to its watery grave.

No, she refused to think that way. He was not dead and he would return safely. He would. He had to. She loved him.

She rested her chin on the hard ledge, no longer aware of the cold or the rain. Lord, she was as crazy as he was to even think such a thing could be possible. That didn't make it any less true. Face the truth, she'd told him. It was time she did the same. The truth was that she was in love with Leon Duvanne. She'd been in love with him, she realized now, for days, weeks, maybe ever since the moment he fell on top of her and she had gazed into the black stars of his eyes and saw things she had been told did not exist.

They did exist. Perhaps not out there, she thought, glancing at the surly sky overhead, but in her heart. Amazingly, the love she felt for Leon thrilled and consumed her more than the heavens ever had, or ever could. Fate.

She loved him. God help her, she loved him. She hadn't understood it at the time, but that was the real reason she had not wanted him to touch her that morning. That was what she had meant when she told him it would only make things harder. How could she have been so wrong? She hadn't understood then that there was no uncertainty about how she felt about Leon and there was nothing he could say or do that would make her love him less, or make it any easier to let him go when the time came.

And the time would definitely come. She understood that. And it frightened her. She, who had vowed never to fall in love, had fallen head over heels, no holds barred, full steam ahead, and she had not even known it was happening until it was too late. She, who had smugly boasted that being older and wiser enabled her to protect her heart from ever being bruised or shattered again, had slowly, methodically, violated every item on her own list of things not to do with a man. She had given her heart and soul and body not just to any man, but to a man who she feared could not, or would not, ever love her in return.

She had fallen in love with a savage.

It was true. The realization was like a blade of ice pressing against her heart. Leon may no longer growl or eat with his hands, but that did not make him any less a savage, or any less dangerous. A man could be taught to hold a fork. She wasn't at all sure he could be taught the process of emotional bonding when he'd spent a lifetime fearing and rejecting any and all such attachments.

It was ironic, she thought, not knowing whether to laugh or cry. The very things that had attracted her to Leon, the darkness and vulnerability that she had sensed in him without understanding what they meant, were the very same things that would hold him forever beyond her reach.

Was he capable of loving her? Was he even willing to try? Could she bear to go on loving him, knowing he might never love her in return? Did she really have a choice? She shook her head, feeling battered on the outside by the elements and on the inside by the raging conflict of her own emotions. Suddenly she, who was never without a common-sense approach to anything, was out of answers.

She had a plan to save her parents from debtors' prison, a plan for marrying Phillip Penrose, a plan for running the Penrose School, but she had no plan, no list, no idea at all of what she was going to say when Leon came crawling back over that cliff and looked her in the eye. *If* he came over the cliff.

Shivering, she picked up his coat, pulled it tightly around her, burying her nose in the thick wool collar and savoring the scent of him that clung to it even when wet. How long *had* he been down there?

What on earth was she going to do if he didn't make it back?

What on earth was she going to do if he did?

She had been willing to marry Mr. Penrose according to a careful plan in which love played no part, confident she could go on to live a perfectly happy and satisfied life. Perhaps she could have with Mr. Penrose. But never with Leon. With Mr. Penrose, her heart was not involved. With Leon it was, and there was a world of difference. It wasn't so easy to say you could live without love, she realized, once you had felt its power.

She brushed the water from her eyes and stared into the distance to where the swirling gray sea collided with an equally gray sky. Perversely, all that gray inspired her to think positively. Leon was going to return safely, she told herself again, and when he did she would be ready. She would do what she always did, what she was best at. She would come up with a plan.

That was as far as she got before the unmistakable

clash of metal on rock commanded her full attention. Leon.

Her eyes went wide with disbelief, followed quickly by a surge of happiness and relief as the sword was tossed onto the cliff beside her. It was long and heavily scrolled and gleamed brilliantly even in the rain, but her response to seeing it didn't compare to the joy she felt seconds later, as Leon's dark, dripping head edged into view.

Ariel grabbed for him. Before he had hitched one leg up she was tugging on his shirt to help him.

"You did it, oh, Leon, you did it," she exclaimed.

He tolerated her efforts, though she had a sense she was more impediment than help. It didn't matter. She couldn't stop touching him. As soon as he had both hands and knees on solid ground, she wrapped her arms around his broad shoulders and cried with relief.

"Hell of a way to greet a conquering hero," he said, breathing hard. "Myself, I had in mind something more like this."

Curling one powerful arm around her neck, he drove her backward with a hard kiss and came down on top of her. Impossible as it seemed, his skin felt even colder and wetter than her own, but his mouth was an inferno and his tongue a rough, welcome invader.

Ariel surrendered to his overwhelming vitality, glorying in the fact that he was there, alive and in one piece, and kissing her like a man who had recently stared death in the face and decided what he wanted out of life. Was it possible, she wondered hazily, that Leon was feeling the same thing she was?

Heat pooled in her lower body in defiance of the weather and the shivers that were passing through her in wave after delicious wave. She clenched her fingers in his wet hair, her senses whirling. She felt his hands on her face and his hips pressing her into the rock.

She couldn't think, couldn't get close enough, couldn't wait for him to claim all of her.

He was reaching down to grab her wet skirts. She felt the cold air on her legs as she slid her hands between their bodies and touched the buttons at the front of his breeches.

Leon trembled and groaned. And froze.

He groaned against the curve of her throat. "What the hell are we doing? What am I doing? Like a damn rutting animal. Out here in the middle of a bloody typhoon."

"Not quite. Typhoons are confined to the Pacific," she said, her tone a restrained counterpoint to the fervor in his.

"They used to be. Then the whole damn world went crazy."

"I think maybe I like the world better this way."

"I don't," he said, and rose gracefully while she lay there wrestling with her sodden skirts and excess of coats and trampled pride.

Reaching down, he burrowed his hands beneath the outermost layers of wool to grasp her in the vicinity of her waist and effortlessly hauled her up to stand beside him.

"Thank you," she said, doing her best not to feel bereft over the abrupt way he had stopped kissing her or the fact that he had already picked up the jewel-encrusted sword and was headed back to the house without her.

She could deal with this, she told herself. Somehow. It wouldn't be easy. *He* wouldn't be easy, but she could manage. All she needed was a plan.

Eighteen

Leon swore the distance between London and Devon had doubled since they'd traveled it last. What else would account for the fact that the ride back from Restormel was taking twice as long as had the trip there?

It only added to his affliction that he couldn't sleep. He was exhausted, his body ached in a hundred different places from scaling those godforsaken cliffs, and his head was pounding in agonizing rhythm with the horses' hoofbeats. Yet whenever he closed his eyes, doubts and indecisions kept sleep at bay. Telling himself that the decision had been made and there was no cause for second thoughts didn't help.

Get up and get on with what has to be done. Those were Ariel's words to him. As much as he'd resented them at the time, he realized now that it was advice worth taking. He had made up his mind about what had to be done, and he was doing it. The sooner he reached London and rid himself of the sword, the sooner he could be on his way back to Hawaii.

He would have started for London the minute he'd recovered the sword, but for the driver's refusal to risk traveling in the storm. Even then he'd been ready to buy a damn horse and set out alone, abandoning the idea only in the face of Calvin's woefully crestfallen expression at the thought of his missing out on the grand tour of Restormel.

So he had suffered through an inspection of all seventy-odd rooms, not to mention another sleepless night in his father's bed, unable to escape the aware-ness that everything he had ever wanted and never had and was afraid to hope could ever be his was sleeping at the opposite end of the hall.

Ariel.

She was like a fever in his blood. The very essence of her beat inside him in a million different ways. To breathe was to think of her, her smile and the softness of her skin and the way it had felt to be surrounded by her silky heat. To think of her was to want her all over again.

And he wanted her more desperately now than he had before he ever put his hands on her. On top of a cliff in the middle of a raging downpour, he had been on the verge of baring his heart and soul to her. That clearly meant he was besotted enough to commit God only knew what kind of impulsive blunder. It had to stop.

There was only one sure way to put an end to it all. He would lay the sword at Lady Sage's feet, accept her pronouncement that he had won the right to be the next Marquis of Sage, and walk away. It wasn't the consummate revenge he'd thought would be his, but it would have to do.

He would walk away knowing that he could have had their precious title, but had chosen to reject it and everything it signified, and knowing that they all knew it as well.

You mean run away, taunted a voice deep inside.

All right, he thought, teeth clenching, run away. If discretion was the better part of valor, there was no shame in running while he still could. He would run away from the danger of losing any more of himself to the one woman who could reach inside him and touch his soul and make him feel the violent depths of emotion he had spent a lifetime avoiding.

When they had reached the outskirts of the city, Leon turned to Ariel.

"We're almost there," he said.

"So are we." Ariel laced her fingers together in her lap.

Now, she thought. This was the moment she had been waiting for. The moment to put her plan, such as it was, into action. She had thought of nothing else for hours now. Then she'd had to wait for Mrs. Farrell to fall asleep so that they could speak with some privacy. Then she had to work up her courage to say what she had to say.

She cleared her throat, shifted her feet, and said his name.

Leon turned to her, his jaw rigid, his eyes narrowed, drawing her attention to the lines that fanned at their outer corners. He looked exhausted, she thought. Why wouldn't he, with all he had on his mind. He was surely thinking of the meeting with his grandmother, the prospect of becoming Marquis of Sage and the countless new duties and responsibilities it would mean. No wonder he was so moody and preoccupied. Ariel wished there were some way she could lighten his burden rather than give him yet another thing to think about. Only the knowledge that this may well be their last time together compelled her to act now.

"What is it?" he asked.

"There is something that has been on my mind for the entire trip back, or, rather, I should say, on my conscience, and I cannot leave this coach without confessing it to you."

He appeared intrigued. And wary. "Go on."

"You asked me a question, after you ... after we ..." She slanted a cautious glance at Mrs. Farrell, who was snoring softly.

"I understand. Go on."

"And I answered you with a lie," she said. "But I fear that while my lie spared me some discomfiture, it may well have burdened you with regrets, and undeservedly so." Oh, why were these things always so much more difficult in practice than when she was concocting them in her imagination? "You see," she continued in an anxious rush, "I lied when I told you that you were the first man I was ever with. There was someone else, a very long time ago."

"Another man?" he demanded. "Are you sure you—"

Ariel clamped her hand over his mouth to silence him. "Of course I am sure," she whispered. "What kind of ninny do you take me for? And will you please keep your voice down? I said I felt an obligation to confess the truth to you, not to all of England via Mrs. Loose-Lips over there."

He nodded and she cautiously removed her hand. Immediately Leon rapped on the carriage ceiling.

"Pull up," he shouted to the driver, waking their chaperone at the same time.

So much for compassion and understanding, thought Ariel. Was the big lout not even going to hear her out?

"Where are we?" Mrs. Farrell asked sleepily.

"Almost home," Leon replied, opening the door. "It has occurred to me that there's no need for you to wait idly while Miss Halliday and I meet with Lady Sage. If you switch coaches here, you can return to the cottage directly. I'm sure you are exhausted from the long journey."

The last was obviously added with dry intent. For an instant Ariel feared he was simply going to boot the woman out in the middle of the busy London intersection and leave her to fend for herself. She needn't have worried. As she looked on, Leon helped Mrs. Farrell from the carriage and escorted her to the curb, where he dutifully waited until she had been safely ensconced in a hired hack, the driver paid, and she was on her way to Paddington.

Was her little test still necessary? she wondered, her heart swelling with tenderness as she watched him. She shook herself mentally. Yes, it was. She had never doubted Leon's capacity for kindness. How could she, when she had seen him adopt a bedraggled rabbit and rearrange his travel plans to indulge the whims of a devoted elderly butler?

Kindness was one thing, love was another. Was Leon capable of loving a woman the way she needed him to love her? Somehow she had to provoke an honest revelation of what was in his heart.

He returned to the carriage, claiming the seat vacated by Mrs. Farrell, and called to the driver to go on.

"There, Mrs. Loose-Lips is gone," he said, making himself comfortable, "I am at the edge of my seat in anticipation, and you are about to tell me why you lied to me about being a virgin."

"Because," she said, disconcerted at being diverted from her prepared spiel, "because I am a coward, I suppose."

"That's not an answer, it's an evasion." He turned his head and glanced out the window. "We don't have time for evasiveness."

"All right." She folded her arms with a disgruntled air. Whose show was this anyway? "I didn't tell you beforehand because, well, frankly, it wasn't any of your business. And I didn't tell you the truth afterward, when you asked me directly, because—" She drew an uneasy breath, her small smile ruefully honest. "Because I didn't want you to stop."

Leon's heart slid sideways, colliding with his lungs and making it difficult to breathe. He wanted to hold her and stroke the hair from her face and demonstrate to her how difficult it was for him to stop then, now, forever.

Instead, he scowled at her. "You little fool, do you really believe that your desirability is as fragile and insubstantial a thing as a maidenhead? That it is something to be claimed, surrendered, used up, and discarded in a single act?"

"No. But I was afraid you might think so. Most men do apparently. You yourself warned that Mr. Penrose would expect me to be a virgin, and be distressed to discover otherwise."

"Get this straight," he snapped. "I'm not Penrose. Nor am I like most men." For some reason, that seemed to please her immensely. His expression eased. "Just tell me one thing, will you? The man who was your first, did you love him? Did he love you?"

She gave a small, mirthless laugh. "I barely knew him, or him me. And he was more boy than man. I told you, it was a long time ago."

"I see," Leon said, not sure if that made him feel better or worse. For Ariel's sake, he wished her first experience had been one to cherish. For his own selfish sensibilities, he would prefer it meant nothing more to her than a bad memory. He would prefer to think that he was the first in every way that mattered.

"I was seventeen," she revealed even as he searched for a tactful way to satisfy his need to know more. "And so was he, the son of acquaintances in the North whom we were visiting that summer. He was handsome and charming and I was—"

"Ripe," he muttered.

She frowned and nodded. "I never thought of it exactly that way, but I suppose you're right. At any rate, we went out riding one morning and got separated from his friends. It started raining, no more than a drizzle really, but he—"

"Let me guess," Leon interrupted, his mouth spread in a thin-lipped smile, "he knew of a place where you could take shelter."

She nodded. "Yes, there was a small hut nearby."

"Of course there was. There is always a small hut, or lodge, or chalet nearby when a man lures a woman off to be alone with her."

"He didn't lure me," she said. "It rained, and the others took off. My horse was slower and couldn't keep up."

"Imagine that." He shook his head. "Trust me, Ariel, if your horse had not been slow, your devious young Galahad would have twisted his ankle or lost his way or experienced a sudden malady that would be miraculously cured once you reached the hut."

"How can you know that?"

"Trust me," he said a second time, a dark, sardonic edge to his voice, "I know."

"You think he planned the whole thing?"

"I'm sure of it. You were simply too trusting and naive to realize it. Hell," he said, noting her incredulous expression, "you still are."

"If that's true, then it was all a ruse, a sham." Her eyes glittered venomously. "That bastard. That lousy, scheming, good-for-nothing lecherous bastard."

Leon started to grin, happy not to be her target for once, until a sudden suspicion had him hunching forward to study her face closely. "He didn't force himself on you, did he?"

She shook her head, looking more indignant than violated, he decided, relieved.

"No. He didn't force me. He didn't have to. I was too much of a sheep. I can see that now. A big, foolish sheep that he herded along, ripe for shearing, just as you said." She stamped her foot on the carriage floor. "He lied, damn his heart. And I fell for it. Oh, I was curious enough at first, I admit, wanting to find out for myself what it felt like to be held and kissed by a boy. But that was all I thought there would be to it." She shook her head, her dainty jaw rigid. "When I tried to tell him so, it was too late. He said to stop him then would—"

"Be inhuman," Leon interjected. "And cause him horrific suffering. He regretfully confided in you about the agony that befell any man who was so thoughtlessly aroused by a woman and not allowed to go on. At which point, your sweet, soft heart was his for the taking. Along with the rest of you." He offered her a consoling smile. "That is what's known as the trump card, sweetheart."

"How do you know all this?"

He shrugged. "Brace yourself. I'm not a virgin either." Before Ariel could castigate him, as she appeared very ready to do, he added, "Let me go on record as saying that I never used such tactics on a woman who wasn't old enough or wise enough to know exactly what she was getting herself into."

"You mean what you were getting her into. Men are so devious."

"Men? Who is it who's plotting and scheming to trap old Penrose in dreaded wedlock?"

She shook her head. "That's different. *If* we marry, it will be a mutually agreed upon and advantageous arrangement. With all the cards on the table up front."

He flexed one dark brow.

Ariel shrugged. "Well, almost all the cards."

"This does explain why you are so well versed on the subject of accidental falls and small vials of animal blood," he remarked dryly.

"I thought I should be prepared."

"You are that," he assured her. A smile of helpless admiration ruffled his mouth. "The most remarkable, amazingly well-prepared lady of my acquaintance."

"You called me a lady. Can I assume that means you do not now consider me . . . soiled goods?"

"Soiled goods?" His eyes narrowed. "What the hell are you talking about?"

"It's a common British term for women who lose their virginity outside of marriage."

"I see." His tone turned sharply contemptuous. "Tell me, what's the common Brit term for men who lose theirs? Buck? Rake? A jolly good out-and-outer?

They all have a considerably different ring, I must say, from soiled goods."

"It is considerably different for a man," she pointed out.

"Do you really believe that?"

"I do now," she replied with a resigned nod. "There was a gentleman, several years ago, whom I trusted was seriously interested in pursuing an alliance with me. Then I made the mistake of telling him the truth about myself."

"How did he react?"

"He *said* he understood, that anyone can make a mistake and that it didn't matter or change how he felt about me, but he suddenly remembered someplace else he had to be. I never saw him again."

"Were you heartbroken?" he asked.

Her small nod made Leon hate the anonymous man for whom she had cared enough to be hurt by his rejection.

"But I got over it," she said. "What I didn't get over was the lesson it taught me. His reaction made it clear that society holds a woman to a different standard than it does a man, and that the mistake I made that summer was something I would carry with me forever." She tossed her head and met his gaze levelly. "I guess you could say that's my scar to bear."

Scarred. Ariel? She had never looked more beautiful to him. She looked proud and defiant and brave. And more fragile than ever, thought Leon, a strange heaviness around his heart. She was fragile when compared to the entrenched strictures of society. No wonder she had settled on Penrose. With him she was confident she had something to offer to compensate for the virtue she supposedly lacked, as if she herself were not enough. Leon knew exactly how that felt.

Soiled goods. Just the words incensed him. That a woman who was everything good and loving and generous in the world should ever, in any way, be made to feel ashamed or diminished for the natural expression of those qualities was beyond his understanding. It was exactly the sort of nonsense he found so uncivilized about civilization.

"So?" she prodded. "Do you?"

"Do I?" His puzzled look quickly gave way to a nod. "That's right, you want to know if I think ill of you for doing exactly what I myself have been doing for years, for doing it *with* me on one momentous occasion, simply because you're a woman?"

"Yes."

It seemed to Leon that she was straining forward even though she hadn't moved. Her avid attention made him hesitate, cognizant of the import of the moment. He searched for exactly the right words to tell her that she was so far above all this petty, self-serving hypocrisy, that none of it mattered, and that any man truly worthy of her would understand that. The way he understood.

The coach rolled to a stop in front of Lady Sage's residence before he found the right words and the groom hurried to open the door.

"What I think," he said at last, "is that it doesn't matter. And that Penrose is the luckiest bastard alive.

He had anticipated striding into Lady Sage's salon like a triumphant warrior, brandishing the indisputable proof of his superiority. Instead, he felt preoccupied, weighted down with concern for Ariel.

How was she going to react to the announcement

that he was leaving? he wondered. Would it bring back memories of the last time she had confided in a man, only to have him walk out on her immediately afterward? He had tried to tell her that the past didn't matter. Too late he realized those were the same empty words her fickle suitor had used. If he left now, she was bound to be hurt. But if he stayed, he thought, anything could happen.

His mind was made up. He had to go. He just couldn't help wishing there were some way he could protect her in the process. He couldn't seem to shake the hellish image of her and Penrose and a preacher. He'd already taken what steps he could to alleviate her financial situation. If only he could do more. If only there were a way he could ensure that Ariel would never have to worry about the future, or the past, ever again.

She walked by his side without saying a word as they were shown in and led upstairs, her expression thoughtful. Only when they stood before the towering gold-trimmed door to the salon, waiting to be announced, did she touch his elbow and flash him a smile so bright, he had to look away or lose all power of concentration.

It didn't surprise Leon particularly to find Lockaby and his mother there already, or that their smug greetings held only the most sheer veneer of politeness. What did surprise him was the sword Lockaby was holding, remarkably similar to the one in his own hand.

"Another offering," exclaimed Lady Sage, clearly enjoying the scene to the hilt. She leaned forward in her thronelike chair, flanked by her faithful pugs. "My, my, this does seem to be my day for receiving presents from handsome young men. And both of you so brisk in your procurement of them. I am quite impressed."

"Please stop cooing, Mother," snapped Elizabeth

Lockaby. "It's unbecoming, and besides, this is not your birthday, you know. Obviously this other sword is a fake."

"One of them is, to be sure," Lady Sage agreed. "But how to tell which?"

"I should think this is where character comes into play," her daughter responded without missing a beat. "One's background, good name, and connections ought surely to be given due consideration."

"They should indeed. But I hardly see where such a consideration will benefit either side here."

With an indignant gasp Lady Lockaby flounced to her son's side to console him.

He shrugged her off. "I was the first to present you with the sword, Grandmother. Doesn't that count for something?"

"No. This wasn't a race, boy, it was a test. Fortunately, I shall be able to determine which of you has been successful." She paused and shifted a wizard's narrow gaze from Leon to Lockaby and back. "And which of you seeks only to deceive me."

"How can you possibly tell which sword is genuine?" Lady Lockaby asked her, paling. "I'm certain I've heard you say that you never saw the thing for yourself."

Lady Sage nodded agreement. "That is true, but if you paid attention, dear daughter, you would have learned by now that men are not the only ones capable of passing on knowledge. I was only a bride when my mother-in-law shared with me what it meant to be the Marchioness of Sage, including a retelling of the family legend. It so happens she had seen the sword, and she described it to me in great detail. And I," she declared with a flourish, "remember every word. Both of you, bring your swords closer," she ordered crisply.

The two men complied.

Lady Sage leaned forward regally to inspect them. "Ah, the jeweled band, the beading, the basket handle meant to protect a swordsman's hand in battle. They both appear to be exactly as described to me." She sighed dramatically. "Now, if they both also have the partial crest engraved on the blade, I fear I will be at a loss to choose between you."

From the corner of his eye Leon saw Lockaby's shoulders flinch slightly, as if he'd been stung beneath his fitted coat.

"What engraving?" his mother asked.

"The knot and the dagger, of course, taken from the Sage crest. It was meant to have the whole crest on it, but that is all there was time to engrave before the first battle, and it was kept that way afterward. For luck."

Lady Lockaby shook her head in disgust. "Really, Mother. I should think that after all these years, any engraving that was there would—"

Lady Sage banged her walking stick on the floor for silence.

"Please turn them over," she directed, her use of the word *please* making it no less a command.

Leon pivoted his wrist, reversing the blade of the heavy sword, and his grandmother smiled as her gaze locked onto the spot just below the hilt.

"The knot and the dagger," she said with quiet, unmistakable satisfaction. She lifted her gaze to meet Leon's. "You please me greatly."

Before Leon could respond, Lockaby hurled the sword he was holding in the general direction of his head. Leon quickly raised his arm to deflect it in midair, the heavy steel blades clashing loudly before Lockaby's sword fell to the floor at his feet, sending the skittish pugs flying.

Lockaby swore and whirled to confront Leon. "You bastard. Who the hell do you think you are?"

"Not a bastard certainly," retorted Leon, aware that his laconic tone was adding insult to injury. He didn't like having swords tossed at him. "Though it might be considered a lucky turn for us both if I was. Cousin."

"Don't call me cousin." Lockaby glared at his grandmother. "So that's it, then? You've had your bloody little test, and now you'll see him with the title?"

"At once."

"Damn you."

"Adam, hold your tongue," advised his mother, trying to take him by the arm. "There are other ways to—"

"To be sure there are ways, you old witch," he said to Lady Sage, shaking off his mother's efforts to calm him. "Ways of wresting more than titles from the likes of you. Go ahead, hand him the title on a silver platter and see where it gets you." He glared at Leon. "Your days are numbered . . . *Lord Savage*. I'll have the title— and the silver platter with it—in the end."

He stormed from the room.

Elizabeth Lockaby started after him, then paused to look daggers at her mother. "I will never, ever forgive you for this," she screamed. "Adam, please wait. . . ."

Her unheeded cries echoed tragically through the salon until the butler appeared to close the door.

"Well, that's that," Lady Sage remarked with blatant zest, clucking to the dogs that it was safe to return to her side. "Good riddance to the pair of them, though if the past is any indication, Elizabeth's 'forever' won't last even through Easter. I wouldn't give undue credence to Adam's threats either," she said to Leon.

"I hadn't planned to," he replied.

"Good. Now on to more pleasant matters." She

smiled broadly. "I shall send word to the king at once and see to all the other details. You have earned the title, my dear boy, and it will soon be yours."

Leon bowed his head to her, savoring the moment. It was as close to vengeance as he was likely to get. Too bad there weren't more in attendance to witness his symbolic spurning of all of England. He would have to rely on the ton's savage rumor mill to handle that for him. "I am pleased to have been able to serve you. However—"

"However," his grandmother cut in, usurping his remark, "there is one more small stipulation I shall have to insist upon before we can seal matters once and for all."

Leon almost laughed out loud. Of course. Why not? Why should things get any easier now? He eyed the older woman with wary indulgence.

"Pray tell, madam, what might that one small stipulation be?"

"You've found the sword," she countered, "now find yourself a bride as worthy and I shall see you declared Lord Sage on the spot."

Ariel nearly gasped out loud. She quickly looked to see Leon's reaction and saw him shake his head, chuckling with dry amusement. Something not even close to laughter was bubbling inside her.

"Pardon me," she said, wanting only to get away from there. She still had no step two of her plan, but if she had, she was certain that it would not include provisions for Leon choosing a bride his grandmother would consider "worthy." "This becomes too personal. If you'll excuse—"

"No," Leon uttered firmly before she had finished. "Stay." He rested the sword against the tall chair to his right, then circled it and idly rested his forearms on the back as he eyed the dowager consideringly. "What concern is it of yours whether or not I take a bride?"

"You were far too quick at your task for me to have time to uncover all the reasons I suspect there are for me to be concerned," she retorted, her eyes bright with mischief. "But during your absence I did manage to discover a few interesting tidbits about you."

"Such as?"

"You are a very wealthy man in your own right."

Leon lifted one broad shoulder. "I've been lucky in my investments."

"So was your father. Thanks to him, you will soon find yourself an even wealthier man."

"Beyond a minimal comfort level, I am not particularly interested in money in general, and," he added, tensing so slightly that Ariel wondered if his grandmother would even detect it, "I have no interest in his money in particular."

"You ought to," she shot back. "Money is the most powerful and steadfast ally a man can have. Try to remember that."

"I'll do my best."

"I also learned that you spent some years in Paris."

"True."

"I have many connections with that city," she told him. "I've asked around. Will your hide sustain plain speaking, or shall I temper what I have to say?"

"Speak plainly by all means. My hide is notoriously thick."

"So is your head at times, I've been told, nor does your notoriety end there. I've heard such entertaining tales of wantonly reckless exploits and audacious whoremongering that I rather regret our paths did not cross sooner. I shall at some point expect a full recounting of what you know about everyone I know."

He gave another small nod. "My pleasure. I'm so glad you approve my style."

"Oh, I don't approve at all," she said, smiling broadly and prompting Ariel to wonder where this was leading. She wasn't sure she wanted to hear the details of Leon's colorful past. She *knew* she didn't want to be in on his marriage plans. "I can tolerate self-indulgence to a point," his grandmother told him, "though I would have hoped for a bit more discretion even from a young man. It's almost as if you were intent on rubbing the pride of Paris's noses in your disdain for them."

"Perhaps I was."

"Perhaps you were." Her gaze sharpened. "I understand your mother was partly of French ancestry."

"She was."

"Her family came from Paris, did they not?"

"I believe they did."

Ariel tensed, hoping for Leon's sake that the dowager would not probe too deeply in areas where he was most vulnerable.

"I see," the dowager said, smiling at him. "Well, suffice it to say you will not be repeating that performance here. I mean to ensure that by seeing you wed."

"On the unfailing theory that married men never whore around?" he challenged.

Lady Sage nodded slowly. "You won't. I can tell. No, I shall be quite at peace once you are married and settled, hopefully with an heir on the way as soon as possible in case you decide you prefer your jungle life after all." She ran an approving gaze over him. "Judging from the vigorous looks of you, getting an heir shan't be a problem."

He shrugged and looked disgruntled. "Who was it who said that looks can be deceiving?"

"A blind man no doubt," she retorted. Her round face grew solemn. "Trust me, Leon, I am not deceived by you in any way."

"Might I say the same of you?"

She laughed. "If you dare. I am an old lady, and old ladies are to be indulged in their sly schemes and machinations."

"Then the deck is stacked against me from the start," he said, shaking his head in apparent disgust as he straightened and came away from the chair.

Ariel couldn't believe they were having this conversation, and in front of her. She couldn't believe that Leon was even entertaining the idea of an arranged marriage. Though perhaps she shouldn't be surprised. A passionless political marriage would present no threat to someone afraid to fall in love. She should know, she had almost settled for one without understanding what she would be sacrificing.

"The deck is not entirely stacked," the dowager was saying. "You shall, of course, have some say in selecting your bride."

"You're too generous," he muttered.

"Provided she meets with my approval. Don't glower," she chided. "London is full of young women eager to land themselves a handsome, rich marquis. Indeed, your stint as a savage has added considerably to your panache. I predict you'll be the toast of the coming season."

"Lucky me," Leon retorted, looking increasingly like a caged tiger.

He obviously wasn't looking forward to choosing a woman to share his bed and bear his children. That provided some small consolation to Ariel as she pictured him with a succession of the haut monde's most prominent belles.

"I daresay," his grandmother continued, "there are any number of young women handsome enough to tempt you and still politic enough to suit me. If it would help, I could make you a list of—"

"No," he uttered, stiffening. "Don't talk to me of lists of all things." He broke his rigid stance and paced across the room.

Ariel glanced nervously at the dowager, who had her eyes trained on his back. As if sensing she was being watched, she shifted suddenly and met Ariel's gaze. At the same instant Ariel felt a warm shiver run up her spine and turned to find Leon staring at her from across the room, one booted foot in front of the other, his elbows resting negligently on the mantel behind him, his expression shuttered.

She couldn't help fidgeting under his intense, unwavering regard, and in quick succession gazed at her feet, out the window, and finally back to the dowager. Perfect, she thought, now both of them were staring oddly at her. Enough was enough. Before she could excuse herself a second time, Leon strode forward.

"I agree," he said to the dowager. "My situation would be greatly benefited by the acquisition of the proper wife."

"Excellent," Lady Sage said, beaming.

Ariel struggled to conceal her surprise and the fact that her heart was breaking.

"And I've decided who the lady shall be," he announced.

She looked away, her throat constricting even as the giant ache in her chest widened. She should have left when she had the chance. It had been easier by far to imagine him with a string of women than to know he had settled on one.

The dowager chuckled. "Better still. Well, don't keep me in suspense. Who is this singular female and when shall I have the pleasure of meeting her?"

"You already have," Leon replied, tilting his head so his gaze collided with Ariel's before she could look away again. "I intend to marry Miss Halliday."

Nineteen

I intend to marry Miss Halliday.

Leon's words engulfed Ariel like a heavy blanket. For a moment it seemed she couldn't see, couldn't hear, could only feel a sort of spreading numbness, overlaid with disbelief. The conversation around her might as well have been taking place on another planet.

"You jest," said the dowager, laughing heartily.

"I assure you, dear lady, I have never been more serious."

Even dazed, Ariel was able to discern the note of utter determination in his deep voice.

"She is comely enough, I grant you," said his grandmother. "And she's been left alone with you far too often. It's too late to remedy that, but think with your head, boy, she is hardly suitable."

"She suits me," Leon declared, implacable. "I have no interest in being marquis unless she is my marchioness. Consider your options and choose. Miss Halliday. Or Lockaby."

Ariel saw the dowager pause, her soft face puckered in consternation.

"Your father is a baronet, I believe?" she asked, looking Ariel up and down as if it were the first time she had ever laid eyes on her.

"Yes. And a physician," Ariel nodded.

The hint of defiance in her tone caused the older woman's eyes to widen expressively. Let them, thought Ariel. She may not be marriage material of the first water in the eyes of the dowager, but she was still a gentleman's daughter and proud of it.

"Hmm," Lady Sage murmured, and sighed. "But without land, I take it?"

"My family owns a lovely house at Clapham Common."

"Clapham Common." She frowned as if the area on the city's southern outskirts was a foreign country. "Clapham Common indeed." To Leon she said, "Your mind is really set on this?"

"Irrevocably."

"In that case . . ." Her mouth curled into a lavish smile which she proceeded to bestow warmly on Ariel. "Welcome to the family, my dear Miss Halliday."

"Thank you, I'm sure," Ariel replied, trying to sound composed. She was still reeling from the shock of Leon's unorthodox proposal. The dowager's acquiescence, reluctant and blatantly politic as it so obviously was, only complicated her predicament. "I am flattered, of course," she told them, "but this has taken me quite by surprise. I shall need time to think before I can give you my response."

Lady Sage reacted with a derisive snort. "Nonsense. What is there to think about?" she demanded, waving her hand toward Leon. "He's rich and handsome and he wants you. That's thrice what most woman in your situation—and of a certain age—can count on. That he will be the Marquis of Sage is icing on your cake, my dear, and I think you're clever enough to see it. Why make him wait when we all know what your response to his offer must surely be?"

Ariel stood her ground as Leon settled indolently into a nearby easy chair. The man was evidently content to let his grandmother do his wooing for him, she noted with chagrin. His indifference at a moment when she longed for an impassioned proclamation, or at the very moment a tender glance, seemed a harbinger of what life with him would be like. Impossible. The prospect had a rapid, clarifying effect on her thoughts.

"Your points are well taken," she told the dowager. "It is simply my nature to approach things in a logical and cautious manner. If you insist on having an answer on the spot, I will, of course, comply."

"I see no reason not to settle it now," said the dowager.

"In that case, I have no alternative but to respectfully decline the offer of his lordship's hand."

His lordship was immediately on his feet, looking considerably less nonchalant than he had a moment earlier. Unfortunately Ariel was too distressed to appreciate his discomfiture.

"Why?" he demanded.

"Because I question your motives, sir."

"*You* question *my* motives? That's rich. And why should my motive matter as long as I can provide you with what you need?"

"Perhaps because I'm not convinced you can."

She spoke quietly, but his jaw tensed as if she had struck him. "Very well, madam." He turned, grabbed the sword, and approached his grandmother, who was observing the scene with heightened interest.

"It appears, Grandmother, that we have both won and lost today. The only woman I desire to marry has rejected my offer, and I in turn reject yours."

"Don't be a fool," snapped the dowager. "Women can be replaced. Blood cannot. What matters is that you found the sword, and with it goes the title."

"Exactly. And now I relinquish both to you. The sword and the title are yours to do with as you please. I am not."

Ariel watched him lay the sword at the old woman's feet and stand, not sure how to intervene or even if she should.

"Come back here," the dowager ordered as Leon turned away. "I've said you are the Marquis of Sage, and my word will bind. You can't simply refuse a peerage and all that goes with it."

"I just did," he retorted, striding toward the door.

"Don't you dare walk away from me. I'll have you know that it's more than a title you're throwing away," she called after him. "It's centuries of pride and tradition. It's your heritage, my boy, like it or not. Doesn't that mean anything to you?"

Leon stopped and turned, meeting the dowager's inflamed gaze with his own. "It means exactly what it meant to me yesterday, what it's always meant to me and always will. Nothing. Nothing at all."

"Why, you impudent, ungrateful . . ."

The dowager's angry tirade continued as Ariel hurried after Leon, completely at a loss as to why he would agree to marry her in order to claim the title one minute, and then toss it back in his grandmother's face the next. It didn't make sense. *He* didn't make sense when he was in this black mood, she reminded herself, worried enough to chase him all the way back to the Penrose School if she had to.

"Leon, wait," she called, lifting her skirt to race down the stairs. "I need to talk with you."

"Then you're out of luck," he said over his shoulder. "Because I'm done talking and listening. I'm done with all of you, with this whole scheming, god-forsaken country."

"What do you mean?"

"I mean I'm leaving," he said, waving aside the butler to yank the door open for himself.

"You can't leave," she exclaimed, her heart lodging in her chest even before the words were out. Of course he could leave. He could do anything he pleased, and would. "Where will you go?"

He stopped and looked back at her, his gaze cold enough to bring her to a halt a safe distance away. "That is no longer any of your business. If it ever was."

"Fine," she retorted, right at his heels as he stepped outside. "Go ahead and leave. Run away. But not until you answer one question."

He glanced at her, neither inviting nor forbidding her to continue.

"Why did you ask me to marry you?" she demanded.

He stared at her for a few seconds before a familiar insolent smile claimed his lips. "So you could refuse me, of course. I needed some pretense to escape the old lady's clutches."

"What if I had accepted?"

"Then we'd both have cause for regret, wouldn't we?"

As he turned away, Adam Lockaby stepped into view from beside the front door, where he'd obviously been waiting. The already painful tightness in Ariel's chest increased as she glanced around for Lady Lockaby and discovered she was nowhere in sight. Judging from Adam's mottled complexion and the manic glitter in his eyes, she could well imagine what sort of angry scene might have driven his mother to leave her precious offspring there to fend for himself.

"A word with your lordship," he said loudly.

"Not now, Lockaby," Leon replied, attempting to step around him on the wide brick landing.

Lockaby quickly blocked his path. "Yes, now. Right bloody now, your blinkin' lordship."

His voice had risen to a shout, and the contempt that rang in every word caused passersby on the street below to slow and glance their way with astonished curiosity. This was indeed high drama, thought Ariel anxiously. The infamous Lord Savage confronted by the thwarted cousin on their grandmother's front steps. It was just the sort of scandalous happening tonnish gossipmongers relished to get the season off with a bang.

Impulsively she reached for Leon's arm. "Perhaps you should step back inside and listen to what he has to say," she suggested quietly.

His muscles tightened until they felt like bands of steel beneath her fingertips. She didn't need to glance his way to know that same tension was reflected in every line of his body and the hard curve of his mouth. She only hoped that all that tension translated into control. He was going to need it to avoid an ugly confrontation with Lockaby, who was obviously licking his wounds and spoiling for a fight.

"No," Leon said bluntly in response to her suggestion. "Under the best of circumstances I have little tolerance for meaningless conversation." His quick glance in her direction underscored the point that these were hardly the best of circumstances.

"Is that bloody so?" Lockaby demanded, his tone

erratic. "Not a half hour a lord, and already his high and mighty-ship is giving his poor relations the cut."

"Don't be absurd," Ariel admonished, cognizant of Leon's growing impatience. "No one is giving anyone the cut. This is simply an inopportune—"

"Who asked you?" Lockaby interrupted.

Ariel felt the muscles in Leon's forearm tighten another notch. "Apologize," he ordered softly.

Lockaby seemed about to refuse, until he met Leon's fiery gaze and his jaw clamped shut. "Sorry," he muttered between clenched teeth. "Though why the hell I should apologize is beyond me, when she's as responsible as anyone for stealing the title out from under me."

"And is this your clever strategy for getting it back?" Leon countered. His small smile was scornful, but his tone remained utterly devoid of emotion in a way that made his comments all the more scathing. "Lurking here and accosting me for a public venting of your grievances? Evidently everything I've been told about you is correct. You are an ignorant, ill-advised young hothead not fit to wield even the smallest measure of power."

The younger man glared at him in disbelief. "You dare to insult me to my face?"

"It's the only way I would insult you," Leon calmly replied. "Very uncivilized of me, I know. As for the rest, I dare to do whatever I please. I have no doubt you've heard the rumors to that effect. You are about to discover the truth of those rumors if you do not step aside for me to pass."

"First insults, now threats? It is you who test my tolerance, cousin. By God, you'll not walk away from this one. I demand satisfaction," he bellowed, shoulders heaving. A titter of excitement passed through the small audience that had gathered on the sidewalk. "Name your friends, sir."

Ariel's stomach turned. A duel, the fool was challenging Leon to a duel. Outlawed and ludicrous, the practice persisted in certain echelons. Lockaby was calling on Leon to name two seconds from among his circle of friends so that his own seconds could call on them in the morning to formally deliver the challenge. Then they would all meet at an appointed hour at some clandestine location to make total jackanapes out of themselves and perhaps shoot each other in the bargain.

"I fear I must disappoint you," Leon responded in that same detached tone that was beginning to frighten her. "I have no friends. Nor will I participate in a farce devised by men without honor in order to prove mine."

Lockaby's eyes narrowed. "Are you refusing my challenge?"

"I am," Leon replied. Ariel began to release a sigh of relief and a triumphant gloat was pulling at Lockaby's lips when Leon added, "But I will satisfy your need for a fight, which is what this is really about after all. On my terms. Right here. Right now."

An excited murmur passed through the crowd at the unorthodox counterchallenge. A bloody spectacle on the sidewalk was fine sport, and the onlookers seemed to press forward for a better view.

"A common brawl in the street?" Lockaby sneered. "That's how you mean to prove your honor? I see that what I've heard about you is equally true. You really are an animal. A pity about the sanctity of deathbed wishes. My uncle would have done better by us all if he had stood by his first instinct and left you in the wilds to rot. That's obviously where you belong."

Lockaby's lips were still moving when Leon lunged forward, grabbing him by the throat. The shouts of the crowd seemed very far away as Ariel's whole world narrowed to the sight of him swinging Lockaby around as effortlessly as if he were a rag doll.

A second later Leon's fist came up and caught Lockaby squarely in the midsection, doubling him over. As Lockaby struggled to upright himself, Leon hit him in the face, in the stomach, in the jaw again.

Ariel had witnessed fights at school before, the awkward advances and retreats, the misplaced punches, the whole affair usually ending with both boys locked in a stagnant tangle on the floor and all too willing to be pulled apart.

What was happening before her now was not a fight. It was a beating, a rapid-fire execution of driving blows and agile kicks that drove Lockaby first into the solid brick wall of the house, then to the edge of the landing, his back to the stairs. In spite of his earlier bravado, it was obvious he was no match for Leon's skill. Or his ruthlessness.

Leon reared back, and the younger man took advantage of the reprieve to grab at him, causing them to tumble together down the stairs. They crashed against the wrought iron rails, splattering blood, most of it Lockaby's to be sure, and landed on the sidewalk as onlookers scampered to get out of their way. If there had been any possible doubt that Leon was now the sole aggressor, it was banished when he hauled Lockaby to his feet and slammed him against the side of the parked carriage and shattered the windows, sending glass raining down on them.

Clutching the rail for support, Ariel made her way down the steps after them. Somewhere behind her she heard the dowager huffing and gasping from the exertion of hurrying downstairs to see for herself the cause of all the commotion.

Please let him stop now, let him stop, Ariel prayed silently. From the second Leon landed the first blow, his words to her at Restormel had been running around and around in her head, harsh and terrifying, slicing through all her attempts to tell herself that men fought all the time, over the most trivial things, and that everything would be all right.

I did not want to use a knife on him, he'd said to her. *I wanted to kill him with my bare hands.*

It took three men to pull me off.

I have a nasty habit of beating men senseless for telling the truth about me.

Yes, and despising himself for it afterward, she thought with great distress. Lockaby had taunted him with the fact that his father had abandoned him. That was the truth. Worse, it was the one unalterable truth from which all the pain and bitterness in Leon's life flowed. Lockaby had unknowingly released the side of Leon that he himself feared most.

By the time she reached the sidewalk, they had rolled into the gutter, grunting and grasping at each other. Their clothes were torn and blood-soaked. Lockaby was pinned between Leon's knees, his face a distorted mask she could not bear to look at and could not drag herself away from. If he was not unconscious already, he very nearly was, and still Leon held him by the tatters of his coat, his own shoulders heaving with each labored breath.

"Say it," he growled.

As if, thought Ariel frantically, there were any words that could be spoken now that would in any way lessen or atone for anything that had happened. Leon was clearly beyond understanding that. Just as the man sprawled under him was beyond speaking.

"Damn you," Leon muttered, and lifted his fist.

He *was* going to kill him, she thought, unless somebody stopped him right then. She hardly needed to glance at the glazed, bloodthirsty expressions all around her to know that if anyone there was brave enough to intercede, they would have done so already.

Without thinking, she jumped forward and grabbed Leon's arm with both hands and was nearly tossed off her feet for her trouble.

He snarled, then halted abruptly at the sight of her.

"Please stop," she said quietly. "You do not need to hurt him anymore."

It seemed to take a minute for him to withdraw from wherever he was and focus on what she was saying. He blinked and shook his head. His hair hung over his face in wet black clumps. He groaned.

Tomorrow he would be glad, she told herself. Tomorrow he would thank her. Once he was himself again, he would be grateful she hadn't allowed him to kill Lockaby over a careless remark. But that was tomorrow. The look in his eyes right then scared her senseless.

His face became shuttered, which alarmed her in a different way. It was like peering in a familiar window and having the curtains jerked closed right in your face.

"Anything for you, madam," he murmured with all the tender regard he might show a speck of lint that dared to settle on his lapel.

He brushed those lapels after removing his hands from Lockaby and standing, his movements as easy as if he had engaged in nothing more strenuous than lifting a pint of ale. He took care to adjust his waistcoat and smooth back his long hair. Not a single onlooker dared to so much as smile.

"A pity," he said to her in that new, stranger's voice. "Had I known you took such a kindly interest in the man, I wouldn't have broken quite so many of his bones."

"I do not . . ." she began, but he was already looking past her to where Lady Sage stood, looking quite aghast.

"I trust you'll see to it that Miss Halliday gets home safely," he said to her.

"Of course," the dowager replied. "But see here, young man, where do you think you're . . ."

He was gone before she could finish asking.

Seven days. Leon had been gone for seven days. A full week. After the second day Ariel forced herself to stop keeping track of the hours and minutes. It didn't help. Nothing helped relieve the pressure in her head and the ache in her heart that turned the days into an endless ordeal to be gotten through any way possible, and the nights into a sleepless battleground of worry and yearning and second thoughts.

What if she had said yes to his sudden proposal? What if she had taken a chance on the love she felt for him and had faith that he would someday learn to love her in return? Even if that never happened, could marriage to Leon and unrequited passion be any worse than being without him entirely?

She returned to her duties at the Penrose School and to her tiny room in the dormitory, but in a strange way, her own life no longer seemed to fit. It was too narrow, too colorless, too safe for the woman she had become. Nonetheless, she went through the motions, an uneasy impostor in her own skin and with an underlying amazement that everyone around her couldn't see it as well.

She didn't belong there, not in the classrooms or the dining hall or the office. She belonged with Leon, wherever he was. Now, too late, she realized that she belonged with him at any cost and regardless of the consequences. Now, when he was gone and she had no idea where he might be or if she would ever see him again.

That gnawing uncertainly dominated her thoughts and played havoc with her concentration. Much to her employer's annoyance. But then, these days the very sight of her seemed to irritate Mr. Penrose, who made no secret of the fact that he blamed her for the failure of Castleton's scheme and consequently his own efforts to curry favor with the earl. Clearly, even if she had been able to summon the heart and stomach to resume her romantic overtures toward him, Penrose would be less than receptive.

Fortunately for both her and her family, Lord Castleton did not hold her responsible for Leon's defection. The day following the incident at the dowager's, she received a letter from him, praising her valiant efforts and declaring her part of the endeavor an unqualified success. She felt a bit sheepish in the face of such accolades, but only briefly. She reminded herself that she had accepted the undertaking in good faith and from start to finish had applied herself to the task wholeheartedly. Perhaps too much so, she thought ruefully, reminded of how big a piece of her heart she had surrendered. She doubted that anyone besides Penrose would argue that she had not earned the generous recompense the earl included with his letter.

Ariel wasted no time in opening an account at the bank and depositing Castleton's draft. It was not a fortune by any means, but it would enable her to pay off her father's outstanding debts and to settle others as they came due. With luck, there would still be a small nest egg left over to supplement her salary, ensuring her the financial independence that had always been her goal.

On Saturday, her usual day off, she sought Mr. Penrose to tell him she was leaving.

"I have a few errands in the city and then I'll be spending the rest of the day at home with my parents," she told him.

He leaned back in his chair and regarded her with undisguised disapproval.

"The nerve of some people," he said. "I should think you've had enough time off from your duties here over the past weeks that you wouldn't be coming to me about a day off until the new year."

Resentment surged inside Ariel. It was the first time in a week she'd felt anything except unrelenting sorrow, and she seized the moment.

"I beg to differ, Mr. Penrose. While it's true I have been unable to attend to my usual responsibilities, during the past eight weeks I have not had any time off from the other duties that you expressly requested I undertake. I do believe that if I were to calculate the time I devoted to the task of tutoring Lord Sage, I would be owed days off, and not the other way around."

Penrose shook his head, his pale eyes reflecting amazement. "You really are incredibly presumptuous, aren't you? Tutoring Lord Sage? Is that what you call dancing the waltz with the man and frolicking about the gardens with him and that detestable rabbit? And while we're on that subject, I am well aware you have persuaded the gardener to build a pen for the creature, the cost of which will be deducted from your salary. Tutored, indeed." His lip curled. "Do you know what I think, Miss Halliday?"

"No," she said. "And frankly, unless it relates directly to my performance as a teacher here, I don't care to. Good day, Mr. Penrose. I shall return in time to supervise the dinner hour."

Let him dismiss her, thought Ariel as she tossed her head and left him sputtering in shock. In fact, the idea of quitting held immense appeal. Her personal situation was only marginally more hopeful than it had been two months ago, but she was radically different. She realized now that if she could teach the little monsters Penrose accepted, and run his muddled affairs—and survive Lord Savage—she could undertake anything.

Perhaps Lord Castleton would give her a reference. Even if he didn't, she would manage. She would sew dresses or bake bread or rake mucky gardens. She would do whatever she had to do to survive. With one exception. Never again would she abandon her pride and flutter her lashes and pretend to be something she was not to attract a man.

The confrontation with Penrose wasn't enough to make her forget her troubles, but it helped. Her spirits were lifted a little more, as much as it was possible for them to be lifted under the circumstances, by thoughts of her first errand of the day. If there was a silver lining to her experience with Leon, she mused, this visit to her father's club to settle matters on his behalf was surely it.

It was midmorning and members had not yet begun arriving for lunch. Mr. Hutchins, the club's manager, invited her to sit in the dining room, where several young men in black coats and starched white shirts were busy setting tables. While Hutchins thumbed through the pages of the gaming book in which members' wagers were duly recorded, Ariel glanced around the dark-paneled room, wondering how many times her father had sat in that same chair, passing a pleasant evening of cards and conversation.

The manager's satisfied tone intruded on her bittersweet thoughts.

"I was right," he said, adjusting his half-glasses on his aquiline nose. His hair was gray and thinning above a high forehead. "I was quite certain I was, but I thought it best to verify my recollection before saying anything. Your father has no outstanding debts, Miss Halliday. They have all been discharged."

"That's impossible," Ariel said. "Please look again."

"I have checked the entries twice already. Here." He swiveled the ledger so it faced her, surreptitiously placing a sheet of blotting paper atop the page that did not pertain to her father. "A check mark in the last column to the right indicates payment in full."

Ariel looked where he was pointing, squinting in the dim light. Sure enough, there was a neat, solid row of check marks in the last column beneath her father's name. It had to be a mistake. There was no way her mother could have paid off even one of these wagers, much less all of them. Her gaze halted abruptly on a line close to the bottom of the page.

"Something is definitely wrong here," she said to Mr. Hutchins. "According to your record, this wager was paid a full two months before the outcome could possibly be known."

"Exactly. That's why I was so sure I remembered correctly. The method of payment in this case was so . . . unusual. The gentleman responsible requested a full accounting of Dr. Halliday's wagers, both past due," he said, lowering his voice, "and outstanding. The very next day he sent someone around to discharge the lot of them. Very unusual."

"It certainly is." She glanced up from the book, her pulse quickening with suspicion. "What was this gentleman's name?"

"I'm sorry, I'm not at liberty to say." As he reached for the book he saw her troubled expression and added, "His lordship made it clear he desired to remain anonymous, and he's not a gentleman I would care to displease, if you know what I mean."

Ariel glanced quickly at the gaming book, this time noting the precise date on which the debts had been paid.

"I know exactly what you mean," Ariel told Mr. Hutchins, getting to her feet. "Thank you for your help."

So, Leon had paid her father's debts, she thought, still struggling to come to terms with that fact as she returned to the carriage waiting outside. In full. In advance. And on the night before they'd left for Restormel, according to the club records. She winced, recalling how she had imagined him out on the town, imagined all kinds of outrageous things actually, when all the time he was busy putting things right for a man he'd never even met. She had no doubt that Leon was the mysterious benefactor. What she didn't understand was why.

Why would Leon put himself out at his very first opportunity, setting off alone in a strange city and spending a considerable sum of his own money in order to help her and her family? And with no reasonable hope of ever being repaid. She had certainly made it plain enough that they had no resources to draw on, nor prospects of any.

Why? She turned the question over and over in her mind. Too preoccupied to bother with the rest of her errands, she asked the driver to take her directly to her parents' house. Could it possibly have been a simple act of kindness on his part? Or had he expected something in return? Had he been setting her up, drawing her into some sort of vengeful plot, even then?

That possibility was not only heart-wrenching, it didn't make sense. If Leon had been setting her up, wouldn't he have sought to increase her vulnerability rather than eliminate it? If he had paid the debts in order to gain some sort of advantage, why keep it a secret? He could have thrown his act of charity in her face any number of times but had not. He'd even held his tongue during those tense moments in his room at Restormel, when revealing the truth would surely have put him in a more favorable position with her.

Why?

Ariel's palms went damp as it occurred to her that if Leon's motive for paying the debts had been genuine, perhaps his proposal had been as well. It was possible that his grandmother's stipulation that he marry hadn't inspired him to offer for her so much as it had provided him with an excuse to do what he wanted to do anyway. The notion might seem far-fetched to someone who didn't know Leon as well as she did. She understood only too well how difficult it was for him to reach out to anyone emotionally, and how devastating it must have been for him when she refused him.

How could she have been so blind? There was only one reason she could think of for a man to go to such lengths to obtain a trump card and then not play it when he had the chance. Leon probably did not know it, and she may never get the chance to tell him, but he was in love with her.

Moments later the carriage pulled to a halt in front of her house, and it appeared her luck might have changed at last. There was a carriage already parked in the drive, an immense black and gold affair with the Sage crest emblazoned on the doors and boot.

Leon.

That was Ariel's single, hopelessly irrational thought as she bolted from the carriage without waiting for assistance and raced into the house. She fully expected to find Leon waiting for her in the drawing room, and couldn't hide her disappointment when instead she found her parents entertaining the Dowager Lady Sage and Lord Castleton.

"There you are, my dear, dear girl," the dowager exclaimed as Ariel came to a dejected halt in the doorway. Faith and Felicity panted excitedly at her feet. "Your headmaster told us you would be coming here, and we've been eagerly awaiting your arrival."

"Why?" Ariel asked. This seemed to be her day for being blunt.

The dowager smiled and beckoned her to come closer. "Because, my dear, I've had my fill of this little game of hide-and-seek. We are going to find my headstrong bull of a grandson, and you are going to tell us how."

Twenty

I only wish I could help you," Ariel told the dowager and Lord Castleton, strategically choosing a seat beside her father on the settee. "Here you go, Papa," she said, retrieving his napkin from where it had slipped to the floor and placing it on his knee.

She smiled at him, her fingers curled anxiously as he peered at her as if she were a stranger invading his home. *Don't let him have one of his episodes now,* she prayed silently. Not when her mother was clearly going to great lengths to impress her guests. She had dragged out the best china and the silver tea service, and the homemade biscuits were accompanied by a carefully hoarded jar of Elise's plum preserves. More important, her mother was smiling the way she used to smile when callers stopped by, and Ariel wished for nothing to spoil that.

Perhaps nothing would, she thought with relief as her father's wary frown gave way to a broad smile.

"Ariel," he said, patting her knee. "What are you doing here?"

"It's my day off, Papa, and I came to spend it with my favorite gentleman in the whole world. Shall we walk to the park together later?"

"Well, yes, I suppose," he said, looking puzzled. "But I thought you were spending the summer in the country with your aunt Matilda."

"Not this summer, Papa," she replied, hoping no one would point out that it was not yet summer, or, worse, ask questions that would force her to reveal that Aunt Matilda had passed away seven years ago.

She turned to their visitors, relieved to see her father return his attention to the biscuits in front of him.

"I'm afraid I have no more knowledge of where Leon, that is, Lord Sage, might be than you do."

"You must," insisted his grandmother. "You spent more time with him than anyone. He must have confided something in you."

Ariel shook her head. "Nothing that would indicate where he might go if he didn't want to be found. My only guess is that he would return to the islands."

Castleton groaned. "You see? I told you it was useless. Even Miss Halliday does not know where he is, and she was our last hope. We've lost him. He's gone forever, I know it."

"Hush. Of course he is not gone forever," admonished the dowager. "Where on earth would he go?"

"Where indeed?" retorted Lord Castleton, his obvious despair fueling Ariel's. He got to his feet, clasping his hands behind him and marching back and forth in front of the dowager as she sipped tea and munched biscuits. "Let us think," he continued, sarcastically, Ariel was sure. "The man is clever and dangerous and devilishly resourceful. I do believe we can all agree on that." He looked around for disagreement and found none.

"He speaks seven languages that we know of, and has powerful connections in a part of the world where our own government wields little if any influence. He has made God-only-knows how great a fortune in sandalwood exports, of all things . . . oh, yes," he said, noting Ariel's surprised expression. "Lady Sage has filled me in on all the details of our Lord Savage's ruse, and his not-so-savage background."

"Are you angry?" Ariel asked.

"Angry? Blazes, no. I wanted him to be a proper gentleman and a lord, and so he is. It is of little import to me how he got that way."

"But you paid me to do a job that in fact was done long ago."

He waved aside her words. "Do not concern yourself with that. You earned your payment honestly. We were all at the man's mercy, and by God if we don't continue to be." He shook his head. "I'd say you hit it right on, madam," he said to the dowager. "With so many splendid options open to Sage, we can do little but sit here on our hands and wonder where on this great big earth of ours he might choose to go."

"I don't care how many languages he speaks, or how much money or influence he has at his command, I want an heir to carry on our family name. Him, for starters, and eventually his son. He will not leave England until I get an heir from him, and that's all there is to it." She banged her walking stick on the floor, sending a sour look Ariel's way. "If only you had accepted the boy's proposal when he made it, married him, and gotten yourself pregnant, we wouldn't be in this unholy predicament."

"What proposal?" inquired Millicent Halliday,

entering the conversation for the first time, her wide, astonished gaze fixed on her daughter.

"I'll explain later, Mother," Ariel said, darting her a look.

"Who's proposed?" asked her father.

"No one," Ariel said. "Have another biscuit, Papa. They're your favorites."

"Who's proposed to whom?" he asked again, more loudly this time.

"I'm not sure," her mother said to him, making a hushing motion. "I believe someone has proposed to Ariel."

"Our Ariel?" Dr. Halliday exclaimed. "Ariel's at Matilda's for the summer. I won't have her running off with some country bumpkin, mark my words." He stood abruptly and glanced around with a perplexed expression. "Where's my bag? I have to get to the office."

With a conspiratorial wink only Ariel could see, Lady Halliday hurried to her husband's side. "Your bag is where it always is," she assured him. "Come along and I'll help you fetch it." She smiled and bowed her head to their guests. "Excuse us, please."

"Of course," said the dowager. When her parents had left the room, she turned to Ariel. "Your parents are charming. And you are a gem for tending to them as well as you do. You might be surprised to learn that Leon confided a few things in me as well." She sighed. "If only you had accepted his proposal," she said again, adding another giant dollop of regret to what Ariel was already straining under, "then all our problems would be solved."

"Begging your pardon, madam," said Castleton, "are you mad? The only way that Sage marrying and siring an heir could solve my problems was if the babe were a prodigy capable of casting a vote in Parliament. Don't you understand? I vouched for him. I gave my word of honor that the Sage seat was secure, and on that basis men have proposed legislation and made investments. Now it appears that scapegrace Lockaby may get the last laugh after all, and it will all have been for naught. And *I,*" he concluded with an embittered flourish, "shall be the laughingstock of the season."

"Stop whining, Castleton, it's most unbecoming," snapped the dowager as Ariel listened in silence, beginning to wish they would just go away. "You and your cronies have lost on legislation and investments before, and I daresay you'll do so again."

The earl looked askance at her. "It's obvious you don't understand the first thing about politics or high finance. It's compromise and investment and capital all in a carefully balanced interplay of mutually interested parties, a delicate, ever-shifting framework built on a single, rock-solid principle. Do you know what that principle is, madam?"

The dowager looked up from her anisette biscuit. "Luck?"

"No, not luck," he bellowed. "Trust. Trust in each other, trust in me, trust that when I give my word that a man is worthy of their confidence, he is as I say he is. When they hear that Sage has disappeared before ever making an appearance in the house, there will be hell to pay. Now do you understand?"

"I understand perfectly," the dowager responded. "We must find him and bring him back. That's all there is to it."

There was a desperate edge to the earl's laughter. "Find him? Just like that, hmm? I'll have you know we had the devil's own duty laying our hands on the man last time, when he did not even know he was being hunted."

"Just the same, he must be found and made to face his responsibilities. I need an heir," the dowager declared.

"And I need his vote," Castleton added.

Ariel leapt to her feet. "Stop it. Both of you. You're doing it again."

Castleton and the dowager exchanged a look of surprise, but their shock was nothing compared to her own as she realized she had just shouted them into silence.

"Doing what?" the older woman inquired.

"Plotting," she said. "Plotting and scheming and thinking only of what Leon can do for you. I've been guilty of it as well, I confess. We all have been, right from the start. You want an heir, and you want an agreeable voice in Parliament and I want . . . oh, I don't even know what I want anymore," she said, clasping her hands together.

That was a lie. She knew exactly what she wanted. Worse, she knew that it had been within her grasp and she had let it slip away, and that made it even sadder and harder to bear.

"The point is," she continued, her voice reflecting the sudden weariness inside her, "that we have all been so busy thinking of what we want, none of us has given any thought to what Leon wanted. If we had, maybe he would still be here."

The British transport, *Recovery*, raised anchor and set sail from Portsmouth with cargo consisting of 207 convicts, an assortment of French laces intended as a gift from the captain to a certain ladybird in New South Wales, and the Marquis of Sage, well into his cups.

The accommodations were dismal and overpriced, the captain having bled him obscenely for the privilege of coming aboard at the last minute, but Leon counted it a bargain at any price. He wanted to be as far out to sea as possible before he sobered up.

It said something about the state he had been reduced to that he saw things more clearly while foxed out of his skull than he did when abstaining. He saw The Truth, that Ariel was everything good and beautiful in the world, and he was everything that was the wretched and unworthy opposite of her. The biggest favor he could do her was exactly what he was doing now, climbing back into a hole in the belly of a ship and putting as much cold, deep distance between them as possible.

He was besotted with the woman, to be sure. He had finally admitted that much to himself. But not so totally enthralled that he would try to swim an ocean to be at her side. At least he didn't think he would. That was not to say that throwing himself overboard and sinking did not hold a certain desperate appeal at the moment.

Thanks to rough waters, he'd managed to nurse his hangover and headache well into his third day on board. Then sobriety and confusion set in. He woke in a bunk narrower than he was, stared at the worm holes in the wooden ceiling a foot above his face, and thought about love.

Despite his rakish past and bawdy, well-deserved reputation, it was a subject about which he had pitiful little knowledge, and none at all of a personal nature. Unless, he thought with raw self-contempt, one were to count that perfect, fleeting stretch of time between the moment in the dowager's salon, when he at last realized he was in love with Ariel, and the moment he'd fucked it all up so royally.

This was not how he had envisioned it ending. Not that he had failed. On the contrary, he'd met his objective with much less expenditure of time and effort than anticipated. He had retrieved the sword and tossed it in their smug Brit faces. Symbolically at least. He should be feeling triumphant and vindicated, he reminded himself, propping his boots on the leather case at the end of the bunk.

"Three cheers for me," he muttered.

It was damn hard to feel like a winner with Ariel hundreds of miles away, left alone to deal with the no doubt scathing aftershocks of his abrupt departure, and him there, unshaven, unwashed, and missing her so much it made his chest ache.

Ariel, he thought, his entire being infused with yearning for her. Hopeless bloody yearning, it was too. He had asked her to be his wife and she had wasted no time refusing him cold. Quite insightfully so as it turned out, since not ten minutes later he was rolling in a filthy gutter, grunting and bloody and out of his raging head, while the dowager's lofty neighbors looked on and laughed and told each other the rumors had been right. He *was* a savage.

He had made a complete ass of himself and shown himself for the raging mongrel he was to the one woman in the world whose opinion mattered to him.

And for what? His bitter snort of laughter rattled around inside the small cabin. Why, because Lockaby had dared to speak the truth to his face, that's why. The truth. That he was an animal. That he did not belong there. The real truth was that he could not face the truth so he had nearly killed the man to shut him up.

As if that could change who he was.

He squeezed his eyes shut to stop images of the brawl from flashing in his head, unable to stave off thoughts of how it must have appeared to someone of Ariel's tenderhearted sensibilities. Well, she couldn't say he hadn't warned her. He had told her what he was. Or tried to. Hearing him say the words was not the same as seeing it for herself, seeing the blazing, ranting, blood-splattering devil-beast inside him set loose.

Groaning, he dragged his hair back from his face, holding it with clenched fists until his temples throbbed. She had thought him a savage when he stood half naked and spat tea in her face. Witless play-acting was all that had been. She knew now what a true savage was capable of.

I am not afraid of you, she told him once.

He would wager she was afraid now all right.

But that wasn't even the problem. The problem was he, too, was afraid. Afraid of falling in love, afraid of admitting it to himself and of revealing what was in his heart to Ariel. He was afraid to want, only to be told no. So he had hedged his bets even as he was asking Ariel to marry him, pretending the dowager had forced his hand when in fact he had been trembling inside as he waited for her answer. No wonder she had questioned his motives. And how had he responded when she did? With more pretense, more evasion, more fear.

What if he'd told her the truth instead? That his motive consisted of doing whatever he had to do to keep her with him every day and every night for the rest of his life. What if he'd told her that she had changed his life, that she had changed *him*? It was true, he realized, not at all dismayed by the fact. Sweet, patient, relentless Ariel had done exactly what she had set out to do. She had tamed the part of him that needed taming the most—his heart.

He longed to have back that moment at the dowager's so he could do it again, but differently. This time he would tell her exactly what he was feeling. But did he have the courage to look her in the eye and risk honesty?

She had managed it, he reminded himself. She had sat across from him in the carriage, her chin held high, and laid bare her soul in order to spare him any uneasy thoughts over being her debaucher, daring him to call her soiled goods. He should have had the guts to follow her example.

Surely he was man enough to face the truth for once instead of trying to crush it. Or run from it.

The way his father had run away, he thought, going cold inside at the realization that the two of them might have something in common after all. His father had also left without either farewell or explanation. Had he also been tormented by his decision? Had he told himself over and over that he was doing the right thing? How easy it was to confuse right with easy.

Leon sought to ease his conscience by reminding himself that there was one significant difference between his father and him. He had not left the woman he loved pregnant.

Had he?

Sweet Jesus. He hurtled to his feet, then gripped the wall as the ship heaved. Panic coursing through his veins, he thought of Ariel alone and husbandless cast aside by yet another man, continuing on with her life in a world where propriety was sacrosanct. Just imagining it made his heart feel like a lead dagger in his chest.

And it left him both stone sober and thinking more clearly than he had in a long time.

While he had needed a hundred sodden excuses to justify leaving, he needed only one reason to go back. That reason had nothing to do with his father or with responsibility. It had to do only with Ariel. He loved her. That was the sole reason that mattered.

He would tell her how desperate he was to make her his own, his lover, his wife. If that was not what she wanted, if she now found him reprehensible and wanted him out of her life forever, let her tell him so to his face.

Two minutes later he was knocking on the door of the captain's quarters. The instant the captain appeared, Leon flipped open the leather case he was holding and stuck it under his nose, waiting for the man's eyes to widen at the sight of all those neat bundles of crisp one-hundred-pound notes, all that remained of the money the dowager had advanced him.

"One question," he said when he was satisfied he had the captain's undivided attention. "How much will it cost me to turn this ship around?"

T w e n t y - o n e

It was bound to happen, and when it did, Ariel wasn't sorry. As Mr. Penrose increasingly seemed to seek out reasons to criticize her, her tolerance for his nit-picking shrank. Her patience finally snapped when he interrupted her in the midst of wrestling with the latest imbalance in his accounts, her incomplete lesson plan for the following week waiting on one side of her desk and a stack of essays yet to be graded on the other, and inquired why she was falling behind on his correspondence.

It was all she could do not to hurl the heavy ledger at his empty skull. She must not have done nearly as well controlling her expression, for he responded to her speechless glare with a loud, indignant, "Humph.

"There is no need to be impertinent," he chided. "If you are not up to the position you hold here, then perhaps I should see to seeking a replacement."

"Do it," she said, her decision and the words

coming in tandem. Far from regretting the impulsive declaration, however, she felt buoyant.

"Have a care, Miss Halliday, I assure you I am not joking."

"Neither am I. Seek a replacement," she said, slamming the ledger shut and standing to thrust it at him. "I wish you luck finding someone willing and able, or perhaps simply desperate enough, as I have been, to do your bidding and endure your petty criticism and clean up your messes and then do her own job as well."

Penrose pinched the bridge of his nose. "What are you saying, Miss Halliday?"

"I'm saying good-bye."

If he had a response or objection, Ariel didn't wait to hear it. She went directly to her room and packed her clothing and few personal belongings. It was of no consequence, and only small satisfaction, that her *former* employer—oh, what a glorious sound that had—caught up with her at the front door and urged, no, begged her to reconsider.

She did not, not even when enticed with promises of fewer responsibilities and an increase in salary. She needed to make a fresh start, and this was it. Perhaps somewhere else, someplace that didn't hold so many unsettling memories, she would be able to shake the heavy emptiness inside that left her unable to sleep or eat or concentrate.

Eager to cut all ties as quickly as possible, she would have refused a ride as well if Penrose had been gentleman enough to offer one. She was content to make her way to the main road at the end of the drive and wait for the post chaise to London. Not until she was halfway down the brick path did it occur to her that along with all the bitter, unhappy memories she had of the Penrose School, she was leaving behind some precious moments as well. Most of them involved Leon, she thought, and suddenly the sight of the cottage was too tempting to resist.

Since Leon left and she'd moved back to her own room, she had intentionally avoided even glancing in that direction. Now her footsteps turned onto the curving stone path almost of their own accord. What harm could there be in taking one last look?

The front door was unlocked. Seeing the house after she had worked her magic on it had apparently inspired in Philip a new appreciation for his former castoffs, and he had been steadily moving furnishings and artwork from the cottage to his new home. Ariel hadn't realized the extent of his plundering, however, and peering around, she almost wished she had left her memory of the cottage undisturbed. The most charming pieces had been removed from the first floor, and those remaining were shrouded in protective white sheets.

It was like being surrounded by ghosts, she mused as she wandered aimlessly around the drawing room. Back in the hallway, she stood with her hand on the newel post, debating whether she was brave enough to go upstairs and see what was left there. Already she was being haunted by echoes of a deep, familiar laugh, and visions of Leon splashing water at her and then trailing the path of the droplets along her throat and chest. Different sorts of ghosts, she thought ruefully. These less easily covered with a sheet and forgotten.

The sound of the door latch was a sharp, metallic contrast to her daydreams. She whirled around, bracing for another go-round with Penrose, who could be there either to offer her further inducements or to tell her to go if she was going.

But it wasn't Mr. Penrose who entered and closed the door behind him.

Everything inside her went still.

It was the third heart-stopping entrance this man had made into her life. Ariel would have thought that by then she would be prepared for such moments. She was not. Breathless, and with what she suspected was a notable lack of panache, she drank in the sight of him.

The wild and bloodied warrior of the other day was gone. He was exemplary in fitted dark gray wool and a freshly starched cravat, standing with one shoulder propped against the drawing room arch. A smile she knew she ought to resist shaped his beautiful mouth.

The silence was paralyzing. The occasional creak of a floorboard sounded to Ariel like thunder. They stared at each other, spellbound, until at last Leon stepped forward to break the mood.

Ariel tensed. She did not want him to touch her.

She did.

Before she could make up her mind, he had sauntered past her for a closer look at the bare walls, barren tabletops, and empty spot where the pianoforte once stood.

"I love what you've done with the place," he said. "Wasn't there a painting about there?" He pointed to a telltale patch on the wall. "A man holding something, I believe."

"Yes. A pitchfork to be precise."

"Rather on the dark side, as I recall."

"One might say that, I suppose, if one were totally ignorant of the subtle play of light and detail in art."

"Just as I thought. On the dark side. I think I prefer this fresh, open look you have achieved." He lifted a small crystal figurine from the mantel and turned it over in his hand.

"This is not my doing," she protested. "Mr. Penrose has decided to enhance his new home with some pieces from the cottage."

"Ah, I see. In preparation for his new bride, I assume?"

"You assume falsely," she told him in a brittle tone.

He tossed the figurine in the air and caught it before meeting her gaze. "So it didn't work out with Penrose? A shame, really, since from the very start that was the point of this whole exercise in futility."

"No, you wretched, ungrateful clod, you," Ariel snapped, snatching the delicate crystal from his hand and replacing it on the mantel. "My intent, from the very start, was to save you."

"To save me?" His brow wrinkled. "From whom, pray tell?"

"From Castleton and the others, from your grandmother, from yourself at times," she added, exasperated. "From everyone who wanted to break you and make you into something you are not."

"How very noble."

"How very pointless," she retorted, turning away.

He grabbed her and pulled her into his arms before she could escape, easily overpowering her efforts to resist. Ariel held herself carefully still, afraid of what his closeness was already doing to her, afraid to believe he was really there.

"Wretched, ungrateful clod?" he said. "Is that what you called me?"

"Yes."

"Is that really the best you can do?"

"At the moment."

"I have spent the past week coming up with much more colorful and inventive words to describe what I am. I could draw up a list for you if you like. It may be of some use the next time I make such a complete and utter ass of myself as I did the other day. And afterward," he added, his voice dropping, as if he were speaking through a wall of pain. "Running away as I did, instead of having the courage to face up to my actions. Instead of facing you.

"As it turns out," he went on without affording her a chance to respond, "I am no better than those I condemned for imposing on your kind nature and generous heart. In fact, I am selfish enough to impose even more outrageously than any of the others and beg for your understanding."

His eyes had never looked so golden to her, or so uncertain. He smiled ruefully as he touched the cameo at her throat. "The wishing mermaid."

"I've been wearing it every day since you left," she said softly.

"And I've been hanging over a ship's rail searching the waves for one so that I might make a wish. Do you know what I would wish for?"

She shook her head, afraid to speak.

"I'd wish that I could turn back time, to before I made such a mess of matters at the dowager's. No, before that even. I wish I could start all over with you." He slid his thumb from the pin to her jaw, stroking it lightly. "But I can't. All I can do is ask you to forgive me for all the stupid things I've done, and for all the misery and unpleasantness I've brought into your life. Can you, Ariel?"

"I could if it were necessary," she replied, her heart melting, swelling, flying. "But since the pleasure and generosity you've brought me outweigh the other, it is not. Either way, my forgiveness means nothing if you cannot forgive yourself."

She smiled up at him and traced the bewildered

slant of his mouth. "You are not to blame for your father's leaving, or the tragedy of your mother's death, or anything else that happened so long ago," she told him. "You are fighting ghosts, my darling, and because that is a battle you can never win, you end up trying to give the rest of the world a bloody nose instead."

He winced. "Lockaby?"

"He will be fine," she said. "You broke amazingly few of his bones after all. Though according to your grandmother, he will not be making any public appearances until the swelling goes down. She also expressed a hope that you had pounded some sense into him."

"The opposite is certainly true, if that is any consolation to her. I am not the same man I was that day."

She laid her palms against his chest, feeling the strong, rapid beat of his heart. "I sincerely hope you are not too changed. I should not want a different man from the one I fell in love with."

He closed his eyes and threw his head back, as if letting her words wash over him. Then he gently pulled away, grimacing. "How can you even say that? That you would not wish me changed."

"I can say it because it's true. You are not only the most stubborn and maddening man I have ever known, but also the kindest and sweetest and most generous, and I shall love you forever whether you are here with me or somewhere far away."

Hope and hopelessness warred in the look he gave her. "If you only knew . . ."

"I do. I know all that matters. For instance, I know what you have done for me and for my family. Thank you, Leon. If you had not settled my father's debts, there is no way I could have done what I did today."

"What is that?"

"I terminated my employment here." She unleashed

a gleeful smile as she nodded at her valise by the door. "More accurately, I told Mr. Penrose to take his hopeless ledgers and go hang."

Leon grinned. "So that's why you were traipsing down the drive, bag and baggage. I thought—" He hesitated, shrugging sheepishly.

Ariel looked aghast at him. "You thought what? Not that I was moving in with Mr. Penrose? Oh, how could you?"

"I thought perhaps he'd offered for you and you'd accepted. I thought maybe you weren't even aware that you were no longer facing a mountain of debts. Mostly I thought it was a damn shame that I had returned to apologize to you for nearly killing one man in front of your eyes and now was going to have to kill another."

Ariel shook her head, reaching out to touch his hand. "You foolish, impossible, wonderful man."

Leon stared at her fingers, so much smaller and more delicate than his own, and marveled at how their gentle touch could so effortlessly lift from him a crushing weight he had been struggling under for years. He burned to sweep her into his arms without any further explanation, carry her upstairs to that bed where he had spent so many restless nights, and do what he had been dreaming of doing the whole voyage back. Unfortunately, he was through taking the easy way out.

He lifted her hand to his mouth and kissed her knuckles, her palm, the soft pad below her thumb. "I do not deserve you. I cannot even promise you that I will always be the man you make me want to be. But I will promise to always try." He met her gaze. "I am not like my father."

"I know. I have always known."

He carefully released her hand and moved away, needing distance to think clearly. He gazed around, seeing a different, far grander room than the one he stood in.

"I keep thinking of Restormel," he said. "I spent hours walking through that place, wandering the endless halls while everyone else was asleep and trying to feel whatever it was he must have felt that bound him so strongly to a pile of wood and stone, trying to see what it was he saw there that was worth more than the woman he loved and his own son. But I couldn't.

"I can't understand," he said. "I'm not sure I ever will. I do know I will never sanction what he did in the name of honor." He turned to her and his weary, guarded look faded into a faint smile. "But I am at last ready to accept it and put it behind me."

"It is behind you, Leon, it always has been."

"No." He shook his head and placed his hand flat over his heart. "It was always right here, and it was all that ever was there, until you made me feel something else.

"Thanks to you, I now pity him more than hate him," he went on. "He found the one woman he would ever love and gave her up for what he saw as his greater responsibility. I found the one woman I will ever love and almost gave her up in a senseless quest for revenge." He went to her and stood before her, not trusting himself to touch her even yet. "I love you, Ariel. I will always love you, if you will let me, if you will trust me enough to give me your heart."

"You have it already. I suspect you have had the biggest chunk of it since the moment I watched you kneel in the mud to feed biscuits to a scraggly old rabbit."

"Prinny." His wry smile pretended to turn fierce. "I sincerely hope, madam, that Prinny was not among the household treasures the Nose saw fit to claim."

"Perish the thought. In fact, Prinny has quite splendid and spacious new quarters to call home. I had a pen built."

"A pen? You mean a cage? I am gone not two weeks and you put poor Prinny in a cage?"

"I'll have you know that poor Prinny is very happy there, with the door ajar so he can take a stroll whenever he pleases. He is ill suited for domestic life and was forever bumping into things and getting himself lost or in trouble."

"Yes, I know the feeling all too well," he said dryly.

"I must confess that the female companion I provided for him has no doubt made his adjustment easier."

Leon smiled. "More gratifying, at least." He cupped his hands over her shoulders and let the pleasure of touching her spread slowly through him. "Is that how you shall cage me?"

"I would not dare to try. Accepting the past is one thing. Making your home in the land that you have spent a lifetime hating is quite another. The choice must be yours."

"Then I choose to make my home here. Not because I share a name and bloodlines with the men who lived here before me, but because this is where you are." He slid his hands the length of her back and pulled every supple inch of her against him. "I choose you, Ariel, now, tomorrow, forever. Will you marry me?"

"Yes, oh, yes." Her laughter was exultant. "I will marry you, here or on a faraway island if that is what will make you happy, whenever and wherever you choose."

"Right away," he said. "That takes care of when. As for where . . . at Restormel, I think. You fell in love with the place right off and I believe in time I can learn to. We will start our own tradition there."

She nodded, understanding, and at last he allowed himself to bend his head and claim her mouth as he had claimed her heart. She parted her lips, welcoming the slow exploration of his tongue, drawing him into her soft heat and holding him there until they were both breathless.

As soon as he lifted his head he wanted to kiss her again and again and go on kissing her forever. He wanted to kiss her hard and fast, and long and lazy, and every way he could discover in between. The heady knowledge that he could, that she would surrender to him the time and the right, was like fireworks inside him, one explosion rolling into the next.

"It is ironic," he said, his forehead touching her. "For all that my father took away from me, he ended up giving me the one thing I treasure most and always will. If I had truly been Lord Sage, and not Lord Savage and in need of taming, I may never have found you."

"I think if you had been Lord Sage rather than Lord Savage, I should not have found you nearly as fascinating," she said. "Or as tempting."

"Tell me again," he urged.

She didn't pretend to not understand. "I love you," she said.

"Tell me how much," he demanded, starving for all the shades and nuances of something he had never had.

"I can't." She cupped his face in her hands, her eyes burning with a soft, steady glow. "There aren't enough words in all the languages that exist. I will have to show you instead, and even that will take a lifetime."

"We have a lifetime," he whispered.

"It may still not be enough. I may need forever."

"Forever," he echoed, and kissed her hard. "You shall have it."

As if he could refuse her anything she desired. She was his heart, his soul, his life.

If it was forever she wanted, forever she would have.

About the Author

PATRICIA COUGHLIN is a former English teacher who quickly discovered she would rather make up stories of her own, thus ensuring happy endings. The award-winning author of over twenty-five novels lives in Rhode Island with her husband and two teenage sons.

DON'T MISS THESE FABULOUS
BANTAM WOMEN'S FICTION TITLES

On Sale in December

HAWK O'TOOLE'S HOSTAGE

by *New York Times* megaselling phenomenon SANDRA BROWN

Another heady blend of the passion, humor, and high-voltage romantic suspense that has made Sandra Brown one of the most beloved writers in America. Now in hardcover for the first time, this is the thrilling tale of a woman who finds herself at the mercy of a handsome stranger—and the treacherous feelings only he can arouse.   ____ 10448-9 $17.95/$24.95

"A spectacular tale of revenge, betrayal and survival." —*Publishers Weekly*

From *New York Times* bestselling author IRIS JOHANSEN comes

THE UGLY DUCKLING in paperback ____ 56991-0 $5.99/$7.99

"Susan Johnson is queen of erotic romance." —*Romantic Times*

WICKED

by bestselling author SUSAN JOHNSON

No one sizzles like Susan Johnson, and she burns up the pages in *Wicked*. Governess Serena Blythe had been saving for years to escape to Florence. Despite her well-laid plans, there were two developments she couldn't foresee: that she would end up a stowaway—and that the ship's master would be an expert at seduction.   ____ 57214-8 $5.99/$7.99

From the bestselling author of *The Engagement* SUZANNE ROBINSON

HEART OF THE FALCON

Rich with the pageantry of ancient Egypt and aflame with the unforgettable romance of a woman who has lost everything only to find the man who will brand her soul, this is the unforgettable Suzanne Robinson at her finest.   ____ 28138-0 $5.50/$7.50

Ask for these books at your local bookstore or use this page to order.

Please send me the books I have checked above. I am enclosing $____ (add $2.50 to cover postage and handling). Send check or money order, no cash or C.O.D.'s, please.

Name _____

Address _____

City/State/Zip _____

Send order to: Bantam Books, Dept. FN158, 2451 S. Wolf Rd., Des Plaines, IL 60018
Allow four to six weeks for delivery.
Prices and availability subject to change without notice.   FN 158 12/96

Bestselling Historical Women's Fiction

❧ AMANDA QUICK ❧

____28354-5 SEDUCTION . . .$6.50/$8.99 Canada

____28932-2 SCANDAL . . . .$6.50/$8.99

____28594-7 SURRENDER . . . .$6.50/$8.99

____29325-7 RENDEZVOUS . . . .$6.50/$8.99

____29315-X RECKLESS . . . .$6.50/$8.99

____29316-8 RAVISHED . . . .$6.50/$8.99

____29317-6 DANGEROUS . . . .$6.50/$8.99

____56506-0 DECEPTION . . . .$6.50/$8.99

____56153-7 DESIRE . . . .$6.50/$8.99

____56940-6 MISTRESS . . . .$6.50/$8.99

____57159-1 MYSTIQUE . . . .$6.50/$7.99

____09355-X MISCHIEF . . . .$22.95/$25.95

❧ IRIS JOHANSEN ❧

____29871-2 LAST BRIDGE HOME . . .$4.50/$5.50

____29604-3 THE GOLDEN

              BARBARIAN . . . . :$4.99/$5.99

____29244-7 REAP THE WIND . . . . . .$5.99/$7.50

____29032-0 STORM WINDS . . . .$4.99/$5.99

Ask for these books at your local bookstore or use this page to order.

Please send me the books I have checked above. I am enclosing $____ (add $2.50 to cover postage and handling). Send check or money order, no cash or C.O.D.'s, please.

Name _____

Address _____

City/State/Zip _____

Send order to: Bantam Books, Dept. FN 16, 2451 S. Wolf Rd., Des Plaines, IL 60018
Allow four to six weeks for delivery.

Prices and availability subject to change without notice.   FN 16 11/96

Bestselling Historical Women's Fiction

❧ IRIS JOHANSEN ❧

____28855-5 THE WIND DANCER ...$5.99/$6.99

____29968-9 THE TIGER PRINCE ...$5.99/$6.99

____29944-1 THE MAGNIFICENT
                ROGUE ....$5.99/$6.99

____29945-X BELOVED SCOUNDREL .$5.99/$6.99

____29946-8 MIDNIGHT WARRIOR ..$5.99/$6.99

____29947-6 DARK RIDER ....$5.99/$7.99

____56990-2 LION'S BRIDE ....$5.99/$7.99

____09714-8 THE UGLY
                DUCKLING ....$19.95/$24.95

❧ TERESA MEDEIROS ❧

____29407-5 HEATHER AND VELVET .$5.99/$7.50

____29409-1 ONCE AN ANGEL ......$5.99/$6.50

____29408-3 A WHISPER OF ROSES .$5.50/$6.50

____56332-7 THIEF OF HEARTS .....$5.50/$6.99

____56333-5 FAIREST OF THEM ALL .$5.99/$7.50

____56334-3 BREATH OF MAGIC ....$5.99/$7.99

____57623-2 SHADOWS AND LACE ...$5.99/$7.99

- -

Ask for these books at your local bookstore or use this page to order.

Please send me the books I have checked above. I am enclosing $____ (add $2.50 to cover postage and handling). Send check or money order, no cash or C.O.D.'s, please.

Name _____

Address _____

City/State/Zip _____

Send order to: Bantam Books, Dept. FN 16, 2451 S. Wolf Rd., Des Plaines, IL 60018
Allow four to six weeks for delivery.
Prices and availability subject to change without notice.   FN 16 11/96